D1002737

DARK SIDE
OF VALOR

Dear Reader:

Dark Side of Valor focuses on teen runaways and the homeless. These are subjects that are dear to my heart and Alicia Singleton courageously explores them with compassion.

Lelia Freeman is dubbed "The Street Angel" and her title is well-deserved as the traumatized former teen runaway transforms into a child advocate. We follow her suspenseful and thrilling journey from New York to Los Angeles to Washington, D.C. to foreign lands.

I commend Alicia for her humane mission to step off the pages and shed light on this challenging way of life that is sadly a reality to many Americans.

Thank you for reading this novel and for supporting the Strebor Books family. We appreciate your love.

Blessings,

Zane

Publisher
Strebor Books International
www.simonandschuster.com/streborbooks

ZANE PRESENTS

ALICIA SINGLETON

DARK SIDE OF VALOR

SBI

STREBOR BOOKS

NEW YORK LONDON TORONTO SYDNEY

SBI

Strebor Books
P.O. Box 6505
Largo, MD 20792
http://www.streborbooks.com

ISBN 978-1-59309-386-0
ISBN 978-1-4516-4519-4 (e-book)
LCCN 2010925101

First Strebor Books trade paperback edition February 2012

Cover design: www.mariondesigns.com
Cover photograph: © Keith Saunders Photos

10 9 8 7 6 5 4 3 2 1

Manufactured in the United States of America

For information regarding special discounts for bulk purchases,
please contact Simon & Schuster Special Sales at 1-866-506-1949
or business@simonandschuster.com

The Simon & Schuster Speakers Bureau can bring authors to your
live event. For more information or to book an event, contact the
Simon & Schuster Speakers Bureau at 1-866-248-3049 or visit our
website at www.simonspeakers.com.

Dedicated to The Lost Ones

ACKNOWLEDGMENTS

To God, my strength, thank you for using me. To Martin, my first and always love, to Davin, my heart, every day I thank The Father for you both. To Mommy, Mimi and Mr. Capers, you always believed in me. To Donna and Kevin Bolk, the sister and brother of my heart, you mean more than words can convey. To my critique partners for the endless hours, days, and years. To Sara Camilli for believing in me, representing me and staying with me over the years. (I've thanked God many times for letting DSV be the lone book in your trunk on a day you had to wait for the repairman.) To Simon and Schuster/Strebor for giving me the chance. To Alhaji Saccoh for the research. To Beverly Alsop and Deborah Sumlin for the wisdom. To everyone who inspired, pushed and prayed, I love you. Thank you.

PROLOGUE

Rats.

Thick and well fed, they scurried along the moldy baseboard, and nosed through debris a few yards away from her feet. Lelia Freeman shifted her position, picked up the worn-down sole of an old shoe and tossed it toward the interlopers, then scoped the dank room once more.

A pile of urine-stained clothes adorned one corner; a pyramid of aluminum, ode to the beer can, lit another. A derelict wooden crate, blunt buds, and a broken crack pipe cluttered the floor. Someone managed to throw some fast-food wrappers into a mildewed box.

Lelia swiped her forehead with her sleeve. Boiling. It was one hundred degrees or better in the boarded row house. And she roasted.

Thick rubber bands shackled her jeans to her ankles, bit through the thick denim and knee-high socks, and held in the heat. She inched the bands down. A necessary evil. Better than roaches, mice or worse scampering up her legs.

She'd been there, in the squat, waiting for three hours. She'd give Megan another hour to show, then she'd head back to ChildSafe.

Megan's father was flying in from Colorado that day, was supposed to pick the child up from the shelter in three hours. Megan had left her home eleven months ago. She didn't flee from a hellish existence like most runaways. "I just wanted to be free from rules and live my own sixteen-year-old life," she'd said.

Life sunk its teeth into that sixteen-year-old, bit back. Crack found another weak slave to control, ruin.

She'd come to ChildSafe after eight months of hell, wanted to clean herself up. Wanted to go home. Lelia helped her, tough-loved her away from the streets, like she'd done for all the kids that stepped over ChildSafe's threshold.

The night before, after lights out, Megan bolted. Lelia's search brought her here, back to Megan's old stomping ground.

Lelia stood and stretched her cramped muscles. The floorboards shifted, groaned beneath her feet. She left the room, moved along the hallway, listened to the scampering, the scratching from inside the walls. She glanced through the holes punched in the clapboard. The reek of human waste, mildew and suffering assailed her. She didn't flinch. The surroundings were a part of her.

High in a corner on the wall, she caught sight of a scrap of wallpaper. Bright as the day it was hung, it stuck out in the gloom. Colorful flowers splashed across a white background.

Déjà vu.

A piece of her past.

On tiptoe, she touched the scrap...

...and remembered.

BOOK ONE

"Fearlessness and trembling are come upon me,
and horror hath overwhelmed me. And I said,
Oh that I had wings like a dove! *For then* would I
fly away, and be at rest."
—Psalm 55:5-6 KJV

CHAPTER ONE

Something scampered across her face. A waterbug, roach or worse. Lelia bolted upright, and almost toppled her makeshift bed. She shook off her clothes. Sweat dampened her honey-chocolate brow. Wild eyes darted about the small, dismal room, tried to draw comfort from its familiarity.

A single, yellowing light bulb hung from the ceiling by a tattered cord. Small bursts of chilly air from the plastic patched window rocked the bulb, and caused its dim light to bounce from one cracked plaster wall to another.

Her clothes were still tidy in the scratched, white laminate bookshelf at the foot of her bed; two stacked milk crates held her thrift-store sneakers and size-too-small flip-flops. The green shag remnant she'd lugged from the carpet discount Dumpster covered the cold wooden floor. The old radiator beneath the window produced little to no heat. Her cross-shaped clock still read 3:35 a.m., and her mama's neatly made cot remained untouched.

Still.

Nothing altered, everything forever in its depressing order. Familiarity of the room brought reality. Reality brought no comfort.

She padded to the curtainless window, rested her forehead on the frosted pane.

Across the front yard, the new dope dealer stood over his latest victim, Snook, the block's newest crackhead.

The street lamp over the court was busted. In the shadows, the dealer held up a small baggie. A madman, Snook clutched for it. The man held it just out of reach, laughed at Snook's desperation.

Snook stopped trying, rolled into a tight ball like a baby. Moans, low, pain-filled, filtered through the thin glass.

The scene was so common, it barely touched Lelia's heart. She flattened her hand against the pane, caught her reflection in the night-blackened glass, noted the change.

Her eyes.

She thought it would take longer.

Years. Decades.

It was there. The look she swore she'd never succumb to.

Staring at her were the eyes of her mama, Rubinell. Rubinell's eyes looked like that when she talked of Lelia's father.

She gazed into the eyes of Little Ray who stood on the street corner, begged for liquor money and ranted about Vietnam.

They were the sad, blank eyes of old Mrs. Sadie, who carried grocery bags of cans wherever she went.

Haunted eyes. Eyes weary of seeing. Tired of living.

Lelia was tired. Tired of being teased about her tattered clothes. Tired of Mama showing up at school drunk.

Tired of being alone. Weariness, slow and hungry, ate at her for months, but she wouldn't accept it. She wouldn't let the hood steal her dreams. Not like it stole Mama's.

She moved to the bedroom closet and retrieved the letterbox she kept hidden beneath the floorboards.

Her box of dreams.

The thin hardwood was padded with care and covered with a cream-colored silk. Dainty, pink water lilies splashed the soft material, trimmed with a narrow gold braid. A small, tarnished locket kept the flap sealed.

Bernard had given her this box. Bernard Samuels was the only decent man her mama ever dated. The only man Lelia thought of as a father.

She pulled out a stack of letters and pictures, all from him. She always wrote, told him her problems and fears. Without fail he responded, always sent a little spending cash and a return envelope with postage.

He wrote about Ohio. He sent pictures of his brothers, sisters and their children who wanted to meet her. He also wrote about his mother who had cancer. He left them to be with her. Lelia understood. Mama never forgave him for it.

He wrote to Mama, too, but she never opened his letters.

He used to fly in to visit them, but Mama refused to see him. After a while, he stopped coming.

Lelia put the money she'd saved from Bernard's letters and her after-school job at the corner store aside.

Housed in a plastic sandwich bag were several withered blooms. She held the plastic to her nose, pretended she could smell the petals' sweetness. The last item in the box was a picture. A photo of Bernard, Mama and herself on a weekend trip. Mama's eyes smiled at her.

Bernard had driven them to North Carolina. He'd planned on buying a house there, and wanted Mama to see it first.

Lelia remembered how the wind felt on her face, the endless miles of fields and trees. The vivid shades of the pink amethyst and yellow wildflowers took her breath away. She never remembered air smelling that good, or feeling that free.

Right before they got to the house, Bernard stopped the car and made them close their eyes. She peeked once, giggled when he sneaked a kiss from Mama.

He counted to three. They opened their eyes. Everything looked beautiful. Green grass as far as she could see, and actual trees growing in the front yard. Huge trees with dark, leathery leaves and big beautiful flowers that made the air smell like heaven. Bernard called them magnolias.

One story, the house's cedar polish sparkled against the cornflower sky. Large windows let the sun and fresh air flow through; a wide porch wrapped the house in a hug. Bernard promised Mama he'd build her a swing on the porch so he could court her properly.

Lelia loved everything about that place, but her favorite thing was the pretty flowers. Purple and magenta scattered around the porch and along the walkway...

Reality doused her. The apartment door crashed in, sounded like thunder.

She flipped off the light, dropped to her knees, and crawled to the radiator. She huddled against the cold metal, afraid to move.

Moments turned to an eternity. Familiar sounds dribbled through the walls. The Peters fighting next door. The Scoggins' loud rent party.

If she screamed, she'd be dead before anybody bothered to wander in to tell her to shut up. Nine-one-one was a fairy tale seen on TV. The cops wouldn't show. Whoever broke in would find her first.

The rustling from the living room grew bolder. The fear fisting her lungs grew tighter.

Lelia eyed the fire escape. She pulled herself to the window. Chips of old paint clung to her sweaty palms. Fingers trembling, she pushed the rusty latch. It bumped along, abused her bloody fingers.

"God, please help me."

She wrenched up the window, threw one leg over the sill.

Mama's cry pealed through the apartment.

"Mama!" Lelia fell to the floor. She worked against the darkness, grabbed the bat from behind the bedroom door, then stumbled into the narrow hallway.

Just past the kitchen, semi-darkness bathed the living room. The streetlight's glow fingered through the rips in the window shade, provided minimal light.

Lelia edged along the wall, listened again for Mama's voice. Scuffling sounds greeted her.

Her fear-washed body trembled anew.

"Mama?"

"Lelia!"

Her mother's strangled pitch reached her as a man's head popped over the back of the sofa.

Lelia cocked the bat, then wailed on him. The heavy wood cracked his shoulder, knocked him to the floor.

Adrenaline pumped fast as lightning. She raised the bat again, rounded the couch.

"You hurt my mother, you sorry..."

The lamp clicked on, a blaze of light blinded her. She adjusted her terrified eyes, slid her gaze from her mother's dumbstruck grimace to the man propped against the wall spitting curses.

"Crazy-ass bitch...!" He staggered to his feet. "Who the hell is this?"

That same question ran through Rubinell Washington's mind as she skimmed her daughter's confused expression and raggedy appearance.

What got into that girl? The kung fu crap was embarrassing enough, but that rat-eaten sweatsuit she had on made Rubinell flinch. And look at that mop of hair or whatever she wanted to call it! Looking like electrified black cotton.

Was she drunk? Just the thought of it pissed her off. If Lelia was drunk, there would be hell to pay, especially if the girl had drunk up her last bottle of Mad Dog.

She would deal with Lelia soon enough. Now, she had to take care of business. Sexiest pout intact, she pulled together the edges of her fire-red sweater dress, took her time buttoning it over her boobs.

That new push-up bra did wonders. Steve was licking his lips, probably already forgot his sore shoulder.

She sashayed up to him. "Steve, this is my daughter, Lelia. She's a little confused right now." She emphasized the word *confused*, hoped Lelia would get the message. She slanted a cold glare toward her child.

"Mama, are you all right?"

Steve was still nursing his shoulder. "Why are you asking her? I'm the one you tried to take out!"

"She didn't mean it, suga." Rubinell leaned against the wiry, balding man, and placed a small kiss at the corner of his mouth. "Did you, Lelia?"

She felt his body relax. Her old charms soothed better than five bottles of Wild Irish Rose.

"Apologize to the man, Lelia." She offered him another kiss. The bat banged to the floor, set her teeth on edge.

"But, Mama, I thought he was hurting—"

"Nobody asked you to think, did they Miss Honor Society?"

Steve tensed again. Rubinell cursed under her breath. She could kiss next week's free dinner with him good-bye. And that O'Jays concert.

She lowered her voice to a threatening whisper. "You know, I only ask once, Lelia."

She loosened Steve's tight lips with another kiss, then turned to confront her daughter.

Rubinell's breath caught. She stilled. Not many things backed her down, certainly not her child. But for a moment, she stared into the eyes of a man she loved long ago.

Defiant. Protective. Loving.

Lelia's fiery raven eyes were so like her father's that for an instant, Rubinell was ashamed of herself.

"I'm sorry, Mr. Steve."

Lelia spoke the words, but Rubinell saw her eyes held no remorse.

The apartment fell into an uneasy silence. For once in her life, Rubinell Washington was at a loss for words.

"Fruit don't fall far from the tree. Do it, Ruby?"

Steve squawked on, mother and daughter continued to eye each other.

"Both of y'all are whacked." He stomped around the sofa and snatched up his jacket. "I'm out."

Rubinell was relieved to see him go. She glanced over her shoulder, didn't try to stop him when he threw open the door. He was just another jerk, and her jerk quota had been filled years ago.

Hesitant, her gaze returned to Lelia, observed the child closely. Unsettling. Her daughter wasn't drunk. To her shame, she silently prayed that alcohol was responsible for Lelia's craziness. Rubinell knew drunk well, could deal with it like a pro, but not with the haunting emotion that simmered in her child's dark eyes. She'd lost too much to that emotion. She'd die before she'd lose her baby to it, too. She needed to stall, needed a minute to collect her thoughts.

Steve wasn't man enough to close the door. At least he was good for something; it gave her an excuse to run from the disturbing standoff with Lelia. She turned away, found him standing in the doorway, his repulsed glare swept the apartment.

"I'd sue to get something back for the eats I paid for, but your ass ain't got jack no ways. Besides..."

Rubinell watched his bored gaze rake her body, then rest on her face.

"...there ain't nothing here I want."

She forgot his words when she slammed the door in his face. Nothing registered anyway. Except panic. Except fear. Drunkenness dismissed, she had to face the truth. Lelia tried to save her life.

It was a fool thing to do, especially if someone was attacking her. The girl could have gotten herself killed. What was she thinking?

She squeezed her eyes closed. Lelia's fiery gaze flashed through her mind. Rubinell had her answer. The girl was her father's child, which meant valor preceded self-preservation, no matter the consequence.

How could she explain to Lelia all she'd lost to valor?

The love of her life. Her parents, her family. The chance of going to college. Bernard. How could a sixteen-year-old understand?

Then again this was Lelia, not some ordinary sixteen-year-old. An old soul. Wise beyond her years. Older than any child her age should be.

She was always there. Cooked the meals, washed the clothes, managed what little money they had.

She took care of everything like she tried to tonight. With a sad smile and tired eyes she would tolerate it because she was Lelia.

Rubinell would lovingly explain to her girl that self came first; chasing dreams was for fools, and trying to save the world would get her killed.

She braced herself, turned to the task at hand. Her child's sympathetic gaze slammed her. The love and compassion in Lelia's eyes was more than she could bear.

Love for her daughter filled her, and just as her mother had taught her, Rubinell expressed love to her child the only way she knew how.

"Just what in the hell did you think you were doing!"

Lelia rubbed her hands down her sweats. "I heard the door crash, and then I heard you scream." She paused, dragged in a breath. "And so I ran in and saw the man."

Her explanation hadn't changed Mama's mad expression. She dropped her gaze to her sock-covered feet, her big toe slipped through the hole on top. "I thought he was hurting you, Mama."

"What were you trying to pull, some of that karate bull Bernard's been filling your head with?"

Rubinell's voice reached a fever pitch. She closed the gap between them. "If you thought someone else was in here, why didn't you go down the fire escape?"

"I was going to, until I heard your voice. I couldn't just leave you, Mama. I had to help."

Lelia's soft-spoken reply proved Rubinell's undoing. She'd stood by, watched the man she loved die like a dog because he tried to play the hero. She'd be damned if she'd lose her child the same way.

"Just like your father. He died in the street at the ripe old age of eighteen. Is that the way you want to end up?"

"Mama, please." Lelia's eyes darkened with pain before she lowered her lashes.

Rubinell snapped Lelia's chin up, then seized her arms and ground out the tale that changed her life. Maybe it would save her daughter's.

"You're going to hear it again and again, until you get it through your head that being a hero don't add up to jack on the streets. You understand?

"Your father was a straight-A student, like you. We both were, for that matter. He'd gone away to Temple University on a full scholarship. He was only gone for a couple of months, but we talked on the phone almost every day. We were in love and missed each other."

Lelia lowered her head, closed her eyes tightly. She didn't want to hear this story again.

"The day he hit town for Christmas break, he rushed over to see me. I'd spent all day primping up. He worked part-time in the library and didn't have much money after paying for our phone calls, so he took me to Pop's Burger Stand. We had a candlelit picnic in his mother's basement and talked about the wedding and the life we were planning after he graduated."

Lelia felt the pressure from her mother's hands ease. She listened to the pain seep into a toneless rasp. It always did.

Usually Mama casually preached the tale when she was a little tipsy. A behavior-modifying sermon. This time was different. Desperation trickled along her mother's hoarse voice, made her feel uneasy. Knowing her mother was sober frightened her even more.

"I started telling him the gossip on the street when he asked about his best friend, Richard. Rich was a good kid, but after your father left, he started hanging with the wrong crowd. Word was out that the boys Rich hung with were going to knock off Sofia's Corner Store that night. I didn't want to tell your father, but we didn't keep secrets. When he told me he had to find Rich, I exploded. We argued. He stormed out."

Lelia shook her head, silently prayed the story would end here.

Mama's blank eyes relived another time.

"I followed him to Sofia's and watched from an alley across the street. He found Rich standing outside the store, being the lookout. He was fussing with Rich to leave when the other guys came running out of the store."

The pressure on Lelia's arms increased. A scary wildness filled her mama's eyes.

"It all happened so fast. I felt my chest tightening and knew something was about to go wrong. The owner came out as I tried to cross the street. Rich saw the man and ran. Your father turned and told the man he wasn't involved, but all he saw was a young, black face.

"He emptied his gun into him. I couldn't hear anything but the cracks of the bullets. I reached the store and the man was still pumping the trigger. Red paint, your father's blood, covered the sidewalk. I held him. Rocked him until the life slipped from his eyes, listened to the click of the chamber over and over.

"A month later I found out I was pregnant. Four months later my parents couldn't hide it anymore, so they kicked me out."

Rubinell let her hands slide from Lelia's arms, turned away, appalled at her child's expression. She didn't mean to scare her, only shake a little sense into her.

Nothing ever worked the way she planned. This wasn't the way she wanted to raise her child. Lord knew she didn't deserve her. The mess she'd made of her life was testimony to that.

Of late, her past and present mistakes haunted her. Dismal warnings tapped her mind, played their incessant tune, denied her peace. Everything was spinning out of her control. God, she needed that Mad Dog.

Weary from life, Rubinell rounded the sofa, moved an ashtray here, straightened a pillow there. Opposite her daughter, she didn't raise her eyes to ask the simple questions.

"Do you want to end up like your father? Do you want to end up like me?"

Lelia watched her mama move down the hall. She snapped off the living room light and followed her to the bedroom.

"Lelia, clean up this mess." Rubinell waved a finger toward the floor before she entered the bathroom.

Lelia made her way to the foot of the closet. A scattered array of letters littered the floor. Her pictures were skewed beneath Mama's bed. The beautiful flower petals appeared as crushed purple snowflakes against the green carpet. Her box of dreams lay splintered on top of the letters, its creamy silk torn from its flattened sides.

Rubinell stopped at the bathroom door, followed Lelia's gaze to the clutter. She caught her child's eyes, found them needy. Her daughter's eyes pleaded for reassurance that things would be all right.

What did the girl expect from her? She was tired and couldn't take anymore.

Not tonight.

Lelia needed her mama's strength and reassurance. But all Rubinell did was try to remove the pins from her hair before she gave up, crawled into bed and closed her eyes.

She walked over to her mother's cot, sat on its edge and started to remove the bobby pins from her mama's curly black hair.

She was tired and couldn't take anymore.

Especially not tonight.

"Mama, I have some money saved. We can leave this mess and start new lives." Lelia prayed that this time her pleading wouldn't fall on deaf ears.

"You can find a job and I can work after school. We can move down South. I read it's not expensive to live down there. We can save for a house with pretty trees and..."

Lelia stopped talking, surprised to see a single tear course down Mama's smooth, copper cheek.

She'd never seen her mama cry. She reached to dry the tear. Mama's fingers clamped over her wrist. Their eyes met, held. Mama aged, her eyes held years of anguish, pain. Years of dreaming of a better life only to settle for this.

"Please, Mama...please?" Maybe this turning point would change their lives.

"Lelia, you were born here, you're going to marry and raise your children here, you're gonna die here. Nothing and no one's going to change that."

Lelia held her shattered box, sat and stared at her mother for hours.

A dreamless life wouldn't be her life.

She placed fifty dollars and a note on the bookshelf. Book bag packed, she brushed a kiss on her mother's cheek, then set off in the snow to follow her dreams.

CHAPTER TWO

"*There is a fountain, filled with blood, drawn from Emmanuel's veins, and sinners plunge, beneath that flood, lose all their guilty stains.*"

Lelia huddled on the last pew in the large sanctuary, listened to the choir softly sing the old hymn. If only the words could be true.

She wiped her nose along the dirt-encrusted sleeve of her coat, caught sight of her filthy hand. Hand of a beggar and thief. How could someone like her lose or be forgiven of such sins?

She hunkered deeper into the oversized coat. She'd burn for sure, as sure as she turned nineteen years old that day. The two years she'd survived in Los Angeles made her feel one hundred and nineteen.

For two years she called abandoned squat buildings and teen shelters home. For two years she panhandled and stole from the markets just to ease her burning hunger. And for two years she fought off Zeek, the man who wanted to pimp her body.

These weren't the dreams she'd dreamed when she left

New York. She wanted to come to L.A., make some money and help people. Help Mama. Yet there she sat, in the same clothes she'd stepped off the bus in two years ago, only fifty-three cents hidden in the bottom of her shoe. Homeless. Hungry. Filthy.

Three nights ago, she'd burst into Cornerstone Baptist's vestibule, barely escaped Zeek's clutches. With hands pressed against the glass of the heavy entry doors, she watched him, bold eyes dared him to walk into God's house.

He'd stood at the bottom of the church step. Their eyes waged a silent war until a passing couple drew Zeek's attention. Part chameleon camouflaged all evil, instantly transformed his tight features. Manicured forefinger and thumb sleeked his sable mustache and goatee. He granted the pair a friendly nod. She watched his gaze follow the couple, finally turning back to her. He blew her a kiss around a thin-lipped grin. Long fingers smoothed the lapels of his cashmere coat before he strolled off.

She rested her head against the cool glass. Then she heard it...the beautiful music. Almost against her will, she was drawn through the stained-glass doors of the sanctuary. That was three days ago. Since that time, each night she'd left her play sister, Joella, to attend the weeklong revival. She'd hunker in the last pew, and try to glean hope for their dismal existence.

Lelia pulled her gaze from her ragged-soled sneakers to scan the front of the church. Large ivory candles around the gold-draped altar provided a warm glow to the sanctum, and filled the air with the aroma of bayberry.

Red and white poinsettias wrapped in green foil, gold bows and holly adorned the pulpit, choir loft and various sconces around the church. The choir wore warm smiles and billowy cream-and-gold-trimmed robes. Their sweet voices rang with joy.

The congregation filled half the pews. It was a mixed crowd...ranged from infancy to elderly, clad from casual to the best Sunday finery. Mothers soothed fussy infants; husbands pulled wives close and stole quick kisses; while seasoned citizens sneaked grands, peppermints and caramels. The strong sense of family made Lelia feel at home.

That night's sermon was on faith. The minister preached about holding on, not giving in to despair. His emotion-filled timbre recalled the many trials he made it through over the years, with God's help.

Head held high, he stepped off the altar, coursed the center aisle. He stopped in front of Ma Ella, the 102-year-old mother of the church. He grasped her weathered hand.

Everyone knew Ma Ella's house burned down three weeks prior. The preacher announced the names of a builder and national lumberyard who volunteered to rebuild her house, free of charge.

Amens and hallelujahs filled the sanctum.

By the time the invitation to join the church was offered, a strange feeling flowed through the sanctuary, one Lelia never experienced. Every night, this was the time she slipped away, but a powerful sense of peace permeated the church, riveted her to the pew.

Many in the congregation stood, their faces toward the ceiling. Others sat rocking. Each member acted differently. One thing held true for everyone it seemed, all eyes filled with tears. Even hers.

Maybe if she knew more about God, had some of that faith the minister preached about, she could change a few things. Have a real life. She and Joella didn't belong on the streets. None of the kids she knew did.

So engrossed in thought, Lelia didn't hear the benediction or notice the people mill past her. There were only two people in the sanctuary when she looked up, herself and Ma Ella, who sat directly in front of her.

Lelia peered through the Coke-bottle lenses that sat atop Ma Ella's nose. The matron of the church held her gaze for a moment, then she widened her ever-present smile.

Ma's slightly lined ebony face didn't show her age. She didn't look a day over sixty. Under the latest Sunday-going-to-meeting hat, her salt-and-pepper hairpiece was neatly styled, as usual. Her remaining ten children, numerous grands and great-grands kept her in the latest duds. Mind and memory razor sharp, her four-foot-eleven frame got about with minimal help, except when her 'ritis flared up.

Lelia couldn't comprehend reaching twenty-two, let

alone 102. She searched for something adult to say, but only came out with a dumb, "Hi."

"Hi yourself, baby."

Ma's warm smile proved contagious. Lelia grinned for no particular reason.

"I've seen you sitting back here trying to hide since the first night of revival, creeping out before Pastor gives the invitation. What are you running from, baby?" Ma's teeth slipped while she spoke.

"Ma'am?"

"I know you're not deaf, child. So I'll ask you again. Why are you running?"

"I'm not dressed for church, ma'am, and I haven't got a place to wash up regularly."

"I've had more dirt on me working the tobacco fields. Nobody in here looks at you strange because of a little smudge."

Lelia didn't answer. Her eyes slanted to her dirt-darkened nails.

Two years ago she chased her dreams. When did she stop chasing them and start running from nightmares? Today, she wasn't sure of anything.

Ma Ella leaned over the pew. "What's your name, baby?"

"Lelia, ma'am."

"Lelia, your eyes tell me you're a good child. You have a kind heart and warm spirit. Baby, maybe if you'd stop running long enough, you'd hear what God is trying to tell you."

With that, Ma Ella raised herself from the pew and waved toward the church's vestibule.

A tall man appeared at Ma's side, nodded a cordial hello.

Ma stopped at Lelia's pew, rummaged through her purse and pulled out a moist towelette and peppermint. She grinned and handed them to Lelia.

"This should help wash off some of that dirt you're so worried about. The mint is for your breath, in case you try that as an excuse for not sitting through tomorrow's service." She smiled at her escort. "I'm ready, Simian."

Lelia watched them take several slow steps before Ma stopped at the sanctum door. She straightened to her full height, head tilted, pride entered her voice. "I've been at this church for seventy-three years. There're good folks here. God sent you to the right place, Lelia. When you get tired of running, we'll be here to help. Night, baby."

Lelia gazed around the empty church, pondered Ma's words, wanted desperately to believe them.

She thought of Joella. The child was only thirteen. She should be going to sleepovers or giggling on the phone with friends. Instead she slept on cold floors in abandoned, drafty buildings, and was sick all the time. How could she last living like that?

Bundled to brace the unusual cold, Lelia scanned the street for Zeek and his boys. The church provided a safe haven, but Zeek still ran the neighborhood.

She stayed off main streets after nightfall, avoided The Strip. Tonight she chose residential side streets for her trudge back to the squat.

With every footfall, Zeek stole into her thoughts, quashed her spirits. Discarded paper and cans littered the cracked, uneven pavement. She trudged through the garbage, the lightheartedness and freedom she'd felt moments earlier insidiously vanished.

Busted street lamps allowed the moon's fullness to brighten the road with an eerie glow. Shadowed porches, trees and vehicles made the neighborhood a sinister photo negative, deepened her dolefulness.

She felt trapped.

The desperate need of a better life brought her bleak existence into painful clarity. Once, the dreadful surroundings seemed ordinary, now they clamped around her, smothered with a frightful intensity.

The pastor's passion-filled timbre dueted with Ma Ella's pointed questions. Both raced through Lelia's mind, kept a rhythmic cadence as her footsteps quickened.

"There is hope for any situation, if you have faith....What are you running from, baby?...This place is not your destiny... Maybe if you'd stop running long enough, you could hear what God is trying to tell you..."

Their words deafened.

Cold wind bit the tears on her cheeks, stung her eyes, blinded her path as she ran. Desperation numbed her usual cautiousness to her surroundings, and almost cost her dearly.

She raced from her specters, rounded a corner full speed, not hearing the punishing, raspy voice until she nearly collided with its distracted owner.

Zeek's suited flunkies, Thero and Weasel, were shaking down one of Zeek's girls, Angel.

Unnoticed, Lelia inched back into the shadows to watch and pray.

Thero rifled through Angel's purse, while Weasel kept sentry by the curb. Zeek never got his hands dirty in the business. Nonchalant, he leaned on an iron-gated store-front, observed the arena.

A typical scene for The Strip, the strong preyed on the weak. Still, this was unusual for Zeek and his crew. Why were they collecting on the street? Everyone who worked for Zeek, even those who didn't, knew his rules. They were simple: bring Thero the proceeds or die.

Heart heavy, Lelia eyed Angel and wondered why she chose to surrender to Zeek. She sorely missed the bubbly young woman named Angela, missed sharing dreams with her good friend.

Lelia remembered the bus ride to L.A. they had shared, the cheap motel they called home for three months.

Five-foot-five, statuesque, shiny raven hair, flawless honey skin. Only Angela's beauty and soft heart surpassed her singing.

Both of them had worked odd jobs. After work they'd meet back in their cramped room, dreaming about their future till the wee hours. Lelia talked of college, of changing the world. Angela talked of taking the record-ing industry by storm.

Angela got her break. She met an agent with all the

right connections. He loved her voice, her look. Fresh, raw talent, that's what he searched for. He wined and dined her. Conjured a new, sexier image. He managed and invested her savings, like he did for all his clients.

Angela's head was stuck in the clouds. "He's hell-bent on making me a star."

Lelia met Angela's agent the night she was to perform for a large-label record producer. Ready to launch Angela's career, he strolled into their room. Tall, handsome, expensive-clothes-down.

Lelia helped Angela with the last touches to her hair, then she hugged her. "I'm so proud of you, Angela."

Angela giggled, headed to the bathroom. The agent leaned against the door, eyed Lelia, up and down. She didn't like the feel of him. Bold, she matched his stare, watched two long, tawny fingers smooth the sable mustache and goatee. He seemed to enjoy the cat-and-mouse chase, broke the folly only when Angela re-entered the room.

He extended his arm to Angela. "Come, sweetness, time to make you a star." He blew Lelia a kiss, opened the door to usher Angela to her destiny, and then he turned back into the room. "Her name's been changed. Now she's my...Angel."

Angela had lived in hell ever since.

Tonight Lelia watched a frightened girl shiver in a short denim jacket, red micro miniskirt, and spiked heels that could impale a roach. Angel. Zeek's property.

Thero fisted the crumpled bills he'd extracted from Angel's purse, tucked them into the breast pocket of his suit. He extended the ragged satchel toward her and offered an apologetic, gold-toothed grin around the stub of his vanilla Mote Rio.

Angel's lips curved a shaking smile, seeming to accept his unspoken apology.

Hesitant, her fingertips grasped the bag's worn straps. Angel's features relaxed when Thero released the bag.

"Please, just walk away." Lelia whispered the prayer.

Thero's hand snaked out, yanked the straps around Angel's wrist, wrenched her arm into an unnatural position. With the homemade manacle wedged in his meaty palm, he jerked Angel's slight body against his iron-wall frame.

Lelia balled her fists. *Fool knucklehead better not hurt her.*

Thero released the purse straps, toyed with Angel, pretended to soothe the hurt, before he snatched her off the ground to his eye level.

Cigar smoke haloed Angel's head. She choked while her eyes begged.

Thero's bulbous glare trapped his quarry. His scratchy rasp lashed out verbal punishment. "Don't have us come for you again, *capeesh.*" He shook her with each word, forced her head to thrash like a bobble-head doll.

Anger overrode common sense. Lelia searched for a brick, rock, anything to bash Thero's bald head in. She spied a banged up metal trash can, pried off its lid. She raced to the corner, breathed fire, but stopped.

Miracles do happen.

Thero bounced Angel on her feet. A disgusted scowl raised his lip. He grabbed her purse. After he rifled through it, he slung it to the ground. He trudged it underfoot as he snapped for Weasel to follow his departure.

Punch drunk, Lelia flopped to the ground, while relaxing her death grip on the metal lid. What would she have done if things had gotten ugly? The preacher said God takes care of children and fools.

She peered around the corner as giddiness turned to loathing. Angel crawled across the pavement, scurried to retrieve her belongings. Zeek pushed himself from the window, and strolled to her.

He hovered, stared at Angel's bowed head. Lelia had never seen such hate-filled eyes.

Angel put the last items into her purse, then looked up to her keeper.

Zeek's features transmuted. Actor-rehearsed sympathy softened his hard face. The epitome of a caring guardian, he stooped to help his Angel.

Angel's soft brown eyes looked like saucers whenever she looked at Zeek. He graced her with a tender smile, gently tucked stray, dull strands of hair behind Angel's ear.

Lelia turned from the nauseating scene. She tried to talk Angel into leaving L.A., going back to Knoxville. Nothing worked.

Angel would be on the verge of going to a shelter for a free ticket home, then Zeek would roll out his record-contract lies and have Angel eating out of his palm again. He'd chastise her for listening to her little friend's fairy tales. Angel would disappear for weeks, sometimes months afterward. All of Zeek's servants followed his command.

Bone weary, Lelia stood, walked the trashcan lid back to its receptacle.

She closed her eyes. Her nerves were shot. Her thin mattress on the squat floor sounded like heaven right about now. She needed to pull herself together before she went to the squat or Joella would know something went down.

Relaxation was a foreign word.

Bernard taught her how to relax, part of the martial arts he studied. Deep-breathing techniques, he called it.

"Standing over a trash can trying out tai chi. Girl, you're tripping."

Still, she started to breathe the way Bernard had taught her.

Inhale through your nose and exhale through your mouth. Inhale through your nose and...

Vanilla.

CHAPTER THREE

The smoky-sweet stench clung to the icy breeze, and danced around Lelia's panic-frozen body. She opened her eyes, peered at a dime-sized ember bobbing a few yards from her side.

"Well, well, well, look what I found here among the trash heap. A sweet little package of...confection."

Thero's scratchy whisper had a clawed-chalkboard effect across Lelia's skin. The moon glowed behind him, obscured his features. Her mind pictured them vividly. The crazy gleam in his bulbous eyes. Thin, angry lips pulled over fourteen-karat-gold teeth. Scratch marks; from one of his victims; marred his shaven ebony head and left cheek. A badge of honor.

Gone was her bravado. Her angry venom of injustice vanished. Only one emotion lingered: fear.

Zeek didn't scare her, neither did Weasel. Thero was different. His eyes held an unnatural glitter. No camouflage. No emotion. Just evil.

"I know a man who's been itching to own a particular

cube of confection. Not just any old sweet..." She listened to the slow inhalation hiss over metal caps. "...but a special comfit, with a specific feel, smell and...flavor."

Sweat moistened her brow. Wickedness seethed along his husky rasp, stroked her with its iced finger. Her body trembled.

"My man will pay big bucks if I deliver this little package. He's already got plans to rename it. Gonna call it brown sugar."

The ember bobbed closer. Lelia prayed for mercy. Thero delivered his loathsome blow.

"Time to go, sweet thing. But before I bring you to my man, we gonna get you cleaned up. You and me are gonna have a little fun, brown sugar."

His nearness cowed her. Slowly she lifted her gaze to scan his face.

Ghastly shadows played over his features, darkened his eyes to bottomless chasms. The blackened hollows beneath his cheeks consummated his skull-bone appearance.

The reaper cometh.

His beefy hand descended at half-speed, the metal reflection of his victorious grin stirred the bile in her stomach. His triumphant bark slammed her senses, jarred her fear-induced stupor.

She swung the can lid toward the reaper's skull, happy to feel pain vibrating through her arms and shoulders, to see the torch of the Mote Rio spin toward the moon. One last swing connected to the reaper's shaven dome.

He dropped, whipped-up drunk on the cold pavement.

Lelia's arms and hands still quivered as she covered her third block at breakneck speed.

It was crazy to charge Thero. When he snapped out of it, he'd be really ticked.

She'd beat him and was alive to tell it. If word of his shameful defeat got out, his bad-fool image would have a costly chink. He'd be useless to Zeek. And useless to Zeek meant death.

Thero would keep it quiet, but he wouldn't forget. It wouldn't take him long to hunt her down, silence her for good.

Fate mocked her as she slipped down side streets and dodged through alleys. The moon loomed high, lit the deserted neighborhood that housed her and Joella's make-shift home.

A working-class community, small, one-story bungalows spread for blocks. People struggled to provide food and shelter for loved ones. Desperate parents tried to keep their children from the lure of gangs, drugs, reaching towards the mirage of a better life.

Everyone in the neighborhood knew she and Joella lived in the abandoned three-story storefront. No one squawked. Two homeless runaways were the least of their problems.

After her tango with Thero, Lelia was happy to see her boarded, dilapidated home. She scanned the street, rounded a corner, trudged to the narrow alley beside the squat. She hated these last steps. There was no other way into the building. Sideways was the only way to get through the tight passage.

From the roof, musty water scaled the sides of the building from a dangling, rust-eaten downspout. The liquid smelled stale, formed a green, slimy film that covered the walls and clung to anything in its path. She slogged through murky puddles, scared off hungry rodents. Commonplace.

In the large walled-off alley behind the building, Lelia rummaged to find the hidden iron railing that availed as her ladder to a boarded second-floor window. She crawled through the broken pane into a hallway, then hoisted up the railing and slid the boards into place.

Pungent mildew twanged the stagnant air. The house's clamminess enveloped her. Outside, the roof lamp flickered, spewed cool blue fingers of light between the slats of wood boarding the window, brightened the top of the dank corridor.

Lelia didn't need the light to see. She knew her surroundings too well.

Marred walls covered with scads of daisy wallpaper lay eroded, filthy with dust. A deserted gallery of closed doors hid battered chairs, two-legged tables, and other debris that once cluttered the hallway.

Dismal to most, but to her tired eyes, it fell a sliver short of paradise.

Almost.

Her weary mind hadn't noticed anything out of sorts. Until now. She eyed the corridor. One usual comfort was missing.

Light.

The end of the hallway was usually aglow. A soft, pale beam invariably spilled from the bedroom she and Joella shared. Like air, Joella needed it. She feared darkness.

Joella was a normal runaway. She survived the evils of the streets, tried to forget the demons that chased her there. Nine months of street life had toughened Joella, but her demons weren't easily forgotten. They invaded her dreams, attacked in the darkness. Nightmares that left her screeching. The terror made her withdraw for days, robbed the pixie mischief that danced in her gentle brown eyes.

Lelia felt helpless. The child wouldn't share her horrors. Besides rocking Joella in her arms until she fell back to sleep, the only comfort Lelia could provide was a small battery-powered lamp that kept the child's demons at bay.

Now the end of the hall was shrouded in blackness.

Lelia ignored the knots tightening her stomach. Her feet sprinted over the warped hardwood. Pain did not exist when her shoulder cracked against the doorjamb. Fear froze Joella's name in her throat as her lips parted in a silent scream.

Numbness engulfed her body at the sight that welcomed her.

CHAPTER FOUR

Rotten clapboard scraped over the brick window ledge facing the alley. Faint rustlings, like a dog scratching hard dirt, floated through the house. It meant one thing.

Lelia was home.

Joella glanced down at the candlelit muffin and tiny plastic-wrapped package beside it. Everything was perfect.

She reached to click off the battery lamp, but hesitated. Sweat-slicked fingers trembled on the power button. Jitters gnawed her stomach, wide eyes darted around the room.

Empty. Nothing to fear.

She held her breath, pushed down the old horrors, and managed to switch off the lamp.

Instinct snapped her eyes shut. She forced them open to slits. Candlelight bathed the beat-in walls. The room wasn't too dark. She wasn't scared. Not much.

Frantic footsteps pounded the hall's creaky floorboards. Lelia skidded around the door frame. Joella sat straighter, so Lelia wouldn't think she was chicken.

"Happy birthday to you, happy birthday to—well now, I know I sound a little croaky but dang, I don't sound that bad. Do I?" All good intentions caught in her throat.

Lelia stepped into the candlelight, eyes big, unblinking as a doe caught unaware.

Pain played just below the surface of her stare. Sadness, despair seeped from Lelia's stiff body, stroked Joella.

She opened her mouth, then closed it. No amount of talking would ease the look fixed on Lelia's face. Joella knew better. She'd seen that same look reflected in her own mirror. She'd lived in the same hell many times herself, almost didn't get out.

Life, cruel and hard, must have whipped up on Lelia, made her draw inside herself like a cornered hare drawn inside its burrow. Best thing to do was leave her be, for now. A burrow was the safest place for her.

Joella was an expert on safe burrows. They made life endurable, harbored your mind, saved you from going mad.

A lifetime ago, they were the only way she'd survived. She used to fill her burrows with rainbows, magic dragons and pretty horned horses. All the things her daddy used to spin tales about before he'd tuck her into bed. She hadn't needed safe burrows when Mama and Daddy were around. But all that vanished when they left.

For a while, Grandma Dell was all she had. Until Cousin Daryl came sniffing around, hard on his luck. Evil took the form of that hard-on-his-luck doper.

Joella thought hell was missing her parents. Cousin

Daryl had other thoughts of hell. He shared them with her daily.

Open-handed cuffs across the face, kicks to the ribs. The thrashings. Still, no hell he executed terrorized her more than the darkness.

Cousin Daryl always locked her alone. In the darkness.

Grandma Dell tried to stop him, but he hit her, too, forced her in her room.

Joella could still hear Grandma calling through her bedroom door, begging him to stop. She still felt fire scorch her skull from his fingers clenched in her hair, still remembered half screeching, half choking on fear as he drug her to the barn. Taught her her lesson.

Sprawled on her stomach, her back ripped raw. Tears puddled mud under her cheek. Dirt and sweat throbbed in her busted lip. Blood and bile sullied her tongue. Unable to move, she lay in the blackness, hushed her sobs, scared he'd hear. Scared he'd come back to teach her more lessons. Those were the times her safe burrows surrounded her, pressed insanity to the fringes of her mind.

One night she ran away from Cousin Daryl while he was sleeping off a high. She'd helped Grandma Dell to Granddad's old truck, and drove off. Her feet barely reached the pedals. They hit a couple of ditches, but they'd made it.

A family friend in the next county took them in. For a few weeks hell disappeared.

It resurfaced when Cousin Daryl tracked them down. Joella took off, never looked back.

Some nights Cousin Daryl still found her, stole into her dreams, locked her in darkness. Memories of Daddy or Mama didn't keep him from hurting her, remembering Grandma Dell's kind words didn't hold him at bay. Only Lelia's soft voice broke through the death dream to save her.

Now Lelia needed saving.

Her friend knelt in front of the candlelit muffin. Zombified, she stared at the burning wick.

Comfort was the only thing Joella could offer. She shrugged the rough quilt off her shoulders, then wrapped them both in it. She rocked like Grandma Dell used to do. It felt like forever. The hardwood dug into her knees, the candle burned, she kept rocking.

For once, Lelia needed her. No matter what, she'd be Lelia's light, 'cause no one should be left in the darkness.

The flame danced before Lelia's eyes. Numbness ebbed through her skin, her muscles, lolled her head to one side.

Time stilled. The room's dismal atmosphere faded. Only the candle's torch existed. It enticed, mocked her. In its flicker danced her anguish. Her shattered dreams. All her terrors whirled through the fire's smoke, until they consumed her.

She rocked. Slow and easy. A hushed melody drifted

through the fog, called to her. Her eyelashes batted against hair, her cheek rested against skin. Burning skin. Lelia blinked again, looked down. Joella was huddled beside her, humming a scratchy tune.

"You're hot, pip-squeak."

"I'm fine." Joella sat up, snapped on the light, her eyes overly bright. "Do you like your birthday surprise?"

Her birthday. Hours ran into months, weeks into years. Lelia lost track of time. Only hours before, she'd reminisced about the day of her birth. She glanced over the fare Joella prepared.

A chocolate-iced cupcake sat on an overturned dresser drawer, pink wax puddled in the center of the icing. The cellophane cupcake wrapper was folded in a neat square beside it.

"I didn't have another candle, but you can make a wish just the same."

Lelia looked into the child's uncertain eyes. The need to protect welled in her chest, made it hard to breathe, stoked her resolve to get them off the streets. She masked her turmoil. "My birthday? I thought you laid out this fancy dig for the President."

The smile she'd hoped for creased Joella's face. "What's this, pip-squeak?" She palmed the small, cellophane package.

"Ain't much." Joella shrugged, looked away.

Lelia turned the tiny present. "Is it a sports car?"

Joella giggled. "No."

"A house with running water?"

More giggles. "Uh-uh."

"I'm stumped."

"Just open it up."

Tongue in cheek, Lelia slowly peeled back each corner, exaggerated every movement. The deep belly laugh she loved filled the room. The child's wet gurgling coughs doused the merriment.

Lelia got up, poured some water from the jug in the corner, then handed Joella a broken-handled cup. "Here, drink this."

The coughing settled. Content, Lelia pulled back the last corner of the wrap.

"Jo Jo, it's your necklace." She held up the delicate gold chain, watched the half-heart pendant catch the lamp's light, spin in midair. "I can't take this. You've never taken it off."

"It's all I've got besides my quilt. Some folks say the giver makes the gift special." She pushed the pendant and Lelia's outstretched hand away. "I wanted to give you something special."

"Did someone special give this to you, Jo Jo?"

Joella's gaze flitted away.

"Look, it's beautiful, but why give away something that obviously means so much?" Lelia grasped Joella's hand. "You're the sister of my heart. That's gift enough."

"I can't explain it, but this might." Joella handed her a piece of tattered cardboard.

Lelia held it up, read the minute cursive.

There was an empty vessel, no love no peace inside.
Hurt was its cork-tight closure, fear guarded every side.
My heart was this lone vessel, pain destined to subdue.
Until the day, God showered down, the blessing that is you.

"I'm giving you half my heart so you'll have one half..." Joella placed her hand over her chest, "...and I'll have the other, so we'll always be together."

"Mmmmm, uh-mmmm, uh-mmmm." Lelia mopped her cheeks with her coat sleeve. "Jo Jo, stop making me cry. You know how ugly I get when I bawl."

"I don't believe I do. I've never seen you cry."

"Trust me, it's not a pretty sight."

"I don't need to trust you, seeing is believing."

"Okay, smarty. I get the message. It's just that no one's ever done anything this special for me. Ever." She finished drying her face, then undid the necklace clasp. "Do me a favor?"

Joella wrinkled her nose. "Depends what it is, I guess."

Lelia rose on her knees and looped the chain around Joella's neck. "Wear it for me. You've been keeping it safe this long. With me on the street so much, somebody might snatch it." She leaned back on her haunches. "All right?"

Joella smoothed a finger over the pendant, gazed at it like a long-lost friend. "All right."

"Let's turn in." She straightened her newspaper-stack mattress into a neater pile. When she glanced back, Joella was staring wide-eyed at the dimming lamp.

"Lelia, did you get more batteries?"

"You know I did."

"Did they cost much?"

Lelia took the heavy pack out of her pocket and tossed them to her. "Found them near the Dumpster in the back of Joe's Market."

"Liar." Large, worried eyes met hers. "Do you think you'll be needing the lamp close...you know, for reading?"

Lelia shrugged, went back to fixing her papers. "Naw. Scoot it closer to you. The light helps keep roaches away."

"Thank you."

"For what?"

Joella plucked at a loose string on the quilt. "Letting me keep my pride."

Lelia lay down, pulled her coat around her shoulders. "Don't know what you're talking about, pip-squeak."

"Liar. And I ain't no pip-squeak."

"You are if I say you are. And *ain't* isn't a word."

"It is where I come from."

Plastic scraped across the floor, the lamplight wavered, shifted. Muffled coughs, soft rustling drifted through the room.

"Lelia?"

"Yeah, Jo Jo."

Silence.

"I love you."

Quiet blanketed the room again. Warmth, peace enveloped her heart. Somehow things would be all right.

"I love you, too, pip-squeak. I love you, too."

Lelia caught a glimpse of the bright smile wedged between chestnut cheeks before Joella rolled over and snuggled under her quilt.

She pulled her wool hat over her ears, stared at the dingy ceiling. It was time to swallow her pride and take Ma Ella up on her offer.

For Joella's sake.

CHAPTER FIVE

"Jo Jo, I've got to go out." Lelia fixed her hat on her head and looked over at the bundled body on the floor. "A woman I trust promised she'd help us find a place to stay, find us a home."

She took the silence as opposition. "We need better lives, Jo Jo. I promise we'll stay together. Jo Jo?"

She knelt beside the child, pulled back the quilt. "Oh no."

Bright red spots painted Joella's cheeks and nose. She placed the back of her hand against her forehead. "God, you're burning up. You need to be in a hospital."

"No."

"Yes, Jo Jo. Your clothes are soaked, you're trembling."

Joella struggled to sit up. "Please, Lelia. They'll send me back. They'll try and send me back." She gripped her sleeve. "I'd die before I go back. You hear?"

Wet gurgling coughs shook Joella's thin shoulders. Lelia raced to the water jug. A dribble of fluid circled the bottom of the container.

She rushed back to Joella's side. "I'm going to get some juice and medicine."

"Where'd you get the money?"

"Don't worry about that." She eased the child's quaking frame under the quilt. "I'll be right back."

"No hospitals, Lelia."

From the door, Lelia held Joella's wide-eyed gaze. She wouldn't make that promise.

She hurried to the hall bathroom, wriggled loose the emergency cash she had stashed in the rusted pipes, then sprinted to the store.

Packed down with flu medicine, juice and water, she stepped onto the last rung of the railing when sounds of strained retching echoed down the hall.

For the second time in twenty-four hours, fear for Joella stabbed her heart. She raced down the hall, found Joella doubled over the dresser drawer, dry heaves shook her torso.

"Jo Jo!"

She bit the plastic tab on the water jug and ripped it off. Next, she dug in her knapsack for her spare pair of socks. She wet the threadbare tubes and looped one over the back of Joella's neck, held the other to her forehead.

Clumps of green mucous tinged the wet spots in the drawer. She rubbed Joella's back. "Are you finished?"

"I believe so."

Lelia pushed the drawer away, eased Joella down on her newspaper bedding.

So intent on comforting her charge, she almost missed

the shadow that fell across Joella's quilt. She jerked her head around as Angel touched her shoulder.

"You scared the—! How'd you get up here?"

"You left the railing down. I came to say good-bye."

Lelia looked past Angel to the large duffel bag and jacket by the door.

Her friend looked different. Not dressed in the fleshy garb Zeek forced his girls to wear, devoid of makeup, she wore jeans, sneakers and an oversized sweatshirt. She looked like the old roommate Lelia grew to call a friend. She looked like Angela.

Angel pushed Lelia aside. "What's wrong with the baby? She looks awful." She peeled back the sock and placed a hand to Joella's brow. At the touch, Joella's drowsy eyes sought Angel's, graced her with a sleepy grin.

Lelia hedged closer. "I'm worried about her."

"Well, what did you expect?" Angel tucked the quilt around Joella's shoulders and neck. "You keep her in this drafty rat trap. She can't help but be sick."

"I'm doing my best."

"Well, your best isn't cutting it. Why didn't you come to me? I've asked you, no, begged you a million times for the two of you to live with me."

Tired of the old argument, Lelia got up and walked just outside the door. Angel hounded her heels.

"You think I could stay there, knowing Zeek kept you on your back to pay the rent? He used you to line his pockets, Angel. Forget it, I don't play that."

"So you'd let her die in this musty, cold hell hole!" Eyes

ablaze, Angel flung a hand toward the room. "Your stupid pride won't heat up the place! It don't generate electricity either, Lelia! All it's doing is killing the baby!"

"I ain't a baby," Joella said softly.

"Shut up, Jo Jo!" they chorused.

Angel pointed a finger at Lelia's chest. "At least Zeek doesn't have me living homeless." She stepped closer, her lips thinned.

"Why do you defend him? His no-account tail treats you like a slave. Can't you see he's no good?"

Angel's gaze fell away. "Zeek doesn't own me."

Every talk about him ended in war, left them furious with each other. Zeek's power over Angel sickened her. Even in his absence, he controlled her.

The last thing Lelia wanted to do was fuss about Zeek. "Look, I'm not going to do this with you. Jo Jo needs help. I can't leave her here. It's too cold."

"You and the baby come to my place."

A raw voice sounded from the room. "I ain't no baby, y'all."

Lelia closed her eyes, rubbed the skin beneath her lashes. There had to be another way.

Angel's voice moved away. "I pay the rent, not Zeek."

Lelia opened her eyes, looked into the room. Angel was shoving what little possessions she and Joella had into her half-empty duffel bag.

"Jo Jo can stay there while you get help. The rent and utilities are paid to the end of the month." Angel's hand hesitated over the bag before she jammed the zipper closed. "It'll be safe. Nobody knows I'm going. Nobody can tip off Zeek."

Torn and out of options, Lelia moved into the room and looked down at Joella. She choked down her pride again and reached to help Angel bundle Joella for their trek to the apartment.

Overhead, clouds stirred, a threatening mix of blue-black and pewter. They made it to Angel's before the heavens opened.

Lelia had never set foot in Angel's apartment. When they crossed the threshold, she wasn't surprised at the surroundings.

The place was a decorator's showplace. Flashy, brash, everything Zeek.

They shuffled Joella into the bedroom, rested her on Angel's queen-size bed.

Zeek's influence didn't touch this room. Bright and cheery, it spoke to the soul of its occupant. Soft pastels colored the curtains and bedspread. Teddy bears and other creatures filled every corner. On the walls, life-size images of Billie Holiday, Ella Fitzgerald and Nancy Wilson kept watch.

Angel broke into her thoughts.

"I'll get her a pair of pajamas. There's an extra blanket in the hall closet."

Lelia ambled to the hallway, swung open the closet door. Mini-skirts and micro-dresses filled the rack, spiked heels cluttered the floor. Zeek's uniform.

Shaking her head, she pulled down a blanket from the shelf and shut the door. Angel watched her from the bedroom archway.

"I couldn't stand to have them where I sleep, is all."

In silence, they helped Joella into red-footed pajamas, coaxed her to sip some juice, smiled at the face she pulled from the taste of the flu medicine. When she dozed, they crept from the room.

In the living room Angel emptied their belongings from her duffel. She slung the bag over her shoulder. "Well, I guess this is it."

Lelia followed her out the door. Angel tripped the dead bolt, then pressed the key into Lelia's palm.

They trudged the stairwell in strained silence. The sad word *good-bye* loomed between them.

Angel stopped at the bottom of the steps. "Maybe I should stay. Just until the baby gets better, until you two get help."

"I found help. We'll be fine." She grasped both of Angel's hands. "You need to get far away from Zeek while you still can."

Angel pulled back. Lelia pressed her thumbs over the backs of her hands, didn't let her retreat. "All right. No more about him. I'll miss you, Angela Price. Wherever we are, we'll be friends. Always."

"Always." Tears pooled in her eyes. "Hey, come with

me? You can find a job. Jo Jo could go to school and—"

"No."

"This feels so wrong. I can't up and leave you two here alone."

"We won't be alone."

"I feel I should be doing something. You're the best friend I have." Uncertainty wavered Angel's voice. "Tell me we're going to be all right, Lelia."

"We're all going to be all right, Angela. I promise."

Misery clenched her stomach. She pulled Angel into a fierce hug. God, it hurt.

"Come on, girl." Lelia eased away. "We have new lives to start."

"New lives." Angel wiped an index finger over her eyes. She pulled a matchbook from her pocket and scribbled something on it. "Look, here's my number in Knoxville. You'd better call me next week collect or I'll be coming back for you. Okay?"

Tears choked Lelia's words, spilled down Angel's face. Their tears turned to sobs. They clung to each other, fear of the unknown kept them bound.

Angel pulled away, held Lelia's hand and led her out the glass entry into the light drizzle.

Silence was all they could share. They nodded their good-bye, squeezed each other's hands, parted. Each looked back at the other until they were out of view.

Angel returning home.

Lelia praying she'd find one.

Lelia pushed the soggy rim of her hat out of her eyes. The church's steeple presented a heavenly sight. Weasel lounging a block away meant hell loomed nearby.

She slipped around fenders and bumpers, skirted into the church's side alley, then stopped. The church's side door stood ajar, a rock jammed it open.

The opposite mouth to the alley emptied onto a busy crosswalk. She craned her neck, cased the tiny opening for Zeek and Thero.

Deserted.

Lightness wrapped her heart. Deliverance stroked her spirit.

She glanced over her shoulder one last time before she started her sprint to freedom.

Something hard, unyielding, smashed into her chest, stole her breath, sent her sprawling.

Her rump smacked the concrete, cold water soaked her clothes, shocked her. The jolt flopped the hat over her face. Heavy hands clamped her shoulders, hauled her to her feet.

Adrenaline raged. Lelia waled on the solid bulk in front of her. He whipped her off the ground, hitched her around the back of his thick waist, fettered her arms and legs with his arms. She squirmed, wiggled, bucked against the biting pressure. He clenched her tighter.

"Let go, bald-headed freak! Help me! Somebody help me, damn it! He's going to kill me!"

He hauled her along. She screamed, cursed at the top

of her lungs, prayed against hope someone would hear. Someone would care.

Motion stopped. He dropped her to a wooden floor.

She clawed, kicked. "Stay away from me, pervert."

He didn't come near. Didn't speak. Lelia stopped fighting the air, heaved in a breath, listened for her tormentor. Sounds of her raspy breathing and quiet clung about her.

Tomb quiet.

"You want some of me? Come get it, mother..." She whipped off her hat, blinked twice, wished the Grand Canyon was near to swallow her whole.

Three hundred or so forks filled with collards, macaroni and cheese and candied yams froze in midair, held by a congregation of openmouthed spectators.

She wasn't in an alley or derelict building somewhere. She'd become the off-color entertainment for Cornerstone Baptist's Honors Banquet.

A child's snicker snapped her from her horrified daze. She scurried to her feet on the platform stage and looked over the crowd.

Some forks lowered. No mouths closed. Church members sat frozen in their best finery, shock etched on their faces. All except Ma Ella. From the head table, she smiled her slipped-toothed grin, saluted her with a drumstick.

Lelia opened her mouth, but her stomach growled a loud solo. Another snicker broke the silence. The laughing imp sitting near the stage got the back of his head cuffed by his mother.

Lelia resought Ma Ella, spied her sending a small child up the aisle toward the stage. The little boy approached. Lelia inched away, backed into a pair of thick hands.

What else could go wrong? She spun around, found herself facing a modern Goliath. Packed solid, the giant's shoulders stretched a city block, arms and neck the size of subways, all topped with a look that would spook the Grim Reaper.

Goliath's deep Barry White bass shook her. "Little sister, we can duke it out again. You'd lose. Besides, my dinner's getting cold."

She took in Goliath's wrinkled shirt and askew tie. God, she'd tried to take out a minister or deacon or something.

Lelia wrung her hat, waited for a lightning bolt to strike her down. "I'm so sorry." She stumbled forward, rambled while she tried to brush the creases from his shirt. "I thought you were somebody else. I didn't mean to mess up your nice clothes, not to say you have bad ones, I just...I mean..."

What did she mean? She was so tired, so worn, she didn't know anymore. Close to tears, she backed away. The hat slipped from her hand when she raised her palms. "I didn't mean any harm, mister."

Goliath stooped down, picked up the hat, pressed it in her upturned hands. Amusement, compassion danced in his eyes. Clearing his throat, he nodded toward the young boy who stood silently at Lelia's side. "Run along now. Ma Ella's sent for you."

Lelia gazed down at the outstretched hand of her miniature chaperone before she looked out over the crowd. Shocked faces had changed to compassionate ones.

She felt a light tap on her thigh.

"Ma Ella says you're family. Come on with me."

Not shy, he placed his tiny fingers in her hand and led her to the vacant chair next to Ma Ella.

A heaping plate of food appeared in front of her. As hungry as she was, she pushed the plate and her shame aside. "Ma Ella..."

"Baby, if you want to do an encore of that gangster rap performance you reeled off, you're on your own." She waved her drumstick toward the congregation. "You shocked them into comas the first time. I don't know if I can hold them back from giving your tail the tanning it deserves next time."

"Sorry about that, Ma Ella. I came because...because I need that help you offered. Well, me and a friend."

"Well, it's about time."

Ma lifted her head as the man that preached the revival entered the hall. Raising her weathered hand, Ma summoned him to their table.

"Pastor Stevens, this is Lelia."

Pastor Stevens was as she remembered. The dark bronze face of a strong young man, the snow white crop and knowing kind eyes of a wise sage. Tall, no-nonsense, yet humble. He held Lelia's hand in a firm grasp. "It's nice to see you've come back, Lelia."

"Pastor, Lelia needs our help. Go ahead, baby, I've

already talked to Pastor about you. We're all here to help."

"Yes, Lelia, we'll help...if you let us."

Lelia looked at the pastor, saw the sincerity in his eyes. "My friend, Joella, is sick. I think she needs a doctor, but she's afraid they'll send her back home. She won't go back there. She needs a real home." She ducked her head, her voice lowered, humbled. "We both do."

Lelia tightened the grip on his hand. "I'd be very grateful if you can at least help Joella. I'll work to pay off the medical bill. Whatever I have to do, just help my friend."

"Where is Joella?"

"At a friend's place about ten blocks over."

Pastor Stevens gave Lelia's hand a reassuring squeeze and set things into motion. All business, he delegated tasks to his members, then called to Goliath. "Brother Thompson, come with me, please."

Filled with relief, Lelia closed her eyes. A light touch under her chin brought her gaze back to Pastor Stevens.

"You have a servant's heart, Lelia. Your good deeds are about to change your life forever."

Steady raindrops pelted the windshield. The gloom didn't infuse the joyful ride to Angel's apartment. Her heart free from shadows, Lelia felt happy, alive. She even laughed when Brother Thompson, Big T, ribbed her about her subdued, lady-like entrance into the Cornerstone Baptist family.

Pastor Stevens chuckled. "Don't worry, Lelia. No one

rode Brother Thompson too long when he tripped down the steps last year and bowled over Mother Beasly. Had the poor woman spread eagle on the pavement."

He cast a side-glance at Big T. "Mother's Easter bonnet lost two begonias and the hem of her dress saw heights she said it hadn't in years. The congregation saw drawers that I'm sure were Civil War relics."

The car stopped in front of Angel's building. "Lelia, we have a ton of nurses, a few doctors and a handful of social workers in the congregation." He cut the engine, then turned to her. "We're family now. We'll get through this together."

"Thank you." She reached for the door handle, hesitated. "Pastor, I need a few minutes to tell Joella what's happening and help her get dressed."

Pastor Stevens looked through the rain-beaded window. "You have exactly five minutes, young lady, then Brother Thompson and I will be up to carry Joella to the car. Informed, dressed or not."

Lelia trotted to the entrance, took the stairs two at a time. She almost ran into a woman bounding down the steps with an armful of clothes.

On the second landing, she passed another woman carrying a toaster and an armful of towels. A man followed close behind, his arms laden with huge images of Billie Holiday and Ella Fitzgerald.

Heart pounding, Lelia raced up the rest of the steps.

Angel's door hung on its hinges. Looters scavenged the apartment, unfazed by her entrance.

"Joella!"

She ran to the bedroom. Two men pushed past her toting the mattress.

"Joella?"

The room lay barren. Only a message remained.

Blood-red letters stained an unholy script across the stark walls.

The Freeze.

The author scrawled his calling card: Z.

Lelia burst through the thieves, half tripped, half flew down the stairwell.

Sheets of rain mixed with tears, soaked her face. Logic gone, she raced past the waiting car, away from Big T and Pastor Stevens' distraught voices.

She ran for Joella's life, to the Freeze...to Zeek.

CHAPTER SIX

The cold deluge beat her, slowed her terror sprint block after block to the dilapidated duplex.

Zeek's crack house. The Freeze.

A high chain-link fence sentried the building. Lelia bound onto the metal partition, clawed the loops. Her rain-slicked soles skidded against the steel. The guard tube was ripped off the top of the fence. Filed spikes twisted up, gouged her hands, sliced her pants when she tumbled over the top.

The ground rose, smacked her with a fierceness that rocked her bones, sent fire through her leg. A deep wound gaped on her thigh. Air scathed over the flesh, razor pain shot down her limb. She clutched it. Rain paled the crimson ooze seeping between her fingers. She ripped her pant leg farther, bound it around her thigh, then hobbled toward the house.

The back door stood ajar. She shouldered it, but something barricaded it from the inside.

She moved through the deserted yard, debris, junk parts littered brown tufts of grass. Around, around she circled the house, peered up at the clapboard-covered door and windows, pounded the walls with her fists.

The onslaught drummed in her ears, blurred her sight, nearly choked her. The heavy smell of rain nauseated her.

She bent her head, shielded her face against the downpour. Something caught her eye. A small basement window was hidden by a rusted fender. She thrust the metal aside, lay on the ground and kicked the glass from its frame.

She crawled through the hole and dropped onto a heap of decayed boxes and mildewed newspapers. The tiny window afforded little light. She searched the musty room, prayed she didn't miss anything.

A rickety staircase led her to the garbage-spewed first floor. The day's gloom moped through the clapboard, cloaked the room in lightlessness.

Hand over hand, the walls as her guide, she stumbled over the clutter.

"Joella? Answer me. Pip-squeak, it's Lelia." She tried to mask the tears in her voice. "You hurt her, Zeek. I'll kill you!"

He answered. A dull light flicked on, filtered down the stairwell from the top floor.

Old needles, a lost man's markers showered the steps. She followed the gruesome map.

Scattered glass and plaster muddled the first room. Light shone from a gaping hole in a connecting wall. Lelia stepped through and found Joella.

"Please, God, no."

Slumped against a wall, the child's body quaked. The tremors lolled her head to an unnatural angle.

"Jo Jo?" Lelia ran her hands over the child's limbs.

Fever seeped through the rain-soaked pajamas. She cupped Joella's face, rubbed the black saucers underneath her eyes.

"Wake up, baby. It's Lelia." She shrugged off her coat, wrapped it around the girl. "Come on, Jo Jo, we got to get out of here."

"You can't leave. The party just started."

Zeek stepped through the door. Thero trailed him. He spread his arms in a grand gesture. "All this ambiance and atmosphere and my soon-to-be protégé wants to cut out? After all I've done to plan this dig? I think that's a sin."

Joella's whimper tore Lelia's heart. She shifted Joella's head from the wall, wrapped her arms around her shoulders. "Shh, pip-squeak, it's all right."

"My, my, my, aren't we the popular one. That popularity will bring in big benjamins."

Lelia stood. "I'm taking her out of here. I don't want your kind of money."

Zeek raised a hand, snapped his fingers. A satisfied smirk curled Thero's thin lips. He strolled to Lelia, towered above her.

Quick and lethal, his hand crashed against her face. The blow flung her to the floor, cracked her head against the wall. Fire burst through her skull. Salt and metal, the telltale twang leaked through her teeth, coated her tongue.

Zeek's voice raked over her. "I don't give a damn what you want! My wants always come first. *Al-ways!*"

Lelia steadied her breath. Unable to keep the hatred from her eyes, she stared at the floor, played his game. "What do you want?"

"You know that answer."

She raised her head. "The hospital first."

Zeek's eyes flashed ice, his smile never wavered. "Haven't you learned yet? Zeek makes the rules, brown sugar. I'll make sure Little Red gets the best medical care out there, but you'll be staying with me. Collateral, you understand." He shrugged off his trench and dropped it over Thero's outstretched arm. "Now, come here."

Lelia glanced down at Joella. Glassy eyes stared back, pleaded with her not to make the pact.

"It'll be all right, pip-squeak." She lifted the sides of the coat around Joella.

"Snap to it! We ain't got all damned day, Florence Nightingale."

Thero's command made her jump. She stood, walked the death march to Zeek.

He rubbed his goatee. "Zeek likes what he sees... always has." He pulled her close, his hand roamed.

She tried to break free. "Go to hell."

Hard fingers dug into her face. Her teeth separated

from the force. "I'm not going just yet. But you keep lipping off and you and Little Red will get a first-class ticket there...tonight."

He clamped his arms around her ribs. "That's what I like about you, brown sugar. You got sass. Some of Zeek's biggest spenders pay fat cash for sass."

The manacles tightened, slowly increased the punishment. She fought against the breath-robbing pressure.

"Watch yourself. With me, you'll be soft and sugary. You can handle that. If not, Thero's got some homemade sass remedies he'll be glad to dole out.

"My patience is hanging by a thread. You ought to be kissing my ass right about now. You owe me." His nostrils flared. "I should have sent Thero to snap your neck and been done with it. Word is you've been filling Angel's head with bull about going back to the sticks. Haven't you?"

He jerked her off the floor. "I don't like people messing with what's mine. Right, Thero?"

"Right, Z-man."

"No one walks out on Zeek." He crammed his face to hers. "No one!" He dumped her on the floor, smoothed the rumples from his suit. His features smoothed as well. "Get up."

She sucked oxygen back into her air-starved lungs. Pain ripped through her thigh as she struggled to stand. Moving to her side, Zeek wrapped an arm around her shoulders.

"Look, forget about all that. Be one of Zeek's girls and Little Red will get the best doctoring money can buy. We'll all go to the hospital. Thero will carry her in, you'll wait out in the car with me. Just say yes."

He squeezed her shoulders. "Sounds too good a deal, doesn't it? But Zeek knows if your mind is worrying about Little Red, you wouldn't have your heart into the customers. I don't share my girls with nobody. Not a boyfriend, mother, or a Little Red Riding Hood. Bad for business."

He turned her toward Joella. The child's chest rose and fell, slower, slower. Her body trembled with each pull to fill her lungs.

"I can make all that pain and suffering go away. Let me take care of you the way only Zeek can."

He pulled her closer, touched his lips to her ear. "What's it going to be? You gonna be a hero? Or die a martyr?" He nodded toward Joella. "Little Red's clock is ticking, brown sugar. So is yours."

From the corner of her eye, Lelia saw a flash of metal, heard the click of a loaded chamber.

Her tongue couldn't form the words Zeek waited for. Her jerked nod appeased him. His low chuckle vibrated through her like a cannon blast.

She stared at Joella, unable to leash the tear that seared her cheek. Zeek's finger trailed the tear to her chin, made her meet his caldron cat grin.

"No need to cry. Not yet. Smile for Zeek, brown sugar."

She refused him. His grin dimmed a watt.

"Smile." He waited, received nothing.

"Later maybe, huh? Now, let's finish our business. First, the doctoring for Little Red, and second, remember." He puckered his lips, blew a silent kiss. "Zeek don't share."

Lelia felt Thero shift. She jerked from Zeek.

Fury, horror raged through her.

An explosion rocked the air.

Darkness devoured her.

CHAPTER SEVEN

Fire.

Hot fury flamed through her. Pain set her body ablaze.

Lelia groped her chest, tried to ease the agony. Something sticky, wet matted her hands. She lifted them. Crimson stained her palms. The smell of blood rolled her stomach.

Joella.

She lumbered to her side, spotted the child still propped against the wall. Still breathing. "Thank you, God."

"It's too early to thank Him yet."

The hard tip of a shoe lodged beneath her ribs. Zeek and Thero hawked over her. Zeek stared with disgust. Thero smirked.

"A waste of a good bullet. You should have smiled." Zeek blew a kiss, extracted his shoe from her side, then walked away.

Lelia strained to hear their movements. Their footsteps echoed faint, fainter, taking Joella's hope for survival with their retreat.

She wouldn't barter with the devil, she wouldn't will

them back. Still, when the footfalls stopped, sick relief washed over her.

Zeek's whisper mocked. "See you on the other side, Lelia."

A heavy object scraped the floor below. A door slammed. A lock rattled into place.

Silence.

The room blurred, shifted, blood rushed, hammered her ears. Lelia crawled to the wall, propped herself beside Joella.

"Pip-squeak, can you hear me?" She lifted a hand to Joella's cheek, winced from the pain, from the blood she'd smeared onto the girl's face.

Joella's sightless gaze fixed on the ceiling. Lelia cupped the back of the child's neck, pulled her forward, rested their foreheads together.

"Jo Jo, talk to me, baby. Please."

Joella's lids jerked. Soft brown irises vanished above bloodshot white orbs. Her eyes closed. Lelia watched the child's lips move, felt the wheezing puffs of air fan her face.

"I can't understand, pip-squeak."

"Take half my heart."

Tears hazed the face she loved so. "No. You're going to keep it safe for me, remember?"

"Take it...promise."

"No, Jo Jo. Please."

Joella's eyes opened slowly. Their intensity bespoke the girl's anguish. "Promise!"

Lelia nodded.

It was hard to focus now. Hard to do anything. Her clumsy fingers unclasped the necklace. Sliding it from Joella's neck, she grasped the pendant. Kept her promise.

Lelia wanted to sleep, to continue to float in the warm light below the darkness.

Something pulled her. Through the fire. Back to the darkness, the pain.

She woke in a daze, dragged her lids open.

Joella lay across her lap, wheezing. Another coat covered the child's shaking form.

Heavy pressure pushed Lelia against the wall, worsened her torment. Hands held a blood-soaked sweatshirt to her chest. Angel's tear-streaked face came into focus. Splotches of red covered Angel's T-shirt. Lelia could barely make out her sob-muddled words.

"There's so much blood, I...I can't stop it. There's too much. I'm so sorry, Lelia. Please forgive me, please."

"Joella...needs...get help."

"The police are coming. I can't let them find me here. God, I didn't know, Lelia. He said he just wanted to talk to you. He promised he was going to help the baby. He promised. He promised."

Lelia heard the words wept over and over until the warm light embraced her again.

She floated. Fast. Carefree.

Unfamiliar faces hovered above. Large squares of lights sped behind their heads, blotted their features. Their voices rung distant; their words unimportant.

"Her pressure's dropping! Start another IV! Run it wide open!"

The harsh brightness blared in her face, burst past her closed lids. Sleep. All she wanted was to sleep. The brashness, the noises wouldn't let her.

Lelia turned her face from the troublesome glare. Her gaze fell on Joella.

"Call the OR to prep a room, stat! Run a type and cross match for four units! Tell 'em we might need more!"

Pip-squeak lay on the other side of a half-closed curtain. She looked so peaceful sleeping. Lelia hated to wake her, but she wanted to make sure her Jo Jo was all right.

"Joella? Pip-squeak?" Lelia mouthed the words. No sound came out.

"It's okay dear, don't try to talk. You've been badly hurt but we're going to take care of you."

A woman clad in white entered Joella's room. A kind, caring expression etched her face. She looked like a cherub. Jo Jo was in good hands. Lelia relaxed.

The woman stared at Joella, laid a tender hand on her brow. Lelia watched the woman. When she looked up, their gazes connected. Lelia started to smile, but stopped at the heavy sorrow marring the older woman's gentle eyes.

She needn't look so sad. Joella was asleep. She was all

right. I promised her everything would be all right! *"There's more blood over here! It's her hand. She's clenching some kinda chain. Damn, her fist is clamped tighter than a pit bull!"*

Lelia tried to speak. Her voice failed. "I have to give Jo Jo her heart back. She gave it to me, but she's all right now. I want her to take it back." She had to touch Joella. If she could just touch her, everything would be all right.

"What the hell! Hold her down! Hold her before she bleeds out!"

Lelia tore her gaze from Joella, implored the woman to make her Jo Jo well.

"Pulse is a hundred thirty, not good, not good!"

The woman held Lelia's gaze. Her face a somber mask, she mouthed the words "I'm sorry." She covered Joella's face with a white sheet and gently closed the curtain.

No! Joella! Nooooo!

Lelia waited beyond the light. It was warm and inviting and free from pain.

Beautiful.

Joella was there, bathed in the brightness, dressed in a pristine gown. It flowed around her ankles as she romped and giggled among the wildflowers.

Joella held her hand up to a man who walked nearby. His face was familiar. His smiling image had been hidden away in Mama's old Bible.

When she looked at him, Lelia saw herself. She saw a man she'd longed for but never knew. Her father.

It was beautiful there, peaceful, serene. So when they held out their hands and beckoned her forward, Lelia stepped into the light.

"Flatline! Damn it, she's gone! We lost her!"

CHAPTER EIGHT

THE PRESENT

The creaking floorboards drew Lelia's attention. She eased to her feet, stood motionless. Through the jigsaw holes beaten in the plaster, between the rotten wooden slats, she watched the child creep along the hallway.

The girl rounded the doorjamb. Wide, guilty eyes clashed with angry, disappointed ones.

The chase commenced.

Lelia dodged garbage piles, leaped over holes in the floor. She finally caught the child climbing through the busted bathroom window.

She hauled the girl inside, spun her around. The teen pushed off her hold.

Lelia ignored the fighting stance. "Oh, it's like that now? You want to fight? Fight for something worthwhile like getting out of this mess. Don't fight to stay trapped in it."

Lelia stepped closer, bumped against the girl's outstretched fists. "What's up with you? Why'd you run?

Huh? I thought you wanted better than this?" She waved her hand around the room. "*I* want better for you than this."

"You think you know everything." The girl's voice trembled. "You don't understand."

"That's a lie and you know it." Lelia softened her tone. "I've been here, I've lived this, remember?"

"Stop tripping. Back off, Lelia."

She covered the girl's fists with her hands. "Or what?" Tears brightened the child's eyes. "Look, I just...it's just..." The fight seemed to flee the girl's body. "I'm scared, all right. Home means all these rules and no freedom. I can't get with that anymore. I'd die before I go back. You hear me, Lelia?"

The words fused present with the past. Lelia stumbled back. Her mind reeled. She conceived full chestnut cheeks, mischief-filled brown eyes. Eyes that robbed her heart when they closed forever.

A decade passed since Joella's death. In two weeks, she would have turned twenty-three. The days leading up to the anniversary of the day she died always spun Lelia's life out of control. Around this time, she always took personal leave just to cope. This year, she had another child in need of saving.

Joella's pixie face ebbed away. Megan "Tweek" Yates' defiant, scared gray eyes stared at her.

Tweek dropped her fists. "You have all the answers, don't you, Lelia? What if Mom and Pops don't want me back?"

"You and I both know when parents don't give a flying leap about their kids. You've seen what lunatics do to their kids when they don't want them. Your parents aren't like that and you know it."

Tweek turned away, folded her hands behind her neck. "Did you tell Mom I'm a crackhead? How did Pops feel about the shoplifting charges and my johns?" She let her hands fall to her sides. "Well?"

"It's not for me to tell. You've been clean for months, so don't use that excuse."

"Am I supposed to be the lucky one, 'cause you're trying to play fix the family?"

Lelia hiked the bill of her cap up to release some heat. "I don't play games and luck had nothing to do with it. You did the hard work on your own."

"Yeah, right. Well, what if I can't cut it back home and all of this is for nothing?"

"I'm tired of this." Lelia snatched the girl to the broken mirror over the exposed pipes where the sink used to be. "Look at me, Tweek. What do you see?"

Indignant, the girl slowly raised her head to meet Lelia's reflection. Head cocked to the side, lips pursed, her street-toughened eyes held fear, uncertainty.

"What do you see?"

"That you're loco. Big time!"

"No. You see somebody who's tired of hearing your trifling pity-party song."

Gray eyes skirted away. Lelia trapped her chin, lifted it.

"I was you. Except my daddy never came looking for me, 'cause he died before I knew him. And my mama couldn't have cared less if I was among the living, as long as I didn't mess with her booze and stayed out of her hair.

"Nobody babied me to a better life, Tweek. I got off the streets, finished school because I wanted to. I had to or the streets would have killed me. Is that what you want, for them to kill you?"

Tweek didn't answer, just stared out the window. A single tear slipped around her cheek.

"You worked too hard to get right. Why'd you do it if you don't care?"

The girl's cold gaze shifted to the mirror. "To get you off my case, okay?"

Lelia let her hands fall away. "You want to go back to breathing, living and dying for your next hit, fine. Just don't lie to me about not caring...and stop wasting my time."

Lelia walked to the door, then stopped. "I'm parked out back. I'll wait five minutes. After that, I'm out."

Her thoughts on Tweek, she made her way through the house. Outside, the sun baked through her thick jeans and shirt. She stripped off her outer layer of clothes, popped her trunk, and wrapped them in a trash bag to be sanitized.

She moved to the lean-to back porch, sat down near the door and waited.

Tweek would make the right choice. The child had come a long way from the strung-out kid she'd stumbled on nine months ago.

The night they'd met, Lelia had just left the shelter. The kids wore her out with their Friday night jam session. All she wanted was a long bath and her bed.

She almost made it to her car when she heard a small voice.

"Help me. I'm tired of hurting."

Behind the Dumpster, she found Tweek, hungry, cold and coming down off a high.

Tweek wouldn't come inside, so Lelia sat on the pavement beside her. They stayed that way for hours. Finally, Lelia stood, offered Tweek her hand. The child had been on the mend ever since.

Come on, Tweek. Come out. We'll get through this together. Instinctively, Lelia rubbed her thumb over the half-heart mark forged in her right palm. Over and over, she smoothed the scar, twin to the pendant around her neck, willed the child to walk out the door.

Five minutes turned to ten. Ten turned to twenty. Lelia pushed to her feet, dusted the dirt from her shorts. Over her shoulder, the door and the hall beyond stood empty.

She swiped the sweat off her forehead with the back of her wrist and leaned into the house. "Look, I know you hear me, Tweek. If you think I'm going to beg you, forget it. You want this, you know where I'll be."

The vinyl seats burned her legs as she slid into the car. She slammed the door. The ignition flipped the customary three times before the engine turned. She revved the motor louder and louder, kept an unblinking eye on the door.

"To hell with this."

Car in reverse, she eased over the uneven hills of dirt in the backyard, all while keeping watch through the slats of the boarded windows.

The wheels hesitated over a large mound, afforded her an excuse to stop the car. Scalding air closed around her, made it hard to catch her breath. Pressure pushed at her chest, forced her to cut the engine and dash back into the house.

"Tweek! Megan!"

She searched the bathroom, then each junk-piled room. Memories of another frantic hunt bombarded her mind, panicked her heart.

"Megan!" Her voice echoed back through the hollow rooms. No one answered. She stood alone. Again.

Not caring about the filth, she flopped to the floor. Blowflies worried a foul-smelling garbage heap nearby. It didn't faze her.

Tears wouldn't come. She felt too numb to cry. After she'd lost Joella, she'd promised herself she'd never feel that much. Not again. Sometimes lies and promises share the same face.

The sun moved across the room by the time she stood and walked from the house. Denying the vise around her ribs, she started the car and drove off.

Random turns down unfamiliar streets led her nowhere in particular. The car drifted to a stop at a red light.

Sticky air oozed in the windows, got stagnant, made

her reach for her homemade air-conditioning system, washcloths soaked in a cooler full of ice. She drew a cloth from the now lukewarm water, laying it across the back of her neck.

Her gaze skimmed the group of corner store loungers to the fenced-in lot across the street. Her stomach dove to her spine. Cruel fate guided her back to the place where she'd lost part of her soul.

The Freeze.

Sunlight ricocheted off the mangled chain-link fence bordering the yard. The house no longer stood, only a pile of rubble and siding remained.

She snapped her gaze away. Like something bewitching, hideous, the lot lured her eye.

Trapped in the crushing stupor, horrid memories seeped into her thoughts.

Torment. Guilt. Pain. Death.

She closed her eyes against the onslaught. Her mind obliged the darkness, pulled her back to the time she'd floated between life and death. The time she begged for death's triumph rather than live a numb, pain-filled existence.

God had decided it wasn't her time. When the nurses checked her belongings, they found a bulletin stuffed in her coat pocket, called the number printed on the front. Cornerstone's.

Lelia awoke to a pair of owlish, wise eyes staring at her from behind thick-lensed glasses. Ma Ella.

"About time you woke up, baby. Stopped feeling sorry for yourself, did you? Not that I mind waiting all this time. They brought me in this cushy recliner and I can watch all the cable I want. Don't have it at home, you know."

Big T and his wife, Naomi, became her honorary parents. The Thompsons, Ma Ella and the rest of Cornerstone became her mainstay.

Best of all, she was reunited with Bernard after her name was linked with the Center for Missing and Exploited Children. Two fathers, a mother, grandmother and an extended family renewed her reasons to live.

The day at The Freeze changed many lives.

Word on the street was Thero had gotten tired of being second man and tried to strong-arm Zeek's territory. Weeks later, they found him floating.

Someone fingered Zeek with the murder. Once arrested, the list of charges mounted. Murder, drug trafficking, solicitation of minors and kidnapping.

News reporters devoured the case, hailed him The Pretty Boy Kingpin and The Cocky Chameleon. Lelia faced The Chameleon, testified against him, endured his winks and blown kisses.

When his verdict was read, Zeek's slow, cocky smile transformed to enraged shock. In Lelia's mind, two life terms seemed light.

In the end, he got his due. His charm, his charisma didn't win him any buds in the joint. His prison mates hated child leeches. Penitentiary guards found The

Chameleon hanging from a second-story railing after his third week in jail.

And Angel.

As mysteriously as she'd materialized that fateful eve at The Freeze, she had vanished. No one knew her whereabouts. The media never disclosed who supplied the information that brought Zeek down, but Lelia knew.

A letter came to Cornerstone weeks after Zeek's death. Lelia's typed name appeared on the white envelope, nothing more. Inside were *Los Angeles Times* articles of Zeek's sentencing and hanging. The typed message, FOR THE BABY, lay among the news clips.

A horn's angry blast swiped Lelia from the reminiscence. The light shone green, then quickly turned yellow. Her mind in a fog, she waited until the speed demons plowed around her, honked their horns and flipped the bird.

She drove through the intersection at a slower pace, tried to leave her nightmare with the diminishing pile of rubble framed in her rearview mirror.

She didn't look forward to explaining Tweek's actions to the rest of the kids at the shelter. They'd put together a surprise going-home party for her. Tweek was the one who surprised them all.

Lelia maneuvered her car through the narrow back entrance of the shelter.

"Just great. I don't need this hell today."

The regional director's Volvo bogarted across the three shelter parking spaces. Lelia backed out and parked on the street. Cheryl Lopez and Pee Wee Dunn stood outside the back door when she walked up.

Pee Wee nodded toward the shiny vehicle. "The jerkoff took your space. Want us to jack his tires?"

Lelia looked over her shoulder. "Not yet, maybe in another hour or two."

Cheryl flicked her cigarette butt into the sand can. "Well?"

Lelia shrugged, shifted the garbage bag off her shoulder. "Well, what?"

"Quit stalling, Lelia. Did you find her?"

"Yeah. She's not coming."

Cheryl kicked the can. "Man, I knew it. I knew she'd freak and skip out." She rubbed her forehead in circular strokes. "Maybe we can find her and talk her through it, you know?"

Pee Wee held the door open. "Sometimes she hangs out at the skateboard ramp. We can check it out."

Lelia leaned against the jamb. "I'll call Jacko's, see if he spots her. Some of the kids get free grub there after the lunch rush."

She watched the teens walk away. "Hey."

They turned.

"If you find her, whatever happens, she has to make her own choice. Okay?"

Pee Wee's shoulders rose and fell. Cheryl lit another cigarette.

Lelia walked through the shelter, glad to see Reginald Albright through the glass office door. Heels of his spotless gleaming tennis shoes kicked up on the desk; he was too deep in his phone conversation to notice her pass.

She left her office door open a crack, then sunk into the tattered chair.

All her kids' photos lined the office wall. She zoomed in on Tweek's picture. Little by little, she felt her control slipping from her well-guarded heart, her life. She palmed her forehead. "God, I don't know what I'm doing anymore."

As if in answer, the picture frames started bouncing against the wall from the vibration of the body-rattling bass blaring from the stereo in the gym. The obnoxious voice from the disc jockey she'd grown to detest followed.

"Yiza! Yiza! Yiza! I know you loved what you heard because I can feeeeel your love vibes shouting cross the circuits. That was Dirty Hams with their number one smash, 'Who Took The Last Slice Of Bacon?'"

"Now time for the newwwws! Zenith has just received the latest scivvy. 'What's happening, Zenith?' you cry. Well, I'm fixing to tell you, home slice. It's about our very own street angel, Lelia Freeman."

One of the kids cranked up the volume from eardrum splitting to fault shifting. Zenith Starr's voice wrapped around her like the flu. "Finding a rich runaway made her a star. How convenient. Who'd have thunk it."

Who, indeed. Lelia remembered the child to whom Zenith referred. Like her other kids, he was afraid, in need of shelter. This child's father, however, was a well-known national news anchor. Son and father reunion spurred the network to do a three-segment special on the epidemic runaway crisis.

Ignoring her protests, the third segment centered on her. Reporters and camera crews went with her to dilapidated buildings, slept with runaways under bridges or in parks. Anywhere she went to get her kids off the streets, they followed. The special got top ratings, they dubbed her the Street Angel, and a star was born.

ChildSafe Foundation's corporate office loved the media blitz. Funding poured in from across the country. Along with the funds came calls for interviews with the Street Angel. As quickly as Lelia refused the interviews, the foundation's public relations director accepted them. Hence, Zenith Starr.

During their interview, the jerk had the nerve to call runaways tourist attractions. She'd walked out on his live radio show, told him where to shove his attraction. He'd been a thorn embedded in her head ever since.

"Able to sleep in abandoned buildings with runaways, can fight kiddy prostitution with her bare hands and re-unites hundreds of families in a single bound. It's a nut! It's a psycho! No, it's Street Angel."

She stuck her head out the office door, pinned one of the kids with the evil eye. "Hey, turn that trash off!"

She closed the door. The barrier didn't block out his voice.

"Hey, Street Angel! I love ya, baby. Legs long as a country

mile and packed in all the right places. Is that how you got the appointment to that highfalutin' Washington sub-committee?"

Silence followed. Lelia ran into the gym. "Turn it back on!"

About to shoot a hoop, Duley Jones held the basket-ball in midair, looked confused. "But you just said…"

She marched onto the court. "Come on, turn it on. Now."

"All right, all right. Stop tripping, Lelia."

Zenith's loud drone commandeered the room. "You heard it right and you heard it here first. Our very own Street Angel is going to the nation's capitol to secretly serve on some committee. We'll miss you, Street Angel."

His fake sobs raked over her nerves.

"Let Zenith give you a fashion tip. It's free, unless you want to pay me. Say…the same way you settled up to get that appointment. Give me a call tonight, we'll work it out. Now for the tip, lose the jeans and the fresh face look when you get to D.C. It's getting old! If you're not down with the glam, scram! Peace ouuuuuuuut! Next up, Foul Zombies with their single 'Your Turn To Clean The Crypt.'"

Lelia whirled a finger in the air, signaled for Duley to turn the station.

A sledgehammer must have knocked her between her eyes. Sharp pain heated her temples, sent her in search of the aspirin in her desk.

Sugar McNeily's worried eyes appeared at her office

door. "Lelia, a guy is out in the lobby waiting for you."

Lelia rubbed her temple. "Can you get Derrick to handle it, sweetie? My head's about to explode."

Sugar stepped over the threshold, then closed the door. "I tried that. No Derrick. He wants *you*. It's Tweek's dad, Lelia."

CHAPTER NINE

The lobby was deserted except for the metal-framed chairs and the tall man standing in front of the painted mural. He turned when Lelia walked in. His eyes mirrored the crystal color of the girl he'd traveled the country to find.

"Mr. Yates?"

"Yes."

Lelia crossed the scuffed linoleum floor. "Hello. I'm Lelia Freeman."

He clasped her outstretched hand, shook her arm like a water pump.

"Miss Freeman. God, I just need to thank you for finding our daughter. Thank you, so much. Thank you."

He released her hand, looked embarrassed. "Sorry. We're so grateful. It's been hell for me and my wife this past year. One day you have the normal adolescent problems, the next your baby drops off the face of the earth. I swore someone had gouged out my heart."

He ran both hands through his blond curls. He turned away. "It didn't start beating again until you called and said Megan wanted to come home. It seems like I've waited a lifetime for this. Bless you, Miss Freeman."

He spun around, palms up, eyes expectant. "Where's Megan?"

Lelia laced her fingers. Her thumb slipped into her palm, traced the marred skin there. "Mr. Yates, Megan's not here."

He looked at his watch. "I'm a little early. My wife called the hotel three times today so I wouldn't be late." He pointed to the empty chairs. "I'll sit here till she comes. I promise I won't get in the way."

He headed for the chairs. Lelia stepped up and placed a hand on his forearm.

"No, Mr. Yates. Megan isn't coming." She slipped her hand to his elbow to guide him to the seats. "Come on, let's sit down."

"I don't want to sit. Where's my daughter?"

"I don't know. I saw Megan a little while ago. She was scared, had all kinds of doubts. When I went back in to get her, she was gone."

He snatched his arm away. "Back *in* to get her?"

"She left the shelter yesterday, didn't show up last night. So I went to where she used to camp out and waited. She came in, we talked, then I left. I told her I'd be outside to give her a ride to the shelter, but she never came out."

A gradual swell of scarlet tinged his face.

"Mr. Yates, I understand you're upset and I'm so sorry."

He swiped the air with his fist. The breeze from the motion puffed Lelia's face. "You can't begin to understand." He got in her face, shoved a finger at her nose. "Look, I don't know what you people have done with my kid. Either you produce her damn quick, or I'm calling the cops and having you all busted for kidnapping."

"Mr. Yates, you can use the phone in my office to call the police. They know Tweek. They'll tell you what I'm telling you. If she doesn't want to be found, she won't be."

"Who in God's name is Tweek?"

Lelia could almost touch the anger and frustration radiating from him. "Most runaways don't go by their real name or just use parts of it. Megan's street name is Tweek."

"What the hell am I supposed to do now? What am I going to tell her mother?" Bit by bit his angry countenance slipped into despair. He walked to the entry doors, then looked out to the street.

"Do you know what it's like to see someone familiar in a crowd, just a shadow of a person you love more than life? You run up to that person, hoping against hope, spin them around and it's a stranger."

His voice shook. "Have you ever heard something in the house that sounds like their laughter, and you run down the steps to find an empty room? Do you know what it's like to breathe a breath, feel your heart beat, know that blood's pumping through your veins, but you're still dead inside?"

Lelia fingered the pendant around her neck, turned her face away. "Yes."

"Miss Freeman, I'm not leaving L.A. without Megan.

I'm begging you, please, find my baby." Tears spilled down his face, darkened his shirt. "Please."

His chin dropped to his chest. Sobs shook his shoulders, sorrow vibrated down his body. "Please."

Lelia watched the man weep against the glass door. She tried to steel herself against the emotions crashing on her, quickly swiped the tears that clung to her lashes.

Someone tapped her shoulder.

"After all these years as director, I assumed you would be able to interface with less emotion and more professionalism. Save that compassion for your interviews."

Reginald Albright moved to her side, flashed his Pepsodent smile to an unseeing Mr. Yates. "Finish up here. I need to speak with you in my office."

Lelia brushed past him. She walked to Mr. Yates, tried to comfort him the best she could. She let him talk about the daughter he remembered. They shared stories and laughed at some of the antics Megan loved to pull. She jotted down his hotel number and promised to be in touch.

Mask in place, she sought out the regional director. When she stepped into his office, he waved impatient fingers toward the door. "Close it. This is private."

He continued to skim their monthly expenditures for what seemed like forever. Lelia knew it was his way of reminding her who was in charge.

Reginald Albright. Ivy League educated, perfect teeth, manicured nails. A speck of lint on his Polo tennis shoes meant all hell was about to break loose. He could not care less about the kids, about the shelter. He needed them to finish his doctoral research—once it was completed, he was foundation CEO bound.

He glided his hand along the top of the ledger, snatched his finger away. "Friggin' paper cut. Get me a Band-Aid before it gets infected."

Lelia peered at the invisible cut he held in front of her, then leaned back in her chair. "Sorry, we can't keep the conditions around here sterile. If it comes to amputation, Duley's real handy with tools."

He swiped a tissue from the box. A smile lifted the corner of his mouth, but didn't reach his eyes. "You don't like me very much, do you, Lelia?"

"Is there a point to this meeting?"

"As a matter of fact, there is. The foundation received a call from Washington last week. Apparently, one of the items on the Presidential agenda is to dole out more foreign aid."

He wrapped the tissue around his finger. "Some East African country recently ended a civil war. Left a lot of orphans. A task force is in the works to focus on relief efforts for the kids. They want someone from the foundation that's dealt directly with post-traumatic syndrome in children."

The cards fell into place, muscles in her shoulders tightened. "Right up your alley. Congratulations, Reggie." She got up to leave. "We'll promise not to blow up the place while you're gone."

"I've told you it's Reginald, and I won't be serving in that capacity." Not looking at her, he flipped another page. "They want you."

"Say again?"

"Your name was emphasized as top choice." He shrugged. "Apparently your fame is...far reaching."

"I can't go. We have a crisis with one of the kids."

"Where's the crisis? She's been a runaway for more than a year."

"The crisis is if we don't get her back soon, we never will. Her mother and father are slowly going insane because their little girl is alive, but she's lost to them." Lelia leaned over the desk and slammed the ledger closed. "You might not give a damn about that, Reginald, but I do."

"Keep your voice down." He glanced past her at the kids who'd stopped shooting hoops to stare into the office.

"Our support means a grant for the shelter." He reached into his briefcase, then slid a memo across the desk. "A very sizable contribution, don't you think?"

Lelia looked at the number with the string of zeros trailing it. "Someone else can go. I'm needed here."

"I've talked to Derrick. He can handle things here. They want you. No Lelia Freeman," he held the paper up, "no grant."

She looked down at the sum again. The money could buy new beds and mattresses to replace the sleeping bags and cots. It could pay for a new water heater so all of the kids could take warm showers, not half of them.

"When?"

"The briefing is Monday." Smug confidence settled on his features. He flipped back the ledger cover. "We'll book you on a flight Sunday morning to give you time to settle in."

"Which Monday?"

He counted off his fingers like he was teaching a first grader the days of the week. "Today is Thursday, Friday, Saturday, Sunday, Monday."

"Does anyone at corporate think of me as anything but a money pitch?"

His eyes moved across the pages. "If Sunday doesn't work for you, we can shoot for Saturday."

"None of this works for me. Are the words *advance notice* in corporate's dictionary?" She sat down. "Neither day is convenient. I'm spending the weekend with my dad."

He waved his hand, closed the book. "I'm sure Mr. Thompson won't mind. He and Mrs. Thompson love the kids."

"Not that dad. Bernard."

"Mr. Samuels is a military man." He secured new tissue around his finger, then started packing his briefcase. "He'll understand."

"I guess you have it all figured out."

"What I've figured is a list of all the things that money can fix around this place." He snapped the latches closed. "I also figure the kids won't understand why you'd deny them what that money can buy just because it puts a snafu in your personal schedule."

He looked up. Lelia could have sworn a trace of shame flitted across his face, but it quickly disappeared. "That was totally uncalled for."

"Lelia, I won't deny I'm envious of you and this appointment." He stood. "This is a once-in-a-lifetime opportunity for ChildSafe, for the shelter, and for you. I realize you don't want to be a star, that you're happiest right here, but this could help *right here* a great deal. Look, give it some thought."

Lelia looked out the glass door. Some kids were trying to reattach the basketball rim to the backboard. The screws in the splintered wood never held for long.

"I don't have to give it thought. I'll go."

"Yes." He picked up the phone. "I'll call for your tickets and book your hotel room. I guess thanks are in order."

She stood and moved to the door. "Don't thank me yet."

"You will be on your best behavior?"

She turned, glad to see his finger poised over the phone push buttons. "I'll be me." She opened the door.

"Washington's not structured for earthquakes."

Lelia let the mumbled crack slide. She gathered the kids to break the news. They didn't take it well. To their credit, they let the director and his car leave the shelter in one piece.

Three hours later, when she pulled onto her street. Naomi Thompson's car was parked in the driveway. Lelia drove in behind the maroon Buick, wondered why she was getting a visit from her honorary mother.

She got to the screened door, smelled the sweet potato cake and collards, and wanted to haul tail. Hell, she'd forgotten dinner. She was supposed to be home hours ago to help cook for Bernard.

Lelia gripped the handle of the door, contemplated leaving the country. Robbing the treasury was probably a cakewalk compared to getting past Nana when you were late.

Underneath the perfect French roll and fashionable garb, Nana was a five-foot-nothing marshmallow. Warm-hearted, stylish, fun-loving. Get her riled and she transformed to a shoe-throwing, wooden spoon-wielding hellcat. Messing with her loved ones or her schedule riled her real good.

The sound of clanking pots rang from the kitchen. Lelia inched open the door, damned the fact she hadn't oiled the squeaking hinges before that day. Her head and shoulders had just cleared the threshold when the clanking stopped.

"Lelia Marie Freeman, stop right there! You are three hours late."

Lelia's life shortened ten years. One foot froze in mid-air, the other demanded a hasty retreat. Nana seemed to materialize in the living room, grim features, puckered lips, wooden spoon poised in hand.

"Nana, I'm sorry. It's been a bad—"

"I don't want to hear it. Telephones were invented to be used."

Her arms were crossed over her apron, and the spoon she clenched kept steady time with the angry tap of her heel. If her toe tapped, she was a little ticked. When her heel tapped, she was ready for liftoff.

Lelia couldn't take anymore. "Nana, I said I'm sorry. It's been really rough today." She flopped down on the couch, dropped her forehead in her hands.

The warmth of Nana's hand covered her shoulder. "Don't worry, Vernon and Bernard are late, too. Seems like nobody wants to eat dinner." She rubbed her hand across Lelia's back. "What's the matter, Peanut?"

"Tweek ditched today. Nobody can find her."

The rubbing stopped. "Well, we just have to pray harder for her. She's a good girl. She'll come to her senses."

Lelia raised her head. The woman standing above her could read through the brave front she wore for everyone else. Over the years, she'd stopped trying to hide her emotions from her.

"Nana, sometimes I feel like I don't know what I'm doing anymore. Like it's all falling apart, you know?"

"Peanut, we get through it every year around this time. We'll get through this year, too." Naomi sat down, hugged Lelia's shoulders. "God's kept you in the past. He'll keep you now. You need to have faith."

They sat for a moment, silence stretched between them.

"I've been trying. It's hard." Lelia hated the pitiful sound of her voice.

The sound of a car pulling up and doors slamming

floated from outside. Lelia shuttered the emotions raging through her.

Nana patted her hand and stood. "That blank face you pull on doesn't work on me. You don't want to hear it, but I'm going to say it anyhow. You need to stop bottling up all that sadness and guilt that's beaten you to a pulp." She cupped Lelia's chin, brought their gazes together. "You've been bearing it too long. Maybe if you'd let us help you get over it, things wouldn't be falling apart. You don't have to go it alone." Her hand fell away, she shook her head. "I know I'm preaching to the choir. You think about what I said. You hear me, Peanut?"

Combined male laughter carried from outside, grew louder.

Nana faced the door, glanced down at her watch, her brows knitted. "Somebody thinks being late is funny. Looks like I have more chickens to fry."

The screen door opened, Big T and Bernard strolled into the house, laid-back like a Sunday evening.

Lelia's mood lifted at Nana's expression. She leaned back in the cushions set to watch the fireworks. Big T could handle himself. Bernard wouldn't know what hit him.

"Wait one minute! Bernard Samuels, what are you doing here now?"

Bernard's neck shrunk into his shoulders. His eyes darted from Big T to Lelia; the helpless confusion on his face was priceless.

Nana crossed her arms. "What time is it, Bernard?"

Bernard looked at the clock on the wall. "Uh-oh. I guess it's CP time." He grinned his best forgive-me smile.

"You were supposed to be at this house one hour ago." Nana's toe started a slow, steady rhythm.

"Well, Naomi, it's like this. I was at the airport and I was thinking to myself, wouldn't it be nice to get Lelia and Naomi some flowers." He pulled two bunches of roses from behind his back.

Nana's eyes narrowed, her toe kept time faster than an M.C. Hammer song. Bernard's smile faded a little.

He held the flowers in front of him. Protection, maybe. "Now I know what crossed your mind. That took all of fifteen minutes. And that's true. But on the way here, I was thinking, I'd like to even things up with Vernon for all those golf games he whipped me at. A couple of tees would be a nice way to unwind after the flight."

His eyes lit up. The confident she'll-forgive-me smile was back in place. "But you see, those were inner thoughts, never spoken aloud. Nope, I didn't utter those thoughts. When Vernon picked me up at the airport, we were talking and laughing, and before I knew it, we were at the course."

He coughed several times like he couldn't get the last phrase out. "He must be psychic or something."

Nana's neck looked like it would snap out of joint.

The smile vanished from Bernard's face altogether. "Well, I have to follow my ride, don't I?" Out of alibis, he leaned over to Big T. "Sorry, brother. It's every man for himself and God help us all."

While Bernard was singing his jailbird song, Big T hadn't mumbled a word. Larger than life, he stood, arms folded across his chest, legs spread apart, watching his wife intently. His hooded onyx eyes sparked fire under his lashes.

Lelia bit the side of her lip, braced herself.

"Vernon T. Thompson, you know what time the concert starts! You bought the tickets. Now we have to choke down my dinner, that's getting cold, and rush to get there. What do you have to say for your—"

Nana never finished. Big T bore down on his wife in two steps. He swept her up and kissed her with the hunger of a newlywed. One of her shoes plopped to the ground, the other dangled from her curled toe.

As always, Nana put up the initial front and beat his thick arms with her open palms. Eventually. As always. She slowly wound her arms around his neck and settled into his embrace.

Lelia shook her head. Big T was the only person who could quiet her down when she flew into orbit. She pushed herself off the couch, then walked over to Bernard. He placed the flowers on the coffee table and folded her in a tight hug.

"You should be on my hit list. Saw a brother drowning and didn't throw a lifeline."

Lelia pulled back to look up at him. "I just pulled myself out the frying pan. I love you, but I'll never be a fool for love."

They watched the couple, knowing from experience the clinch would last a while.

Lelia laughed. "I don't know why she fusses at him. She knows what's coming."

Bernard's smooth chuckle vibrated with hers. "Maybe that's why she fusses. Now, how you been, baby girl?"

He held the daughter of his heart at arm's length and reminisced. He pictured the scrawny girl who used to follow him closer than a shadow. Cottony black pigtails catching the wind. Silent, curious doe eyes, unbreakable spirit. Fearless. He loved her like his own. From child to woman, his baby girl swelled his chest with pride. Still fearless, still unbreakable.

He surveyed her short, tapered curls and radiant mocha face. She had her mother's flawless skin. "You're more beautiful every time I see you."

She glowed at the compliment. She always did.

Bernard took a deep breath. He hated what would come next. It would wipe the radiance away. The question he'd asked many times before would cause pain. He'd die rather than hurt her, but he needed an answer. God help him, it had gone on long enough.

"Baby girl, have you written or tried to contact your mother?"

There it was. He felt her shoulders tense beneath his hands. Her gaze skirted away. When she looked back, stiff indifference masked her face. If he pushed, he stood to lose everything he loved. "Baby girl?"

"Bernard, please don't. I can't."

Lelia hated the question. She didn't have the answer Bernard wanted.

Unable to bear the pleading of his eyes, she glanced away. Her mama was lost to him, yet he still loved her.

He didn't realize Lelia yearned for the same love, shared the same misery. She cloaked her emotions from the world. Bernard couldn't. He didn't talk about it, but it was there, in his eyes coupled with another emotion. Desperate hope.

She pitied them both.

For her, desperate hope vanished long ago. Nine years earlier when Bernard came charging into her hospital room thanking God she was alive, Lelia had hoped her mama would feel the same.

Not so.

Day after day she lay in the hospital, and she wrote to her mama. She found the courage to mail the letters once she was settled in with the Thompsons. Like a child on Christmas Eve, she waited for a phone call or letter. Any sign Mama cared.

Rubinell's response was immediate. She returned the letters all unopened, her unmistakable cursive scribbled across the top. *Return to sender!*

Each week Lelia wrote. Each week the letters came back, unwanted. Soon, Mama didn't take the time to write on the envelope. A sterile, blue return to sender stamp was her only correspondence. Lelia still wrote, hoped one day she'd open up the envelope and read the words, *I love you, Lelia*. Hoped things would change between them.

Things did. The letters stopped coming back altogether.

Keeping her shameful secret was easy. When she lived with the Thompsons, she'd snatch the mail from their mailbox every morning, plucked the returns before anyone saw them.

Now she sent cards on Mother's Day and Christmas. Out of respect. Not hope.

Bernard grasped her chin, returned her gaze to his. "Baby girl, she's your flesh and blood. Can't you put the past behind you?"

Big T's bass sounded behind her. "Little sister, forgiveness unlocks the chains of pain."

Bernard's gaze turned firm, demanding. "We'll end this discussion here. You have four months until I visit again. Then you won't run, you won't skirt the issue."

He dropped his hand from her chin. "You'll contact your mother. Come hell or high tide, you'll deal with this." He stepped back. "And so will I. Love heals, Lelia. Remember that."

"Love heals what, Bernard? Mother and child relationships? Family ties? How can you heal something that never existed?"

She turned, not able to bear the pain in his eyes. She stopped just past Big T and Nana.

"I never stopped loving, Mama. She forgot to love me."

CHAPTER TEN

Lelia sat in the cold, arena-shaped boardroom. Listened to the same no-account bull she'd heard for the last week and a half.

"Ladies and gentlemen, today we'll be reviewing slides on Sudania's conditions."

She raised her hand toward the committee director. "Excuse me, Mr. Silas, but we've been hearing about the conditions in Sudania for the last eight days now."

All eyes turned her way. She felt glare daggers bounce off her skin. She'd gotten used to them.

"Where are the statistics from the World Health Organization? We were supposed to get them last week." She tapped her fingers as she ticked off items. "How can the dietitians make up a diet? And what about initial food drops, medical supplies, building materials?"

The grumbling started. Lelia looked around the room at the other committee members. Papers rustled, eyes shifted. Typical. A third of the committee seemed to agree with her. Hushed-mouth disease struck them mute. The others ignored her or treated her like a leper.

She turned a non-blinking gaze to Paul Silas. His fingers flexed above the light switch. She didn't understand him. Sometimes he seemed genuinely concerned for the orphans. Other times he followed the useless program doled out by the powers that be.

"Well, Mr. Silas?"

His Adam's apple bobbed. "I get where you're taking us, Ms. Freeman. I think everyone wants to jump right in to help the children. Some of the information you're asking about is included in this presentation." He pointed to the wide projector screen. "I've been told the rest of it will be forthright in the morning. No later than the day after tomorrow."

The freckle-faced man next to Lelia tossed the pencil he'd been tapping on his lips at her feet. He stretched over the armrest to pick it up. "Ms. Freeman?"

She scanned his carrot-hued hair. "Yes, Dr. Willis?"

"We'll be working together for Lord knows how long, right?"

"That's the general idea."

Deadpan eyes met hers. "Exactly how many cups of Java does it take to lighten you up?"

"Two. Right now all I want are some straight answers."

"Hell, I'll bring you three tomorrow if it'll help." He sat back, slouched to one side. "We're on the same team, remember?"

A red tint colored his cheeks. "Why'd you stop coming to lunch with us? Gourmet grub's got to be better than those peanut butter sandwiches and hot dogs you chow down on. Be more social and maybe we'd back you."

He glanced toward the front of the room, sat straight in his chair. "Chill on the interrogation. Your boyfriend just walked in."

Lelia turned toward the door, couldn't stop her eyes from rolling.

Eugene Frankel strolled to the podium. The secretary of foreign affairs was a rude piece of work. Flushed puffy cheeks crowded his small, close-set eyes. More overbearing in person than on television, his tight jaw and impatient brows buckled the strongest man's knees.

Despite his persona, he'd been a staying power in the Senate for years before moving to his present office. Part of a good old boys network that reigned power term after term.

The secretary rocked on his heels. "How is Team Sudania today? Any concerns I can address while I'm here?" His frost-green stare met every eye in the room except hers.

Lelia stood. "As a matter of fact there is, Mr. Secretary."

Boredom settled over his features. "Ms. Freeman?"

"I have concerns about the timeliness of the statistics from the World Health Organization. In my opinion, we're wasting valuable time. Can someone contact the Sudanian government? It must have some preliminary reports on the children's condition. Or maybe representatives can be flown in to assess the situation so we can get some first-hand accounts."

"Are you hinting at a vacation, Ms. Freeman?" He pushed the knot of his tie closer to the folds in his neck. "That's not the way things are done here in Washington."

"I understand that, but we can't move forward until we receive that information."

"Ms. Freeman, you did your master's thesis on post-war traumatic syndrome in children, correct?"

"Yes, but…"

"Well, that may have been several years ago." He turned to Paul Silas. "I think the heads on this committee will understand if you feel your competency is lacking after all this time." Campaign grin intact, he looked around the room. "Not to worry. There's a long list of candidates that would be more than honored to replace you. If you don't feel comfortable with this appointment, that is?"

"Mr. Frankel, that's not what I…"

"Good day, everyone. The reception starts at seven o'clock sharp. President Deng is eager to meet all of you. See you there." The secretary walked out of the door.

"I told you to chill on the interrogation," Dr. Willis said from the corner of his mouth without looking her way.

Lelia plopped down in her chair. "This is ridiculous."

Paul Silas pushed his rimless glasses high on his nose, had the decency to look embarrassed. "Yes, let's pick up where we left off." He switched off the lights, thumbed the slide projector's remote control. Aerial landscape pictures flashed on the screen.

"Sudania, ladies and gentlemen. About the size of

Montana, it once held vast wealth and resources. Sudania's military recently ended a two-and-a-half-year civil war."

Soldiers dressed in fatigues held up the country's flag. "They defeated the militant faction that opposed the government's regime. After two-and-a-half years of war and a two-year drought, the country is desolate."

Another slide filled with statistics clicked onto the screen. A red pointer highlighted the numbers. "The World Food Program calculates forty percent of the Sudanian population lacks up to fifty percent of the normal diet.

"From the initial assessment of the medical coordinators of Doctors Without Borders, one-fourth of the children seen are severely malnourished and in desperate need of care. Quoting the transmission, 'Many are traumatized from the war. There is no food. Now, people are starving.'

"One of President Deng's objectives is a comprehensive wellness program to heal the Sudanian children both physically and mentally."

White light bounced off the empty projection canvas. Paul Silas stepped to the center of the screen. "These next slides are disturbing at best." His voice faded a little. "The photos emphasize the orphans' plight better than any report."

The room stilled. Lelia dropped her gaze to her lap, pressed a hand to her rolling stomach. The facts she'd waited for were finally in front of them. The pain, the destruction would be vivid, jarring. Things she didn't want to see. Fate forced her gaze back to the screen.

The longest fifteen minutes of her life followed. Picture

after horrid picture flicked before her. She studied each one, trembled.

War, in all its horrendous glory was captured splendidly, imprisoned in the desperate, fearful eyes of the Sudanian children. The last photo was purposefully placed. It exuded doom, was horrible in its symbolism.

A child, two or three, stood naked in the middle of a dirt road. Her belly was swollen, her hair the color of red ash.

Alone, she looked over her shoulder at the camera. Her large eyes, clear and tear-free, not laden with desperation or fear. Numb acceptance haunted their infant depths. In the background, through the hot, dusty haze, armed soldiers marched toward her. Her back faced the approaching troops. She stood still, seemingly waiting for the inevitable.

God help her, she was just a baby.

Lelia turned her face from the miniature countenance, her own cheeks wet with the tears the baby couldn't shed.

Light filled the room. Paul Silas moved in front of the screen, kept the child as his backdrop. He scanned the room. "We have crucial work to do, ladies and gentlemen. That's it for today." He removed his glasses and rubbed his eyes. "I think we've seen enough to last a lifetime."

They gathered their belongings in silence, left the building through the revolving doors.

Once outside, Lelia let the others pass.

Dr. Willis stopped beside her. "You catching the shuttle?"

"No, go on. I'll walk. It'll give me time to clear my head."

"I know how you feel." He switched his briefcase to his other hand. "Don't forget, they pick us up in two hours for the reception."

She nodded, and began trekking back to the hotel.

Alone with her thoughts, the caving pressure she'd felt for the past weeks pushed against her chest, screamed in her mind.

The fact that Joella's birthday was three days away intensified her urgency to help the Sudanian children. She knew for every day they wasted, more children suffered.

Repeated calls back home deepened her misery. No one had seen or heard from Megan.

Everywhere she turned, the world seemed to fold in on her. In her soul a clock ticked louder and louder, kept cadence with each footfall, mocked that somehow she was running out of time.

The hotel's frigid air conditioning spread goose bumps on her arms. A few people milled around the posh lobby. Lelia made her way to the secluded phone booths. She pulled out her phone card, then dialed the shelter.

"Hello?"

"Derrick. It's Lelia."

"Woman, don't you pick up your messages? I left four today."

Tingling numbness stole over her skin. She dropped her purse to the floor. "What's wrong?"

A long pause followed. Lelia heard her assistant giving one of the kids instructions on the duty roster.

"Derrick, what happened?"

"Dag, girl, don't take my head off. It's a good thing." His awestruck chuckle boomed through the earpiece. "Duley found Tweek. Now don't go getting excited. She's not here."

Her lids slid over her eyes. "Where is she?"

"Still on the street. But Duley said she's still clean. Said she misses her dad and mom. That's good news, isn't it?"

"Yeah." She felt a smile spread on her lips. "The best news I've heard all day."

She promised to pick up her messages more often, then hung up and called Big T and Nana to tell them the news. Bernard was next.

A muffled greeting hummed over the line.

"Bernard?"

The line buzzed dead. After a few seconds, a recording informed her to make a call or hang up.

She peeled the cellophane off another calling card and redialed the number.

"Hello?"

"Hi, baby girl." A smile warmed his voice. "My mind's been on you."

"Hi, yourself. Did you just pick up the phone? I thought I heard...oh, never mind."

"So how are you faring, baby girl?"

Thoughts of Megan lifted her spirits. "The last hour hasn't been so bad. The jury's still out on the rest of the day." She filled him in on the committee. "It's like we're circling and nobody wants to land. I don't get it at all."

"Maybe you're not supposed to." Silence deadened the line.

"Bernard?"

"Just thinking to myself. Baby girl, maybe you should go with the flow for right now. Or better yet, let that Albright fellow take your place."

"You're joking, right? I'm not going to go with the flow. They have enough yes men in there already. Something needs to be done for those kids." She rubbed the burning at her temple. "Look, Bernard, I'm sorry. I didn't mean to flip out. I see all these needy little faces and I feel so useless."

"I know your heart's in the right place, but D.C. isn't the place for soft hearts. I don't like the smell of it. I've had a bad feeling since you told us you were going. Got some friends who are still serving. I'll do some checking. Whatever's going on, it don't feel right."

She could almost see the worry lines etched in his forehead.

More silence clutched the line. "Forget this battle, baby girl. Come home."

She tried to find the words to reassure, but couldn't. His mood wouldn't allow it. He'd been like this once before. When she lay recuperating in the hospital. He stayed by her side night and day, getting snatches of rest only when Big T visited.

When she'd ask what was wrong, he smiled and waved

it off. But his eyes glinted a warning to every new face that came too close to her for his liking.

Ma Ella had noticed it, too. "The old folks used to say people like your Bernard have cat senses, can feel and sense things the rest of us can't."

Lelia cleared her mind, glanced at her watch. "Geez, the shuttle left twenty minutes ago."

She gathered her purse and attaché. "Bernard, I have to see this thing through. I can't let this go now. I can't let down my kids either. That money will be good for the shelter. I've got to go. I'm a big girl. So stop worrying."

"You know I can't."

She pushed the bifold door open, and smiled. "I know. I love you. Bye, Bernard."

"Bye, baby girl."

She hurried across the polished marble lobby tiles. Outside, she flagged down a cab, then slid into the seat and closed the door.

"Where to, sistah?"

Lelia picked her brain, tried to remember the location of the reception. "I think it's called the Whin-tom?"

"The Wyndham. That a fancy dig." A light Caribbean accent stroked his words. "Pretty lady like you is deserving of such finery. When you got into my cab I knew heaven was smiling on me."

Lelia pulled a deadpan stare. "Look player, save the slow jam for the sistahs who want to hear you croon. I'm not the one."

"Ouch! You slice a brother deep, don't you?"

At a red light, he turned, hooked an arm over the seat. His eyes grinned. "What's your name anyway?"

"Lelia." She lifted an eyebrow. "And what happened to your Jamaican accent?"

He nodded toward the floor. "You cut me so bad, it all spilled out. See it oozing down around your feet?"

She chuckled. "You're from Brooklyn. I can hear it."

"Guilty as charged." He wrapped both hands around the steering wheel, slowly inched the car forward. "My stepdad's from Kingston. The way he talked was the slickest vibe I'd ever heard so I picked it up. Ladies love it." He shrugged. "Most of them anyway."

He pulled into the circular drive of a block-long hotel, stopped in line with the limos and cabs dropping off passengers. "You going to need a ride from here?"

Lelia paid the fare displayed on the meter. She glanced at the massive gray-granite building. "Probably. I don't think I'll be long."

He trailed the other vehicles until they reached the entrance. "Here." He handed her a card. "Call me when you get ready to go. I'll come back.

She read the print. "Romeo?"

One hand cupped around the rearview mirror, he slicked down his eyebrows with his left index finger "Gordon turned the ladies off. Romeo Jones sort of rolls off the tongue." He wriggled his eyebrows. "Don't 'cha know, my sistah?"

"Whatever, *Gordon.*" She placed the card in her purse and stepped onto the curb. "See you in a few."

The bellman ushered her through the hushed, glass-etched entry. The concierge directed her down a short secondary corridor. Two men stood in front of large ornamental brass doors.

"I'm here for the Sudanian relief effort reception."

"Name, please?"

"Lelia Marie Freeman."

"I need to see your driver's license and your committee credentials."

Lelia pulled out her license and the badge she clipped to her chest every morning.

He inspected the cards, then lowered his head to talk into a radio. While he did his checking, Lelia watched the floor-to-ceiling waterfall cascading in the massive lobby.

Minutes later another man appeared from behind the doors.

"Ms. Freeman?"

Lelia eyed the Tommy Lee Jones replica. "Yes?"

He held the door open. "This way, please."

She trailed Tommy Lee around a corner and down a posh corridor. In front of heavy mahogany doors, another man sentried an X-ray machine.

Tommy Lee held out his hand. "Bags, please?"

She handed them over. He opened her purse, rifled through the small compartments. Her attaché was next. His sidekick stepped up.

"This way, Ms. Freeman. Lift your arms."

Lelia complied. A handheld metal detector hovered above her body as she watched Tommy Lee plop her items on the conveyer belt and let them run through the machine.

He waved for her to retrieve her things. Items from her purse cluttered the end of the belt. She tried to snatch the lipstick and tampons that rolled out.

She straightened, lifted her chin. Thankfully, Tommy Lee held his emotionless demeanor.

"Follow me."

He led her to a set of elevators, fished a thick gray-backed card from his pocket and swiped it into a turnstile. The lights on the contraption flashed green and he motioned her into the carpeted lift.

The door opened on the thirty-fourth floor. Muted music drifted into the elevator, brought with it the fragrance of herbed meats and fresh baked breads.

Tommy Lee escorted her through the only door in the corridor, left her with an, "Enjoy the night, Ms. Freeman."

Lelia stood at the periphery of the bejeweled event. Candlelit tables bordered the room. Three crystal chandeliers dripped from the center of the arched ceiling.

Cream linen serving stations lined either side of the ballroom. Rimmed with live flowers, centered with ice sculptures, each table garnered white-capped chiefs.

A white-coated waiter broke into her thoughts. "Something to drink, ma'am?"

"A root beer, thanks."

"Root beer?" He drew out the words like he didn't understand the language.

"If you don't have it, a Coke is fine." She slowed her words to the tempo he used. "Like in rum and Coke, just drop the rum."

She turned back to the crowd. Committee members socialized with people she'd only seen on the news or TV, others she didn't recognize. She walked farther into the room.

"Your root beer, ma'am."

She lifted the gooseneck flute from the tray. "Thank you."

"Such an exotic drink. Perhaps I should consider one."

Lelia turned toward the lightly accented voice. Ink-colored eyes regarded her. A gaze so intense, so unsettling, she stepped back.

The tall lean man inclined his head. Smooth chocolate skin stretched over the sharp, stark features of a hawk. "I apologize. I did not intend to frighten you."

"No need. You didn't frighten me, you startled me. I didn't see you standing there."

The lie fell from her lips too easily. When she'd turned, glanced into his disquieting eyes, she *was* scared. A chill idled over her skin.

"Very good. It would distress me to cause you any displeasure. Are you enjoying the festivities?"

"Actually, I just got here." She stuck out her hand. "I'm Lelia Freeman."

Long, cold fingers wrapped around hers. "I am pleased to make your acquaintance, Ms. Freeman. My name is Mawain Boll Deng."

"As in President Deng?"

Pinpoint lights shone at the center of his dark pupils, increased their disturbing potency. "I am he."

"The pleasure's mine, President Deng." Another lie dropped from her mouth. The chill became unbearable.

"President Deng, can we get a picture?"

Before Lelia could step away, a photographer snapped a photo. The harsh flash bounced dots beneath her lids.

She slid her hand from his grasp. On impulse, she rubbed her hand over her skirt, tried to warm her palm.

The movement drew his eye. "Has something made you uncomfortable?"

"Why do you ask?"

His sharp gaze returned to her face. "You look disturbed."

She quelled the urge to move away. "What are your goals for the orphans?"

He looked puzzled, but answered the question with ease. "I have recited my wishes to your government officials numerous times. I will, however, repeat them as I am in such distinguished company."

Like a man accustomed to his orders being followed, he waved two fingers toward a waiter. He placed his half-empty brandy snifter on the serving tray, and then immediately turned back to her.

"My country never knew the meaning of this word

orphan. The people of Sudania believe the rearing of a child is the responsibility of the entire community."

Suave, he laced his fingers. "The adult population has dwindled due to the war. The children have no one to raise them. The Brotherhood Alliance has nearly wiped out a generation."

"President Deng, I'm not interested in discussing the political tone of your country, just the orphans."

Her response amused him, but the smile curving his lips didn't soften his features. "I have heard you are a warrior for the underprivileged."

"President Deng, do you realize no concrete plans have been set to get food and medicine to the children?"

His brows drew together. "How can that be? Have you discussed your concerns with Mr. Frankel?"

Bionic hearing must have been a reality. From across the room, the foreign affairs secretary's head appeared through the tangle of milling bodies. His close-set gaze collided with hers. Lelia sensed he sniffed trouble. He parted the sea, made his way to them in record time.

Frankel turned to the President, smiled his greasy charm.

"President Deng, I hope things are going well?"

"No, Mr. Frankel, they are not. Miss Freeman recently informed me of disturbing information."

"So introductions aren't necessary?" His too-bright voice belied the warning in his eyes.

Lelia tapped the bottom of her glass against her palm. "We've met."

"I see."

President Deng inclined his head toward Frankel. "Perhaps, I need to forgo conferences about oil for one day to observe exactly how the relief committee is helping the children of my country?"

Lelia stopped tapping her glass. "Oil?"

"Miss Freeman is confused." Frankel stepped between her and the President. He extended a meaty hand toward the wide veranda doors. "Perhaps we can discuss the progress of the committee in the garden?"

President Deng tilted his head toward the doors. "Yes, we should, Mr. Frankel."

Lelia watched them turn away. Someone touched her shoulder.

"You do look confused." Dr. Willis reached in front of her to pluck a few hors d'oeuvres from a waiter's tray.

"I am."

"Judging from the expression on your face when the oil issue came up, I take it you don't have a clue?"

Lelia lifted her glass to her lips, tried to hide her embarrassment. "Guess I don't. A clue about what?"

Dr. Willis popped a shrimp into his mouth. "What the average Joe doesn't know is Sudania is one of the richest oil-producing countries in the world. That little fact was left out of the presentations." He chewed the last bite, stuck the toothpick between his teeth. "Now that the war's over, it opens the door for trade negotiations. That's one way to eventually bring down those crazy prices at the pumps."

The pieces of the puzzle jarred into place. The Sudanians

needed food, medicine and shelter. The United States needed oil.

Lelia looked to where Frankel guided President Deng through the garden doors. Fury churned the pit of her stomach, threatened to choke her. Did anything ever come free? She looked around the room at the decked-out guests laughing, drinking top-shelf, wondered how much grain, milk and seed could have been bought and shipped instead.

Her root beer suddenly tasted sour. She deposited the glass on a nearby tray, then maneuvered through the partyers.

Hard-toed shoes kicked the back of her ankle, pulled the shoe from her foot. Clumsy hands clutched her arms, tried to keep her from falling.

"Sorry. My feet don't listen to my brain sometimes. I was trying to keep up with you, but you stopped short."

Even in the dim light, Lelia could see the flush spread across Dr. Willis' cheeks. He fumbled one of her shoulder pads into place, pulled down the other, then shoved his hands in his pockets. "Hey, you leaving so soon? You just got here."

She stooped to nudge her shoe back on. "I need some fresh air."

"Yeah, I hear you. Hang on, I'll go, too. You shouldn't be out this time of night by yourself."

She laid her fingers on his arm. "Thanks, but I breathe alone. It's been a long day and I need some space."

"Look, be careful."

"No problem. I'm a city girl."

Lelia rode the elevator to the lobby and walked to the concierge. After they'd called Romeo, she went to stand out front.

The air breezed warm, she shrugged off her jacket, flipped it over her shoulder.

Impatient horn blasts, transit bus roars, the constant energized buzz of the city surrounded her. Familiar smells, exhaust fumes, expensive perfumes, joggers' sweat, all reminded her of home.

Washingtonians were out in force, enjoying the city's cosmopolitan culture. She followed the throng down the sidewalk.

A short distance from the hotel entrance, a man sat propped against the wall.

Even in the heat, layers of clothes wrapped his body. Holes peppered the worn garments. Age-cracked athletic shoes encased his feet. All his belongings seemed to be in two black garbage bags snuggled close to his sides. His legs drew to his chest, arms rested on his knees. His face was hidden from view.

He rocked back and forth, moved a fraction at a time. The movement so slight, it was almost undetectable.

People strolled by, relishing their night out. They didn't acknowledge him. For them, he was invisible.

In him, Lelia saw herself or one of her kids.

She hurried to the late-night deli across the street. She came back with a half-smoke and a soda. The man hadn't budged.

She walked over and sat beside him. "Pretty nice tonight, huh?"

The rocking stopped.

"I just bought this food, but I can't finish it." She waved the bag in front of his knees. "I'd hate it to go to waste."

"Go 'way." The rocking resumed.

She kept quiet for a while. The rocking ceased again.

"Said go 'way."

"All right."

She pulled some bills from her wallet, placed them under the half-smoke on top of one of the bags. She put the soda by his foot, then stood. "There's always hope, my friend. I've been there, I know."

She walked back to the entrance.

A horn blared from the street. "Hey, Lelia." Romeo opened the door of his cab as she approached. "Your chariot awaits." She tossed her purse onto the seat, then glanced back at the man.

Their gazes connected.

Shadows obscured his face. Head lifted, he held the half-smoke in one hand, soda in the other. He raised the cup. Lelia nodded, then allowed Romeo to fold her into the cab. She twisted in the seat, watched the man until the cab rounded a corner.

Romeo broke into her melancholy. "The night's still young. Should I take you to a club, or how about somewhere in Georgetown?"

Lelia turned in the seat, pressed a finger to the throbbing pain at her temple.

"There's a boatload of drugstores along the way if you want to get some aspirin or something?"

She met his eyes in the rearview mirror, then dropped her hand. "I just realized I hadn't had much to eat all day." Her stomach rumbled to confirm it. Countless high-end eateries passed in a blur. She'd had her fill of that food the first few days she'd been in D.C. "Do you know where to get some good home cooking?"

Romeo stopped the car. He pulled a tube of lip balm from his shirt pocket, smoothed the tip over his lips. "Depends on your home. Anything and everything you want to eat is up and down Georgia Avenue. Now there's this one place Carib Delight. They make the best curried goat roti this side of the West Indies."

Lelia grinned around the headache. "I was thinking more like soul food."

"Well, that's a no-brainer. You've got to go to Pop's. He's in Northwest, but he makes a slamming smothered pork chop sandwich and collards. His banana pudding would make you slap your mama."

She tried, but couldn't stop her chuckle. "That sounds like the place."

"Pop's it is."

She glanced out the window. Block after block of cosmopolitan marble-and-glass buildings melted into the neighborhoods of D.C. Corner convenience stores, carryouts, and small porched houses bordered Georgia Avenue.

Romeo pulled in front of a small shop. The lighted

shingle hanging over the door sporting bold black letters, signaled they'd made it.

"Just tell Pop I sent you." He leaned over the back of the seat to palm the fare Lelia handed him.

"I'd go in, but..." His head wove back and forth as he tried to get a better look into the shop. "...he's still ticked at me. I had a thing going on with his daughter. It didn't work out. You know what I mean?"

Lelia opened the cab door. "I'm scared to ask."

"Yeah, I was scared, too. Pop packs a mean-looking shotgun. Hey, call me when you're done."

He rolled down the window as she shut the door. "You know, maybe you should wait to tell Pop I sent you until after he fixes your food." The smile he flashed shone pure innocence. "Just to be safe."

"Sure, Gordon."

She stepped into the small shop, inhaled the soul-cooked fragrance.

High-backed booths lined one wall of the narrow restaurant. A red Formica countertop lipped the cashier area. Swinging doors behind the counter led to the kitchen. Old fashioned candy and cookie jars crowded the corners of the counter. Lelia walked farther into the shop, sat on a cracked vinyl barstool.

The pudgy man behind the counter wiped his hands on a dish towel. He tossed it over his shoulder. "Welcome, young lady. This your first time here?"

"Yep. Your smothered pork chop sandwich and collards

come highly recommended. The banana pudding's so good I hear it'll make you slap your mama."

He slid a laminated sheet across the counter. "Let me guess. Romeo."

She grinned. "He told me to tell you he sent me, only *after* you fixed my food."

"I guess he thinks sending me business will get him off the hook. That boy's a mess." He moved to clean away the dishes from another customer. He swiped the dollar off the counter as he sponged the crumbs away. "Well, what'll it be?"

Lelia set down the menu. "The pork chop sandwich, collards and banana pudding, of course." She tapped the menu with her thumb. "Oh, and a side of macaroni and cheese and a root beer to wash it down."

"Will do."

He disappeared behind the flapping kitchen door. Ten minutes later, Lelia slumped against the back of the stool, licked the savory gravy from the corner of her mouth. She closed her eyes, wolfed down her third mouthful. Anything that tasted this good should be a crime.

"Miss Freeman?"

The thick accent vibrated over her. She turned, assessed the stiff-backed young man sitting next to her.

He held out a tattered manila envelope. "Please."

Anxious energy bounced off him. He kept a nervous eye on the door as if he expected someone he knew to walk in.

He was one of Frankel's stoolies, no doubt. That comment to President Deng may have been over the top. She knew she should have stayed to defend herself, yet here she sat greasing on a pork chop.

The foreign affairs secretary was probably back at the reception laughing his head off. These were her termination papers telling her to go home, don't call us because we won't call you.

She wiped her hands on the napkin, opened the seal and removed the sheets from the envelope. Her fingernails bit into the back of the slick paper. Bile burned her throat, the smothered pork chop re-entered her mouth. She pulled her eyes from the photos, looked at the young man. "What do you want?"

"For now, your full attention."

CHAPTER ELEVEN

Lelia stared at the grotesque pictures. Women and children were imprisoned in cages that shouldn't house animals. Men brutalized beyond recognition. People were sprawled on dirt floors of small, crowded rooms, barely clothed, their gaunt faces desperate for help. Salvation. The shiny photos trembled, her hand quaked beneath them.

"Miss Freeman, please. May we speak privately?"

The urgent voice broke through her thoughts. She looked up at the nervous young man. A Redskins baseball cap hid his brow. He wore baggy jeans and an oversized red-and-gold T-shirt. A typical Washington sports fan.

Pop lingered nearby. "Is everything all right, young lady?"

She pushed the photos back in the envelope, flashed the brightest smile she could muster. "Yes, Pop. Everything's delicious. My friend and I are going to sit at one of the booths."

Lelia lifted her plate, signaled for her companion to

carry her drink. They settled in the last booth. She slowly reopened the envelope.

Picture after picture of human torment cried from the sheets. She looked at the last photo, slipped the pile back into the envelope, then put it on the table. "Who are these people and why are you showing me this?"

"These are the people of Sudania, Miss Freeman. The people you were sent to aid." Bitterness edged his dark eyes.

He eased to the end of the booth, glanced toward the door. "I can explain in more detail, but I must leave. Can you meet with me later?" He pulled a napkin from the dispenser and scribbled down an address.

Picking up the envelope, he slid the napkin in its place. "The truth must be revealed to stop the suffering of my people."

"Look, whatever your name is. You've got the wrong person." She pushed the napkin back toward him. "There are dozens of world organizations that deal with war crimes like these."

"These are not war crimes, Miss Freeman, and I have the right person."

"Go to the media. They'll run the story."

He scooped up the napkin, pressed it into her palm and folded her fingers around it. "Please, meet me. Do not fear. It is a public place. I will explain at that time."

He slipped from the booth and left the shop.

Forty-five minutes later, Lelia sat staring at her cold plate of food, her banana pudding still untouched.

"Hey, it doesn't look like my cooking cut the mustard." Pop glanced over the half-eaten food.

"Oh no. Everything was wonderful. I just got full."

"Worry can fill a stomach quicker than food." He piled the plates in his arm. "Let me box this."

"Thanks, Pop." Lelia wrapped her fingers around the flat root beer. "Would you call Romeo, too, please? I'm ready to go."

"Will do."

She gulped the last of the watery soda, mulled over what she should do.

Pop lifted the carryout bag off the counter. "You're set to go. Romeo's on the way."

She moved to the cash register, paid the bill, then took the bag from Pop.

"Come back and see me soon, young lady. Next time don't meet with anybody who'll spoil your appetite."

Romeo pulled up as Lelia stepped outside. She got into the cab, rolled the addressed napkin between her fingers.

"Everything was good, wasn't it? You don't have to say yes because I know it was." He threw his arm over the seat. "I figure right about now you're ready to go back to the hotel and sleep off that good cooking, huh?"

Silence filled the cab. "Actually, no, Romeo. Can you take me here?"

He smoothed out the napkin with his thumb, took a quick glance at the writing. "Club M? Going down by the water for some party time? So, who'd you get the napkin from?"

"My cousin."

His eyebrows raised in the mirror. "Yeah, I got a lot of cousins, too."

Romeo drove for a few minutes and finally pulled in front of what looked like a refurbished warehouse. "It's not swank, but they do know how to throw down. Well, I guess you won't be needing me anymore. Your *cousin* will probably take you back to the hotel."

"Actually, wise guy, I will need a ride. I'll call you when I'm done."

He walked around and opened her door. "I'm off to-morrow morning."

She got out, slapped his shoulder.

"Okay, okay." He held up his hands. "Call if you need me. I'll hang around for a while." He pulled a vial of breath freshener from his pocket, shot three sprays onto his tongue. "Just in case. Don't want to offend the honeys."

Lelia shook her head and moved to stand behind the red velvet rope sectioning off the waiting line to the club.

Salt and sea tweaked the air. Humidity rolled a blanket of mist along the District's wharf. Across the street, heavy fog concealed the water lapping against the con-crete barriers.

"Miss Freeman. Thank you for coming." The young man from Pop's stood behind her. "Come with me, please."

He stooped beneath the sagging rope, then lifted it for her to maneuver under. She trailed him to the front of the line. Perturbed voices called after them, angry that they'd butted.

The thick-armed bouncer at the door nodded to the young man. "What's up, dog?" He lifted his chin toward Lelia.

"It's okay. She is with me."

The bouncer held out his fist. The young man mimicked the movement, tapped his clenched knuckles against the bouncer's, then stood aside for Lelia to enter.

Heavy bass house tunes bounced off the walls. Romeo look-alikes leaned against the bar, waited for the next available female. Gyrating bodies packed the wide dance floor, bopped to the music. Lelia shouldered her way through the thick crush.

The young man led her through the kitchen to the storage room. He punched numbers into the keypad beside the door. The lock clicked open. He ushered her inside.

The room's coolness felt good against her skin. Liquor crates and boxes lined the walls and muddled the floor of the massive storage area. Thick plastic strips hung from the ceiling of the loading dock, covered the metal delivery door.

"Thank you again for coming." He moved to a tall wall of crates, reached behind the stack and pulled out a case. He flipped it open. "Here, Miss Freeman, look at these. They were taken one week ago."

More inhuman photos. These worse than the others. Lelia thumbed through them, closed her eyes against the suffering.

"Our government, our president has been feeding your

media lies. He enslaves us and covets the riches of our land while the people of our country starve."

Lelia let the pictures fall to her side. "None of this makes sense. President Deng is here to help his people."

"No. He is here for greed." He spat the words. "The profit from Sudania's oil is enough to feed and clothe all its people. Because of Deng's greed for power and money, only himself and his puppets live. We die."

He pulled off his baseball cap. He could be no more than eighteen. His work-weathered hands, the lines etched in his chocolate skin, the silver streaks in his straight raven hair aged him.

Lelia held out the pictures. "I've met the man. It's a little hard to believe."

"Does not the devil walk among us, Miss Freeman? Your Bible says he walks to and fro seeking whom he can devour." His eyes flashed his urgency. He took the pictures and shook them at her. "You have met the devil. Deng is a master deceiver."

"Why don't you go to the media?"

"We have tried. The information is never made public. He captures our families, tortures the ones that stand up to him. The meek he enslaves in his drilling sites. They work until they drop."

He pulled out a newspaper. "See." He slapped the caption with the back of his hand. *Militant Faction Attacks Innocent Gathering; 14 Die.*

"He has tainted the media with his lies. He will not

Dark Side of Valor 139

allow people to assemble. If they do, his troops shoot them down, slaughter them like sheep. The next day the media will report that we were responsible. That we held the guns. That we were the murderers."

Lelia ran a hand over her nape, tried to collect herself. "Who are *we*?"

"We are the Brotherhood Alliance, Miss Freeman. We are the ones asking for your help."

"Why me?" Lelia took a step toward the door.

He followed her action. "You are on the relief committee. You are reputable. There are many Sudanians in the United States who feel you can be trusted. We can use that to our advantage."

"I won't be used."

He smiled a sad smile. "It is too late. Why do you think you and the others were appointed to the committee? You are all respected leaders at the top of your fields. People value your opinion. And you. You are an American hero of sorts. People admire you. They trust you. It is easy for them to believe President Deng is a living martyr fighting for his country's survival if the relief committee, especially you, say it is so."

He crammed the cap on his head. "We do not have time to seek out another to help us. Unless you bring this to light, no one will know he initiated, fought, and concluded this so-called civil war to obliterate us. If he triumphs, no one will remain to oppose him. The dead do not speak, Miss Freeman."

He fisted the pictures and shoved them in front of her. "Please help us end this slaughter. You are our last hope. We have run out of options."

Lelia turned her eyes away. "Go to the government. They would help."

He lifted the photos directly in front of her face. "Our government is not to be trusted. With millions of lives at stake, can you trust yours?"

She placed her palm over his fingers, lowered his hand, the pictures from her view. "What can I do?"

Relief eased the lines around his mouth. "There are many family members and comrades of the alliance who are imprisoned. Once we free them, we will contact you."

He placed the photos and the newspaper into the envelope and sealed it. "Once we do, take these to this person."

He handed her a name with an address printed beneath it. "She is employed at CNN. She can be trusted."

He laid the envelope in her palm, placed his hand over it. "We will not meet after today. Handle these with great care, Miss Freeman."

Lelia zipped the envelope in her purse. She didn't know if she believed the young man, or what she'd do with the information.

He stepped around her to punch the entry code beside the door. "Thank you again, Miss Freeman. Now you are Sudania's angel as well."

A deafening blast ripped through the room. The delivery door slammed up. Barrel-chested giants charged in, guns drawn.

The young man hauled her behind his body. Instinct and fear controlled Lelia's feet. She ran between boxes, wedged herself between two crates.

One of the crates was pried open. She crouched in the empty space.

Through the narrow slits between the wooden planks, she saw the young man. One hulking monster grabbed his shoulders, held him in the cage of his arms.

The young man's face settled into a mask of calm defiance. His chest rode up and down with each breath.

The giant turned him to face the delivery doors. Pitch blackness back-dropped the plastic loading dock slates. There was movement there. The young man saw it, too.

His features contorted. Rage flared his nostrils, bulged his eyes. "*Shaitan! Shaitan!*"

A hand pulled back the plastic strips. President Deng stepped through, walked into the room as if it were his kingdom.

He strolled over to the young man, spoke to him in a whispered hush.

The young man quieted, his eyes fired with hate. He spat at the President's feet. "*Shaitan!*"

The muscle-bound ape holding him twisted his hands up into his shoulder blades, then wrapped his log-thick arms around him and carried his bucking body through the delivery doors.

The young man continued to screech the word over and over. Lelia would always remember the haunting cry.

The President waved his hand. The men spread around the room.

She kept her gaze on Deng. As if sensing her, his intense eyes met hers through the slats. A corner of his mouth lifted. The pinpoints in his eyes danced. He inclined his head. Lelia shivered, felt something cold touch her.

She shoved her purse under the packing hay piled in the corner, then shouldered her weight and rushed the front of the crate.

Pain burned through her shoulder and back. She ignored it and ran through the plastic slats. The street lay deserted, except for the limousine idling by the curb.

"Seize her." The quiet, chilling command grated along the mist.

She sprinted out of her pumps down the deserted pavement. Pounding footsteps clamored on the pier behind her.

Past the street lamp, the heavy blanket of fog obscured the wharf. She saw nothing but the faint lights of the docked boats, heard nothing but her ragged breaths, lapping water and the giants gaining.

Humid air and fear glued her dress to her skin. Debris cut her feet.

A loud crack erupted behind her. Then another. Harsh shouts meshed with gunfire. She ran harder, toward far-off headlights burning through the fog.

The scuffling footfalls echoed louder. She felt their nearness.

The headlights veered, vanished in the smothering mist. She cried out. Despair doused her knotted stomach. A heavy crush pummeled her from behind. The weight squashed her to the ground, snatched her breath.

Pain rocked her skull. Shards of light exploded behind her lids. Parts of a shattering mirror, each piece carried an image from her past: her mama, Zeek, Joella.

Like rain, they fell into a black void churning below her.

Leila fought, groped away from its depths. The pain imprisoned her, intensified.

Conquered, she sank with the broken pieces into the abyss.

CHAPTER TWELVE

A cloying touch stoked her from the abyss. Down her cheek, along her jaw, it skimmed, feathered over her throat, her collarbone. Its coolness, gentle, giving.

Crushing pain scorched her head, wouldn't allow her peace. She tried to move from the agony.

"Well done, Miss Freeman. I am pleased to see you are on the side of the living."

The voice was close.

"Save your strength. You will need it to recover."

"President Deng?" Her throat felt clawed. Dry as dirt.

"Correct. Open your eyes fully and look upon my face."

Lelia struggled to focus through the halos of light. She forced her lids apart. The brightness caused another explosion in her head.

President Deng's gaze bore into hers. His image filled her view. The coolness from his fingers continued to stroke her throat.

"Don't touch me." She flinched, tried to lift her arm

to knock his hand away. It wouldn't comply, stayed limp by her side. The eerie coldness in his eyes scared her. "Look, call me a cab, now. Let me out of here and we'll forget this happened. Okay?"

His knuckles grazed around her ribs to her breast-bone. He gouged them into her skin. Harder. Harder. She moaned under the pressure. His eyes sparkled the unhallowed sheen of black pearls. He threw back his head. Unnatural, mirthless laughter poured from his lips, bounced around in her skull.

As quickly as it started, it stopped. He pressed her body into the mattress. His nose almost skimmed hers.

"Mr. Frankel was correct. You are confused. No cab will travel the distance for your rescue. Now, you reside in my world."

He leaned back, moved off the bed. Her eyes followed his movements until he disappeared.

Thin netting encased the king-size bed. She fisted the material, jerked it aside. She blinked, wondered if the blow to her head had knocked her insane.

The ceiling was arched and covered with murals. Proud eyes of ancient tribesmen peered at her from their por-traits hanging on the walls. Arched doorways led to endless connecting chambers.

Lelia dragged her legs to the edge of the bed. Her feet dropped to the floor. She held her head with both hands and inched her bottom off the mattress to stand.

The room tilted. Her knees knocked like wooden clack-ers. She closed her eyes, tried to stop the spinning. When the earth slowed, she raised her lids. Her eyes fell on a woman standing across the room.

Lelia cleared her throat. "I need a cab."

The woman bowed her head, but kept silent. Her face, head and body were hidden, wrapped in yards of black material.

Leila took a shaky step. "Please, if you point me toward the phone, I'll make the call myself."

"She will not aid you unless I command it." President Deng's voice echoed from one of the archways.

Lelia ignored him, walked closer to the woman. "Look, this lunatic sent his goons to kidnap me. Call the police, the front desk, somebody. Tell them what happened."

The woman remained a statue. Her silence rang loud, drew goose bumps across Lelia's skin.

"Save your pleas." Deng's breath raked the back of her neck. He dangled her purse in front of her face, then draped an arm over her shoulder. "Does this belong to you?"

A slow-moving pendulum, he swung the purse back and forth. Lelia closed her eyes against the damning motion.

A smile rode his words. "The contents were very enlightening. It appears you were conspiring with a known murderer."

"Yeah, I talked to you for a few minutes at the reception, but don't be so hard on yourself. You didn't mean to kill all those people. Shit happens."

His fingers bit into her arm. He spun her to face him. "Crossing me is a dangerous thing." He pitched the bag across the room. "Do you know what I am capable of?"

"Pictures don't lie, Einstein. They were very...enlightening." She yanked her arm free. Palms up, she shoved his chest hard enough to knock him off balance. "This party is over." Lelia tried to pass him.

"Witch!" The back of his hand sliced the air, cuffed her face, sent her reeling. Smug, he stood over her, adjusted his jacket. "You will learn what true obedience means."

Pin pricks flamed her cheek. Anger torched her spine.

Teeth grinding, she kicked out her leg. Her calf smashed across his knees. The vibration of his body and head smacking the floor rattled a vase on the nightstand.

Her body tingled. She dragged herself to her knees, arched over him.

"Your sorry behind." Hands fisted, she landed windmill punches to his head.

The front door crashed in. Two of the goons that chased her down rushed the room.

Blunt fingers plowed through her hair, dug into her scalp, brought her to her feet. Dazed from the fire shooting down her body, she slumped against the goon. A gun lodged in her cheek, bunched her skin into her eye. The other helped Deng to his feet. He shoved him aside, then ran a finger over his swollen lip.

Icy eyes stared her down. "Leave us!" He snapped his fingers toward the man he'd shoved and the silent woman.

They slipped from the room. Deng nodded for the man gripping her to stay.

Once they were alone, the President waved his hand to the mangler. "Release her."

The vise loosened. Lelia crumpled to the floor. Hammers pummeled her head and neck. Unseen fingers squeezed her lungs, robbed her of air. The room echoed her ragged breathing.

She raised her eyes, worked to still the waves crashing against her eardrums.

Deng towered above her. Blood beaded in the corner of his mouth. He swiped it, glided his finger over the tip of his tongue. His eyes gleamed as he smiled a cat-to-mouse grin. "Do you read the newspaper?"

He stepped back to a marble table to pick up a paper. Paper in hand, he walked back to her. "I insist you read an article from your country's *Washington Post*. Excuse the late date."

Dread churned in Lelia's stomach. A large black-and-white photo of the two of them shaking hands monopolized the front page.

The image was deceiving. He looked the concerned leader of a struggling nation. She, an opportunistic American waiting for her ship to come in.

LA Street Angel Appointed U.S. Goodwill Ambassador to Sudania

"You look shocked." He held the paper close to her nose. "Perhaps your vision is impaired."

Lelia skimmed the article. The lies bounced off the page.

Unbeknown to many, Los Angeles' popular homeless advocate, Lelia Freeman, has recently been appointed Sudania's Goodwill Ambassador. President Deng and Freeman apparently had a lot to discuss. Sources close to President Deng say he is pleased with the appointment. "Miss Freeman has the heart of a warrior. She will be a tremendous asset to the Sudanian people." Freeman was not available for comment. She traveled with the Sudanian convoy back to Sudania yesterday.

Lelia's eyes snapped to the upper corner of the paper. It was dated the day after they'd hunted her down.

"You appear to be confused again. The paper is a week old." He moved closer, lifted her chin. "Come, come, Miss Freeman. Do not look forlorn. Do you know how many people would die to be in your position?"

She snatched her chin away. Fury brought her gaze back to his face. "Why?"

"In the future, you will not question me." His fingers flexed as if he wanted to slap her again. "I now allow it only because I will take great pleasure watching your lovely face as I detail your fate." He strolled to the vanity chair and sat. Long legs stretched, one ankle crossed the other.

"When I came to the United States last year, I had the opportunity to read about a courageous warrior who saved children on the streets of Los Angeles. I was intrigued, however, I had other immediacies to attend to."

He fingered his lip. "The civil war in my country had ended, yet it had not served its purpose. It was necessary to rid the country of pestilence. The Brotherhood Alliance. They are, however, more resilient than I anticipated. Over the years, I discovered, to my chagrin, my followers had lost faith in me. The Brotherhood Alliance had spread untruths, told the people they should have more liberties."

He steepled his fingers. "Such lunacy. The people of Sudania are helpless sheep. They require guidance for their very existence. They cannot survive without leadership. Without me. I am their salvation."

He looked at her as if his statement made perfect sense.

"The alliance rallied the people. To protect them, I forbade public gatherings. The alliance began to raid our military compounds." He spread his hands. "They had to be abolished.

"A worldly man, I realize other political leaders do not share my administrative style. The need arose to conceive an amicable resolution to the situation. So I initiated the civil war to eliminate my opposition. They became casualties of war, you would say in your country."

He uncrossed his ankles and planted his feet on the floor. "The tactic worked well for some time. The finances for replacement arms were costly, however, and the revenue from our natural resources were dispensed in other venues."

"You mean you stole the money to make yourself rich."

"You are too gullible, Miss Freeman. You should not believe the words of a criminal."

He smoothed his palm over the arms of the chair. "It

was necessary to obtain more arms to end the alliance's influence over my people. Your country was interested in oil trade. They frowned upon the violence of the war, therefore I ended it."

He shrugged. "Now your country will receive Sudanian oil and I will obtain the finances for the weapons needed to quash the alliance. Then I will receive the acknowledgment I deserve. That is where your services are needed."

He stood and walked to her. "I have painstakingly guarded my reputation with the media. Heroism and my name are not synonymous, however. You, Miss Freeman, are here to make me a hero. You will tour my country. Photographs will be sent to the media. Reports, sent by you, of course, will go forth stating the Sudanian government is doing everything in its power to heal its people.

"I wanted you because, in an odd way, the people of your country view you as a savior. They believe in you. That is why I wanted you for this venture."

Lelia cut him off. "I don't give a damn what you want. You've picked the wrong one. My family knows I wouldn't run off without discussing it with them first. They'll drop on the State Depart-ment like the plague."

He slipped his hands into his breast pocket and pulled out a small booklet. "What is the euphemism in your country? A leopard cannot change his spots? You ran away from your mother and family before. Did you not?"

Lelia's heart skipped. In all the years the media hounded

her, she never mentioned running from her family, never mentioned Mama.

Satisfaction spread over his face. "Surprised? I know about your drunken mother, Rubinell, and the others in your family. I even know the kind of undergarments that fill the inexpensive oak dresser in your single-level home. I know the very soul of Lelia Marie Freeman."

Slowly he flipped open the cover of the pad. "Vernon Thompson. Fifty-six. Occupation: supervisor, Able Roofing Company. Employed there for eighteen years. Resides at 1709 Willow Creek Drive, Los Angeles, California. Married to Naomi 'Nana' Thompson, fifty-three, for thirty-one years. Her occupation, owner of Naomi's Beauty Salon. They attend Cornerstone Baptist Church. Address: 11 Cardinal Street, Los Angeles, California. Bernard Samuels…"

"Stop it." She moved toward him. The mangler clamped down on her shoulder. The power struggle was short-lived. He forced her to her knees.

"Hurt one hair on any of their heads and I swear…"

"You are in no position to dictate demands." He stared at her knees. "You are in a position to worship me, which you will do, joyfully for the media, knowing I will spare the lives of the ones you love."

He folded the booklet back into his pocket. "You initiated this. You asked Frankel to send a representative to my country. The request was ignored.

"You have yourself to blame for your predicament. Your

untimely rendezvous with Kofi, shall we say killed two birds with one stone and sealed your fate. Kofi can no longer speak untruths. He will not show treasonous pictures to the media. Nor will you."

He patted his pocket. "I am thorough. I leave nothing to chance. Once the media hails me a savior, your purpose will be fulfilled." He attempted to look sad. "Unfortunately, you will be gunned down by the alliance. However, your obedience in this endeavor will save your family. You will die knowing your loved ones will live."

He gripped her chin again, jerked her to his gaze. "Do you understand me?"

Lelia's stomach rolled. Nausea tugged bile to her throat.

"The venom in your eyes intrigues me. It will please me to groom your obedience."

He let her go. A frown bunched his brow, he fingered the collar of her dress.

Cool fingers traced the delicate chain of the golden charm that rested between her breast.

She tensed. The guard stilled any movement.

Deng lifted the heart with two fingers, sent it into a gradual sway. "Beautiful in an inexpensive way. From the emotion firing your eyes, this is a gift from a lover, perhaps?"

A harsh tug snapped the chain from her neck. He held it suspended, twirled it in front of her eyes. "Now Sudania is your lover."

Lelia's heart twisted, then broke.

Forgetting the mangler, she sprang toward Deng. The guard's fingers dug into her flesh.

The President enjoyed her display. He drew back and struck her face.

"Obedience. It will be painful only if you make it so."

The mangler let her drop to the floor. He stepped over her and left the room. The President lagged inside the entrance.

"What did you voice previously? This party is over?"

Lelia lifted her head. The grin she'd grown to hate settled on his face.

"Contrary to your belief, this party is not over. It has just begun."

CHAPTER THIRTEEN

President Deng stood in his office, surveyed the sparkling lights of the small city miles below.

His kingdom.

He possessed it all.

Every man, woman, every child. The livestock, the homes and yes, even the grains of sand were his.

None of the minions residing below or within these walls were worthy to serve him. Their menial labor, however, proved necessary.

He ran his knuckles over his chin, his thoughts lingered on his most coveted possession.

They called it Black Gold. The lifeblood of his country.

Oil.

The ebony liquid bolstered his power with the outside world.

The commoners below did not understand power or wealth. Why squander precious resources on serfs? He did them a service, allowed them to live, even though the alliance polluted their minds with a nonsense concept they did not understand or deserve.

Equality.

Everyone had their place. His was to rule. Theirs, to attend his needs and revere him. The Brotherhood had their uses as well. Their negligible attempts to undermine him were amusing. He permitted them to survive only to serve his design. Once his purpose was complete, he would destroy them.

He walked over to a delicate, ornamental chessboard atop his desk. He eyed the porcelain figurines before picking one up. He plowed the figurine on top of the another, crushed both with the blow.

Checkmate.

"President Deng?"

The quiet inquiry startled him. "You dare enter without permission!" He glared at the stiff man standing before him.

General Saccoh did not move from his military stance. His eyes never shifted from the man he addressed. To show weakness was a mistake.

"My apologies, President. A critical matter has arisen. The Alliance raided Area Three weapons hold and commandeered the arms."

Saccoh watched the President's eyes. Cold, and ruthless, they danced, plotted another torrid game to lure the Alliance to slaughter.

Saccoh had fought many wars, had been face-to-face and battled beside every devil imaginable. In his fifty-five years he'd never known a more cunning military mind than the President. Nor one more evil. Saccoh feared no man except Deng.

The short pause drew out the game Deng loved to play.

"Who will pay for this infraction?"

Saccoh knew the payment Deng required. "The punishment has been carried out, President."

"And the infiltrator?"

"Eliminated."

"Very good, Saccoh. I will locate another weapons hold. You will secure it." A long silence tightened the air like a noose. Saccoh read the underlying meaning of the quietness. Another game commenced.

"And the needed weapons, President?"

"Make the call."

"Yes, President."

CHAPTER FOURTEEN

He'd gotten the call.

Standing in the airport, Elijah Dune wondered how things would unfold. He hadn't planned on this stroke of luck. Nor did he plan on the meddling man and woman blocking his path.

"What's up with you, man? Aunt Dee says you've lost your mind. She's at home climbing the walls worrying about you." His cousin Marcellus stood in front of him, larger than life.

"Mama's fine."

Elijah stepped around his cousin. Marcellus moved into his path. Nose to nose, they stared each other down.

"Mind your business and get out of my way."

Marcellus' voice raged just above a whisper. "I'm making it my business. You can sucker Aunt Dee, but it's me you're lipping off to now."

Elijah bared his teeth.

His cousin's big mouthed drawl blared on. "Yeah, I'm in your face, and I ain't moving 'til I get some answers."

"Marcellus, man, either step out of my way or I'll go through you."

"Wait one minute!"

Elijah felt small hands pry between their bodies.

Pint-size shoulders wedged them apart. Feeling the hard tug on his collar, he drew his eyes away from Marcellus' challenging, concerned stare to look down into angry doe eyes he'd always loved. His other meddling cousin, Marcellus' sister, Sierra.

"Need I remind you I'm still the oldest around here. I don't know what's going on in that hard head of yours." She jammed a finger in his chest. "But I do know you've got Aunt Dee frantic that you're about to do something stupid."

"Hold up, I'm going on a trip. Is that allowed?"

"Sure. As long as we go with you."

"The hell you are!"

"The hell we're not!"

Elijah eyed Sierra and Marcellus saw the overnight bags slung on their shoulders.

"All right. I'm just flying to Texas for a couple of days of R and R." He couldn't stay mad for long when Sierra was around. He bent to kiss her flared nose.

Her suspicious eyes gave him a once-over. "You're not off the hook yet, Boopy." She moved the strap of her bag higher on her shoulder. "You still have a lot of explaining to do once we hit Texas."

Marcellus touched his sister's shoulder. "Go call Mama

and tell her we'll be gone for a couple of days, then call Aunt Dee. Tell her everything is all right and we'll keep an eye on the hard head." He gently moved her toward the pay phones. "We'll get the tickets and meet you back here."

Elijah watched her turn and march off. Conversation halted until her five-foot-one frame merged with the crowd.

He turned to the man who'd grown closer to him than a brother. "I can go it alone."

"Not while there's breath in my body you won't. We can stand and fight it out like old times, but Sierra will be back soon."

Elijah nodded. Marcellus followed him across the concourse. "Now, where are we really going?"

Elijah leaned his head against the headrest and gazed through the airplane window. Across the night sky, the moon's brilliance glowed above the cloud cover.

He was traveling back to the Motherland, one of his many trips to Africa.

He thought of Sierra and the hell they'd pay for leaving her behind. But he drew comfort knowing she was safe. He had no doubt she could have taken care of herself. She could outshoot, outrun and outsmart him and Marcellus both. He couldn't risk it.

He didn't want Marcellus along either, but logic won

out. He needed him. If things got too hot, he'd find a way to ship him home. Elijah couldn't have his mind muddled with worry. Not now.

Now only one thing mattered. One thing had become the basis of his life.

He'd waited an eternity for it. Now he was closer than he'd ever been.

His veins pulsed with it. Soon it would be his.

Vengeance.

CHAPTER FIFTEEN

"How long has she been in this state?"

The bright light hurt Lelia's eyes.

"Not more than an hour. This morning, she awoke from the sleep they induced."

The voices hung close to her face.

"Idiots! There is not one functioning brain between them all." The male voice sounded angry.

"Excuse me. Would you stop hollering? And move that light out of my eyes. Please."

The light shifted. Lelia let her eyes adjust. She focused on the people who framed the bed. The silent woman stood on one side, a short stooped-shouldered man on the other.

The man touched Lelia's wrist. "Bring me the vials and bag you spoke of."

The silent woman left.

He lifted Lelia's arm, then rolled up her sleeve. He snatched something sticky off her skin. The hair on her arm went with it. "Ouch. Hey quit it. That hurts."

"Sorry, Miss Freeman."

Gentle fingers poked and probed the tender spot on her arm. He clicked his tongue as he inspected the glass vial and plastic bag the woman handed him.

"Fools. If the IV had not infiltrated, they would have killed her." He folded her hand in his. "Miss Freeman, explain to me what you are feeling."

Lelia eased her hand from his, then looked at the woman.

"This is Dr. Kanu. He is only here to help you." The woman's voice fell soft like spring rain.

Lelia tried to relax, rubbed the center of her forehead. "My head hurts and I think I'm going to upchuck."

His eyebrows bunched. "Upchuck?"

"Like in vomit."

"Oh yes, I see. That should subside momentarily."

His fingers slid around her wrist to her pulse. "I need to ask you some questions. They may seem trite, please bear with me. How many fingers do you see?"

Lelia stared at his hand. "Three."

"What is your name?"

"Lelia Marie Freeman."

"Where are you?"

"In Washington D.C. where some crazy-tail psycho carted my black behind to some bourgeois hotel to do Lord knows what…"

"I think she will be just fine." The doctor tucked her hand underneath the covers. He looked at the silent woman. "Inform me if there is any change in her condition."

The woman nodded and led the doctor into the bathroom. She returned alone.

Lelia eyed her as she glided from room to room. The carpet hushed her steps. The woman piddled around for half an hour, then moved down the main corridor. A door clicked shut somewhere in the suite.

Lelia eased out of bed. The movement caused heat to flash over her body, bile to bitter her tongue. She sat on the edge of the bed, swiped the sweat from her forehead and nose.

The waves of fire receded, she looked down the main hallway. Empty. She padded to the corridor, peeped around the first open door.

Recessed lighting brightened the room-size closet. An array of clothes hung on the racks. Shoes in every color filled hand-crafted cubicles.

A suitcase sat close to the door, it was the same brand and color she'd bought three years ago. A loud yellow, daffodil-shaped ID tag hung from the handle. She remembered buying it from the dollar store last summer. She flipped the tag over.

Her name, her address and her phone number stared back at her.

She walked over to the racks, pushed aside the garments. Her jeans, dresses, skirts and tops crowded the hangers. Other clothes were there. She reached for a pair of khakis, turned the waistband and flipped back the tag.

Her size.

She snatched down a top, then a skirt, inspected the tag. All the same. She ripped the rest of the clothes from the hangers, pitched them to the floor, then hurried from the closet.

The endless catacombs of rooms boasted artwork and furnishings from Africa. Everything exuded the persona of her captor.

None of the rooms had outlets, only the doors she entered through. The walls pressed in around her. Hysteria tightened her chest, tears flooded her eyes, blinded her way.

The last room had a large glass door on its far wall. Sunlight streamed through the panes. She wiped the wetness from her face, took clumsy steps toward her freedom.

The door handles were warm underneath her palms, invited her entry. They clicked. The doors swung open.

A lush garden lay before her. Tropical trees stretched toward a cloudless sky. Bushes and flower-topped cacti had been planted with care. Sculptured statues stood among the foliage, intricately bricked walkways led in all directions.

It could have been Eden.

Lelia's gaze followed the towering path of the trees. Two armed men walked on top of a high-bricked barrier wall surrounding the garden. Her jailers glanced down from their posts—then continued their sentry.

At the end of the garden stood a narrow, heavily barred gate. Numb, Lelia stumbled toward it.

Her knees trembled as she stared through the gaps between the black iron bars. An ocean of sand spread as far as the eye could see. Miles below the dunes, a city sparkled like a small diamond.

Slowly, she wrapped her hands around the hot metal. Tears of desperation, of doom spilled down her face. Her body mimicked the path of her tears and slid to the flat-stone earth.

Instantly, her mind conjured the young man from Pop's. The word he'd shrieked rang through her skull. A warning heard too late.

"Miss Freeman."

Lelia let go of the bars and straightened her spine.

"Miss Freeman?"

She recognized the silent woman's voice. Its calm brought new tears to Lelia's eyes. Blinking them away, she shifted, kept her eyes trained on the sand.

"What's your name?"

"Asha. Miss Freeman, if you feel well enough, please allow me to draw your bath. Sitting in that fashion will bring aches to your body."

"Asha, what does *shaitan* mean?"

A long pause tightened the stifling air. "Miss Freeman, please let me help you back to your chambers. Perhaps you will feel better after a short nap?"

"What does *shaitan* mean?"

Lelia felt Asha move. Out of the corner of her eye she saw the woman sit on the ground beside her.

"Long ago, upon the creation of man, the dust was to be the tool for human formation." Her voice sounded like a haunting cadence. "The Supreme Angels were gathered. They were called to bow down and submit to the very clay from which the blessing, man, would be created.

"One, Iblis, was disobedient. He refused to bow to mere clay, he felt the task beneath him. For his disobedience, he was reviled, cast down from the heavens. He was permitted to keep his life until the day of judgment. But he pledged to walk the earth, to corrupt those who are weak in heart. Still today, he walks. Tormenting the weak."

Lelia glanced at the woman. Her back was ram straight, her head turned toward the bars.

"When he sat among angels, he was called Iblis. Today, he is Shaitan." Her voice lowered as she finished. "To Christian believers, his name is Satan."

Lelia squeezed her lids shut. The young man's contorted features appeared as clearly as if he were there with her. Had he known her fate? She couldn't stop the tremors that attacked her body.

She stayed in the garden long after Asha left. She'd moved from the gate to a chair beside a small patch of cactus and flowers.

She sat, gazed into the flowerbed. A spider perched there, still atop its snare. Its web attached to the leaves of a desert bloom. Sunlight danced through the silvery mesh, illuminated the embroidered crystals of water along the strands.

She watched the spider stun an insect, then quickly entomb it. The spider and its snare. How appropriate.

The spider destroyed another insect. Then another. Lelia sat helpless, watched her own fate unfold. Hours passed, maybe minutes. Despair impeded any semblance of time.

Coolness invaded the air, caused chill bumps to rise on her neck. Lelia spun from the chair.

Enter the serpent.

Deng stood in the doorway, hands folded over this thighs. The perfect host.

Lelia raised her foot and kicked the chair, sent it skidding toward the door.

The pin-points in his eyes gleamed. "Still the warrior, Miss Freeman?" He stepped toward her. "By will or force, you will submit."

"President Deng." Asha stood behind him, head bowed.

"You dare disturb me?"

Asha did not raise her head. "Forgive me, President. Your guests have arrived."

His eyebrows lifted. "Why did someone not inform me sooner?"

He adjusted his perfectly knotted tie. "I have pressing matters to attend to. Tomorrow, you will have the privilege of being formally introduced to my administration and other associates."

He seemed amused by her silence. "Contain your excitement, Miss Freeman. There is more. Beginning this evening, you will be tutored in the language and history of my people."

His eyes skimmed her rumpled dress. "In addition to the clothing we acquired from your home, I have provided supplementary garments and footwear in your appropriate size. You will dress according to your position."

He turned to leave. "Be a good pupil, Miss Freeman. Teacher is watching." His laughter mocked her from the corridors.

Lelia balled her hands.

"Take care, Miss Freeman."

Startled, Lelia jumped, then turned to the soft voice. Asha had snuck up on her with those catlike footsteps.

Lelia tried to assess the woman, but could only imagine what she looked like. Still wrapped in a black shol, even her eyes lurked behind round black glasses.

"Do not provoke his wrath."

Lelia couldn't control the sista snap of her head. "Don't provoke his wrath? He kidnapped me, threatened my family, said he's going to kill me, and I shouldn't provoke his wrath?" She started to pace. "I don't give a rat's a—I couldn't care less about his wrath."

Asha stopped in the doorway. "Come, Miss Freeman. Rest. Your mind cannot defend a body that is failing."

Lelia followed the woman through the hallway. Back in the dressing room, the clothes she'd thrown on the floor had been neatly rehung.

Asha opened the bathroom door. "I will prepare a bath for you. If you direct me to the clothes of your choosing, I will assemble them."

Lelia rubbed her hand over the sweat on her throat. "I know it's your job, but I don't want anybody waiting on me, Asha. I'll run my own water."

Lelia turned, then hesitated. "I'll wear the clothes I arrived in."

Not waiting for a response, she closed the door.

Two hours later, she walked into the bedroom. The cinnamon silk dress she'd worn lay on the bed. Her underwear and bra were folded in a pile beside the dress.

She dressed, looked down, noticed her bare feet. Her pumps were probably in some D.C. trash pile.

A muffled knock filtered through the front door. Thick shags of carpet piped through her toes as she walked to open it.

A heavy-shouldered guard was posted halfway down the hall. A child, no more than fourteen, stood a few feet from the door. Her arms were weighted down with heavy books. Her chin was buried in her chest.

Queen of Sheba's twin stood by her side. Head at a royal tilt, spine bold, her perfect cocoa skin matched her immaculately braided bun. A vibrant African-print suit snuggled every curve. Her full lips pulled a pleasant smile. Her eyes shot poison, drew the lines of an adversary.

"Good day, Miss Freeman. I am Nylu. This is Makol." She tilted her head toward the child. "We are here for your tutorial."

Her tone insinuated Lelia should bow for the privilege. "Makol will conduct your lessons in Sudanian history and language." She flicked a finger at the girl like she was a stray mutt. "She is a mere child. However, I think you will find her knowledge...refreshing. Although she does not look it, she has the IQ of a genius."

Lelia tried to draw blood with the look she threw the woman. No wonder the child looked petrified.

Nylu motioned the girl forward. "Makol will begin with her instruction. I will return in two hours to teach the proper etiquette for tomorrow's reception." Nylu's gaze skimmed Lelia's body, lingered on her bare feet.

Her condemning gaze shifted to the girl. "Makol!"

The child's body jerked like she'd been shot. She nodded.

"Remember what you have been told."

Fake smile in place, Nylu looked back at Lelia. "In two hours, Miss Freeman, we will transform you into the liaison Mawain, pardon me, President Deng desires you to be."

Regally, she inclined her head and turned. Lelia forgot her as soon as she stepped away.

Lelia moved aside. "Makol, why don't you come in?"

When the girl stepped over the threshold, Lelia reached to take some of the books. "Here, let me help with some of these."

Makol cowered from her hand, tripped over the yards of black material wrapping her legs. Books flew everywhere. The girl dropped to the floor. Like a frightened mouse, she scurried to grab them up.

Lelia knelt beside her, watched the girl's trembling hands. Picking up a book, she placed it on top of the child's haphazard stack. Cautiously, she reached over to grasp the girl's quaking shoulder. "It's all right, Makol. No harm was done."

The child kept her eyes averted. Lelia felt the girl's muscles bunch beneath her fingers. She eased her hand away, saw the girl look over her shoulder. Lelia followed her gaze. Nylu's had stopped midway down the hall. Her hard stare could've severed stone. Lelia stood, walked to the door. With eyebrows raised, and lips pursed, she slammed it.

Lelia bent and scooped up an armful of books. "I think studying in the garden would be nice." She walked toward the garden, hoped the girl followed.

"Makol, come sit down." She pulled out a chair and sat. "I don't bite, unless I'm hungry."

The girl backed up two steps and bumped into the door frame. Lelia didn't think the child's eyes could stretch any bigger.

"Makol, it's a joke. Come on now, do you actually think I'd bite you?"

Makol's head shook a negative response, but ended bobbing. "Yes."

"Why'd you think a crazy thing like that?"

Lelia watched the girl shift from one foot to the other then look back over her shoulder.

"Makol? I promise I won't let anybody hurt you." She

patted the empty seat. "Come over here and answer my question."

Makol inched to the table but wouldn't sit. "I have heard you are a brutal soldier. That you make the streets your home. I hear you are not like normal Americans. You rule those under your command through evil means. Your habits are carnal…" The girl's eyes ran down Lelia's wrinkled dress, then cut to her bare feet and wiggling toes. "…and strange."

She put a hand beside her mouth and lowered her voice. "The news of your arrival has traveled quickly. Most in the household believe you are wicked."

Lelia mimicked the girl's action. "Am I supposed to have a tail, too?"

Makol's eyes skidded away.

"Well, I guess that answers that one." Lelia sat back and wrapped her toes over the edge of the empty chair. She absorbed the infor-mation, then burst out laughing.

Poor Makol. The child had the most ridiculous expression on her face, like she smelled something awfully funky. Then she had the nerve to twist her face up like she was mad because Lelia was laughing at her. That made the whole mess more comical.

When she finally pulled herself together, Lelia wiped the tears from her cheeks, and tried to push down any loose snickers. "Thanks, Makol, I needed that. I haven't had a good laugh in weeks."

She stood and walked over to the girl. Taking the books

from the child's arms, she placed them next to the others. She slid the chair out, coughed around another snicker. "Makol, please come and sit down. I promise to suppress my carnivorous appetite for someone with a little more meat on their bones."

Makol seemed a little less cautious and more than a little put out as she sat down.

"Look, Makol, I don't usually dress like this, but it's the only thing I brought to wear. I also don't walk around barefooted. I don't have any shoes."

Makol's eyes narrowed. "I saw the clothing and footwear the workers brought here for you. Have you not seen them? There are enough garments to clothe the city."

Lelia smiled, gauged her answer. "Yes, I've seen them. My pride won't allow me to wear anything I haven't earned. My pride keeps me barefooted and wearing the same wrinkled dress."

Makol's chin dropped. When she raised her face, her eyes were hollow, confused. "Mistress Freeman, I do not understand because I do not know what pride feels like."

Lelia's heart trembled.

"Makol, you have so much to be proud of. You're smart, kind, and I bet there's a beautiful smile in there somewhere. You just need something to smile about."

Makol looked down at her hands. Lelia raised the girl's chin.

"A wise friend once told me, 'Baby, don't let anyone tell you you're not a walking miracle.'" Lelia could almost hear Ma Ella's voice. She stood and pulled Makol to her feet. "Makol, you are a walking miracle. Say it."

The girl shook her head.

"Come on, say it."

"You are a walking miracle."

Lelia dropped her hands from the child's arms. "No, Makol. Say I am a walking miracle."

"I am a walking miracle."

"Well, that was weak. If you don't believe it yourself it won't work." She straightened the child's shoulders. "Now say it again, this time with *oomph*."

"I am a walking miracle."

"Good, again. Put some soul in it." Lelia put her fist on her hips and cocked her head to one side. "I said, I'm a walking miracle."

Makol copied her movement, her voice grew louder. "You heard me. I said, I'm a walking, talking..." The girl shrugged.

"In your face."

Makol wagged her head. "In your face."

Lelia folded her arms across her chest. "Don't make me repeat myself."

"Don't make me repeat myself."

"Miracle."

"Miracle." Makol's smile beamed like sunshine.

Lelia hooked their arms. "Now on to pride lesson number two."

Lelia became the teacher, Makol the pupil. The rest

of the lesson flew by. It didn't include Sudanian history and language. At the end of the two hours, Makol had passed her "you go, girl" pride lessons with flying colors, and Lelia had an ally.

They pushed the chairs back around the table. Makol shuffled the books in a neat stack. "Miss Freeman?"

"What is it, sweetie?"

"I have thought a lot about your bare feet, and your reasons for not wearing the shoes provided for you." She scratched the tip of her nose. "I have two shols and one pair of slippers. Still, I think I would rather wear my slippers than to have riches and a bought soul."

Lelia looked into the girl's charcoal eyes. "That's called pride, Makol. You may only have a few things, but at least you earned them honestly. Tomorrow, we'll work on another pride lesson. Self-esteem."

They stacked the books in their arms, Asha's voice sounded nearby.

"Miss Freeman, Mistress Nylu has arrived for your next lesson."

Lelia saw Makol's shoulders hunch. The child stared down at her feet.

"Thank you, Asha. I'll be there in a minute."

Lelia raised the girl's chin and looked into her eyes. "Makol, remember what I told you about walking miracles?"

A faint sparkle tweaked the child's eyes. She took a deep breath, shifted the books in her arms.

Lelia called out in her best military canter. "Chin?"

Makol turned. Her young face a no-nonsense mask. She lifted her chin. "Up."

"Shoulders?"

The girl straightened her spine. "Back."

"Hand?"

Makol juggled the books to one arm, then lifted her palm out. "Talk to it because the ears aren't listening."

Lelia grinned and hugged her. "That's my girl. Lesson number one, A-plus."

They trailed Asha down the hall. When they entered the bedroom, it was empty. Lelia shrugged toward Asha.

Asha motioned toward the door. "Much to her displeasure, Mistress Nylu waits in her proper place. The hallway."

Hard pounding shook the door. Lelia walked over and opened it.

Nylu's chest was puffed out. Her eyes raked Lelia, then Asha. She flicked out her wrist, sneered at her watch. "I have been standing here for fifteen minutes. You have waylaid my schedule." Nylu took a step into the room. Lelia blocked her path. She stretched her neck, crowded her face in Nylu's, glad to see the woman's head jerk back. Not blinking, she called for Makol.

"Yes, Mistress Freeman?"

"I'll see you tomorrow. Remember what you've been told."

Lelia repeated Nylu's earlier words. From the corner

of her eye, she watched Makol move toward them. The child's chin trembled, her eyes blinked too often, but she kept her head high and her shoulders back. Finally proud.

Nylu caught sight of the girl. Her mouth dropped open. She turned her head to follow the child's path down the corridor.

Makol didn't look back. She got to the corner of the hall and pivoted a military turn that would make any general proud.

Nylu looked like she'd sucked on a prune. "We will begin at once."

"No, we won't." Lelia stepped back into the room. "You are dismissed." She closed the door on Nylu's sputtering features. Lelia leaned against the door, closing her eyes to the dull throb in her head. When she opened them, Asha stood in front of her, hands folded.

"You have made a fatal adversary in Nylu."

Lelia waved a hand. "Whatever, Asha. Nylu needs to check herself. She scares the socks off that girl. If she tries to hurt Makol, she'll have to deal with me. Nylu doesn't want that action."

Lelia might have imagined it, but she swore she heard a smile in Asha's voice.

"I am pleased to see the warrior within you is still alive. Be wise in your battles, Miss Freeman. Nylu should not be your concern. Her day of reckoning will come."

CHAPTER SIXTEEN

"Miss Freeman, President Deng is ready to receive you."

Lelia stared at the ragged-edged shoes on her feet, shoes Makol had sneaked in during their lesson that day. Earlier they represented a joyous gift. Now they held little comfort. Soon they'd walk her into a madman's deception.

She looked up at Asha, then pushed herself from the plush chair. Lelia couldn't pick up any emotion from the woman. The veil and dark glasses still hid Asha's face.

"This way, Miss Freeman."

She followed the woman out of the waiting room, down a long portrait-filled corridor. A quiet melody strummed along the hall and grew louder. Chopin. She'd never associated "Fantaisie Impromptu" with an executioner's cadence.

She rounded a corner and came face-to-face with the executioner's assistant. Nylu. No doubt the woman was still pissed because Lelia slammed the door in her face again that day. Mouth bent, as usual, she skimmed Lelia's dress and the rag-tag shoes.

Lelia maintained a ghetto-fabulous air until she passed. The woman's attitude plucked her last nerve. "Why is she always tripping?"

Asha glanced over her shoulder. "She trips because she perceives you as a threat." With a nod, the woman motioned Lelia toward a wide decorated door. "It is time, Miss Freeman."

Shoulders back, Lelia walked through the doors. A rising fanfare accompanied every step.

"Allow me to introduce Sudania's goodwill ambassador from the United States, Mistress Lelia Freeman."

A violin struck an off chord as she walked through the ballroom. Gasps and whispers seeped from the crowd. Masses of primped-up people parted like she was Moses or a leper. The first gaze her eyes clashed with gleamed dark and cold.

It irked her, but she followed the command of Deng's outstretched hand, and walked toward the raised stage he occupied. She looked over his vulture-like face. He masked his features well. For his guests, he appeared the placid savior.

Lelia knew better. She was close enough to see the veins pulsing on his temples. She didn't miss the way his eyes flicked down her body to her shoes.

He clasped both his hands around hers, then pulled her closer for a regulation political pose. An easy smile spread over his lips. "You will pay dearly for your folly."

He turned her to face his guests. "The country of

Sudania is honored to have such a fierce servant of the people. We must, however, keep her from the servant's wardrobe."

Lelia ground her teeth, listened to the crowd's laughter. She tried to jerk free. Deng's long fingers bit into her upper arm.

He waved the people from the stage. "Enjoy the festivities."

His breath clamored against her ear. "Do not cause a commotion. My anger would force me to retaliate in a most unpleasant way." He straightened, ran a hand over his tuxedo jacket. "You are so transparent, Miss Freeman. I have determined you hold no regard for your own life. However, your antics may prove fatal to someone else. Bernard Samuels, perhaps? Now smile and wave to my people."

Lelia stopped struggling. She raised her free hand and waved. The fake smile almost cracked her face.

"Very nicely performed. You will greet my guests with that same pleasant smile or your father will pay for your disobedience."

She looked up at him.

His fingers gouged deeper into her flesh. "Your eyes hold an intriguing challenge. Would they hold the same challenge after you view the mass grave of your relatives? Do not try my patience. Annihilation of them is a mere telephone call away." He propelled her down the side steps toward the milling crowd.

Servants smiled as they balanced golden trays on their shoulders. Champagne flutes and hordes of hors d'oeuvres whisked around her. The food should have smelled heavenly. The aroma and Deng's closeness made her stomach roll.

He dragged her along like a pet, occasionally tightening his vicegrip on her arm. They circled the elaborate ballroom. Deng exchanged niceties. She stayed quiet.

Dignitaries and socialites smiled, shook her hand. Some politely indifferent, others outright snobs. She ignored their contempt.

Deng pulled her to the periphery of the room. He snapped toward a servant holding a champagne tray, then jammed a flute in her hand.

"I don't want it."

"Drink it! Perhaps it will stabilize your intolerable demeanor until I can mold your behavior. Personally."

She squeezed the stem of the glass, pushed down the urge to punch him.

His expression brightened. She could feel someone standing behind her.

"Ah, good evening, Mr. Dune. I assume your suite is adequate." Deng's shoulder brushed her arm. "Mr. Elijah Dune, this is one of your countrymen, Mistress Lelia Freeman."

Lelia sat the untouched champagne on a nearby table. Smile chiseled in place, she turned.

Narrowed eyes, the color of liquid fire, watched her.

Lelia reached for his outstretched hand. His callused fingers engulfed hers, held on too long.

"Miss Freeman." His voice rolled low and distant like thunder.

She couldn't answer. She nodded, then disengaged his grip. He lifted a short tumbler to his mouth. Over the lip of the glass, his cognac eyes held hers.

She matched his stare, looked him up, looked him down. A few inches past six feet, dressed in black, mini dreads. A full goatee, cropped close, snaked a slim line up to neatly trimmed sideburns and mustache. She knew the type. A bad behind, a roughneck. Quiet, fierce, bad news.

Deng cleared his throat. "Mr. Dune, we have not been introduced in the past. However, you appear vaguely familiar to me."

"I have one of those faces."

"Mr. Dune's associates helped us quash The Alliance, Miss Freeman." He held up his champagne flute toward the American. "How is Mr. Hobbs? Not to slight your expertise, Mr. Dune, however, I was looking forward to *his* visit."

The man took his time answering. He lifted his tumbler to his mouth again, then again. "Cecil will pull through."

Lelia felt Deng's body stiffen. "Mr. Hobbs informed me you were bringing another associate. I wish to meet him."

As if on cue, a muscle-thick Mack truck with legs

ambled over. Without turning to see who stood by him, Dune took another swallow of his drink. "This is my cousin, Marcellus Dupree." He pointed with his glass. "Marcellus, President Deng."

Marcellus' shoulders bunched as he shook Deng's hand and nodded his greeting. Unlike his cousin, his face wasn't blank. Lips compressed into a thin line, his eyes screamed his distrust. He broke the contact, then turned his full attention on her.

A slow smile lit up his face, caused his brown eyes to twinkle, almost vanish in his dimpled cheeks.

He stepped closer, grasped her hand, and bought it to his lips. His Creole drawl, obvious. "A flower abloom in the desert. Who is this beautiful blossom?"

Deng's smile was tight. "This is my goodwill ambassador, Mistress Lelia Freeman."

"A pity," he said softly. He kissed her knuckles and winked at her.

Lelia slipped her hand from his, smiled at his shamelessness.

Deng wasn't smiling. "Gentlemen, I anticipate your stay in my home will be enjoyable. If there is anything you require, my servants will attend to you."

He pulled Lelia away from the two Americans and propelled her toward the center of the room. Political mask intact, his smile covered a thousand lies.

His voice was low, clenched. "You dare prostitute yourself before my guests. Acting like a common whore. You should not have refused Nylu's instruction on proper etiquette. You will regret that decision."

"Prostitute myself? Look you..."

He vised her flesh to the bone. "Guard your words."

She winced from the stab of pain. It nearly killed her to humble herself. "President Deng, I didn't kiss Mr. Dupree's hand. He flirted with me."

He waved at a couple, then resumed his pace. "You are too intelligent for trite games, Miss Freeman. Dupree's behavior was juvenile at best. Your reaction to Dune's ogling was incorrigible."

They reached the center of the room. His grip loosened. "For your infraction, I will begin your lessons in obedience this evening after my guests have retired." He turned her loose, then pivoted from her. "My esteemed guests, the meal is prepared."

The dining room could have been in any five-star hotel. Lavish tapestries and chandeliers dipped from the ceiling. Heavy cherry-wood chairs surrounded a long, formally set dining table. A server pulled out a chair for her at Deng's right.

The guests milled in. Lelia stared down at her plate when she got tired of returning their fake nods.

She felt someone watching her. Probing, searching. A silent coercion so strong, it made her lift her eyes.

Mr. Dune sat beside her. His judgmental eyes studied her, wouldn't leave her be. She cocked her head, lifted a what-the-hell-are-you-looking-at eyebrow.

Except for his breathing, he didn't move. He eyed her for a while, then lifted his glass toward her in salute.

Lelia pursed her lips and shifted away from him. She picked up her fork and stabbed the food on her plate.

Once the guests were settled, Deng leaned forward.

"Mr. Dune, Mr. Hobbs revels you a hero. Is that true?"

The air stilled. The man leaned back in his chair. "Hobbs talks too much."

"Come now, your military career is astounding. Numerous rescue missions, hero's honors. My guards were apprised of your skills. All of them are jealous...and watching."

The threat was plain. Deng drew a line in the sand, waited for the man to cross it.

"Like I said, Hobbs talks too much."

Lelia got tired of their pissing contest. The movement of the servant filling Deng's water goblet drew her attention.

A small, trembling hand reached to fill Lelia's goblet. The servant's eyes watched her from above the veil covering her nose and mouth.

Makol.

Lelia shot the girl a wink. The child looked down at the borrowed shoes. Pride glimmered in her eyes as she winked back.

Lelia looked up to see if anybody noticed the exchange, came across Marcellus Dupree's warm, mischief-filled face.

The flirtatious giant sat across from her. His dimpled grin was contagious. She tried to keep a blank face, but couldn't.

"Imbecile!"

Rage contorted Deng's features. He bore down on Makol. "This water is icy!"

Lelia could feel the fear radiating from the girl's body. Makol's small hands shook. Water sloshed onto the tablecloth when she placed the pitcher down, then tried to back away.

"You will never again foul a task so intelligible." Deng's hand slashed across Makol's cheek. The child reeled to the floor.

Marcellus shot out of his chair. He reached for Deng's arm. Like lightning, Deng's goons materialized from no-where. Two pressed pistols to Marcellus' temples, then hauled him away.

Everything happened so quickly, so coldly. Lelia sat frozen. She blinked once, again. Makol's crumpled body faded from view. Deng's rage. Smirking guests. All evaporated. Time enacted a cruel trick, drug her back to her darkest hell.

Now, wet clothes plastered her skin. Wood splinters from the warped window frame dug into the back of her skull as she slid to the needle-littered floor.

Fire punched her chest. Darkness crept along the edges of her mind.

Through the haze Joella stared sightlessly at the

caved-in ceiling. Lelia cradled the child as best she could before blackness drowned her.

Helpless then. Useless now.

Makol's whimpers snapped her from the haunting.

Lelia tried to stand, but Elijah Dune towered over her, his large body blocked her chair. What the hell was he doing? Didn't he understand? She had to save the baby.

"Let me pass." Lelia raised her hands to push him aside. She looked up, then stopped.

Killing. That's what she read in his eyes. Hands fisted, he leaned over her toward Deng.

The quiet click of triggers exploded from every corner. From the balconies, behind half-opened entrances, guns aimed toward the man blocking her way. Lelia let her eyes slip to where Makol fell. Asha knelt beside the girl, silently soothed her.

"Take her away."

Deng's order shook over Lelia's skin.

Asha bowed her head and helped the girl to her feet. They moved to a set of wide doors at the end of the ballroom.

Deng reverted to being the consummate host. He waved to his other guests. "Please ignore the disruption. The girl is young and has not mastered the rules of the household."

The chatter resumed as if nothing happened. No one seemed affected except her and Dune.

A servant righted Deng's chair. He sat, spread a new

napkin across his lap. "Mr. Dune, I know the ways of my country are foreign to you and Mr. Dupree. I will overlook your ignorance. All of the servants are aware that I cannot tolerate icy liquids. Obviously, my specifications were not passed along to the girl.

"Nonetheless, I have done her a great service. In the future, she will remember." He motioned toward the soup being served. "Please sit and enjoy your potage."

Dune didn't drop his stance.

Deng's eyes danced. "I have forgiven your confusion of our ways. Do not be foolish, however, and test fate, my friend."

He dipped his spoon into the bowl, then brought the soup to his mouth. "Mr. Dupree was detained for his own protection. Now sit, Mr. Dune, and do not attempt any heroic stunts. My guards will execute you before you inhale your next breath."

He leaned over the bowl. "You may be good, Mr. Dune..." Victory edged his voice. "...but are you that good?"

Lelia saw Dune hesitate, then lower himself into his chair. His eyes stayed on Deng.

Unobstructed, she pushed back from the table. "Excuse me."

Deng clamped tight fingers over her wrist. "The festivities are not over, Miss Freeman."

"I'm not feeling well." She pulled back on her wrist. "I'd like to find Asha and return to my room."

"I regret the servant's blunder has left you ill. I must

remember to discipline her further for the discomfort she has brought you."

Lelia tried her best to blank her features. "The disruption didn't make me ill. The medication I got on the plane ride from the States still seems to be in my system. I've been ill ever since."

He let go of her wrist, his eyes warned her to shut up. "Of course. I will apologize for your absence."

He stood and pulled her chair out farther. She tried to slip past him. He captured her sore arm as if he were helping her, then ran his thumb over her skin.

"As I promised, I will come to you after my guests have retired. Lesson number one will commence promptly thereafter. Until then..."

She pried her arm away. Her gaze fell on Dune.

His molten eyes unsettled her, judged her. Hooded, seemingly omniscient, they burned like liquid fire between his lashes. Those eyes held something more. Something she couldn't decipher...nor did she want to.

She pulled her gaze away and headed for the double doors, feeling his eyes tracking her retreat.

She pushed the doors open and stepped through the back entrance to the kitchen. Servants bustled in and out of the swinging front doors. Cooks shouted orders. Behind the storage racks, she stood unnoticed.

She peered through the shelves, tried to figure out where Asha had taken Makol. Her eyes ran across a large schematic of the guests rooms pinned up on the main wall.

Her name was there, grease penciled on one of the

larger suites. The Americans were bunked in a wing by themselves.

A young man came rushing in through a side door. He lifted an armful of napkins and left the way he came.

Lelia eased along the wall, through the preparation stations and followed him into a dark, barren corridor. She ran to catch him, then tapped his shoulder.

"Where is Makol?"

He turned, his lips and eyebrows bunched into a sour expression. When he looked into Lelia's face, his eyes grew as large as basketballs. He bent at a ninety-degree angle.

"Forgive me, Mistress. I did not know who you were. These are the servant passages."

"Tell me where she is."

The young man straightened and bent again. Half the napkins fell to the floor. "Please, Mistress, do not inform Mistress Nylu of my mistake."

Lelia stooped to pick up the cloths. She touched his shoulder, urged him to straighten. "Don't worry, I won't tell the Wicked Witch of the West."

He took the napkins from her hand. "Strange. I assumed she came from the Southern part of the country."

"Look, never mind." She softened her voice. "I need to know where Makol is."

He raised the pile of napkins. "There, Mistress. Around the first corner. Makol will be in the first room on your left."

Lelia half walked, half ran down the shadowy hallway.

She pounded on the door. Before Asha fully opened it, Lelia pushed her way into the room.

"Where is Makol?"

Asha closed the door, stepped farther into the room. "Miss Freeman, you could have summoned me. I would have escorted you back to your suite."

Lelia started to trace her palm. "I didn't need an escort, Asha. Where is Makol?" She glanced around at the skinny sleeping mat, the pile of books stacked against the wall. "You didn't let Nylu take her, did you?"

"Mistress Freeman."

Lelia spun toward the small, timid sound. Makol stood in the doorway of a tiny stall. Head bowed. The cotton slip she wore had been washed down to the threads.

Lelia stepped closer. Hands shaking, she reached down to touch Makol's face. A single tear rolled down the child's cheek to wet her fingers.

The thin leash Lelia had tied around her emotions snapped. The floodgates corroded, swept her into a dark maelstrom. She folded the child in her arms and rocked.

"I'm so sorry, Makol. So sorry. I gave my word that I wouldn't let anyone hurt you. I need you to forgive me. Will you ever forgive me, pip-squeak? Please?"

She didn't know how long she stood there rocking. When Asha touched her shoulder, Lelia eased Makol away, held her at arm's length.

A dark, red handprint welted the girl's cheek. Deng's brand.

She reached out to touch the mark. Makol's eyes met hers. For the first time in her life, Lelia felt uneasy under a child's gaze. The girl's eyes were filled with admiration and praise. Honors Lelia didn't want, couldn't handle.

"Mistress Freeman, what is a pip-squeak?"

The question slammed Lelia like a fist.

"Wha—?"

"You said, will you ever forgive me, pip-squeak? Is it another name for a walking miracle?"

The sunshine in Makol's timid smile burned Lelia's heart. She couldn't take anymore. Palms out, she turned away from the hero worship in the girl's eyes.

She felt someone step around her.

"Makol, Dr. Kanu will be here soon. Follow his instructions and rest today and tomorrow," Asha said.

Makol's voice quivered. "Yes, Mistress. Mistress Asha, I can no longer stay here. Please, I humbly ask for help. I need safe transport to the city."

There was a moment's silence. "Wait for my instruction. When it is time, I will send for you."

"Yes, Mistress."

Lelia felt her hand wrapped by smaller, frail ones.

Makol smiled up at her. "Mistress Freeman, I will never forget you. The warrior who taught me about pride. Moments ago it had fled me. When I saw you, it returned. You are a walking miracle."

Guilt squeezed Lelia's throat. Her lungs wouldn't expand. She slipped her hand from the child's grasp. "I'm sorry. I can't...I just can't." She backed to the door. Tears blurred the girl's face. The doorknob slipped in her sweaty palms. She fumbled until the latch clicked, then snatched it open. Lelia gasped, jumped back from the tall shadow that lurked just outside in the corridor.

The figure stepped into the light. "Good evening. I take great pleasure in informing you, no one will be leaving."

CHAPTER SEVENTEEN

Nylu loomed in the doorway. Statuesque, regal, and annoying as hell.

"I heard about your little tête-à-tête."

Asha slipped in front of Lelia. "What exactly did you hear, Nylu?"

"Asha, you need not protect this one." Nostrils flared, lips curled down, Nylu shouldered Asha aside, looped Lelia's arm, then drew her into the hallway. "I know she's been filling that scamp's head with fantasies. I heard the girl just now. Walking miracle indeed."

Nylu turned to face Lelia. "Makol deserved to be sanctioned. She was becoming too haughty. The girl needs truth, not fantasy. She will never be anything more than an ugly, book-smart troll."

Still battling ghosts, Lelia stayed silent. The royal pain looked pleased with herself.

"And as for you, President Deng will be incensed to learn his precious street warrior is poisoning his servants' minds." She nodded past her shoulder toward Asha. "Even the most loyal."

She snatched Lelia's arm. "You are coming with me."

Something inside Lelia snapped. "I'm about to slap you into next week." She jerked her arm free. "Put your hand on me again and I'll break it off."

Nylu backed away, didn't look so sure of herself. "It is amusing that you have chosen those words. After I inform the President of your involvement in that scamp's escape, it will be your hand that is broken off." She lifted an eyebrow. "In our country, stealing…"

Lelia watched the woman's eyes roll back in her head. She collapsed to the floor as if her bones had vanished from her body.

She stared at Nylu, wondered if she was dead. "Oh my Lord, I made her have a heart attack." She stooped, felt her wrist. The woman's pulse beat slow and steady.

Asha stood above them, hands laced.

"We need to get a doctor, Asha." Lelia looked toward Makol's room, but the door was closed.

Asha raised the material of her shol above her feet and stepped over Nylu. She strolled down the corridor, left Lelia holding Nylu's wrist.

"I will have the guards take her to her room."

Lelia likened Nylu to a stomach virus, but this was cold. "Asha, we need to make sure she's not dying."

Asha paused, looked over her shoulder. "She is fine. She will not die. Not yet."

"We should do…something."

Asha resumed walking. "The guards will make their

hourly checks shortly. They will see Nylu to her room."

Nylu's chest rose and fell. She cracked a loud snore. The woman was out like an overstuffed holiday guest. Lelia laid her wrist over her stomach, then hurried to catch up with Asha. "What if she…"

"She will not tell of Makol's departure."

"You sound so sure."

"I am."

Asha's statement ended the conversation. They walked in silence.

Dark, twisting passages tossed Lelia back to another time. White-washed walls turned to mildew-laden brick. They closed in, pressed tighter. Sewage ran from the old drain spout, soaked her coat again. The stench of rotting garbage. A rusted handrail ladder. A cupcake.

A single candle burned in her mind. Jo Jo's face loomed in the flame. The baby's eyes held sanction. Blame.

Tears welled, spilled down Lelia's face. She didn't bother to wipe them away.

Asha opened the door to the suite, then stepped aside. Numb, nearly beaten, Lelia walked to the bathroom. Behind the closed door, she peeled off her dress. Her underwear followed. Nakedness didn't free her. The haunting continued…and she succumbed.

The tile jarred her knees when she fell. She cupped her hands over her ears to block the verdict echoing through her head.

Guilty!

She lay on the floor, bare, hurting. Smothering pressure clamped her lungs. She heaved for breath, then stilled. What did it matter?

Pain splintered her temples. A soft, childlike singsong echoed in her mind, repeated the conviction of her appeal.

Guilty as charged!

Sentenced, she curled into a fetal position on the cold tile...and for the first time in nine years, she sobbed...

...and gave in to the ghosts.

"Baby, where is your fight?" The familiar voice beckoned, enveloped her in warmth. "This isn't the tough little nut I watched grow into a proud woman. The child's death wasn't your fault. It was her time, not yours, so get up and fight!"

Filled with wisdom, the words flowed over her. "I've watched you pine away with blame. Put a sock in it and stop killing your spirit! Lelia, wake up, baby. Know the truth. Tell it and shame the devil. The child is in a better place. She's with me. Now, that can't be all bad?"

"Ma Ella?"

"Yes, baby. Get up like I taught you, fight with your mind, your fists if you have to, but remember..." Lelia's eyes snapped open. Her ears peaked in time to hear a faint whisper. "...you're a walking miracle."

She shot up. Shifting positions, her eyes skirted around the empty bathroom, her body trembled.

Ma Ella's voice sounded so real, so powerful.

Several years back, Ma Ella had sat in the audience as Lelia marched across the stage with her bachelor's.

After the graduation, they hugged. Ma's weathered hand cupped her face.

"You've done real good, baby. You keep on stepping. Ma's tired, so I'm going home, but I'll be keeping my eye on you." Ma motioned to her escort , and turned back to Lelia. "Now give me some sugar for the road."

She obliged, kissed Ma's cheek, then watched her walk out of the auditorium.

Ma had slipped away to Glory in her sleep that night. Folks said the peaceful smile on her face must have made the angels sing.

Was she losing it? Lelia closed her eyes, took a deep breath, then pushed herself to her knees. A thin coverlet slipped from her waist to the floor.

Her hip ached from where the tile bit into her flesh. She rubbed the indention on her skin, limped over to the sink.

She leaned over the vanity and turned on the spigot. Cold water spilled over her hands. She cupped her palms and splashed her face.

As she reached for a towel, she caught a glimpse of her eyes. Hollow, emotionless, hopeless. She didn't recognize herself.

Where is your fight, baby? Where is your fight?

She couldn't let Deng destroy her family. She'd find a way out, even if she died trying.

She looked around the bathroom, her eyes focused on the thin blanket.

Asha.

She dressed, raked her fingers through her hair, then pulled open the bathroom door. The woman stood by the dresser.

Lelia hesitated, then crossed the room and held out the blanket. "Thank you."

When Asha took it, Lelia covered the woman's hand and squeezed it.

"Asha? I need to talk to you. But I don't know how to start."

She let her hands slip away and turned her back. "Where I grew up it was a given, trusting the wrong people got you killed; asking for help flagged predators. Leeches who turned helpless people into victims because they needed victims to survive."

She shrugged. "I don't ask for help often. I trust even less." She stopped pacing and faced the woman. "Asha, I need your help. I need to trust you."

Silence. Lelia withstood it, attempted to gauge the woman's emotions.

Nothing.

"I won't let him hurt my family and I won't be his slave." Her voice hitched an octave. "If you won't help me, if I can't trust you, then tell me now."

The quiet lingered.

"Asha, I don't have anyone else to trust. I can't leave on my own." Lelia came close to the woman, raised her palms. "I need your help, Asha, I need a friend." She touched the woman's arm. "Please?"

Asha didn't say a word.

Lelia dropped her hands. "Forget it."

She turned, walked into the bathroom, and closed the door. She leaned her forehead against the wood. If Asha ran and told Deng, he'd kill her family without blinking an eye.

Where's your fight, baby?

Lelia grabbed a towel and a bathing suit from the closet. She strode through the bedroom. Asha had vanished.

Bold, head high, she snatched the suite door open and pinned the guard with a snobby stare. "Where's the pool?"

The guard didn't look at her. He kept his eyes forward. "Which one, Mistress?"

"Which one?" She folded her arms over her chest. "All of them, of course. I'll decide which one I want to use."

"One is here in the presidential wing, down this hall and to your left. One is on the pavilion level and one is in the guest wing."

She stepped around him. "Thanks."

He moved in front of her. "I have instructions that you are not to leave your room."

Lelia drummed her fingers on her arms. "And I have permission from President Deng that I can use the pool anytime I want."

He unsnapped a leather flap on his utility belt, pulled out a two-way radio. "I did not hear of this."

"Go on, call him. He'll be tickled that you interrupted his dinner to confirm instructions he's already given."

She lifted her chin toward the door. "Do you think Asha would let me leave if it were wrong?"

He looked at the door, then at his radio.

"Look, buddy, you're holding me up." She held out her hand. "Give me the radio, I'll call him. I'll even let you speak to him. How do you pronounce your name again? I want to make sure I get it right."

He shoved the radio back in the pouch, stepped back to the wall. "If the President already gave instructions..."

"He did. Like I said, would Asha let me leave?"

"She will deal with the consequences."

She flipped the towel over her shoulder. "There won't be any because I won't tell the President that you held me up."

She didn't exhale until she was around the corner, out of his view.

Lelia crouched behind the door, eyed the passing guard through the cracked opening. He talked into his radio, then moved from her line of view.

The clack of his utility belt grew softer until the corridor was quiet as a tomb. She stayed still a couple of minutes more, then eased the door open.

One hand wrapped around the door handle, the other on the frame, she pushed against the hydraulics, cringed at the loud click when the latch took hold.

She sneaked down the hall, tried to picture the schematic from the kitchen. First, second, third door's the charm.

She rapped on the carved mahogany. No answer.

The door handle didn't budge when she pushed it down. She smoothed a hand over her neck and glanced down the hall. Empty. Reaching through the neckline of her dress, she snagged the two paper clips she'd tucked in the seam of her bra, straightened them out. Fifteen seconds later the handle clicked beneath her palm. She was getting rusty.

She eased into the room, glanced around. It didn't look occupied, nothing out of place. She walked through a sitting room. Past a high archway, the bathroom door stood open. Sounds of shower spray drifted into the room.

Sweat broke out on her nose. She swiped her palms down her dress, grabbed a thin vase from the coffee table, and tiptoed into the bathroom.

Steam rolled thick enough to cut. Even in the misty heat, goose bumps rose on her skin. She lifted the vase, inched toward the glass shower stall.

She felt him then. Watching.

Over the sound of the shower's spray, she heard the bathroom door close. Her heart pounded her ribs. She raised the vase higher, then turned.

A dark figure banked against the swell of steam. Over the mist, thick brows bunched, hooded his eyes to slits.

He parted the vapor, stalked closer, caused her breath to stop.

Lelia took a step back. She took another. Running from the panther initiated the chase.

He lunged at her. Slammed her body against his. A thick arm clamped her arms to her waist, he jerked her to him.

A long knife sliced the steam. He thumbed the handle, whipped the blade between them, pressed it to her throat.

"Scream and you're dead."

CHAPTER EIGHTEEN

The threat chilled Lelia's bones.

Warm, wet metal pinched the skin at her throat. Fiery eyes bore down into hers, made her want to haul tail.

She couldn't let him see how much he scared her. She flared her nostrils, thinned her lips. "Get off me."

It didn't seem possible, but his eyes grew narrower. He eased the knife away. "When I'm damned ready."

She glared at him, struggled to yank her arms free.

"Don't think about it. I hit back. Settle down and lose the vase."

She gripped the vase harder. "Not on your life, Shaft."

"Don't like taking orders, do you? You're not on the throne yet, princess. You came to me so you'll do what I say." He jerked his arm up into her ribs. "Drop it."

Needing air, Lelia let the vase slip from her fingers. The sturdy pottery shattered. Tiny fragments bounced against her legs. He moved them several steps away from the shards, loosened his grip, then pushed her away.

Her hands automatically fisted in front of her. One of

his hands whipped out to snag both her wrists. He yanked them over her head.

"You…"

"Shut up or I'll shut you up."

He planted the knife between his teeth, then reached out for her. His large hand skimmed her body. Over her shoulders, under both arms. She tensed, tried to jerk away when he palmed her breast.

He watched her, didn't move his hand. "You know the drill."

Standing board stiff, she withstood the humiliation. He wrapped his rough fingers around her knee. He moved his hand up her thigh.

"I'm clean!" Against her will, her thigh muscle tensed; she pulled her leg back. The urge to kick his teeth down his throat was too strong to fight.

"Don't try it."

He roughly ran his hand up one thigh and down the other before he stopped his search. He straightened, gripped the knife by the handle, then released her. "What do you want?"

He hadn't hurt her, but Lelia couldn't stop rubbing her wrist. "I want to hire you to get me out of this place. Deng threatened my family. I need to get home and keep them safe."

He reached over to pull a towel from the rack, then slowly tucked it around his waist. "Save the spiel. The answer's no."

Lelia reached out to touch his arm, drew it back at the look he shot her.

"What's your price? I can make it worth your while. Ten thousand dollars." It was all the savings she had.

"I cost a hell of a lot more, lady. You have to come better than that. I know how deep big daddy's pockets run."

"Big daddy?" The implication slapped her face. She didn't have time to set him straight. "That's all I have."

"Not all." He latched on to her wrist, brought her closer. "Show me what Big Daddy Deng got for getting you appointed goodwill trick. If it's worth my while, I'll consider it payment along with your chump change."

"I don't have a clue what you're talking about. When you get me back home, I'll get the ten thousand; maybe three thousand more."

He released her wrists, stepped back a pace. His voice scratched like sandpaper. "Take off your clothes."

"No."

"Take 'em off."

The knife's steel had misted over. Part of the edge caught the reflection from the lights, enforced its owner's threat.

Lelia lifted her chin. "Do you have a problem with two-letter words?"

He slid the edge of the knife toward her. "Afraid, Miss Freeman?"

"No."

"That's not what your pulse says. The heart doesn't

lie." He ran the tip across her jaw, down along her throat. "Right now, you should be afraid." He tilted her chin up with the blade. There was no compromise in his eyes, no bartering.

"Off."

Her body trembled. She took a careful step backward, eased her chin from the knife. Turning her back to him, she reached to pull down her zipper. The fabric fell off her shoulders. She held it to her breasts for a moment before letting it slip down her body to her feet.

He circled around her, waved a casual finger toward her bra and panties, then continued his prowl.

Lelia stood still. She wasn't taking off her underwear. He could go straight to hell.

A swift breeze lit the sweat on her back. Deft fingers grabbed her bra strap. Before she could move, she heard the slice of the knife, felt the garment pop.

Reach for the falling swatch or cover her breasts? She chose the latter.

A buyer sizing up cattle, he strolled around her. His eyes didn't miss a thing. She followed his prowl. After the longest minute of her life, she stared straight ahead.

He stopped, inched close to her face.

"You'll need more money."

Lelia gasped, ready to cuss him out when Deng's commanding voice cut her words.

"Mr. Dune."

Lelia spun toward the door. Forgetting the dress chucked

around her feet, she tumbled toward the floor. Modesty forgotten, she reached out to cushion her fall. Strong hands grabbed her up.

"Expecting company?"

"No." She shook her head. "Please don't tell him I'm in here."

He released her arm and walked over to flip off the shower. Without a backward glance, he headed out the door.

She scooped up her dress, jerked it over her head, performed contortionist moves to pull up the zipper.

She pressed her ear against the metal door.

They weren't saying a word. Was Dune racking brownnose points with Deng? Was he stooging her out?

She stepped back, looked around the steam-filled room for a place to hide. There was nowhere to run.

If she'd misjudged Dune, only God could help her now.

Elijah forced his thoughts off the woman he'd left in the bathroom. He let the bayonet slip to the carpet inside the connecting archway, then went in to meet his tormentor.

Deng sat on the bed, flipping through Elijah's daybook on the nightstand. Elijah eyed him, held down the urge to wring his neck. The arrogant SOB thought he was God.

Elijah strained to hold his peace. Keeping Marcellus

alive and getting them both the hell away from this ass was all that mattered now.

He smoothed the edge from his voice. "You should have called first, Deng. If I'd known you wanted to shower with me, I'd have waited."

Deng continued to flip the pages, then closed the book. His gaze fell to the obvious bulge underneath the front of Elijah's towel.

"It appears you can do some things by yourself, Mr. Dune."

"Let's cut the crap, Deng. What do you want?"

"You are in no position to be obstinate." He folded his arms across his chest. "I do find this a rather amusing little game. I realize you would like nothing better than to murder me. There lies the dilemma. What of Mr. Dupree?

"Yes, Mr. Dune. Think about your cousin and his travails if you allow your temper to go awry."

Long fingers ran over Deng's chin. Ice danced in his eyes.

"By mere accident, Mr. Dupree could lose fingers, then perhaps a hand. Feet, legs and arms would certainly follow, all while he is very much alive, feeling every agonizing cut. Think of the slow, pain-filled death your cousin will endure, Mr. Dune. Think of the terror you can stop."

Deng dropped his arms and stood. "You will ensure that my weapons will be delivered tomorrow by noon. My men will accompany you to your drop location. And of course, I will extend my hospitality to Mr. Dupree until your return."

He opened his arms wide as if he were giving out Christmas presents. "I will give you one-fourth of the agreed-upon payment, the rest will be compensated by the sparing of your lives."

His fingers pushed out the edge of his ear. "Nothing witty to say, Mr. Dune? Allow me to complete my demands. If you do not agree to my terms, I will keep you alive long enough for you to watch Mr. Dupree's dismemberment. Then you will follow with your own demise."

A smirk bent his mouth. "Have I made myself clear?"

"Crystal."

"You disappoint me, Mr. Dune. Allowing love of family to muddle your plans. I thought you a more worthy opponent. Say something, Mr. Dune."

Deng laughed as he walked to the door. He twisted the handle, then glanced over his shoulder. "Tell me, Mr. Dune, how does it feel to be owned?"

Lelia waited until the adjoining rooms fell silent. She crept through the sitting room. Elijah stood with his back to her, looking out the large balcony door. She could feel the rage bouncing off his stiff back.

"See what a lunatic Deng is?" She moved closer. "You need to keep your cousin safe. I need to safeguard my family, too. Will you accept my offer?"

She stepped to his side. "Dune, I need your help. Will you help me?"

"Leave."

He never looked at her.

Lelia's mind whirled. She'd left Dune's room knowing her family's future hinged on one man. She couldn't stomach those odds.

She rounded the corridor to the servant's quarters, then ducked back. A small group was gathered halfway down the hall. Nylu's pitiful voice echoed in the corridor.

"Please, do not treat me this way."

"You are a servant in this household." Deng's words dripped with contempt. "Nothing more."

Lelia peeked around the corner. Nylu was kneeling in front of the tight-faced President. Two guards flanked his sides.

"I used to be more than a servant." Nylu reached up to grab his arm. "I love you. Allow me to be the woman by your side, not that vagrant American hoodlum."

He brushed off her hand like lint. "You speak nonsense." He sounded bored. "Your wishful fantasies have overtaken your mind once more."

"I have devoted my life to you, to the future of our country, our people." Her pitch rose from pitiful to hysterical. "Remember...remember the information I obtained from General Kafu? It strengthened your military hold, helped defeat our enemies and..."

"Lies. You lay in Kafu's bed of your own accord. Sharing

your favors proves you to be a harlot. Now my guards find you sprawled in my corridors, obviously taking one too many sleeping pills again. And you expect gratitude?"

Tears slipped down her cheeks. "Please, my love. I did those things for you. I only belong to you."

"Me? Why, when the smell of you makes me nauseous?" He snapped his fingers. "Take her out of my sight."

"No, wait. Please. There is something I must tell you." Her voice trembled, sounded confused. "There is something about that woman. Something...I...I cannot remember."

Lelia eased away, diminishing sobs echoed down the hallway. She retraced her steps through the north wing. Thankfully the same guard manned her room. His head dipped. "Mistress."

She walked past him into her room. Asha was probably avoiding her. Figured.

She went into the bathroom, leaned on the vanity.

Helplessness settled over her shoulders like a musty quilt. Something she'd never been able to get rid of.

What would she do now?

She reached to turn on the tap, then splashed her face.

"Ten thousand bills isn't enough to keep me waiting."

Lelia spun around.

Dune stood a few feet from her. Like a child caught striking a match, she rushed to explain. "I couldn't get back through the...how did you get in here?"

He tilted his head past his shoulder. "I took notes."

Asha's voice rose from the back of the bathroom. "The President has returned to his guests. He will, however, be ending his festivities soon." The silent woman stepped around Dune. "The time to leave is now."

He turned his attention to Asha. "I'll ask again. Where is my cousin?"

Asha moved to the far end of the bathroom. "I will free Mr. Dupree."

"Like hell you will!"

"If we are stopped, the guards will not question me."

"I'm going."

"No, Mr. Dune, you cannot. The risk would be too great. For everyone's safety, I will go to Mr. Dupree. We will meet in thirty minutes on the loading bays. The transportation will be waiting as we discussed."

"Why?"

"I do not see the relevance of your question."

"I think you do. I think there's a lot you see behind those shades. Why are you doing this? Helping us?"

"Not for you, Mr. Dune. I am keeping a promise..." Her gaze fell on Lelia. "...to a friend."

Dune's gaze stayed riveted to the woman. "Don't try to screw me. Hell would be an easier trip." He stepped closer to her. "Thirty minutes, on the loading docks. If you're not there, I'll hunt you down."

"I have no doubt, Mr. Dune." Asha ran her hand over a portion of the wall. A panel slid open, revealed the gaping black mouth of a cave.

She turned to Dune. "Allow me twenty minutes, Mr. Dune, then follow the map to the loading bays."

The cave's darkness swallowed Asha's small frame before the passage closed.

Lelia eyed Dune as he trudged over to a large duffel bag, swept it from the floor and moved to the spot where Asha disappeared. He ran his hand over the wall.

"What are you doing?" Lelia grabbed the straps of the bag. "She hasn't been gone a minute."

He yanked the strap from her grip. "I follow my own rules. If Deng's men catch them, Marcellus won't stand a chance."

"I trust Asha."

He ignored her, continued running his hand over the wall. "Damn it, where did she touch?"

"We may mess up her plans if we show up off schedule."

"There is no we. You stay here." He placed his bag on the floor to search with both hands. "I don't need you traipsing around tipping anybody off. We'd be lynched while you're back in the palace playing teacups with big daddy."

Hands balled, she stepped between him and the wall. "Look, buddy, you're not leaving me. We have a deal."

"We don't have squat until I say."

"I'll find the loading docks myself and…"

Air whooshed from her lungs when he tackled her at her waist. With one fluid movement, he hoisted her into the air, anchored her over his shoulder.

"Put me down!"

He carried her toward the closet. As they passed the threshold, she grabbed the door frame, tried to hold on for dear life.

A joke.

Dune kept walking. Her fingers snapped from the frame. Arms flying, she knocked into a stand, sent it crashing against the tile floor. Ticked at being manhandled, she pounded his back, but nothing stopped him.

"Look, can't we talk about this like two level-headed adults?"

He marched over to the rows of inlaid dressers. He rummaged through the drawers one by one. Apparently satisfied with what he found, he carried her to the center of the closet.

It was time to take a stand.

"Okay, now it's on!" Lelia took a handful of his shirt for leverage and sunk her teeth into his back.

The low grunt he emitted held a moment's satisfaction. He heaved her up and dumped her on the floor. A sack of potatoes would have gotten better handling.

Before he could grab her ankle, she scrambled to the shoe shelf and snatched the first thing her hand ran across.

She jumped to her feet. One fist jutted out, one hand clutched a thick-soled boot. She stared at the panties and stockings spilling through his fingers.

"Excuse me. What do you think you're going to do with those?"

He shook the panties toward her mouth. "First, shut

you up." He lifted the stockings. "Then try my hand at hog-tying."

She raised the boot higher. "Good thing the shade matches your skin, 'cause you'll be wearing those hose by the time I get through with you."

"Mistress Freeman?" the guard called from the bedroom. "Are you well? I heard a loud noise."

Dune placed a finger over his lips. He slid into the shadows behind the door, threw her a warning gaze, then clicked off the lights.

"Mistress Freeman?" The guard stood silhouetted in the doorway. He stepped over the threshold, flipped on the switch.

Light slashed across the room. The guard took in Lelia's stance. His gaze locked onto the boot still clutched in her hand.

His body stiffened. His narrowed gaze strayed around the room. "Are you well, Mistress?" He lifted his elbow, moved his hand toward the gun at his waist.

Too late. Dune sprung from his lair, took his prey. The guard's gun spun across the carpet, his radio followed. Lelia turned her face away and hurried from the room.

She paced the bathroom tiles, traced her palm. Grunts, sickening sounds of fists pounding flesh tore from the closet, made her skin crawl. Sounds she'd known well, had grown to hate.

An ear-popping crack bounced around the walls. A door slamming? A bullet killing?

The room fell silent. Chills ran down her body, sweat

beaded her forehead. She didn't know Dune. Still, the thought of him lying hurt or dead iced her blood.

She drew in a deep breath, forced herself to look at the closet door.

The door had slammed shut. That's all.

The heavy wood vibrated. Another thud rattled the hinges. Silence followed. She moved to the door, pressed her ear to the wood. "Dune?" She knocked. "Dune?"

The door whipped open, two hundred pounds of ticked-off fury filled the threshold. Blood trickled from his nose, a thin cut sliced his cheek.

Lelia stepped away. "Dune, look, I'm sorry. You okay?"

Geez, she'd really screwed up. His eyes signaled he wanted to squeeze the life out of her.

She wrung her hands. "The guard, you didn't kill him, did you?"

His fingers flexed. She backed up farther. He shouldered past her, a sinking feeling settled in the pit of her stomach. He was going to leave her.

She followed at a safe distance, watched his raw-knuckled hands skim over the wall.

"Dune, I promise I won't mess up again. Just say something. Please, don't leave me behind."

The panel opened, beyond the jagged mouth, blackness. She looked up at Elijah as he bore down on her, then turned away. He snatched up his duffel. "Dune, don't you leave me!"

He spun on her, fisted the neck of her dress. "We have

five minutes. Slow me down again, and I'll drop you myself."

With a commanding yank, he propelled her into the stifling cave.

She followed him, a leap of faith into complete blackness.

CHAPTER NINETEEN

Marcellus stalked the dingy cell like a caged animal. Again, he ran sore hands over the stone-roughened walls, pressed each section, tested its strength.

He moved to the bars. Without tools he couldn't jimmy the locks. Pulling at them in frustration, he let his fingers slide down the smooth metal, then turned away.

Since he'd been hauled in, he'd been over the bars and walls of the cubicle a hundred times, only the back of his hand was more familiar.

He avoided the dusty mattress in the corner of the cell and lay down on the floor. Bed lice didn't make good sleeping partners.

His thoughts traveled to his cousin. Mostly he wanted to knock him into next Sunday. What the devil was going on? What was Elijah doing with a snake like Deng and why was he so closed-mouthed?

None of the pieces fit.

Just thinking about the mess got him madder than a

bulldog. The dust-caked floor that bit into his shoulder blades pissed him off even more.

Cuss words rolled around in his head, tumbled off his lips, each one described Elijah better than the last. "Hushed mouth, hardheaded, son of a—"

Then as always, humbling memories crept along the edges of his mind. A lifetime ago, he'd been shot up, left for dead. Through fever-induced hazes, a figure kept watch, hovered over him. Marcellus found out later that someone had strapped him to his back and drug him out of a living hell, willed him to live.

Elijah.

He pinched his lids with forefinger and thumb. No matter what all this boiled down to, Elijah needed him, whether his bull head knew it or not.

A soft rustling noise, quiet as a church mouse, pricked his ears. Marcellus sprang to his feet. He backed into the corner. Crouched.

He watched as a piece of the back wall slid open. A small, scarf-covered figure stepped into the cell. The person turned gracefully toward him, as if instinct told her where he was.

Marcellus couldn't see her, but the alluring fragrance enfolding her spoke her identity.

She'd helped the little girl Deng struck to the floor. All of the domestics looked alike, covered and servile. He hadn't thumbed any of them, couldn't see their faces.

But he remembered her.

Her sweet smell could make a man drunk.

He waited for her to move. She stood still as a wood post.

The seconds ticked off in silence until he grew tired of the waiting game. "What do you want?"

She didn't respond straight away. When she spoke, her voice flowed soft, smooth as honey. "Mr. Dupree, I have come to aid you."

Not knowing if Deng sent her, he watched.

He could take her down, try to get out the way she'd come. For now he'd hold tight and play along.

"Aid me in what?" He allowed suspicion to slip into his voice.

She tilted her head. "Once Mr. Dune has delivered the weapons, President Deng will not let you leave Sudania alive."

"Weapons!" What in the hell had Elijah gotten himself into? "Where's my cousin?"

The woman nodded toward the opening. "We are to meet him shortly, then I will aid you in leaving the palace."

Marcellus stuffed his thumbs in the belt loops of his pants. "Just out of the kindness of your heart? Come again, honey. Cash, grass or ass, nobody rides free."

The woman bowed her head. "I have one request."

Marcellus waited, studied every subdued nuance.

"There will be two others traveling with you. One, a young girl who will be taken care of. For the other, I will need your word of honor. Your promise to protect her, escort her to America."

Marcellus shrugged. "Who?"

"Miss Freeman."

"Why?"

"A promise made to a friend."

"Obviously, you're hip to a few things. And obviously you know my cousin is in charge. You've made plans with him. Why not ask him to protect your Miss Freeman?"

The cell fell to a long hush before the woman answered. "Although Mr. Dune is competent for the task, his soul is not at peace. I cannot entrust her care to one with such a troubled spirit."

"I won't trust someone I can't see." Marcellus took another step toward her. "Maybe I shouldn't trust you at all. Me, my cousin, the little girl and the Freeman woman, rescuing all of us is a tall order." He threw her a practiced grin. "What's your name, Harriet Tubman, or should I call you Little Moses for short."

He jerked his head to the opening of the cave. "Is Deng waiting for us on the other side of that wall?"

"Asha."

"What?"

"My name is Asha. We do not have much time, Mr. Dupree. If we are to survive, we must leave now."

"Is that so? Well, honey, like I said, I don't trust what I can't see. Uncover your face, then I'll think about coming."

Slowly she reached up and removed the veil that curved her mouth. Next she unwound the cloth on her head. A thick rope of braids fell over her shoulder, its sun-kissed highlights caught the glow from the dim light.

Marcellus exhaled. He hadn't noticed he was holding his breath. No, her beauty had stolen it from him. She was breathtaking. Perfect.

He moved closer, raised his hand to take off the dark glasses that hid her eyes.

Quick as lightning, her fingers curled around his hand. They squeezed gently.

Numbness shot up his arm. His hand dropped away. "What the hell?"

He grabbed his hand, tried to knead the pinpricks from his fingers as he watched her disappear into the cave.

For his cousin's sake, for their freedom, he had no choice but to follow.

As soon as he stepped into the tunnel, the wall closed behind him, threw them into darkness. Once his eyes adjusted, he followed her fragrance until he felt a small hand touch his wrist.

"Please, wait here."

He moved to where the small hand directed, but instead of obeying her order, he flipped her hand around and captured her wrist.

"Don't double-cross me, honey. You won't like the mean side of me."

"That is not my intention, Mr. Dupree."

She twisted free of his hold. A panel swooshed open, he watched her step into a corridor.

Before the wall closed again, Marcellus jammed his shoe in the threshold. The wall stopped, left a crack just large enough for him to see what she was up to.

She stood still, her ramrod back to him. She took a step away from the wall and glanced to her left. Marcellus could hear someone coming. Someone moaning, low and gritty.

An old woman shuffled into view. Head bent, her gnarled hands were loaded with linens. Asha sidestepped, but the woman ran smack-dab into her. The linens spilled to the floor.

The woman crooked her neck to look up at Asha, jabbed an arthritic knuckle in Asha's face.

Marcellus couldn't decipher a word, but the way the old granny was carrying on, Asha was getting reamed out real good.

As Asha bent to help the granny pick up the pile, the old woman stood and knocked her head underneath Asha's chin. The dark glasses flipped off Asha's nose and hit the floor.

Marcellus ran his palm down his face. "Please tell me this ain't the rest of the rescue squad."

The old woman's terrified shriek could have scared a dead man. Marcellus snapped his head up. The old woman was staring up at Asha, her aged, stooped shoulders shook like a leaf in a lightning storm. Horror twisted the woman's features, bulged her eyes, iced Marcellus' blood.

Hands flung out, she moved away from Asha until her

back struck the wall. The woman covered her face. Low, pleading moans floated toward the cave. She was begging for her life.

Asha hadn't moved throughout the weird incident. She raised an open palm toward the woman. The woman railed back, her moaning turned to screams.

Marcellus crammed his fingers between the crack and tried to move the wall back. "Hey, what the devil is going on out there?"

The woman grew hoarse. Above her wailing Marcellus could barely hear Asha's soft canter. She stepped closer, placed a hand over the woman's head.

Through her gnarled fingers, she peeked at Asha again. Terror-filled eyes slowly changed, widened slightly, then filled with another emotion. Reverence.

Her face lit up like a Fourth of July night. She reached to the wall for balance. With slow, jerky movements, she lowered herself to her knees. Clutching Asha's hand, as if it were the most precious diamond in the world, she dipped her forehead over Asha's knuckles and started chanting the same phrase over and over.

Asha helped her to her feet, picked up the rest of the linens and placed them in the woman's upturned palms. From beneath the pile, the woman grabbed Asha's hand once more and bowed.

She stepped away. The woman never took her gaze from Asha's face. Such adoration perked their aged depths, Marcellus could have sworn she was looking at a savior.

Asha bent to retrieve her glasses, then scoped both sides of the corridor before walking back to the wall. It slid open.

"Mr. Dupree, we must not tarry."

He stepped out of the cave, reached for her arm, then changed his mind. "I'm not going anywhere with you, Rapunzel, until you tell me what kind of spooky crap is going on here."

"The choice is yours, Mr. Dupree. The guards will notice you are missing momentarily."

He watched her glide away, then followed at a wary distance, wondering what in the hell just happened.

Strong fingers pressed into Lelia's arm as Elijah dragged her along. They'd fled through the stifling tunnels for what seemed an eternity.

She could barely see. Harsh, rumbled commands forced her on as the suffocating heat, the airlessness crushed around her.

Her dress snagged against the jagged walls. She heard the rip, felt the sweat-soaked material sting her cuts. Yards back she'd lost one of her slippers. Hot gritty earth pounded her sole raw.

She ground her teeth, choked down the curses piling up in her mind.

Dune stopped. She plowed into his back, knocked out what little air she had left in her lungs.

"Damn it. It's a dead end."

The warmth of his hand fell from her arm. He vanished. She stood alone.

Seconds lingered to minutes. He hadn't reached for her. Hadn't come back.

Arms raised, she took a shaky step, then another, until her fingers brushed the jagged stone. Hand over hand, she moved along the rough peaks, tried to inch her way to something familiar, a wall, a door, Dune.

"Dune? Dune?" She hated the weakness in her voice, hated the fact she needed him.

"Dune, you answer me!"

"Hush."

Warm fingers wrapped her arm. Relief eased the tension in her body when he pulled her to his side.

Heavy whiskers scratched the side of her face.

"No funny moves."

She held her breath, waited to see what lay behind this wall. Deng's men, another dead end, or freedom?

Lelia felt his muscles bunch across her back as he reached for the panel. The stone moved slowly, revealed a peek of the brilliant quarter moon, but then stopped. He muttered a curse under his breath and moved to shoulder his way through the crack, carrying her along with him.

A cool breeze ran over her sweaty skin, circulated the reek of garbage. Dumpsters aligned one wall of a large receiving yard, covered trucks filled another. A loading dock never looked so good.

"What took you so long, cuz?"

From behind a large bin, a low Creole drawl floated across the bay. A tall figure stood and moved toward them. Marcellus materialized, a slow, dimpled smile creased his face.

Dune's voiced sounded behind her.

"You in one piece?"

Marcellus' grin widened. "Of course. How could anybody harm a face as pretty as mine?"

A motor started across the yard, cut all conversation. A truck pulled out from the line of vehicles. Marcellus ducked behind the bin. Lelia was wedged close to Elijah's body as they rounded a small rift in a far wall. The truck backed into the bay. The engine idled, the driver didn't leave the cab.

As they waited, a door at the end of the bay opened. Asha stepped through.

"Miss Freeman, are you well?"

"Yes." Lelia tossed a glance over her shoulder. "I'm fine."

Asha nodded toward the truck. "Then you must not tarry. The President will check on you momentarily."

Asha snapped her fingers and Makol shyly stepped through the door, her eyes wide with fear, anticipation. The child handed a large knapsack to Lelia.

"Hi, sweetie." Lelia clucked a finger underneath Makol's chin, let her eyes run over the girl's face.

Asha nodded toward the bag. "Some provisions for your journey, Miss Freeman. A change of shoes would be appropriate." She turned to Marcellus. "Mr. Dupree, your belongings are on the other side of the door. Makol does not have much to carry. Her journey with you will be short."

Dune stepped between them. "You're damned right it will. She stays here."

Asha didn't budge from the threat in Dune's tone. "Mr. Dune, Mr. Dupree has given his word. He has promised to escort Makol and safe harbor Miss Freeman back to America in exchange for assistance in leaving Sudania. Whatever arrangements you made for leaving the country are null. President Deng has no intention of you or Mr. Dupree leaving the palace alive."

She waved a hand toward Lelia and Makol. "I can assist in your departure, provided you meet the terms Mr. Dupree agreed to."

Both men eyed each other.

Asha's voice filtered over the tension. "We must hurry."

The driver stood waiting with the flap of the bed drawn. Elijah cursed, then swung toward the truck. Marcellus followed.

Awkwardly, Makol hugged Asha. "Thank you, Mistress Asha. I'll never forget you." The child ran after the two men.

Asha motioned toward the truck. "Miss Freeman, please."

Lelia couldn't leash her emotions. She reached out to hug Asha. "I'll never forget you either."

Strange enough, the soft-spoken woman returned the embrace before moving Lelia to arm's length.

"Miss Freeman, a word of wisdom if I may." Asha pressed her palms together. "Do not be deceived by momentary calm. Your spirit will only know true peace when your forgiving is complete."

Puzzled, Lelia opened her mouth to ask what Asha meant. The question died on her lips when Dune nudged her shoulder.

"We don't have time for this mumbo-jumbo crap."

Before Lelia could say a word, Asha turned to Dune.

"I offer you the same words. Only when the forgiveness is complete, Mr. Dune."

"Whatever, lady." He pulled Lelia away. "Come on."

Asha's words rolled through Lelia's mind. She snatched her arm away and glanced over her shoulder. The loading dock was empty.

The driver hustled them around several large crates in the back of the truck. He slid open two panels and motioned Makol and Lelia into the tiny space concealed by the driver's seat. He sputtered something to Makol, then slammed the door.

Makol's little hand clasped hers. "Mistress Freeman, do not be alarmed. Soon we will reach a safe destination."

Small spouts of light spilled from three round holes bitten out of the truck's metal.

Through the openings, Deng's palace disappeared behind the jerk of the closing security wall. With one last lurch, the wall clinked shut. Inside its stronghold, Joella's last gift lay lost to her forever.

Instinctively, Lelia reached to cover the place where the pendant used to dangle at her throat.

Now her only link to Jo Jo lay in her scarred hand and her heart.

BOOK TWO

"For *it was* not an enemy *that* reproached me;
then I could have borne *it*: neither *was it* he that
hated me *that* did magnify *himself* against me;
then I would have hid myself from him:
But *it was* thou, a man mine equal, my guide,
and mine acquaintance."

—PSALM 55:12-13 KJV

CHAPTER TWENTY

They'd run for three days, traveled under the guise of night, hid in the scorch of day. Corroded vehicles and rundown shacks were their refuge.

A day ago, they'd left Makol with a man and woman at an abandoned bunker. Heart heavy, Lelia hugged the child, allowed herself to be guided away by Marcellus' insistent hand.

Now, she stared through the open mouth of an aged helicopter. They flew over dense treetops, Zaire. Adjacent to Sudania's border, it was the closest and safest place to wait Deng out, so Dune said.

"Your sugar daddy won't follow you. Zaire's government renounced him. He's not dumb. He won't cross the border."

"How would they know if he did?"

Dune ignored her. Tired of talking over the beat of the rotor blades, she dropped the subject.

His put-down attitude irked her. She glared at the back of his head. The hard urge to knock some of that attitude down his throat boiled inside her. She checked herself. God help her, she needed him.

Daydreams of doing him bodily harm ran rampant, she couldn't help but smile. She watched him turn his head slightly toward her. Like a guilty convict, she snapped her gaze away.

Damn it, Lelia, this was crazy. He can't read your mind. But looking at him, she wasn't so sure.

She ran a hand over the frayed leather belt that anchored her to the homemade metal flip seat, then looked out at the blue-black sky past the chopper door. Its dark beauty didn't quell her unease.

Like a shadow, they skimmed the jungle canopy. Marcellus killed the landing lights and donned night-vision goggles. "To keep big papa off our asses," he said.

Lelia leaned her head back and stole a glance out the windshield, wondering if they'd make it out alive. The fighter in her screamed *yeah!* Her common sense whispered *no*.

Endless days of running, of hiding, pulled her into a fitful sleep. Deng waited there, boosted his power over her. Dune was there too...never far away...always watching.

An uproar clawed through her dream. The eerie howl chilled her. Lelia woke to the deafening whine of the propeller. She looked around the cabin, took in the bedlam. Dune gripped the sidebar, his body drawn rigid. Marcellus' taut features looked grim.

"What's happening!" No one answered. The loud pitch drowned out her voice.

Dune's intense eyes caught her gaze. She read his silent

command. She copied him, wrapped her fingers around the sides of the seat. The craft shuddered, jerked, thrashed her body. Each lurch slammed her head against the metal hull again and again. Pain and fire ripped through her head and neck. She stiffened to stop the impact. Nothing helped.

Lelia tightened her grip around the seat. The metal cut into her fingers.

A wild mixture of hysteria and terror rioted her mind. Would her life end here? Had she come this far to die like this? "Jesus, please. Don't let us die like this."

She felt them plunge. The treetops rushed closer.

A scream worked its way up her throat, burst through her lips, unheard.

The bone-jarring blow brought the silence it demanded.

Blood.

Its metallic tang filled her mouth, nauseated her. It was the first trespass that assailed her senses. The strong cabin light that burned through her lids, the second. The warm, firm hands that roamed her body was the third.

The gentle fingers massaged her skull.

"Ssss, that hurts." She winced when they kneaded the sore spot at the back of her head. They smoothed over her shoulders, down her arms, up her rib cage. Deft and sure they assessed, missed nothing.

Marcellus always looked out for her, always made sure

she was safe. She opened her eyes, expected to see his face etched with brotherly concern. Instead a shadowy figure stood beside her, leaned in close to press his palms over her calves and knees, then up her thighs.

She tried to push his large hands away, but the sudden movement brought more pain. He held down her hands in one of his and continued his assessment.

"Get your hands off me." She attempted to look anywhere but at the hand that roamed her body. She squinted at the cabin light, then cursed it for the increased heat it caused. She stared at the sand on the scarred aluminum floor, still her gaze came back to his hand.

She clenched her teeth. "I said, get off me."

When he finished, he leaned close enough for her to see the lashes of his bored molten eyes.

"Gladly."

Dune moved away and she sagged into the seat. The sound of his voice ran the tension back up her spine.

"You're going to be fine, buddy. Hold tight. I'll be back."

Lelia struggled forward. Marcellus' still body was propped against the pilot's door, his head lolled back in an awkward position.

"Is he all right?" The cabin remained silent.

She undid the belt at her waist, then fell to her knees. Wedged between the seats, she reached to touch his neck. Her fingers smeared the crimson drops that trailed from his forehead and disappeared beneath his collar.

Marcellus groaned. Lelia let out the breath she held.

He was alive. His pulse beat steady beneath her fingers. Despite the situation, she grinned like a fool.

Dune appeared at the pilot window. "I don't see a damn thing funny." His words cut like a whip, wiped the smile from her face.

She didn't lower her eyes from his hard stare. "I smiled because he's alive. When I find people alive, I smile... most of the time."

It felt good to see his eyes narrow, watch the muscles flick in his jaw. She raised an eyebrow to bring home the point, then sat back on the cabin floor.

His gaze moved to Marcellus, and his demeanor changed. With gentle care, he maneuvered Marcellus from the helicopter.

"Easy, easy." His voice took on a smooth texture, it seemed to quiet Marcellus when he groaned.

Lelia reached through the seats. "Do you need any help?"

He ignored her, again.

She sat alone, tried to move her sore body. As best she could she looked around outside. It seemed like a long time since Dune left.

Too long.

The rhythmic chatter of unseen creatures floated through the cabin. The constant clicks, ticks, the soft whoops and quiet snarls grew louder.

She tried to give herself a pep talk. "Animal sounds are normal. You're in the jungle, lived with rats and water-bugs for years, now you're scared of a little noise. Pull up, girl." She scanned the cabin again. "He'll be back."

Chatter. Chatter. Click. Tick.

Her finger circled the scar. She pulled herself to her knees and peered out the windshield, then out of the side of the chopper where she'd last seen him.

Nothing.

"Dune?"

Chatter. Click. Tick.

"Dune? I'm...I'm sorry for what I said, you know about the smiling thing?"

Click. Chatter. Tick.

She looked out the window again. With the cabin light blaring down, she could barely make out what was outside. Maybe she shouldn't have made that last crack. Here she was, in the middle of Timbuktu, insulting her only way out of this mess.

Click. Tick. Grrrrrrr.

"Elijah Dune!"

Dune stood at the cabin door and she could have hugged him. Almost.

"I was just calling to see if you needed help. You know...with Marcellus."

He didn't look her way. What was new? She thought it best not to provoke him anymore. Beneath lowered lashes she saw him gather his and Marcellus' supplies that were strewn over the floor. She watched his jerky movements, his closed expression. The fearful sense that he would leave her to fend for herself welled inside her.

She grabbed the end of his duffel bag as he tried to

zip it. "Look, I said I'm sorry." She strained to keep her voice calm. "We have a deal, ten thousand, remember? You promised Asha you'd get me safely back to the States."

"I didn't promise you or her a damn thing. The decision is mine to make. You haven't paid for jack yet." He jerked the zipper closed. "And you damn well better be sorry." He snatched the duffel bag out of her grasp. "I'll think about dragging your ass through the jungle. I may need the spare change one day. Now get out. We have to camouflage the bird."

Lelia knew he wouldn't help her out of the chopper. And she vowed not to give him the satisfaction of seeing her true pain.

Tight-lipped, she crawled to the door. Her muscles felt like an hour-old fast-food burger, rubbery and worthless. The bass drum in her head kept pounding a fast-paced rap tune.

Tall grass hid the ground, but it had to be close. She could do this. She eased herself out the door down into the waist-high grass. The decent was slow, lacked grace, was humiliating. She stood for a moment, gripped the metal hull, waited for the earth to still.

There. She'd done it without his help. She tried to keep the smug look off her face when she glanced at him. "I need to...relieve myself, then I'll help you."

She took a step and her wobbly legs collapsed. With no choice she released the hull and sprawled onto the ground with all the delicacy of a junkyard frog.

"Not a good place to take a whiz." Dune's voice rung

right above her ear. She felt the breeze from his shoes when he stepped over her. "Catch your z's later. We have work to do."

Lelia lay there, the taste of crow sour on her tongue. She tried to pull air back into her lungs and spit dirt from her mouth at the same time. Able to breathe again, she struggled to her feet. Relief washed over her when she caught sight of him. He crouched by a small fire, his hand rested on Marcellus' shoulder.

Now that she had him in sight, she stood for a while, trying to pull herself together. She looked around the large clearing, but the quarter moon barely lit the starless night.

"Ten thousand bones doesn't include a mansion tour. I said, we have work to do. Let's go."

For the next two hours, her bladder hollered for release. Elijah cut leafy branches, and she hauled them back to the helicopter. When they'd covered the craft to Dune's satisfaction, Lelia collapsed next to the fire beside Marcellus.

Her arm felt like lead when she raised a hand and placed it on Marcellus' forehead. He looked peaceful, a tall stem of grass stuck out of his mouth. When her hand moved to his cheek, a smile creased his face. One of his eyes blinked open. It sparkled in the fire's light.

"Are you two finished covering the bird, yet?"

"You fake! I've been working my tail off and you've been here watching?" Her arms hurt too much to punch him.

"Aww, come on, sweet cheeks. You looked so cute dragging those branches across the field."

"We almost die in a crash, I can hardly move my body, and you think it's cute?"

Marcellus leaned up on his elbows. "It wasn't all bad. You have to admit, I did give you the ride of your life."

"You...!"

Forget the sore arms.

He dodged her wayward swing, winked, threw back his head and laughed. Lelia tensed when he grabbed one side of his head and fell back to the ground.

"Good-night-a-me, my head hurts like a son of a bitch..."

"How you feeling, buddy?" Dune's voice floated over her head.

"A little worse for wear, cuz, but I'll survive, now that I see the face of this beautiful bloom."

Oh, brother. She couldn't take anymore. She crawled over to her knapsack and pulled out the cotton blanket Asha packed.

She threw it near the fire, sprawled on the material, and fell asleep.

The heat baked her skin, woke her from the dead. Lelia tried to regain her sleep, but couldn't. It felt like she was in an oven. She stretched a little. Marcellus' voice drifted through her sleepy haze.

"We're not far off track. Have to walk a little farther, about half a day."

"They shouldn't have migrated since we left." Dune's voice ran over her. "What about the bird? Will it fly?"

"Maybe, maybe no. It needs more fuel. One thing's for sure. I won't fly it without the gas cap and that missing lanyard. Fool thing must've been held on by a thread. It looked fine when I checked it. Kinshasa's the best place to find it. It's big enough to get lost in, plus I can dig up Lumbumba's sorry tail. He owes me one."

Dune cut in. "Once you collect your favors, how much time are we talking?"

"Getting there, waiting for the part, bumming a ride back with the fuel, two weeks tops."

Lelia heard enough. She got up, looked around. The clearing was a cookie cutout. Thick leafy trees and brush bordered it. Tall grass bent under the sun's heat, looked beat and brittle like scorched yellow straw.

Marcellus walked over to her. "Hey, sweet cheeks. Thought the buzzards were going to start circling. You looked dead gone."

"You seemed to have come back from the dead after the work was done last night."

"I'll make it up to you. I'll go check the brush, vanquish any wild beast with my bare hands, so you can take care of your most delicate necessities." He bowed and stuck his hand out like a royal servant, then grabbed his head and stood. "Damn, this kick hurts like a mother."

"It serves you right." She reached up to place a hand over his bandage. "You should take it easy."

He put his hand over hers, his lids shuttered a couple of times for effect. "Ahhh, the touch of an angel. I'm cured."

She couldn't help but grin at his drama. The smile eased when she felt Elijah behind her.

"Cut the bull, Rip Van Winkle. Unless you're calling this home, take your whiz so we can move out."

Lelia let her hand fall. She didn't look at Dune, but instead she marched over to the tree line, did what she needed, and came back to her escorts in record time.

Marcellus tossed her a small can, then motioned to a spot near the pile of ashes that used to be their fire. "Pop the lid and enjoy breakfast. Have a seat, sweet cheeks." He started toward the helicopter and said over his shoulder. "Keep Elijah company."

She busied herself with the can, dug through her knapsack, tried to ignore Dune's stare. She could feel his gaze on her skin as sure as if he'd touched her. Her eyes skimmed to where he sat. His pant leg was raised. Her eyes riveted to the gun strapped to his calf. She stared at the polished metal, wanting but unable to turn.

"You have a problem?"

She did. Guns were her poison, her curse. They sparked an uncontrollable fear, always brought back the darkness.

Nightmares of when she'd been shot, of when she'd lost Joella started haunting her again the night they'd left the palace. The dream was one she knew well. The guard's gun brought it back full force.

"Let's get moving." The voice snapped her from her daze.

She felt someone touch her shoulder. Marcellus stood above her, his eyes held concern. Both men had their gear. She looked down and realized she still held the open can of food.

Silent, Lelia packed her things and trailed behind Dune to the edge of the clearing. She nearly ran into him when he turned to face her.

"Stay between Marcellus and me. Wander off, you're on your own."

She gave him a stiff nod and followed him into another world. A world filled with animals she'd only seen on TV or in geography magazines. Insects, some as big as her fist and birds with feathers so colorful they'd make a rainbow jealous. She watched every movement, listened to every sound. But still kept one eye on Dune.

He pushed them hard. The only time he stopped was to confer with Marcellus about directions.

After the first two hours, all the awe Lelia felt toward the jungle's inhabitants vanished. The muggy, humid air squeezed around her like a size-too-small bra, and her feet screamed for mercy.

She plucked at the soaked shirt plastered to her body. Grit and sand scratched and bit in places she couldn't decently reach. She could only imagine what sort of jiggers had slipped into her shoes.

Giant leaves smacked her face, insects feasted on her arms and neck. She felt whipped. She wiped the sweat that trickled in her eyes, tried to get a better view of Elijah. Before she knew it, she'd trampled on something hard again.

She looked up into his deep scowl, then stepped back.

"Sorry," she said. It was the ninth time she'd kicked the back of his boots. Her sore toes were witnesses.

Marcellus chuckled behind her. "You don't have to trample him, sweet cheeks. I'll make sure he doesn't leave you."

Yeah, whatever you think. She drowned out Marcellus' chuckles, let Elijah take a few steps, then hurried behind him. If he got out of her sight, she knew he'd walk out of the jungle and leave her.

The sound of rushing water piqued her ears. The trees got smaller, the mosquitoes and jiggers got bigger.

Elijah held up a hand. "Wait here."

He left for a minute, then stepped back through the brush and motioned them forward. "It's safe."

Lelia followed him into a narrow clearing. She dumped her bag next to his, and walked the short way to the river-bank. The heavy bag put kinks in her back. She stretched, the movement sent her shoes swishing deeper into the boggy black mud of the bank.

The river moved slow, flowed the color of weak coffee. It still looked cleaner than she felt.

"Hey, sweet cheeks, you can go in and wash up. I checked. It's okay."

He didn't need to tell her twice. She glanced around for

Elijah. He'd disappeared. Marcellus made himself scarce.

She stepped out of the baggy pants, kicked them away. She'd wash them later. Now, she only wanted to feel the water on her skin.

"Hey, sweet cheeks, not too far, all right?"

"I'm no fool." Lelia waved a hand and waded into the water. Chest deep was her limit. She unbuttoned her oversized shirt and tied the sleeves around her neck. Lukewarm and mucky, the water flowed around her chest. It wasn't Calgon, but it still felt like heaven. She scrubbed and hummed, happy to get rid of the grit.

Her feet shifted a little in the riverbed. She took a step toward the bank and continued to hum. Her feet slipped again. She tried to move, but the mud slid and took her feet with it.

She opened her lips to scream. Water filled her mouth as the current snatched her beneath the surface.

Lelia struggled to regain her footing, but couldn't feel the bottom. The darkness of the river clouded around her. Through the murky blur, she saw the sunlight past the surface.

She pushed her way up, broke the water's hold. The air on her face lasted only a second before she felt herself whirled around and snatched down by the current's grasp.

A strong band clamped below her chest. Confused, she struggled against it. She felt air on her face again. She gasped it into her lungs like a beggar.

"Stop fighting."

The rough command stilled her struggles. She allowed

herself to be pulled from the water. Flung over someone's shoulder like a wheat sack, she coughed and sputtered. Her chest burned like she'd swallowed fire.

"Man, where the hell were you?" Marcellus' voice whipped behind her.

"I hauled her out, didn't I?"

She could feel Dune's chest rumble as he talked.

"I'll go get something to put on her," Marcellus said. "Just lie her down by the fire."

She was set on the ground none too gently. She looked across the wide stance of Dune's bare feet and knew he was pissed. She dragged in a deep breath and ventured a look.

Hands planted on the soaked waistband of his pants, he towered over her. Water dripped from his clenched jaw, glistened along the grooves of his chest. His eyes glinted. They raked down her body, then up again.

Instinct made her cross her arms over her bra. She saw his eyes register the movement. When his stare returned to hers, his eyes were hard, accusing.

"No fool?"

Stung, she cast him a challenging look. "Why save me at all?"

"It takes more effort to dig a grave."

His glare dared her to comment. Even if she wanted to, what would she say? Thank you for saving my life? I'll be your humble servant forever? Are you always such a jerk, my lord?

Her neck hurt from craning it. She longed to drop

her eyes, but she held his stare. Unwelcome tension stretched between them, tied knots in her sore stomach. When he leaned down and closed the short distance between them, the knots turned to rocks.

His arm brushed her shoulder. She drew back from the warmth of his body. That warmth seeped through her skin, kindled something she didn't want to ponder.

He paused beside her, infused her with more of his warmth. "My shirt."

Confused, she looked behind her and saw she sat on the pale cotton oxford. She lifted off the material. He snatched it. Not giving her a second glance, he turned, then strode away.

Soggy and shaken, she stayed there until Marcellus returned with one of his shirts and wrapped it around her.

"Hey, Che, how you feeling?" He rubbed circles on her back as if she were a wayward puppy.

"I'm okay." She sounded like a bullfrog. Embarrassed by her stupidity, she shrugged Marcellus' hand away. "I said, I'm okay."

She hated to admit it, but Dune was right. She had been a fool. She'd put herself and everyone else in danger. And threw herself in Dune's debt again. Now she was taking her turmoil out on Marcellus.

She took a deep breath. "I'm sorry, Marcellus. I just want to be alone."

"Come on, sweet cheeks, talk to me. Uhh...you're not going to cry...are you?"

"Not likely."

She sat and stared at the ground in front of her, rocked to ward off the chill. *Lelia Freeman, you will not cry. You will not cry.* A tear fell anyway, then another.

"Aw, hell. Don't cry, please. Come on, darling, give Marcellus a sunshine smile."

She tried to smile, but the effort was too great. She just wanted to be home. Wanted to be safe.

Marcellus' booted feet paced in front of her. For the first time, she noticed his boots sloshed with water and his clothes were drooping and soaked. He walked away and came back seconds later.

"It's not tissue, but I can't stand tears."

He started mopping her face with some leaves. She put a hand on his arm and tried to comfort him with a weak smile.

"Please. I'm okay. My pride stings, that's all."

He dropped the leaves. "All right. I'll be nearby if you need me."

Left alone, Lelia stewed for half an hour, battled a war of indifference. She should go and thank Dune. After all, he did save her life.

She stood and walked around the fire, debated, pondered. The pros, then the cons, of going to Dune weighed down on her.

He didn't have to save your life. She was warned not to go too far. It wasn't his fault she didn't know how to swim.

Everybody couldn't be good at everything like the prolific Mr. Dune. Just who did he think he was, treating her like she was a child?

By the time she'd decided to confront him, the cons outweighed the pros by a long shot. Her fingers went instinctively to her palm as she built up her nerve. It was now or never.

She marched through the brush where he'd disappeared. She stomped into a clearing and stopped at the very edge of a large, quiet loop of water. Lelia opened her mouth to call him, but stopped short.

Her eyes riveted to a body floating face up in the middle of the pond. The body lay still, no movement except for the buoyancy of the water.

Fiery eyes that always watched were closed. The hard planes of features that always scowled were relaxed, serene with a deathlike calm. Dune drifted with a lifeless still that scared her.

"No," Lelia said softly. "No!"

She started to plunge into the water when a large hand snagged her arm.

"Hey, sweet cheeks, you can't swim, remember?"

Lelia tried to snatch her arm away. "Something's happened to him."

"You're telling me."

She turned to Marcellus, angry to find him grinning. "Why are you smiling? It's not funny. He needs our help."

"I only have one set of dry clothes left. I can't go in after you again." Marcellus reached under her arms and plucked her out of the water. "Elijah's not drowning, darlin'. He's fine, leave him be."

Lelia looked over her shoulder again. "But..."

"Come on." Marcellus patted the ground next to where he'd plopped down. "Unless you want another one of his tongue whippings."

She didn't answer him. Her nerves were still raw from what she perceived. She hesitated, then moved over to sit next to him.

His grin widened. "That's my girl."

Marcellus' presence took away the fear for Elijah's safety. Her eyes were still drawn to the figure in the water.

Marcellus nudged her shoulder with his. "What had you so fiery hot? You were ripping through here so fast, I could barely catch you."

Lelia knew who ignited that fire. The same person who'd made her heart leap with fear a few seconds before. She squared her shoulders when she remembered the way she'd been roughhoused. "Your cousin is a...he's a..."

"Bully." Marcellus seemed pleased to help.

"Yes!"

"Mean."

She shot an eye in Dune's direction. "You got it."

"Overbearing."

"My thoughts exactly."

His eyes sparkled with mischief. "I kind of like it when you talk..."

She threw him a murderous look until he threw up his hands in mock surrender.

"Okay, okay."

She couldn't resist his teasing, smiled in spite of herself. She watched as he looked out to the water and shook his head.

He chuckled. "I'd like to knock the teeth down his throat sometimes myself." Marcellus paused and returned his gaze to hers. He tipped his head, his smile sobered. "He also has the kindest heart of any person I know."

Caught off-guard, Lelia opened, then closed her mouth. "Yeah, and I'm Rockefeller on safari."

He didn't smile. His changed mood made her somber. "I know he's your cousin, Marcellus, but I really don't see it."

He looked at her. His eyes held challenge. A challenge she'd love to take on, but knew she'd lose. She glanced away.

She'd seen the kindness. Seen the emotion in Dune's eyes when he found Marcellus standing outside the palace. The care he took with Makol. Even saving her from Deng, from drowning.

She wasn't ready to admit it to Marcellus. In her mind, Dune's attitude overshadowed his scraps of kindness. She picked up a nearby stick and poked holes into the black soil. "What's he doing out there anyway?"

"Calming."

"Calming?"

"Elijah loves water. Always has." Marcellus nodded toward his cousin. "His mama used to lay him on his back in a tub of water when he was colicky. She said as soon as he felt the water, he'd stop bawling, spread his arms and legs out and float there in her arms for as long as she'd hold him. Then he'd be okay. The water is a balm to him. He would never admit it." He turned and smiled at her. "Too stubborn."

Lelia wrapped her arms around her knees. "Has he always been that way?"

"Stubborn, yeah, he's hard-headed..."

"I was referring to the water."

Marcellus' eyes twinkled. "No. When he met Dawnett, all of that changed. She was his balm."

Lelia couldn't explain the sharp quickening in her stomach. The mention of a woman's name shouldn't affect her. What did she care?

"Dawnett?"

"His wife."

"I guess when he's away from his wife, he needs the water to turn him from Mr. Hyde back to his half-human state."

"You're almost right, it's therapy. Dawnett died years ago. That's where the water comes in."

Lelia felt like scum. She turned her face from Marecllus' profile to gaze at Elijah. A piece of the puzzle fell into place.

She'd seen the same behavior in her kids. They were alone and hurting, pushed everyone away. They were afraid that if they felt again, they would hurt again. Dune was no different.

"Hey, don't look so sad. He's just being Elijah."

Marcellus stood, looked down at her and winked. "I'm going to fix a dinner fit for a queen. Seared snake and water grass."

Lelia heard his retreating whistle. She kept her eyes on his cousin. She saw Dune's chest rise and fall. He submerged himself. Seconds later, he surfaced near the water's edge and walked to the embankment.

Now he didn't look so menacing. She watched him turn toward the water and crouch down. If this journey was to be bearable, maybe she needed to be the bigger person. She could do it. After all, he was just like one of her kids.

Lelia got up and brushed the dirt from the back of her legs. She circled around the embankment. Dune was still crouched, his wrist rested on his thighs, his face tilted toward the tree canopy.

She approached him, noticed his eyes were closed. She silenced her footsteps, then quietly sat near him.

She tried to keep her eyes trained on the water, but they always drew back to him.

Through lowered lashes her eyes swept him. Water dabbled along the muscles of his stomach, delved into the deep grooves of his chest. Her gaze wondered past his corded neck, then turned upward.

A glimpse of sunlight escaped the awning of leaves to kiss his face. His face tilted higher, seemed to welcome the sun's caress. No furrow marred his brow. His jaw didn't ripple in anger. His lips weren't drawn into a hard line. They were soft and slightly parted.

Captivated, Lelia watched the sun shift across his face.

The supple change in the light enhanced a thin, almost invisible line. A crystal drop of water topped the raised skin. It trailed a path down his temple, around the ridge of his cheek, flowed to disappear with the scar beneath his jaw.

What caused the marring? The cut had long healed. The man had not.

In the past she'd helped heal so many scarred lives. All they needed was a touch. A touch to heal.

Unconsciously, Lelia lifted her fingers toward the scar. Before she realized, Dune caught her wrist in midair. Molten eyes seared her, imprisoned her gaze.

His large hand engulfed hers, held it in place. The grasp felt different, firm, not punishing. His eyes where watchful, intense, not scornful. Their color changed, burned lighter. A warm liquid blaze, not the angry inferno she'd grown accustomed to.

He didn't speak, just watched. The intensity of his gaze, the warm firmness of his touch, hypnotic. She was pulled by the blaze, the touch. They filled her with a warm heat she couldn't free herself from.

He drew closer. His eyes lulled, but still held her trapped in their gaze.

Her mind spun. She should stop this.

Her body betrayed her. She was wanting from a mere touch, a mere gaze. The low heat thickened her blood like a gradual narcotic.

A breath away from her mouth, she watched his lips part.

Her eyes fluttered shut. She waited for the feel of him. She felt his breath brush warm against her lips.

"Never touch me unless you're invited," he said.

Lelia snapped her eyes open.

The warm blaze was gone.

Her voice belied her inner turmoil. "Don't flatter yourself."

Hurt and embarrassed, she stood and tried to free her wrist. He held her fast. His eyes glinted a challenge. She balled her fist and yanked again. This time he let her go.

She snapped her head up and walked around the embankment. She'd die before she let him see how he'd hurt her. She would lick her wounds in private, then never, never be vulnerable to him again.

Elijah watched her march away.

Damn her.

He reached into his pocket and pulled out the gas cap and studied it.

This thing he'd begun would be seen through. He'd waited too long to taste the sweetness of vengeance.

He fisted his palm around the metal, then pitched it deep into the jungle.

No matter the cost, he'd get what was owed him.

He would finish it.

CHAPTER TWENTY-ONE

L elia stared into the fire. Her fingers moved back and forth over the place where Elijah branded her skin. She still felt his touch.

"Universe to sweet cheeks. You've been staring into space for a while. Sort of makes a brother question his sparkling wit and fine looks."

Lelia pulled her gaze from the flames and looked at Marcellus. "I'm sorry."

"Don't be." He nodded to her wrist. "You hurt?"

The hard glint in his eyes spoke volumes. She knew what he was really asking.

"Yes. Uh, no." She mentally kicked herself, let her fingers fall away. "Is dinner ready? Whatever's in that pot smells good."

His eyes showed relief. "Best thing you'll taste while we're here." He poured some of the concoction into a tin cup, then handed it to her.

"It's hot, now. Watch you don't burn those pretty lips of yours."

She pulled a face, blew over the thick greenish liquid and tasted it hesitantly.

"Mmmm, this is good. Do I add great cook to your list of attributes?"

"Well, when you've got it, you've got it." He stirred the brew and removed it from the fire. "But I have to give props where they're due. Thank Elijah for this tasty delight. He taught me how to cook from roots and plants."

Lelia choked. Her eyes watered, she tried not to spit out the soup.

Marcellus laughed. "Hard to swallow? Believe it or not, cuz can turn plants into just about anything you can think of. He's one of the most sought-after botanists. The boy's a natural."

A natural pain in the butt. She didn't voice her exact thoughts. "A rose planting, gunrunner slash mercenary? I can't contain myself."

Marcellus dropped his gaze. "I'll have the meat ready in a sec."

Dune walked through the brush, his expression was drawn tight. Lelia wondered if she'd thought him up. If she did, maybe she could think him gone.

Marcellus looked at him. "You almost ready for supper?"

Elijah opened his bag. "No. Pack up. We're leaving."

Marcellus poured the soup into the cups he'd lain out. "Three cups of sweet root soup to go." He moved to smother the fire.

What was going on? Hands on hips, she stood and

waited for Dune to acknowledge her glare. "I am hungry. Would it hurt if we took five minutes to eat this...this stuff?"

He pulled on a shirt, then picked up his bag. He walked over to the cups, lifted one to his mouth and gulped down the contents. "Good job, Marcellus."

Marcellus followed suit. When he finished he graced them with a loud smack. "Dang, I'm good." He took the two empty cups and handed the last to her. "I'll rinse these out. Bon appétit, sweet cheeks."

She listened to Marcellus' retreating footsteps, all the while glaring at Dune. He glared back. She would have refused to drink the soup, but her stomach rumbled so loud, she couldn't. She turned the cup up and drank.

She'd finished about half when Dune whipped the cup from her and pitched the rest on the ground.

"Your five minutes are up." He walked over to her bag, picked it up and tossed it at her feet. "Let's go."

Again, she trudged behind him for hours. He only stopped for a ten-minute break, then pushed them more.

Half-delirious, her clumsy hands tried to keep large leaves and branches from hitting her face. Her legs burned after the first hour, now they felt torched.

She tripped over something jutting from the ground and ran headfirst into Dune. The impact left her sprawled on an upshoot of gnarly tree roots.

Someone lifted her from the ground, steadied her on her feet. Dune stood in front of her. His hands circled her waist.

She'd grown accustomed to Marcellus' brotherly touch, his guiding hand, not the warmth that ran through her stomach whenever Dune touched her.

An unreadable expression crossed his face. She knew instinct, not kindness, made him reach for her.

She pulled away. "I'm fine. How much farther?"

"We're here," Marcellus said softly.

Dune turned and stepped in front of her. She looked back at Marcellus. He stood still, his eyes transfixed on the brush. Threat laced his gaze.

She peered around Dune's shoulders, searched the undergrowth. A slight movement snared her view. Dark eyes caught her gaze, assessed her. Lelia backed away and bumped into Marcellus. He placed a hand on her back.

"Just follow Elijah's lead."

A wiry man stepped through the thicket. His forefinger wrapped around the trigger of a rifle. He stuck his tongue between his teeth and let out a low-pitched whistle. Four other men stepped out from their camouflaged hideaways. All of them held machetes or rifles.

The lead man nodded for Dune to trail him. Dune fell in step.

Fear negated her discomfort. She looked around at the guns surrounding them. She wanted to push through Marcellus' hand to run. He urged her forward.

Soon they came to a crystal stream. A four-log bridge bound with thick vines connected the banks. Lelia balanced herself and walked the length. Past the bridge, a gaped-mouth opening in the foliage revealed a village, a picture throw-back in time.

They followed the man into the football field-sized clearing. A wide dirt road separated a flock of straw-roof huts. Kente-clad villagers stopped their activities and moved in to gawk.

Everyone piled into the middle of the village. The press of people made the scorch of the sun unbearable.

The crowd separated to allow a broad-shouldered mountain through. He stood in front of them swathed in kente, a gold triangle-layered halo adorned his head. All talk ceased. His face, a chiseled mask of stone, his voice boomed when he spoke to Dune.

To Lelia's surprise, Dune answered him in swift dialect.

The man nodded, grinned, then clasped Dune into a strong embrace.

Lelia tried to follow the events. She turned to Marcellus. "What's going on?"

"Just protocol, sweet cheeks. Elijah has to ask chiefy there if we can bunk down in the village, and the chief has to give the okay."

"You know them?"

"Sure. We did a job last year for a big diamond retailer. Someone killed some of their carriers and stole the take. The big cheeses sent Elijah and me in to check things out.

"One of the carriers got greedy and whacked the others. He was long gone, covered his tracks well." Marcellus' lips tightened, his eyes filled with anger. "We found something else. Workers slaving in conditions not fit for a dog. They risked their lives in mud pits for half-peanut wages while the retailer got fat pockets. The retailer didn't like the report we called in. We threatened to take it public back in the States, address some civic organizations to boycott the retailer until they did something about the workers' conditions.

"We pissed somebody off. Things got heated. They sent messengers to quiet us down. We did what we had to do, pulled back, lost ourselves. We ended up here."

Lelia didn't want to know what they had to do. She nodded toward Dune and the chief. "Dune can speak their language?"

Marcellus' smile held pride. "Elijah can speak just about any language. That's one of the things he does best."

"Can you understand what they're saying?"

His smile faded a little. "Uhh, not really, but Elijah taught me a couple of phrases. Important things I need to know."

"Like what? Anything that can help us understand?"

Several young women scurried up to them. They covered their mouths and giggled.

Marcellus' dimples deepened. His lopsided grin intact, he uttered a few words in slow, Creole-tinged dialect and capped it off with a wink.

The women's eyes widened, they giggled again, then ran away.

He winked at her, then turned to where the women gathered, pointed in their direction. "See, sweet checks, it doesn't matter where you are, the language of love is the same all over the world."

"What did you tell them?"

"I said they were more beautiful than any jungle bloom." He spread his palm over his chest. "Africa, the Caribbean, Brazil, wherever. Women can't forget The Creole Thrill."

Lelia rolled her eyes. "Oh, please."

She shifted her gaze back to Dune and the chief. The chief snapped his head down and up, then pointed to her and Marcellus. Three women hurried into nearby huts. They came out, hastened to Marcellus and handed him several brightly colored pouches.

Marcellus accepted the gifts. "Thank you, ladies." They blushed under his scrutiny and moved away.

Dune guided the chief over. The man grasped Marcellus' hand and pumped it. He said something.

Marcellus returned the shake, smiled and nodded, obviously clueless to what the chief said.

The chief tossed back his head and roared with laughter. Marcellus kept a smile on his face, but between his teeth, he said, "Why the good chief always smiles and laughs when I'm around is beyond me. I don't even like him."

Dune turned to the chief and said a few words. The

chief nodded to Marcellus, before he left. The villagers dispersed, but kept an eye on them.

Marcellus looked at Dune. "Well, cuz, it's time for me to cut out. Hey, come walk a brother to the tree line."

Marcellus glanced over his shoulder to Lelia.

"Come on, sweet cheeks."

She followed the men a few paces. "Are we going back to fix the helicopter?"

Dune ignored her and spoke to Marcellus. "The chief said the nearest village market is a day's walk. They have trucks for hire that can take you to Kinshasa."

Lelia wouldn't be ignored. "What's in Kinshasa?"

Marcellus stopped and turned to her. "Old contacts. I can get some equipment without attracting attention from the government, also ask about our buddy, Deng."

"We're leaving now?"

He stooped to open his bag and deposit the gifts into it. "Not we, sweet cheeks. Me. You and Elijah are staying until I get back."

She shot a quick look to Dune. An uncomfortable chill ran along her spine. "Why can't, I...I mean couldn't we come with you?"

"It's better if I go it alone. I won't have to worry about keeping you safe. You'll be here with Elijah."

She moved closer to Marcellus and lowered her voice. "Can't he go and you stay here?"

"Logistics and patching things up are the things I do best, sweet cheeks. I'll have the bird fixed in no time, so it can fly us out of here."

Wary, Lelia glanced over her shoulder and met Dune's shuttered stare. Her thoughts tumbled through her lips. "I wish you wouldn't leave us here alone."

"Ahh, sweet cheeks, I didn't know you cared." He laughed at the look that she speared him. "Don't worry. Old Elijah will take care of you."

"But you promised Asha you'd protect me." She knew she sounded desperate. Her rising alarm threatened to choke her.

His eyes softened. "You're in good hands. I'd trust Elijah with my life." He bent and kissed her forehead, then shook his cousin's hand.

Marcellus could entrust Dune with his life. But could she trust him? Something stirred deep inside her.

Lelia followed Marcellus a few steps. He turned, his ever-present smile intact.

"Sweet cheeks, I'll be back before you can miss me. Be a love and go on back to Elijah now."

She watched him step away from her, move through the interior of the trees until the jungle veiled his tall figure.

Alone.

With Dune.

She threw a cautious glance over her shoulder. He stood there, stared at her intensely.

She walked a wide-girthed circle around him, held her head high and trudged the path back to the village.

Lelia walked to the middle of the road. A few children followed her footfalls. She stopped, stooped down and smiled into their curious eyes. They smiled back, swayed to and fro the way children do.

Something behind her caught their attention. Their small eyes grew wide with fear. They ran away.

Lelia stood. Even in the heat, she felt a humid swish of air curl across her neck. She turned. A fierce-looking man stood inches in front of her.

His deep-set eyes pierced her. She'd seen eyes like those before. Every emotion churned there, insanity never far from their depths. His left cheek ticked a compulsive twitch.

Goose bumps rolled over her skin. She moved back.

He clipped a short phrase and stepped close to her, invaded her space.

She took another step back and raised her hands. "I don't know what you're saying, mister."

She looked around the village. People stood a good distance away. No one moved. Their chatter ceased.

Predator and prey, the man stepped up to her once more, clipped off the same phrase.

This time she didn't back down. "I don't understand what you're saying, now back off."

Before she knew it, he clenched her arm.

Lelia tried to wrench it free. "Let me go!"

He jerked her forward and looked around into wide-eyed faces and proclaimed something in a loud voice.

Lelia stepped back and collided with a solid frame. She looked up. Dune stood behind her. His eyes narrowed, his gaze pinned the man holding her. He said something to the man. His voice rumbled low, deadly.

The man pulled her arm harder and repeated his earlier proclamation.

Dune reached around her and grabbed the man's wrist. She could see Dune's fingers tighten around his flesh. She felt the man's meaty fingers loosen on her arm, his hand trembled, caused her arm to shake.

His crazed gaze swung from her to Dune before his hand fell from her wrist. Dune moved in front of her. The two men eyed each other. Now that the hoopla simmered down, the villagers gathered around them.

The chief surfaced, sandwiched his arms between the two men and shouted an order. The man who'd accosted her looked at the chief, pointed to Lelia, then brought his hand to his chest.

The chief looked to Dune, who nodded and said something that sounded like a threat.

The chief seemed pleased. He clasped Dune's shoulder and made a loud proclamation. The villagers cheered and smiled at them, some of the men patted Dune on the back. Everyone seemed happy, except the man Dune pulled off her. He glared at Dune, spat on the ground between them, then pushed his way through the villagers.

The chief smiled at Lelia. He pointed and gave orders to the people around them. He clapped twice and the crowd started singing. One by one they milled by her and Dune to shake their hands. Eventually, they drifted off.

She and Dune stood alone.

Bewildered, Lelia looked at him. "What just happened?"

His expression stayed shuttered. His response stopped her breath.

"We're getting married."

CHAPTER TWENTY-TWO

"Married!"

Dune inched to Lelia, glowered in her face. "Are you deaf?"

She crossed her arms over her chest. "I'm not marrying you!"

"Suit yourself. Mubadu has other plans for you anyway."

The crazed look of the man who'd grabbed her flashed through her mind. She tried to keep her voice calm. "What kind of plans?"

"In this village an unmarried woman is open game. Any man can ask for her hand. Since you have no family to deny his claim, you can become Mrs. Mubadu." He lifted his gear on his shoulder and strode away.

She ran to block his path. "Wait a minute. I don't live here, I'm an American."

"You'll live here for as long as it takes. They outnumber us one hundred to two. I'll be damned if I'll risk my neck because you want to burn your bra." He stepped around her. "You're on your own."

She caught his arm. His glare riveted to her hand lying against his skin.

"Sorry." She released him. "Can't you say you're my brother or something?"

He moved to leave and again she blocked his path.

"Okay. Okay. What do we do? Tell the chief we're married and make goo-goo eyes at each other for two weeks?"

His features changed. He didn't like the comment. Well, here was a news flash: She didn't like the idea either.

She threw her hands up. "Well, what's next?"

He nodded to someone behind her. A small band of women gathered around them and whisked her away. Over her shoulder, she glanced back at Dune. He watched her, his brows knit tight over his angry eyes.

They ushered her toward a hut. The straw roof slanted over thick-stripped branches that formed a lean-to porch. Past an animal skin flap, the inside of the hut wasn't what she expected.

Sun filtered through a cutout window. Dried palms covered the ground, provided a natural carpet. An intricately carved stool stood in one corner, a matching table, sprinkled with flower petals lined one wall. Woven mats lay on either side of the small room.

One woman motioned for Lelia to sit on the stool. The other women smiled, bustled in and out, their colorful print skirts swished around their calves.

Lelia glanced down at her dusty pants, dirt-caked sneakers and mud-splattered top. She ran a hand over her hair and felt the explosion of tight curls, sand and grit. Her last touchup went south long ago. She'd kill for some shampoo and a kente head-wrap.

The women didn't seem to notice. They bought in small wooden bowls and motioned for her to eat and drink. The liquid was warm and sweet, the food smelled wonderful. Before she knew, she'd stuffed herself.

"Thank you. Thank you." She nodded and smiled, hoping they understood the gesture.

They smiled and left the hut. Lelia moved to follow them. A young woman with kind eyes appeared and blocked the door. She smiled and motioned for Lelia to lay down on one of the mats. Lelia nodded and turned back into the hut.

She walked to the window and looked over the village. If she was going to be there for two weeks, she wanted to explore. She moved to leave again. The friendly jailer came to the door and shooed her over to the mat.

The young woman stood there until Lelia sat. Lelia watched the woman place her cheek over her hands and tilt her head.

Lelia drew out every word. "But I'm not sleepy."

The woman didn't move.

"All right, all right." Lelia lay down and received a wide smile. The woman nodded, then left.

She flipped on her side. "Married...humph!"

She closed her eyes and dreamed of a long white satin

dress, an African violet bouquet and the angry eyes of her future husband.

Something old
Something new
Run like hell
Or reap your due

Lelia bolted up. At first she'd forgotten where she was. The interior of the hut brought it all back.

She stretched, wondered how long she'd slept. A flurry of motion at the door drew her attention. Despite herself, Lelia's jaw dropped. She closed her eyes and opened them again. "Someone tell me I'm dreaming."

A salt-and-pepper-haired woman stood in the doorway. Her stance commanded respect. Dressed in a fluorescent hot-pink T-shirt with *Mean People Suck* scrawled across her chest, she sported matching miniature basketball earrings of the same eye-wrenching hue. An ankle-length, lime-green skirt skimmed sunshine yellow high-topped sneakers. Bangles of every color adorned her wrists and jingled when she threw her hands on her hips.

Lelia wasn't sure what to make of the color blast standing in front of her. Had she died and gone to...where?

She blinked again and smiled to keep from blurting something stupid. She nodded and lifted her hands. "I-am-sorry-I-do-not-speak-your-language."

"With your broken English, I am glad I speak yours." Surprised, Lelia stared at the woman. "You speak English?"

"Is that not what I said. One question." The woman raised a finger. "Why do Americans speak slowly, their words dragging for an eternity, thinking that people who do not speak English will miraculously know the language?"

Lelia tried again. "I apologize if I offended you, Ms…"

"I dare not tell you. The thought of you butchering my name will surely plague my dreams. You will call me Aunt Lou."

"I can handle that." Lelia grinned, stood and shook the woman's hand. "I love your T-shirt, Aunt Lou."

Aunt Lou's smile showed a good number of missing molars. She held her arms up and spun around. "Yes, I have many shirts with different sayings. I collected them on my last trip to your country."

"Will you be traveling to the United States soon?"

"No. That journey was my last. My people need me here."

Lelia blanked the disappointment from her features.

Aunt Lou seemed to assess her with a knowing eye. "You are very quick and clever, a good match for the forest son, your Elijah. I know these things. I teach young women the lessons of being a good mate. The grooming starts early in adolescent life. You are old for such lessons. Your mind has chosen its course. Yet your eyes tell me you are wise and will learn quickly. By the end of our lessons, you will make the son a competent mate."

Lelia wasn't sure whether she was insulted or not.

"Exactly what does that mean?"

Aunt Lou held up her hand and ticked off a finger for

each job. "The woman's duties are to cook, fish, gather the fruits, build the dwellings and take care of the mate's other needs, then there are the children, of course."

"If a good mate does all that, why have a man?" It was time to end this farce. "Look, Aunt Lou. I need to explain something to you."

"Hmmmph, there is nothing to explain. We must hurry." Aunt Lou waved a dismissive hand. "The mating dance is tonight."

At the door, she turned back to Lelia. "It is natural for you to have fears. I watched you and the son together. Make no mistake, you are his mate."

Lelia followed Aunt Lou's bustling figure down the dusty center path of the village. Aunt Lou pointed out structures as they went.

"Those are the kitchens." She motioned to two huts with blue smoke billowing through their straw roofs. "That is where we smoke our meat."

Aunt Lou waved to a woman who monitored boys pounding small tree trunks into some kind of rounded out box. "They are making fufu. You will taste it later. And there..." She waved over a large table spread with fruits of different shapes and colors. "...is the beginning of the feast tonight."

Lelia slowed her pace to look at the work being done.

Impatient, Aunt Lou waved her on. "You can ogle later. We have work to do."

Past another hut Lelia heard children's laughter.

At the edge of the clearing, under the shade of a sprawling tree, Dune sat amid six chattering, giggling pixies.

Two of the little girls busily wove flowers in his dreadlocks, others sat close by and followed his instructions on how to make mud cakes. The smallest child slept cradled in his arms.

Aunt Lou chuckled. "They would follow him to the ends of the earth. They'll be under foot for hours or until their mothers come to his rescue."

One girl wrapped her small arms around his neck. She kissed his cheek, then whispered something in his ear. He threw back his head and laughed. He actually laughed. The rich, deep sound vibrated across the air, touched something deep inside Lelia.

Patient, kind, soft. The warmth in his eyes was foreign to her, but it radiated from him, seemed as natural as breathing.

When his head came down, he glanced into Lelia's eyes. For a moment he forgot to shutter his expression. His eyes lit a tender glow. Then angry flames licked in their depths.

Lelia swung her gaze away. She would never understand him.

Aunt Lou took her arm and hurried her along. "There will be time for that later."

They walked along the path until it narrowed and entered the forest. "There are a few things I must retrieve before we begin."

Aunt Lou trudged into the brush. She stooped down to a leafy gnarl of vines, then pulled a cloth from the pouch hanging from her waist. She removed the pouch, opened it wide, and handed it to Lelia.

Cloth in hand, Aunt Lou gently broke off deeply ridged emerald leaves from their stems. A bright red blotch colored the center of each leaf. Intrigued, Lelia reached into the pouch.

Aunt Lou snatched Lelia's hand away. "Do not touch these with your bare hand."

"I'm sorry. I've never seen leaves like those before. They're very beautiful."

"Yes and very potent." Aunt Lou continued to harvest the leaves. "I must dry these, crush them to a powder, then boil them. It is a brew I am making for Mudala's sick child. The drink will cut the fever and purify the body of poison."

She stood and pulled the strings of the pouch closed. "The leaves or powder on the skin will cause itching that feels like fire." She walked away, left Lelia with the bag.

Lelia hurried behind her. "Aunt Lou, about this marriage thing with Dune."

"It is not a thing. It is your chosen walk. He is your soul mate, the spirits have chosen him." She stopped and put her fists on her hips. "Now I would oppose your mating with the other."

Lelia tried to think of what other. "Marcellus? He is very sweet."

"Humph, and very strange." Impersonating Marcellus, Aunt Lou squared her shoulders, grinned and winked, then spouted the phrase he crooned to the young women. "He always tells the young ones that he likes to kiss the backsides of monkeys, and he winks and smiles widely as if he is the man every woman dreams of."

Lelia laughed. Marcellus' ego would be crushed. She sobered when she thought about Dune and what was going to happen.

"Aunt Lou, about these lessons and all of this..."

Aunt Lou waved her off and turned away. "Be patient. Tonight, after the mating dance, you will be alone. That will be your time with the forest son."

That's what frightened Lelia most.

Elijah loved the night. The smells. The sounds. Things were hidden in darkness, painful things the sun exposed in the light.

He turned up the carafe of palm wine and let it soothe down his throat, burn the edges of his tension away.

Now, nothing mattered too much. Deng wouldn't cross the border and risk assassination, and Aunt Lou kept the Freeman woman out of his sight most of the day.

The wine gave his senses another smooth stroke. He settled by the village meeting fire.

Through the flames, Elijah spied the wrinkled face of the storyteller. The men of the tribe gathered to listen to the tales with great interest.

Moisu was one of the best talesman in the jungle.

Graced with recanting the history of their people, their gods, their struggles and triumphs, he held a revered position in the village.

Tonight his hands moved slowly, his face grew shadowed with emotion from a haunting tale. The men sat mystified, leaned toward him, listened to every eerie detail.

"There, in a land past the great father forest's reach, lived a mighty warrior. He was handsome and strong and son to the great Chief Nabu. Many fawned over the warrior, but his heart belonged to only one.

"He'd first seen her by the great river. She was beautiful and soft and he vowed to have her. He would follow her to the river every day and watch. He dare not approach for she was the granddaughter of the shaman of the Botu tribe, the sworn enemy of Chief Nabu and his people.

"One day the girl fell on some slippery rocks and plunged into the river. The warrior ran to save her. When he pulled her from the water and held her, she fell in love with him, too.

"Their love was forbidden so they planned to run away. On the set night, Chief Nabu came to bring the warrior good news. His son was to marry a girl from his tribe.

"The warrior told his father that could not be, that his heart belonged to the shaman's granddaughter. Chief Nabu forbade the warrior to leave. The warrior ignored his father. Then Chief Nabu flew into a rage and killed his child.

"For shaming his father and his people, the warrior's body was carried to the rim of the father forest and left for the spirits to determine his soul's fate.

"The shaman's granddaughter waited for her love. When he did not arrive, she ventured to the Nabu village. On her journey, she found her lover's body.

"That was a terrible day for the Nabu. For the shaman's granddaughter came from a powerful line. Her blood flowed deep with sorcery and magic.

"She damned the Nabu generations with the curses of oneness and of seeing. The surrounding tribes feared to look upon them and banished them to exile. They could not even look upon one another's faces, those that did lost their minds. They walked by night to escape Father Sun's clarity, but even the moon, which hides many creatures, refused their ally. They were lost even to the night."

Elijah finished the wine. The fire roasted warm on his skin and the drink soothed the knots out of his gut. The reason for his journey lay in the far corners of his mind.

He relaxed. The Freeman woman was somewhere with Aunt Lou, Deng was a country away, and Mubadu was banned from the village for his outburst.

The storyteller stopped his droning. The drums picked up a slow, heady beat.

Movement caught Elijah's attention. Over the fire, he spied an entourage of women exiting a large hut and forming an aisle. Aunt Lou appeared next, a large, regal headdress of colorful feathers and wooden beads adorned her head. Wrapped in lively kente cloth, she glided toward the fire in time with the drum.

She stepped to the fire. Sharp and fierce, her eyes speared him. She raised her hand, then struck it down hard over the flame.

The flames flared high. The fire banked. The drum stopped.

The Freeman woman stood before him just beyond the flames.

He couldn't tear his eyes away. Gone was the travel-dusty scamp he'd pulled through the jungle. An African enchantress stood in her place.

Her hair danced with small colorful forest flowers. Earthy colored kente cloth swathed her breasts. A wide expanse of painted beads played across her smooth neck, dipped into the swell of her cleavage. Her bare stomach swayed. A low-riding cloth hugged her hips and opened to show a long stretch of her leg.

The lone drumbeat sounded, then again. She raised her slender arms along the sides of her face, then stretched them to him.

Inviting.

Waiting.

The drummer started a sultry beat. Her arms moved to the rhythm, stroked the air, skimmed her body, led his eyes to follow.

The drum beat bolder. Her slim shoulders rolled with

the pull of the music. Her hips trailed the motion, moved fluid, full and sensuous. She left her spot and glided toward him. His eyes stroked each dip, every soft curve. Her body beckoned him.

She'd bewitched him.

She danced in front of him now. Her skin glistened a mocha sheen, satiny like chocolate silk.

The drumbeat quickened. Heat shot through him.

Damn her! He wanted to take what she offered.

Elijah set aside his carafe and rose. He hadn't noticed the drum had stopped. Hadn't heard the boisterous call of the people surrounding them. All he felt was the tight band clamped around his chest, the fiery heat melting his insides.

He gazed into her dark, vulnerable eyes. Her lips parted, compelled his eyes to feast on their softness. His mouth longed for her taste.

A hard slap on the back jolted his senses. The hoopla around them was deafening. The chief urged him toward the hut the women had exited.

Aunt Lou tugged on his arm. "I told you, forest son, she is the one for you."

Elijah looked around the fireside at the dancing, the joviality, irritated at being manipulated, furious at the low heat still surging through him. His eyes caught a movement at the periphery of the village. A still figure stood watching, motionless.

Mubadu.

He latched on to the Freeman woman's hand and dragged her behind him toward the hut. The calls of the villagers echoed around them.

He cleared the entry, thrust her away from him, then lit into her. "What the hell was that?"

Lelia's mind was muddled. She remembered talking with Aunt Lou, remembered drinking and eating that evening. After that, everything went hazy. She saw herself led out of the hut.

Then she only felt.

Felt the beat of the drum pulse through her, the warmth of the flame against her skin. She felt the fire of Dune's eyes as they moved over her.

She'd had no control.

His bold gaze raked her body. Why was he so angry? His full mouth pressed in a firm line, his nostrils flared, his chest heaved.

What had she done? She put up an arm to cover the scrap of material over her breasts.

He stalked closer. Yanked her arm away, then jerked her to him. The hard press of his body stole her breath.

Energy. Hot, urgent, throbbed from him.

He tightened his grip. "Answer me."

"I don't know." She shook her head. "I can't remember."

"Here's a refresher."

Elijah's lips punished hers.

He didn't want her to be this intoxicating, this supple. Pure honey. He pressed harder against her mouth. Her lips flowered under the pressure. He molded her soft body to his, pulled her closer. Inhaled her essence. The temptress wove her magic.

The grizzly raged in him.

No!

Vengeance regained its rightful place in his soul. He banked the fire coursing through him. He couldn't lose control.

Not now. Not this close. Not ever.

With an arm still around her, he slid his hand to the back of the waistband beneath his shirt. His fingers wrapped around the warm handle of his bayonet. He pulled it out. His eyes mirrored in the blade he'd sharpened that morning.

Her lips still clung to his. He tilted his head. Like a lamb, she followed.

Her eyes stayed closed. She couldn't see the knife inches from her throat. His only regret, being denied the satisfaction of watching her eyes the moment he took her life.

He wanted what was owed him.

The time was now.

He positioned the blade over her jugular.

"Elijah." She whispered his name.

Soft hands smoothed up his chest, her arms tenderly wrapped his neck.

His breaths ceased. He looked down into the soft glow of her trusting face and froze. God help him.

He flipped the blade around and shadowed it behind his back.

"Damn you." He shoved her away, then stormed from the hut.

Elijah ran from the village with the devil on his heels. A nine-year-old devil that stole the joy from his life, the laughter.

Again, pain crashed heavy on him. Again, bitter loss tore at his heart. Again, the three faces he'd grown to despise invaded his mind.

He fled through the night. The leaves slapped his face, the past chased his footfalls.

He'd hunted them all. Had planned their demises. He still remembered the others' deaths as if it were yesterday, not years gone.

For months he'd followed the first. Learned his moves, memorized his habits. When the time was right, he made his move.

Elijah squatted in the rafters of a warehouse along the wharf. His target sat alone, counted his take for the day, a cigar planted between his gold teeth.

A couple of thugs came into the musty building. They were all part of the same clan. They took the bastard out before Elijah could reach him.

They'd offed their own boss.

When they finished, they threw the slime into the harbor. Long after they'd left, the scent of vanilla polluted the air. Elijah watched Thero's corpse bob along the black ripples of the water.

The other, Zeek, had been taken out in jail by his cell mate.

Now, one remained. She'd masqueraded, played the world for fools. They dubbed her a hero, not a crack hustler who led his baby to her death.

They stole Joella's life.

He'd lived to make the last minutes of their lives hell, to see the life die in their eyes just as Joella's had years ago.

Exhausted, he fell to his knees along the water's edge, hoped for the soothing that always came.

It didn't.

Something happened.

She wasn't supposed to be so sweet. Her eyes belied his truths. In her arms, his rage fled. Bitter injustice ebbed away. He only...felt. She'd worked her hustler charm yet again.

He plunged into the water. A long pain-filled cry tore from his throat, echoed back from the trees.

For a lifetime he'd existed for this moment.

For his sanity, for his baby's blood.

The hand was dealt.

Life offered no options.

He'd play it.

CHAPTER TWENTY-THREE

Lelia hated the night. Night brought predators, old feelings, old pains, phantoms that wouldn't stay exorcised.

She stared at the straw roof, tried to match patterns with objects she knew.

Noises drifted through the thatch-mud walls. Every chatter, each howl clawed her nerves. The earlier haunting animal cry from the jungle still chilled her skin.

A small pit fire cast long shadows through the thin kente flap, further edged her unrest.

She flipped on her side and eyed the elaborate getup she'd found herself in. Aunt Lou's medicine pouch lay beside it.

Events still fogged her mind. That day she'd watched Aunt Lou pick plants and herbs, then mix powders and potions.

Together they tended the sick. When they finished, Aunt Lou ushered her into her hut. Other women brought food and drink.

Slow, insidious her mind hazed. Fervid images flitted through her head. Her body had been on fire, throbbed with life. She'd moved toward a flame. Whispers, music whirled about her, impelled her to dance.

Then all was silent. Everything faded.

Except his gaze. It impaled her, beckoned.

She'd swayed toward the pull, then stood before him. Elijah.

His lips tightened into an angry line. But his eyes held a different spark. Or had her stewed mind conjured it?

No. She remembered.

She still tasted his mouth, her body still pulsed from his touch.

Where was he now?

As long as he wasn't there, she was content. She tossed to her back, plucked the sweaty tank from her chest.

Hours dragged, the moon ambled past the window. Still haunted, she traced her palm, instinctively reached for the stolen charm.

What was happening to her?

The door flap kicked back. King of the crib, Elijah strode in. Not sparing her a word or glance, he dropped his duffel at the other side of the hut and unbuttoned his shirt.

She yanked the cover to her chin. "What do you think you're doing?"

No answer. He pulled out his drop cloth and spread it over the other mat.

"I asked you a question."

He slid off his shirt and tossed it across his cloth.

"What are you doing?"

"You adding blind to your dumb act?"

"You need to check yourself and find your own place to bed down for the night."

He sat and untied his boots. "This is my place."

"Did you bump your head out there? I said, get out."

"Keep yapping. Mubadu's still sniffing around." He plopped his boots at the foot of his cloth. "He's welcome to you."

She wrapped the cover around her, then scrambled to her feet. "I am not sleeping here with you!"

"The door's that way." He jerked his thumb toward the entrance. "Remember, out here accidents happen all the time."

She backed away from the edge in his voice.

He lay down, shadows obscured his face. The slow, steady rise and fall of his chest screamed he wasn't pressed.

High-handed jerk. She sure as hell knew where the door was.

She snatched on her pants and top. With mumbled curses she stomped around, gathered her things, made as much noise as possible.

All her unspoken bravado was useless. He didn't budge.

She marched out the door and stopped. Stillness enveloped the village. Paths and porches stood deserted. Two men talked quietly at the central fire.

The moon lazed behind the clouds, then eased free.

Statue still, Mubadu stood on the main path. Pale light etched his emotionless features.

Lelia rubbed her arms, backed into the hut. She leaned on the wall, her eyes found Elijah. She sensed he wasn't asleep. Probably gloating.

Poised for a miserable night, she mimicked his actions, dropped her bag to the ground and moved to her mat.

Time lugged like a prisoner's ball and chain.

Her senses absorbed him. His quiet breathing, his nearness, his scent besieged her. He was too close. Too dangerous.

Denied sleep, by dawn, tension clutched her every muscle. Gravel coated her lids. She glanced at Elijah. He lay there, big, unmovable, calm as Valium. She wanted to scream.

She turned away from his back. Aunt Lou's pouch caught her gaze. A shameful thought tickled her mind.

Silently, she reached for the small satchel. She leaned over just enough, and sprinkled the dirt-brown powder along the back and sleeve of Elijah's shirt. Job done, she pulled the strings closed, returned the pouch, then turned to check her devilment.

Busted. Molten eyes slammed her. Nervous, she eyed the fraction of sleeve that stuck out underneath his body.

She licked her lips, searched his face. "You scared me."

Needing to escape, she stood and grabbed her bag. He latched on to the other end, held it firm. His eyes demanded an answer.

"I'm going to wash." She tugged at the straps. "Do you mind?"

He turned it loose, allowed her freedom.

Heavy dew coated the foliage as she raced to the stream pool.

What had she done? Childish, mean, petty, the words beat in her head.

With a careless toss, she dumped her bag on the bank and glanced down the path to the village.

Why care? He deserved whatever he got.

Didn't he?

After a quick look around, she shrugged off her clothes. Bra and panty clad, she waded into the bowl-shaped pool.

Lukewarm water slid over her breasts. She dipped her head back, allowed her arms to stir the water.

Leaves swayed above. Birds called, flitted from one branch to another. The tranquil surroundings didn't ease her conscience. Guilt ate at her. The weight of shame lowered her head.

Elijah's words cut deep, but that wasn't reason to harm him. She'd go back to the hut, try to make it right. Her gaze drifted up.

Elijah stood at the water's edge. Wide-legged, clenched fists, eyes ablaze. Red welts covered his chest and arms.

Dusty pants rode haphazardly on his hips, the fly half zipped.

His fiery gaze seared her skin. Lelia stopped breathing. Fear clawed her insides. Frantic, her darting eyes searched the shore. There was no escape.

His fatal lure pulled her gaze. His eyes impaled her, consumed each movement. A steady, pulsing muscle clicked in his jaw.

She backed up one step, then turned to make a dash for the shore.

The boggy base mud dragged her pace.

He sprinted around the bank. When she was thigh deep, he bounded into the water.

"I'm sorry!"

He prowled.

"I'm sorry, Elijah!"

Closer.

She spun, ran for the opposite shore. Splashes erupted behind her, merged with her fearful sobs.

The water whirled around her shoulders, pulled her legs like quicksand.

She didn't want to go farther, but plunged on. Death by drowning horrified her.

She feared Elijah more.

Quiet.

The silence before the kill, the splashing ceased.

"I'm sorry."

Fighting for breath, she snapped her gaze around the pool and shore.

Gone. He'd disappeared.

Still, she felt his presence.

Hard, warm shackles gripped her ankles, snatched her beneath the surface. Water rushed through her lips, killed the scream in her throat.

She clawed at his heavy arm clamped around her waist. He held her still, punished her. Blood pounded in her ears. Her lungs craved air; the pressure burned.

He hoisted her to the surface and threw her over his shoulder. Red welts slashed his lower back. The sight stopped her struggles.

"Please put me down so I can apologize to your face."

His silence frightened her. Mud splashed her arms as they neared the bank.

Conversation denied, she grabbed below the seat of his pants and yanked hard. Both of them tumbled into the black soup. She rolled off his prone body and backed away. Jesus, he was going to kill her for sure.

He flipped over and sat up, dragged his arm across his mud-covered face. Molten eyes popped open.

Boy, she needed a camera. What a sight. He looked like a cartoon character blown up by dynamite. All he needed was the peeled back barrel planks around his face. The giggles started low in her stomach. She rolled her lips between her teeth, tried to stifle her laughter. Comedy won out.

His eyes narrowed, he pinned her with a murderous glare. A low growl rumbled from his chest, wiped the grin from her face.

Intent on escape, she flipped to her knees. His iron grip bit around her ankle. He hauled her through the sludge, then twisted her to face him.

"You...you...!" Indignant, she sputtered to get the mud from her lips.

He sat less than a foot away. "Yes?"

Anger gone, his eyes lit with mirth. Beneath the mud, his lips twitched. A full grin creased his face, he threw his head back and laughed.

Warmth seeped through her. She'd only seen his hard mouth soften into a smile once. To hear his rich, deep laughter, see the glow in his caramel eyes, was a gift.

He was beautiful.

Elijah felt a sliver of ice melt from his heart. Her eyes shone like black pearls when she smiled. Her mouth curved soft, welcoming. He'd witnessed her smile before with the children, Marcellus, with Aunt Lou. Never him. He hadn't expected it. Hadn't wanted it.

Now, with their legs tangled, her smile shining into his eyes, he wanted her warmth to infuse him. Wanted his heart to melt a fraction more.

He wanted to forget the pain.

Elijah didn't know when their laughter stopped, when their smiles turned to heated awareness.

His hand slid beneath her thigh, pulled her closer. She tensed, her breath caught. Her eyes widened, shimmered a rich sable. Petal-soft lips parted.

She was beautiful.

His hand trailed to the small of her back, forbade her escape. The grit of mud against her silken skin seemed a sacrilege.

He eased them into the pool. Water lapped her body, rinsed some of the mud from her skin.

His fingers ached to touch more of her. He wouldn't be denied the pleasure.

He bathed her face, lingered his thumb across her lips. Hands cupped, he cascaded water over her shoulders, her throat. The silken smooth beneath the grime set his fingertips ablaze. Her pulse raced under his touch, matched his own.

He needed more.

Gently, he lifted her to him, let her softness cover him. Heat thickened his blood.

Her soft eyes widened, she stiffened against him. She shielded her hands in front of his chest, but didn't touch him. He loathed himself for the words that caused the action. He wanted her touch, yearned for it.

"Shh, shh." He took her hands in one of his and slowly brought them to his chest. Her touch was intoxicating. Famished, he lowered his mouth. He yearned for her taste.

He knew he should stop this insanity. He'd gone too far, was helpless to free himself from the hunger.

Her hands pressed against his chest. She turned her mouth away.

"No, I haven't invited you to touch me."

Her voice smoothed low and silky, stirred the flame burning through him.

He cupped her chin and turned her face. "Your lips lie. Your eyes tell the truth."

She shook her head. With a gentle hand, he stilled her

and took her lips. They bloomed tender, quivered with uncertainty and...innocence. The kind of innocence that belied his truths about her.

Elijah moaned and stroked his tongue across her lips, sampled her sweetness. She trembled beneath his hands.

It pained him to slowly ease her away. With the tip of his finger, he traced her parted lips, watched a pearl of water glisten across their softness. His body screamed to take her mouth again; he banked the urge.

His hands dropped away.

She scrambled from him. When she was a safe distance, she lowered her gaze. Too late. Moments before he'd seen the heat ignite in her sable eyes.

He watched her circle her palm with her thumb, the telltale sign she was nervous

Her lips trembled. "I'm sorry about the powder. I was angry. I know it was childish. I...it won't happen again."

She sounded as if he'd punished her. Not trying to wash the rest of the mud from her body, she turned her back to him and waded to the shore.

Elijah let her go. He turned and dove under the surface.

Her softness haunted him. The water wouldn't work its magic and soothe him.

She'd made him feel again. He didn't want to feel. He wanted blood for blood. Under her spell, he'd forgotten the pain and felt.

Just felt.

He tried to deny her tenderness. He couldn't face that he'd been wrong.

He wouldn't.

A quiet, damning voice asked, "Is this the real woman?" If so, this woman stirred his blood, scared the hell out of him.

He surfaced for a breath, then plunged under again. The water surrounded him, blocked out the world.

His mind still raged. He didn't want to feel her, breathe her, taste her. He wanted her cleansed from his thoughts, his blood.

He'd lived to end her life.

Damn it, he wanted vengeance. Yet her beguiling sweetness had begun melting the ice from his heart.

God help him.

What the hell was happening?

Lelia walked into the village. Aunt Lou nabbed her with a glare. Brows crunched, the woman marched across the village like a general.

What ticked her off? Lelia didn't know and didn't care. She just wanted to stop trembling and forget the name Elijah Dune.

"Look, Aunt Lou, I didn't sleep last night. Just took a bath and I want to lay down for a couple of hours."

Aunt Lou veered off, picked up a bowl from outside the smokehouse and continued toward Lelia until they stood toe-to-toe.

"You are not supposed to sleep. That is the purpose of the mating dance. And that..." She gave her a critical once-over. "...is not bathing. It is mud rolling. You are dirtier than a warthog. Here." She thrust a large bowl of water and a cloth into Lelia's stomach. "Go clean yourself. You have wasted too much time today. There is much to learn."

Lelia almost dropped her knapsack. "But we..."

"I do not want to hear the details of your mating. All night and again this morning is enough for any man and woman. You must eat, so you must work."

"But we didn't..."

"Didn't what?"

Lelia felt like she was the star of a bad commercial. All eyes were on her. "Uhhh."

Aunt Lou clapped her hands. "Wash quickly. We must start." She turned and left.

Lelia went back to the hut and washed.

Aunt Lou stood outside. She held out a woven shoulder bag. "Come, we will start picking fruits and nuts."

The only fruits and nuts Lelia had ever picked were off the grocery shelf. She followed Aunt Lou to a clump of tall trees and picked the fruit from the ground and dropped them into the bag.

"No, those are rotting." Aunt Lou dumped out the melons. "We must climb for the good ones."

"We?"

"No, you. I know how to gather, you must learn."

Lelia looked at the high branches. She bent, picked the fruit from the ground and put it back in the bag. "I know how to gather, too." She held up a big melon. "See?"

Aunt Lou plucked it from her hand. "No. We must climb."

"There's no we in it. No disrespect, Aunt Lou, but you have lost your mind if you think I'm going up there for some funny-looking cantaloupes." Lelia took the fruit from her and put it back in the bag. "No way. The kid's not going."

Aunt Lou snatched the bag and jammed a finger toward the branches. "The kid will go, or the kid will not eat." She dumped the fruit to the ground and kicked it. "Go."

Lelia's stomach protested. She grabbed the bag and headed for the tree. Handle straps between her teeth, she climbed to the branches Aunt Lou pointed out.

"The one to your left. Yes, that one will be very sweet."

Her foot slipped. "Look, Aunt Lou, this bark is slippery."

"I cannot understand you with the straps in your mouth. I said the one to your left."

"Yeah, yeah." She eased over a little more, not letting go of her death grip around the trunk. "So help me if I fall out this treeeee..."

The ground slapped hard the first time down.

Hands on hips, Aunt Lou stood over her. "You did not get the fruit. We must try again."

The next three times her numb butt, knees and elbows barely felt the jolts. So Aunt Lou said.

The last trip down, Lelia lay sprawled, the bag on her stomach.

Aunt Lou plucked up the bag and peeked inside. "These are lovely." She headed toward the village. "The next time I will teach you how to climb down properly. It is less painful."

Lelia got up and limped behind her. Determined to take a nap, she headed for her hut.

Aunt Lou turned back to her. "Lelia, you are going the wrong way. The river is this way."

"River? Oh, I'll wash the fruit later or eat it dirty." She hobbled on.

"No. We must fish now."

"Fish!"

Aunt Lou raised her hand like the newly added torture made all the sense in the world. "Yes, fish."

"We?"

"No, you."

"I'm a vegetarian."

Aunt Lou walked over and grasped her arm. "The forest son is not."

"And?"

"And, it is the woman's job to gather fruit, fish, repair the..."

"Yeah, I've heard that song before."

"Then we must not tarry."

Hours later Lelia trudged along the path back to the village. More water sloshed in her shoes and clothes than she'd left in the river. The branch Aunt Lou gave her to carry her catch was empty.

She plopped on the ground and wrung the water from the ends of her shirt and her shoes. "What next?"

An answering clap of thunder shook the ground. She eyed the sky through the trees. One drop plucked her forehead. Another drop plopped in her eye. Seconds later the deluge pounded her river-drenched body.

God did have a sense of humor. She must be the punchline of the month.

Water streamed down her face, weighted down her clothes, puddled around her newly wrung shoes.

She licked the rain on her lips. There was a sunny spot to this latest drama. Aunt Lou might not holler too much because she didn't catch dinner.

The excuse tumbled through her head. *It's raining, I couldn't catch a thing. What can Aunt Lou say?*

God laughed again.

The rain stopped. Sunlight filtered between the leaves.

Candid Camera must be in on the ha ha, too.

One of the village children trotted by. He carried three sticks, each strung with at least eight fish. He smiled and waved.

Lelia managed a tight smile.

Showoff.

He skipped a wide turn and headed toward her. Males must love to gloat. He stopped in front of her, examined the empty stick perched in her hand.

Without a word, he slipped three eel-like fish on her stick, grinned a shy smile and trotted off.

Lelia looked toward the sky. "Thank you."

Half bloodhound, Aunt Lou lay in wait for her. Arms folded, face set in stone, her eyes drawn into questioning slits.

"You caught those?"

"Well, Elijah didn't."

After a non-believing once-over, she clasped Lelia's hand. "Now comes your lesson on repairing your dwelling. The thatch leaked. We must fix it."

Lelia swore she could hear her bones scream in agony. Aunt Lou, who granted her a moment's reprieve, was off somewhere mixing medicines.

Dusk settled over the village, Lelia's three borrowed fish cooked on a skewer over the fire. Smelled good, too.

Right now she didn't care about eating. She wanted to find a rock to crawl under and sleep for a month, maybe two.

The flames lulled her lids. If she could close her eyes, just for a minute.

The heavy screech sent her heart racing. Aunt Lou stood over her, pointed to the fish. Compared, charcoal was a shade lighter.

"You are not watching. You will burn your man's meal. And this time Abu will not have extra fish to save you."

Lelia stood, tried to appear in control. "Blackened Cajun is very tasty."

Aunt Lou spun on her heels and marched away.

Tired beyond reason, Lelia reached for the flaming fish.

The fire licked her hand. She snatched back from the pain and watched the fish fall into the blaze.

Helpless, she stared at the pyre, wishing pizzas were delivered out there. She flopped down, held her hand. Darn it, she wouldn't cry! One tear slipped around her lashes.

Aunt Lou's voice boomed overhead. "Why should you cry? Look at the fish. They should be crying. Forest Son," she said, "come. Wash her hand, apply this to the burn and wrap it with this. I must tend to Etou's infant."

Lelia ventured a look. Elijah stood by Aunt Lou.

Not him, not now. "I'm fine."

"If that is so, why do you still hold your hand?" Aunt Lou handed him a jar and a cloth. "Tend to her. I must leave."

Elijah stooped and reached for her. He cradled her hand in his. Instantly, her skin heated, brought more discomfort.

He poured water from the dipping pot. It ran cool over her hand, through her fingers.

She tried to pull her hand away. "I can do it."

He held on. He dipped his fingers into the balm. Sure and gentle, he massaged the ointment into her palm.

Too gentle. Too sure. Too unnerving.

The massage stopped. He eyed her palm, traced the scar. "What's this?"

She tried to close her fingers. "Nothing."

An edge sharpened his voice. "What is it?"

She'd never talked about that night at The Freeze. Never uttered the horror that still haunted her.

She gave her standard dodge. "You wouldn't understand."

He kept her hand imprisoned. "Try me."

She looked at the scar, traced it below Elijah's fingers. Thought of years past.

The Freeze, Zeek, Thero, their terror didn't invade her mind. Kinder memories filled her thoughts.

"I was young, on the streets. I had this friend. I guess you could say she was like a sister. She was sort of young to be on the streets, but they show up younger and younger every day."

She looked past Elijah's shoulder, tried to crush the tension clenching her muscles. "You can tell the new kids. Their clothes are spic and span, shiny new backpacks, terrified eyes. This girl fit the bill. Except her eyes. They weren't fearful...just sad."

Lelia folded her leg beneath her. Elijah occupied himself with ripping the bandage. "I felt sorry for her so I told her she could hang with me. At first she was quiet, didn't say much. After a couple of weeks, she started to open up." She smiled. "We lived in this abandoned corner store. The only way we could get in was to rig an old steel railing as a ladder to the top floor.

"One day I was climbing up and my pants got caught on a nail. I didn't feel them snag. They were two sizes

too big and matched the baggy underwear I had on. I'd
gotten them from a mission. The crotch reached to my
thighs, I had to knot them on each side of my waist and
at each leg opening, but they were clean and in a package.
What could I say?"

Lost in thought, she chuckled. "I took a step up and
the pants fell down around my ankles. When I looked
down at what happened, I was hot. I had two pairs of
pants. Those were the good ones, no holes.

"I started back down to unsnag myself, telling off the
nail as I went, then I looked down at my friend. She was
holding her sides, hooting. She pointed to me and said,
'If them ain't the ugliest drawers I've ever seen, I don't
know what is.'

"Boy, was I steamed. I called her everything but a child
of God. I was pulling at the pants. My underwear were
going south, too, and she was on the ground in hysterics.
The more I struggled, the angrier I got, the more she
laughed.

"I yelled at her, told her she sounded like a raggedy
junkyard car stalling out, *uh he he he heeeee.* I was so ticked,
I wanted to choke that kid. But when I really looked at
her, her eyes glowing, tears of laughter spilling down
her cheeks, she stole my heart."

Elijah rolled the ends of the bandage. "She sounds...
special."

She touched the scar under the balm. "I'd never seen
much laughter. Never seen someone laugh with every-

thing they had. From then, every chance I got, I'd try to make her laugh. It was probably more for me than her. Seeing her laugh, her smile was like watching heaven open. She gave my life purpose again. Made me remember the dreams I'd lost."

Lelia stopped tracing the scar, moved her finger away. "Heaven closed for me the day she died."

The words trapped for nine years spilled out. "She'd been sick a lot. I was trying to get us off the streets, make a new life for us. I went to get help and they took her."

"They?"

"Zeek and Thero, a drug lord and his sidekick. They preyed on anybody they thought was weaker than them. I went to find her. They had her in Zeek's crack house. He told me I could save her, if I..." The words were still hard to say. "Pimped for him. Her breathing was so bad. I had to get her to a hospital. I told him yes. They moved to shoot her anyway. I jumped in front and took the bullet, here." She rubbed her upper chest. "When I woke up, they'd shot her, too.

"She had this half-heart necklace. It meant the world to her. One time she tried to give it to me for my birthday, but I wouldn't take it.

"After they shot us, I was holding her, telling her it would be all right, praying for God to make my words true. She made me take her necklace. Later, the nurses told me they couldn't pry the pendant from my hand. I guess I was still trying to hold on to her.

"I tried to die for her. She didn't deserve any of it. She was a baby." Her voice trembled. "I couldn't save her."

Elijah never met her gaze. She was thankful for that.

"Now you try to save every child you can. Try to purge your guilt?"

She knocked his hand away. "No. You're wrong."

"Am I?"

Lelia looked toward the sky for answers. The truth choked her. She couldn't answer him.

His voice sounded distant. "Guilt can destroy. Sully the most honorable intentions."

They fell silent. Elijah wrapped her hand.

"What was her name?"

"What?"

"Your friend's name...the child who died. You never said her name."

Lelia hadn't spoken her name since that day in the hospital. There wasn't a day that name didn't ring through her mind. To utter it was never an option.

The slight pressure to her fingers bought her gaze to Elijah. His head still bent over her hand, he was securing the wrap at her wrist.

"Joella." The name was a whisper on her lips. "Her name was Joella."

It pained to speak it. Unconsciously, Lelia reached to cover the puckered scar on her chest, rubbed it as if the action would ease the hurt.

Had she seen Joella in every kid she'd pulled off the

street? Had she cared for those kids at all or was she trying to save her own soul, her own sanity? Was her life a lie?

She never needed reassurance from anyone. She needed it now. Needed it from him. "Maybe scarred hearts can heal, too?"

He fingered back the edge of her shirt, reached to touch the welted skin, but withdrew his hand.

He stood, stared down at her. The empty depths of his gaze bought fresh tears to her eyes. He turned and walked away.

His hollow, quiet words floated after him.

"How can you heal something that's already dead?"

CHAPTER TWENTY-FOUR

Bone weary, Leila crawled into the hut. Even her eye-balls hurt.

The past three days had been hell. No exit. Eternal torture. Climb the trees. Patch the hut. Scrub the clothes, again. Torment had a new name. Aunt Lou.

Lelia slumped across her mat, and her eyes skimmed Elijah's cloth. Another name for torment filled her thoughts.

How can you heal something that's already dead? The words played through her mind like a scratched record. Hollow pain ripped through her after he'd walked away. The pain hadn't subsided.

His actions only intensified the hurt. He'd avoided her, been like a ghost. She felt him near, yet he stayed barely visible. A glimpse of his back from across the village, his distant profile at the center fire, was all the visual contact he allowed.

Throughout the days, Lelia fumbled through her chores, toiled to make sense of Aunt Lou's orders. Then Elijah would appear, lend a hand here, lift something there. Their shoulders would touch, their hands brush. Before she'd utter a thank-you, he'd retreat.

Again a shadow, he'd enter the hut after she slept and leave before she woke. Worked half dead, she'd never hear him enter. A shift to his duffel, fresh burn ointment to her palm, were the only indication he'd been there.

Well, her hide-and-seek days were long over.

She pulled off her pants, unhooked and slipped her bra through her tank.

The washing pot sat in the corner, bid her to rinse the day's grime away. The pit fire crackled, delivered the aroma of roasting heartwood, an easy breeze floated through the flaps, lulled her. Thinking dirt never killed anyone, she drifted to sleep.

Killing.

Death.

They pulled her to The Freeze. Cold. She stood before Zeek, pleading. The gun raised. Her body lurched. Fire ripped through her shoulder, her chest. Crimson pooled around her.

She looked up. Zeek faded. Thero vanished.

A vague figure stood before her. His finger squeezed the trigger again. He stepped from the shadows, her cracked lips screamed his name.

Pain tore her flesh. Blackness swept her into a pit of doom. One more horrifying than she'd ever known.

She turned from the terror. Strong bands surrounded her, curled her in safety. A familiar warmth chased away the horror. In the haven, she floated into a protected repose.

Leila snuggled closer. The cocoon rewarded her, tightened its heavenly shelter. Safeguarded, she burrowed farther into the embrace. The contented purr drifting about was her own. Dreams never felt this good. Not hers, anyway. She'd string this one out, relish it as long as it lasted.

Hard fingers curled around her hips, molded her to their firmness.

Still not enough.

Beneath a soft, worn shirt, muscles rippled under her fingers. She pressed, melted her body against the firmness.

"Any closer and you'll be behind me."

The gruff words slapped the dream from her psyche. Her eyes snapped open.

Beneath half-closed lids, Elijah's eyes flashed a golden cognac. Wrapped in his arms, she lay fused to his body. Every groove, each hard plane welded against her. A flush washed over her. Warmth smoldered, waves curled low in her stomach.

His touch ignited the fire. His scent stoked the blaze.

How did she end up like this? Heat choked the question in her throat. She searched his face, hoping for answers.

His gaze rested on her lips. "This time your invitation was...obvious."

"You're wrong."

"You lie. Again."

She wedged her hands between them and pushed against his chest. Unmovable. The action slid her into the wall. His fingers tightened on her skin. He leaned closer.

She drew away. The coarse wood scathed her shoulder. "Please, Elijah. I need to get up."

"One day you'll run out of lies." He moved back a fraction. "Then what will save you?"

Work-roughened fingers trailed along her back and straightened her skewed tank top. His other hand smoothed a heated path down her thigh, then fell away. He propped himself on his elbows, then stood. Thank God he slept with his clothes on.

He loomed over her, near enough for her to still feel his heat. His eyes probed, made her feel naked. "Last night you tossed and turned. You seemed afraid."

Careful not to touch him, she sat up and searched for her cover. "It was a nightmare. It comes and goes."

"What nightmare?"

She flipped her hand in the air, consumed herself with the cover search.

He stooped down on his hunches, his thighs jailed her. "What nightmare?"

The low demand told her he wouldn't drop the subject until he was satisfied.

"I dreamed of the night my friend was killed. Sometimes it just comes, sometimes things trigger it."

"You were whimpering. You called out to me so I held you, calmed you down. Is it always that bad for you?"

She looked down to where her fingers worried her scar. The husky concern in his voice was too much. "Last night was different, is all."

"Why?"

Lelia lifted her eyes and regretted it instantly. His clear gaze was laced with emotions she'd never seen from him. She closed her eyes against them.

He captured her chin and turned her face back to him. "Why?"

She felt his gaze pulling her to answer. "I always dream the same dream, us being shot, me holding Joella, but last night, I...it was different. Thero, the man who shot us, didn't pull the trigger."

The words sounded broken. She clasped his wrist, not wanting to finish. The assuring pressure against her jaw forced the confession from her lips.

"You did."

The silence grew thick, stifling. She couldn't force herself to open her eyes. She didn't want to see the hurt she'd inflicted.

When had she start caring if she'd hurt him? When had things changed?

The pressure of his fingers still warmed her jaw. Hot tears rolled down her cheeks, trickled around his fingers.

"It was just a crazy dream, Elijah. I...we...."

"Shh."

His thumbs wiped the dampness from her cheeks. The

coarse pad of his finger strummed her lower lip, left a salty wetness. His finger lingered over her mouth before it fell away.

Quiet rustling, hushed movements scrimped the air.

When she opened her eyes, she was alone. Moments later, Aunt Lou's voice cracked around the hut.

"Your face is drawn down to the dust. The world is not ending, all is well."

Lelia rested her head against the wall. A hollow ache tugged her insides. "Not today, Aunt Lou."

"Yes, today." The woman clapped her hands like she was smashing a bug, a gesture Lelia had grown to dislike. "Dress and meet me by the smoke hut."

She stood, stretched the aches that bit her cramped muscles. Sponged down and dressed, she trudged to the smoke hut. Aunt Lou was stringing small scarlet feathers to the end of a thin, needle-size spike.

"Those being added to my daily torture routine?"

Aunt Lou pinned her with a deadpan stare. "This is for Etou's child. The other mixtures have not worked. We keep her body cool, yet that is not enough. This is our last option."

She returned her focus to her task. "The inside of the child's body races from the illness. This…" she pointed to a clear jade liquid staining a shallow wooden jar "… will slow the racing down so the other elixirs can work."

Lelia eyed the concoction. "Sounds deep."

"It is. Too much and the inside of her body will boil.

To take this in, without the Eboga root to weaken its effects, is to die a slow, stabbing death."

Aunt Lou barely dabbed the needle tip into the mixture. With a surgeon's precision, she flicked her wrist and tapped the needle three times against the rim of the jar.

Carefully, she laid the needle in a small, brightly painted box. "The blood feather warns of the danger." She snapped a lid over the box and tightly screwed a cap on the jar. "I must store these."

She marched to her hut, then returned smiling.

The torment maven looked happy with herself. Wary, Leila pushed her hands in her pockets, then poked at some kindling with her toe. "What's up, Aunt Lou? What kind of torture are you going to lay on me today? Baiting a gorilla trap? How about fishing for piranha?"

Aunt Lou turned and headed out of the village. "Smart-ass."

Lelia couldn't believe what the woman mumbled. It sounded like...no, that couldn't be right. She trotted to catch up. "What was that?"

"I said I learned many things while visiting your country. Piranha are found in South America."

"So where are we going?"

"To gather the Eboga root by the water."

Lelia pointed over her shoulder. "But the pond is that way."

Aunt Lou kept walking. "Not there. This is a sacred place. We only venture here for healing and refuge."

Leila trailed Aunt Lou, listened to the woman's clucking. They entered the tree line. Forest shade breathed cool across her sun-baked skin.

Rich and earthy, the jungle's heady aroma surrounded them. Snarls of green, leafy vines tangled the ground. Jigsaw-barked trees shot toward the heavens. Yellow-eyed lemurs curled their toes and fingers around the high branches. Lelia watched the spooky-looking creatures follow her movements with their creepy eyes.

They'd walked quite a way when Aunt Lou bent to a rounded white flower.

"Perfect." She expertly dug around the root and withdrew the plant. "This is the Eboga." With great care, she placed the plant into a leather pouch and tied the strings to Lelia's belt loop.

"I do not want you to bruise the bark by carrying it in your hand."

"I'll be careful. Now if you have me doing Tarzan stunts in the ripe fruit trees, you might as well take it back now. By the way, I'm not climbing anymore…"

Aunt Lou held out her arm, silenced her words. A gazelle listening for an unseen predator, she stopped, slightly turned her head. Leila followed her stare.

Almost obscured from view, Mubadu stood a few yards away. He broke his stance, walked toward them, and stopped in front of her. The foul tang he gave off could knock out King Kong. Lelia stomached the smell, didn't back up an inch. She looked him up, looked him down.

He bared his teeth. She returned in kind. He must not have liked her go-to-hell smile. He knocked into her shoulder and stormed off.

"Jerk!" Leila watched his retreating back. "I'd like to knock the taste out of his mouth."

Aunt Lou grabbed Lelia's arm. "Do not provoke him. Stay clear of his path."

"I'm not afraid of him like everyone else around here."

"Then you are a fool."

The woman moved forward. Leila trotted a few steps to catch up. "Aunt Lou, you don't strike me as being afraid of anybody."

"I do not fear Mubadu."

"So why not stand up to him? He's just a bigheaded..."

"No." Aunt Lou faced her. "He was not always the man you see."

The older woman walked several paces, then turned her face toward the tree canopy. "His father and mother loved the sunshine that brightened their son's eyes, his smile. They loved each other as well. A love like no other."

Lelia jerked her a thumb in Mubadu's direction. "That thing smiled? Hmmmph."

"You may not believe my words. They are true, however." She brushed her hands along her skirt. "Years ago, Mubadu's father was the chief of this tribe and his young wife ruled by his side.

"Despite their wealth, she longed to see what lay beyond the ring of the village, beyond the Father Forest. She heard tales of dwellings that touched the skies, of giant vessels that brought men from one part of the earth to another. She yearned to see those things. Her husband forbade it. He felt the other world held demons and clung to the ways of his ancestors."

Shooing aside a bug-eye lizard, she sat on a sandstone slab. "The wife obeyed her husband. Still dreams of the other world filled her head. She talked to others in the tribe about her dreams. Her husband learned of this and was furious. He believed that demons had possessed his wife and exiled her from the village."

Lelia sat beside her. "That bites."

Lost in the story, Aunt Lou nodded. "The wife was not allowed to take her infant son with her. The day she was banished, Mubadu screamed for his mother, a scream that cracked the sky."

Aunt Lou fell silent and closed her eyes. Leila placed a light hand on her arm. "What happened next?"

The woman took a deep breath. "The chief was eventually removed. He was allowed to stay in the village, however, he was never the same. His dethroning ate at his mind. He grew sick, his brain filled with insanity.

"With no one else to care for him, Mubadu nursed his father until his last days. Others in the tribe disregarded the old chief's sanctions and ventured from the ring of the village to trade with the Bantus and the markets. All except for Mubadu and his few followers. They do not pass the bordering streams. He still holds on to the old beliefs his father valued."

Her voice grew distant. "The sunshine has fled him. Now he is like a wounded animal. That is why he is dangerous. He has called upon his right to challenge the forest son for your hand in the old way."

The pain behind the words sliced Lelia's heart. "What happened to Mubadu's mother?"

A thoughtful smile bent the corners of Aunt Lou's mouth. "After many years of exile, she returned. She brought the knowledge she hungered to bring to her people, yet she was only allowed outside the village ring."

She pushed a bushy fern back and forth with her toe. "One day two strangers entered the village. One had words smooth as palm oil, the other had eyes the color of fire. The man with the flaming eyes was badly injured, shot here." She patted her thigh.

"He bled large amounts from the wound. His companion's healing powers were good and the injured man had great knowledge of roots and plants. Mubadu's mother was better. She healed the stranger. Because of her kindness and healing power, she was granted back into the tribe.

"The strangers stayed, became one with the tribe. The one with the eyes of fire learned the language. Mubadu's mother grew fond of him. He permitted her to heal him and, in return, she was reunited with her people. Because of this she named him her forest son."

Aunt Lou fell silent. Lelia saw the moisture on her cheeks before she could turn away. Ankles crossed, the woman gazed into the treetops, looked as if the weight of the world pounded on her aged shoulders.

The past was a powerful warden. Mindful not to disturb her, Lelia slipped away. She headed back to the village. The gurgling babble of water drifted through the brush. She'd never been to this secret place Aunt Lou spoke of. Curiosity got the better of her.

Sun peeked through an opening in the trees, filtered down to sparkle on the lazy waves. Scattered furry moss dripped from sprawled branches to tease inches above the water's flow. The stream's sandstone base looked the color of rosewood. This place was mystical.

Elijah shoved the cleaning rag into his pocket, then rested the pistol on his knee. His eyes drifted over the alcove. This sanctuary used to calm him. Now, its soothing softness reminded him of a softness he longed for, but couldn't have.

Hell, it wasn't only this place that conjured her.

Everything did.

Rage and pain used to mesh with her image. Damn it, he still couldn't bring himself to say or even think her name. Now, his hands itched for her suppleness. To hold her, feel her curve around him.

This morning hadn't been enough. His heart demanded more. But his heart beat a rhythm his mind didn't want to accept. Acceptance of the tender woman who controlled his thoughts meant acknowledging he'd become a self-consumed beast.

That truth stared him in the face daily. It was ugly, warped, hostile. His mirror image. He'd been so wrapped in his hate-filled world he hadn't seen the true woman, all he saw was the monster his grief-rattled brain needed her to be.

He'd wished her harm and in return she'd given him a gift, told him Joella hadn't been alone the last year of her life. That eased a part of his soul, gave him a semblance of peace.

His baby had actually laughed on occasion. She actually sounded like his child when she mimicked Joella's laughter. God, his daughter had to leave home in order to laugh.

He inhaled a deep, shuddering breath, closed his eyes and conjured up Joella's small face. "She laughed." A half smile formed his words.

A snapping branch pulled him from his thoughts. Several yards away, she stepped out of the trees. The look of wonder on her face told him she hadn't seen him. Her awestruck gaze trailed across the water, her petal lips formed a small circle.

The thin scratches on her arms, her burned hand angered him. She'd been through hell, a good part of it he'd dished out. She never stayed down though. Always fought back. Even gave him hell on occasion. Hell, he deserved.

Now he knew she was an innocent in this mess, didn't deserve what she got. How could he make things right with her?

The answer was simple. He couldn't.

He'd protect her with his life, see her back to the States, then steer clear. That was the best he could offer.

He tongued the spice twig to the other side of his mouth, watched as she took off her shoes, then stepped into the stream. She raised her pants legs. Glory, her legs could sight a blind man.

She lifted her face to the rays and closed her eyes, content to bask in the warmth. His gaze slid over her tranquil, unguarded features, remembered how those parted lips flowered beneath his mouth. Sweet torture.

If she saw his face, that don't-come-near-me look would bunch her brow, her body would draw stiffer than starched drawers. He used to get in her face just to see that look, see her squirm. He hated it now. He kept her in his sight, but stayed away.

Stay away, that's what he planned to do.

Who was lying now?

Sweat slicked his palms as he spit out the twig and snapped the clip into his gun. Tranquility withdrawn, she jerked her head toward him, her gentle smile faded.

That look. He'd earned it.

He nodded toward the stream, kept things light. "The sandy-colored rock you're on is ancient. It underlies most of the African continent."

Skittish, she licked her lips, caused his eyes to rest on her mouth again.

She glanced past her shoulder, quickly eyed the water, swept her gaze back to his. "It's beautiful."

"Yes, beautiful."

To hell with keeping it light, to staying away. He rose, moved toward her. Her eyes darted to the gun. Fear dominated her features.

He knew she hated guns. All they'd done was bring her pain. He realized it during the fiasco in the palace. When the guard enter the bedroom, he'd pulled out his gun. She ran out of the room like hell was on her heels.

It comforted him to know, even when he planned to harm her, he kept the gun from her sight. Protected her from that pain.

He wanted to soothe the fear from her eyes, now he wedged the gun in the back of his waistband. He neared her. She turned her back to him, ready to flee.

"I have to get back to Aunt Lou."

The street-tough act fell into place. Her back straight, head high. If he hadn't witnessed the terror in her eyes, she would have fooled him.

He should leave her be. He wasn't good for her.

Hollow loss gutted him. He couldn't stand to see her run from him.

He couldn't let her go.

"Lelia."

Flutters strummed her stomach. His low, needy pitch vibrated through her. Chains of velvet, it wrapped her, held her immobile. Her body betrayed her.

She didn't know what scared her more. The gun. The man. She should be tearing tail? Yet...

"Lelia."

He'd never spoken her name before. His deep voice caressed it, almost cherished it.

"Please. Don't run from me."

She felt his warmth on her shoulder. Her breath caught, her mutinous body trembled. She couldn't turn, afraid of what she'd see, what she'd want.

Aunt Lou's gray crop popped around some bushes.

"There you are."

Saved. Relief washed her. Lelia could have kissed the bossy woman.

"Good morning, Forest Son. Lelia, thank you." She crooked her finger. "Come, I will show you a good place to gather snails, and I saw more ripe melons in the tree."

Lelia seized the opportunity. "Don't want to miss out on that."

The strong, gentle fingers on her shoulder applied enough pressure to stall her movement.

"Aunt Lou, Leila and I need to talk."

Aunt Lou gave a quick nod. "Later. Come along, Lelia."

"We need to talk now."

The woman waved, granted her permission. "Lelia and I have much to do. I can spare you a minute. No more. Speak."

"Alone, now, Aunt Lou. I'm not asking." An edge laced his voice.

Raised brow, she pinned Elijah with a glare. "Fine. If you have no meal tonight, it will be your fault." She stomped off through the brush. Over her shoulder, she said, "You have one hour. If you have not delivered her to me, I will have your head."

Quivers seized Lelia's stomach as she watched the jungle envelop Aunt Lou's stark figure. "Do you have that effect on all women?" Leila needed to quell the rising panic.

"There's only one woman I want to affect."

He moved closer. His broad chest hard against her back, his thumb stroked a circular beat at her nape. Heat. Potent, strong, dangerous sizzled around her.

"Will you let me talk to you?" His breath fanned her ear, caressed her neck.

She licked her lips, which had gone dry. "I'm listening."

He turned her, trailed his fingers down her arms, guided her palms around his waist.

Hard metal brushed her fingers, she tried to snatch her hand away. A douse of cold water, the gun wrung the heated sensation from her body.

"I'm not going to hurt you," he said.

He released one hand, cupped her chin and raised her gaze to his. She couldn't stop the tremors that claimed her.

"Does my touch scare you?"

Half-lies spilled out. "It's not you. It's the gun. It's too much...."

"Guns by themselves don't hurt, don't kill."

"I know that."

"Then don't run. Face the fear."

Brave words didn't stop terror. He slid her quaking hand beneath his shirt and wrapped her fingers around the butt of the gun. He held her hand, then turned her around and cradled her back against his chest. Strong arms caged her.

"Let me help you. Together. We'll do this together."

Unable to speak, she nodded. She could beat this. He pulled out the gun, she lost her nerve, jerked her gaze away.

"Look at it."

Her body jolted. "No. I can't."

"Look at the gun, Lelia."

Her heart banged against her ribs. "Please don't make me do this." Sweat dripped a steady path around her brow, down her cheek. Seconds trudged before she was able to peer at their hands.

His large palms shielded hers completely. She focused on his strength. With him there holding, protecting, the fear receded.

"Let's take out the clip."

Together they pressed the clip release. The weight of the cartridge tapped her palm before he retrieved it, and then moved it out of sight.

"The gun alone can't hurt you. It's the bastard behind it who does the damage."

The easy cadence in his voice soothed some of the edge off her nerves. One hand sprawled across her belly to ease her stark body flush against him.

"Don't let him win. He can't hurt you anymore."

Slow and sure, he maneuvered her finger around the trigger.

She turned her face away. "Please, don't make me do this."

"Shhh. I'm right here."

He rocked her. They held the gun poised until her trembling ceased. He eased her hands apart, removed the gun. The clenching tension spun away, she sagged against him.

"You won." He fully wrapped her in his embrace. "You faced your fears. Now, I need to face mine. I've mistreated you." His chest expanded, his body stiffened. "Please forgive me."

It was the last thing she expected.

It was the very thing she wanted.

The revelation shocked her. Words couldn't convey the emotions rushing through her. She needed to show him how she felt, hoped to ease the tension from him.

She reached up and crossed her hands over his arms, felt his slow exhale.

The rough scratch of his chin dusted her jaw, then her cheek. Whisper-soft lips brushed a sensitive spot behind her ear, trailed the column of her neck, set her body flush with fever.

He turned her in his arms, yearning burned in his eyes.

"I didn't want this to happen. I fought it, but now touching you, wanting you is as natural to me as breathing.

"I need to taste you again." He lowered his head, his breath fanned over her lips. "If you don't want this, stop me now."

She stretched on tiptoe to close the maddening space.

His lips feathered over hers, soothed, teased. Thick whiskers pricked a gentle tattoo above her lip. His warm breath blew quivers across her skin. He rubbed his mouth back and forth as if savoring her flavor, then drew her bottom lip between his teeth, stoked it with his tongue. The suckling motion mimicked the low pull swelling in her stomach.

He coaxed her lips open, delved his tongue into her mouth. The bold taste of cinnamon, of Elijah exploded on her tongue. Succulent. She ran her hands up the curve of his chest and locked them behind his neck.

His mouth eased away. Uneasy, she stole a glance. Hunger, desire, scorched his heavy-lidded eyes, unleashed wild flutters in her stomach.

His breath blew across her lips. "I'm going to kiss you again."

She closed her eyes and nodded, melted into him, waited for the delicious sensation to repeat.

Waited in vain.

Passion drugged, she nudged the wariness away, held on to the warm glow strumming her veins.

His body stiffened. The warmth of his mouth moved away. Tension pinched the air.

Thoughts of being used clouded her mind, quashed

the glow he created. Why did he play these mean games? Why was she stupid enough to fall for them? Hurt clawed her. She opened her eyes. A hard glint stretched across his features, made her flinch, retreat a step.

Elijah turned his back on her.

Dread replaced her hurt.

The object of his wrath stood near enough to touch.

CHAPTER TWENTY-FIVE

Mubadu.

Elijah held out his arm and pushed Lelia behind the wall of his body.

Fists balled, she resisted the force. "Don't push me aside. This fool has worked my last nerve."

"Hush."

Mubadu stepped closer, glared a blinkless stare into Elijah's eyes. Nose to nose, neither opponent moved or spoke. Mubadu's body drew stiff with rage. In and out, each angry breath swelled his chest, bobbed his clenched features centimeters from Elijah's face.

Elijah said something to Mubadu, his voice held a guarded calm.

Mubadu's nostrils flared. He jabbed fisted knuckles toward Lelia, his words rang hostile. He side-stepped and latched on to Lelia's wrist.

She wrenched her arm. "So help me..."

Elijah wedged between them. "Shut up."

"Say what?"

Holding his hands in front of him, palms up, he repeated his words to Mubadu as if he were attempting to disarm a rabid dog.

Mubadu ranted again, his voice escalated, sounded rapidly out of control.

"If you don't let go of my arm, you'll have to get my foot cut from your…"

Elijah nudged her with his shoulder. "I said, shut up. Do not fight him."

"Why the hell not?"

"Be still, damn it." His gruff command set her teeth on edge. "I don't want an arrow through my skull. Any way you cut it, five against two are crappy odds. If we walk away from this, hash things out in front of the chief, it will make worst things worse. I'll be called the equivalent of a punk for not fighting. At least your pretty neck will be saved."

"What are you talking about? Odds are that funk bomb here's about to get a beat down."

Mubadu retreated, dragged her with him. His stare never left his enemy. Lelia looked back at Elijah. Every step Mubadu took, he followed.

The dance commenced, Mubadu quickened his pace, left Lelia stumbling after him. In a possessive gesture, he spread his fingers wide and banged his chest with his palm twice.

Oh hell no! Cave woman wasn't her style. She jerked her arm, unbalanced him. "I said, let go!" She swung with everything she had. Bone and teeth shifted beneath her fist, pain rapped her knuckles, shot up her arm. Mubadu sprawled in the dirt.

She stood over him, rubbed her hand. "You let go then, didn't you?"

Strong fingers bit into her arm. Elijah's voice whispered in her ear. "You just sealed our coffin."

"Me!"

She followed the direction of his nod.

Preying jackals, one by one Mubadu's followers emerged from their hidden places. Each face held a different emotion.

Hostility, boredom, scared to hell, mania.

A chocolate-colored Charles Manson spat in Lelia's direction, then let out an eerie bawl. They advanced, watched their leader for instruction. Mubadu righted himself, his eyes crazed.

Lelia's bravery drained away.

"The honeymoon's over." Elijah positioned Lelia behind him.

Sweat pricked her brow. "We can run back to the village for help."

"We'd have to go through them. We'd be dead before we ran a hundred feet."

Mubadu inched to his feet. He twisted his head from side to side, ran his fingers over his jaw. Behind him, his men moved in. He thrust his palm back. Puppets, they stopped.

A muscle twitched a psychotic beat under his left eye, lifted the corner of his mouth into a deranged grin. Insidious, he eased a jagged-edged blade from a strap holster. Its golden edge mirrored a band of sun as he scathed the teeth over his fingers. Crimson dripped from the cut, flowed slow trails around his hand, down his arm.

He brought his fingers to his mouth and smeared the blood over his lips and teeth. He tipped his head back, a crazed shriek filled the air, chilled the small alcove with echoed madness.

Elijah's fingers circled her wrist. He unsheathed his knife. She clung to his arm.

"What are you going to do?"

"Slow them down."

Mubadu twirled his blade, palmed the handle in an underhanded grip.

The deadly challenge engraved on Elijah's features didn't falter. Pressure from his fingers tightened on her skin, then he pushed her away.

"Run," he said softly.

She rushed back to his side, reached for his hand. "I'm not leaving."

Mubadu's glare latched on to their clasped fingers. His eyes condemned Elijah. He jerked back his blade, lunged.

Everything raced forward in a mind-crushing blur. Enraged grunts, sickening slaps from pummeled flesh clamored around her.

Hawkeyed, Mubadu's men stood around the alcove, geared to pounce.

Frantic, she searched the ground, picked up a stick thick enough to knock a hole in Mubadu's skull. She wielded it back, a flash of gold skimmed by her face. Her gaze followed the sharp whip of air, Mubadu's blade vibrated in a tree not far behind her. Ready to dish out a beat down, she spun. Her heart missed a beat.

Deadly rage stoned Elijah's face. Swift and lethal, his hand whipped across Mubadu's shoulder, then arm. He peeled back Mubadu's flailing arm and jammed his fist up into Mubadu's ribs. The skin-chilling crack of breaking bone, the pain-laden scream bounced off the trees before the silence.

Mubadu doubled to the ground. Arms wrapped over his ribs, mouth gaped, he barked up blood as he raked his face across the dirt.

Mubadu's men moved in. One rushed to his side. The others rushed Elijah. He thrust her away. "Run!"

Anger boiled through Lelia's veins. Elijah was holding his own, but for how long? She'd make damn sure the odds were better.

Running toward the fray, she bent, picked up a handful of dirt and flung it into one of the ruffian's face. Another wail rent the air. He stooped over, dragged his arm across his eye.

He was right where she wanted him.

Arms and legs pumping, she vaulted onto his back. With an arm clamped around his windpipe, she locked her hand onto her shoulder and squeezed. Free fingers gouged his tear-drenched eyelids; she wrenched her grip into his sockets.

Eyes bulged, reaching blindly, he staggered wide legged like a Friday night drunk. He twisted, bucked, whirled, tried to shake her off. Pit-bull ferocity, pure adrenaline kept her fused to him.

Steel fists hammered her back. Knifelike fire shot across her spine, pain weakened her leg grip around his chest. Her heels scathed down to his groin.

"Payback is a mother." She jerked her heels back with her remaining strength. Tiny Tim screams bounced in her ears.

"Screaming like a girl. Getting your behind whipped by a girl." With each panted word, she clenched her heel, then kicked in high. When he thrashed his head back, she ground her teeth into his ear, tasted the metallic twang of his blood.

Her captive reared back and crashed on top of her, knocked the wind from her chest. He rolled to his side spoon fashion and cupped his privates.

Black stars swam in Lelia's view. Before she could drag air back into her lungs, large hands hauled her up and propelled her to the tree line. Elijah's voice boomed. "Move it!"

Trees and leaves whirled vertigo around her. Blood rushed in her ears, almost distorted his clenched teeth words.

"Stubborn, bullheaded woman. I didn't need your help. You damn near got yourself killed."

Her lungs expanded, allowed her to heave in a ragged breath. "You're welcome."

"Save your breath. Come on."

Angry shouts erupted behind them. Pounding foot-falls crushed foliage, narrowed the distance between escape and death.

Spiking prickles gnawed at her muscles, numbed her feet. He dragged her along. Clumsy, weary, she stumbled after him. Her foot snagged under a wide root. She fell to her knees, tough bark ripped through her pants, bit into her skin.

Unrelenting, Elijah scooped her up and forced her on. Leaves, branches bounced off his frame, beat her face, her arms. Humidity pressed around her, slowly con-stricted the clamps on her lungs.

The hammering footsteps receded. Her labored breaths were the only sounds she heard.

"Elijah, please stop...I can't..."

"No." He plunged them farther, ran them harder.

Water.

Its heavy smell pinched the air, rushing gurgles followed. They were almost to the stream, almost past the water bordering the village. A high-pitched whip of air whizzed by her face, cooled the sweat on her cheek.

Elijah continued full speed, plunged them through the stream. When they reached the other bank, he hoisted her over the overhanging ridge, then surged through the tree line. He resumed the killing race. After a few hundred yards, he slowed.

Lelia couldn't voice her thanks; her abused lungs wouldn't allow it.

Weary, too, Elijah's chest heaved. He plodded a few steps with all the grace of a weight-footed astronaut before he stopped.

Fear raised the hairs on her arms. She searched the jungle behind, around them. No Mubadu. No henchmen. The forest seemed peaceful.

Elijah's sweat-slick hand squeezed hers. Together they'd made it. The pent-up tension left her body. She laced her fingers through his and returned the comforting pressure. They'd been through hell and back. She ventured a glance his way.

The respite ended.

Elijah weaved back and forth, his body pitched, his legs buckled. The heavy tow from his fall pulled her down on top of him.

She scurried off him. "Elijah?"

He didn't move, didn't speak. She grabbed his shoulder and grappled him to his back.

"Elijah!"

A ruddy flush stained his cheeks and nose. Unfocused pupils tried to hold her gaze. He pushed her away. "Leave."

"No." Hands cupped, she felt his face. Fire danced along his skin. "God, you're burning up."

She ran her hands down his body, over his legs, searched

for a snakebite, stab wound, anything. She rolled his arms over, examined them. Dread clenched her chest. A colorful crimson plume slipped between his slacking fingers.

He tried to move her away, but his hand dropped limp to his side. His words came between short, catching breaths. "Leave. Find the markers. Go to Marcellus."

"I won't."

"Leave, damn it."

No. She couldn't desert him. She wouldn't let Mubadu win.

Droplets of sweat started to bead Elijah's nose. The directions Aunt Lou drilled in her head flooded her brain.

"Cool the body. Cool the body."

She chanted the mantra as she scoped the ground for what she needed. A large melon tree stood not far away. She scooped up a melon and slammed it against a jutting sandstone. The rind split open.

"Cool the body. Cool the body."

She retraced their steps back to the stream, shoveled out the meat of the fruit as she ran.

She leaped off the ridge and landed on her hands and knees in the water. The rind tumbled down stream in the current. She reached it, filled it with water.

A watchful gaze prickled her skin, alerted her psyche. She glanced across the water. The chocolate Charles Manson stood partially obscured by the trees, his bulged, maniacal stare swept her. A crimson plume twirled between his fingers.

Lelia spun, almost slammed into the ridge. Careful

not to spill the water, she eased the gourd on top of the high embankment. Feet plowing into the loose black soil, she struggled over the high mound of earth. She turned. He'd vanished; she still felt his presence. She swooped up the gourd and dashed through the trees. Manson's deranged cackles trailed her.

Heady and full, the heavy scent of rain pinched the air. She needed to lower Elijah's fever, and then build a lean-to before it stormed.

He lay there, lips compressed, nostrils flared, brunting the boiling anguish. When she touched his arm, he turned his face toward her. The pain in her chest threatened to choke her.

"Cool the body. Cool the body." Focused. She had to stay focused. She needed heavy cloth to soak up the water. Her pants leg would have to do. She tried to rip apart the thick seam. The coarse material rough-burned her sweaty fingers.

Elijah kept his knife behind his back. She leaned close to his ear.

"I've got to turn you over to get your knife."

She bunched his shirt underneath his chest and hip and used it as a lever to turn him. At his waist the sheathed knife was tucked opposite his gun. Her heart pounded, old horrors returned. Elijah's hoarse, choppy breathing sliced through the fear. She dragged her eyes from the gun, drew out the knife, and eased him back down.

She butchered one of her pants legs into strips, then soaked them in the sticky gourd water.

The red flush spread down his neck now. Her hands trembled as she placed the soaked strips over his forehead, pressed them behind his neck.

A tremor jolted his body. He bucked once, gritted his teeth, but didn't utter a sound. She ripped open his shirt, the buttons sprayed in all directions.

"You will not die on me. You hear me, Dune! Don't die on me."

Tears blurred her vision. She shoved the shirt past his shoulders, wet more strips. She lifted his arm to lodge strips beneath his armpits. The long golden chain he wore caught on his shirt, tightened against his neck. He winced from the pressure.

"I'm sorry." God, she felt useless. She was only adding to his pain.

She pulled the chain free. A sparkling gold object swung at its end.

Her hand quaked as she reached for the pendant. It dangled over her fingers, then slid to rest in her palm. The small half heart perfectly completed her scar.

Icy dread washed her. Her insides clinched. Her lungs vised, refused to take in oxygen.

She stared at the heart. Its twin so familiar, she knew each engraved stroke, every fine detail.

Like a burning coal, Leila dropped the charm to his chest. Distraught, she studied his features. Every second she searched his face, she beheld what her pain-shuttered eyes rejected.

Traces of her lost friend.

"Who are you?"

Unchecked tears soaked her shirt. She looked into his eyes. They were opened, laced with pain—filled with remorse.

"Why?"

"I can't...hurt you." The words seeped from his mouth, his lids drooped.

Fear scrimped over her skin. She cowered from him.

A panther sensing fear, his eyes snapped open. With strength that belied his pain filled gaze, he imprisoned her wrist, prevented her escape.

"I love you." His voice was weak, strained.

"Why did you bring me here?"

Three words echoed through her mind. All sound ceased. Her heart shattered, then died.

"To kill you."

CHAPTER TWENTY-SIX

Pain. Raw and complete, it depleted her.

Where was she?

Run. Get away. Her vexed soul prodded her. Unseeing, Lelia stumbled through the forest for hours, maybe minutes. Dazed, she spun, plodded in another direction. The shrubs, the trees pressing around her looked different.

Safety? Haven?

She burst through the brush. Hell had navigated her course. She'd come full circle.

Back to Elijah.

Heavy raindrops leaked through the tree canopy, pelted her. She walked over to stand above his supine figure, watched his chest heave, watched the heart-pulse pound at his neck.

The man had killed her heart. Each deadened beat pumped agony through her veins until she was consumed. She eyed the pendant on his chest. It glinted its brilliance, mocked her. Drops pebbled over its face, grouped together, formed one cascade. Not raindrops. Tears.

Escape eluded her. Despair triumphed.

Beside him, she sunk to her knees, buried her face in her hands and wept.

Baby?

Lelia didn't answer the voice that calmed her when desolation exhausted her.

I know you can hear me. Ma Ella's whisper padded soft as falling snow.

Lelia clamped her arms over her ears. "Go away."

Don't sass me, child. That boy needs your help.

Cold rain plastered her clothes to her body, raised chill bumps on her skin. She bowed fetally, something rough bit into her back. Bark? A tree? She slumped against the trunk, not remembering how she got there.

"I can't get away from him. Help me...."

Baby, I know you're hurting. He is, too. He's a good man. Guilt won't give him peace. Won't give you any either. Trouble is, guilt shouldn't lay on either of your shoulders. Look at him, baby, he needs you.

Not lifting her head, Lelia shifted her gaze to Elijah's frame. Rain darkened his clothes, pushed his parted shirt from his chest. He jerked, writhed. The strong cords in his neck pulled taunt, looked as if they'd snap. His brow knitted, yet he didn't cry out.

Anguish squeezed her heart tighter. Fresh tears spilled, mixed with the rain coating her face.

Listen to me, baby. He was dealt a hard life.

"And I wasn't?" Sobs wrenched her chest. She wrapped her arms around her stomach, rocked. "Ma Ella, it hurts so bad. God, it hurts bad."

I know, baby, but it's time to stop the hurt. Time for healing. He needs you, Lelia. You need him.

"No. Please, Ma, I can't...go away."

The heart can't lie, baby. When it speaks to you, you're hearing the voice of the Lord. Follow your heart and always ask yourself, what would Jesus do?

Lelia.

She filled his waking thoughts. The urgent need to touch her, hold her sliced through him. He had to find her, protect her.

From what? Who? He couldn't remember. Where was she? Damn it, where was he, for that matter?

Pain rioted his muscles. And what the hell had trampled him? Questions clamored his muddled brain. Elijah trained his mind quiet. His senses absorbed his surroundings.

His body was too tired to tremble. Fire warmed his left side. The crisp aroma of burning kindling spiced the air. The loud pop of water cooking off the wood, the heavy moisture pressing around him, confirmed it rained not long before.

Nightfall. He could hear the night crawlers' twitter escalate, then fall to a silent chirp.

He felt someone nearby, watching him.

Through slitted lashes, he spied Lelia sitting next to him, silhouetted by the fire.

She palmed his pistol, aimed its barrel at his head. Knees pointing to the sky, her arms bowed loosely on them. She held the gun steady. Her other hand held his chain. The pendant spun carefree, caught the fire's glow in its dance.

Memories slammed hard.

He opened his eyes fully. Gritting his teeth, he turned his head to look into her eyes.

Cold, dead calm washed their depths. A death he'd caused.

He tried to speak. His mouth was drier than packed cotton.

"Lelia."

"Shut up."

"Please, I..."

She snapped the gun on each ground word. "I said, shut up!"

She glared at him. Her eyes grew wide with rage, hurt, loathing. She was still feeling. Relief trickled through him. If he'd killed her fire, her passion, he would've died himself.

His gaze swept her. Dried mud spattered her face. Dirt caked her limp clothes. One of her pants legs had been hacked off. His bayonet was strapped to her bare calf.

He lifted his head. Red dots washed his vision, forced

his head to the ground. Bile seeped onto his tongue. He closed his eyes against the threatening nausea, then opened them, tried to focus on her eyes.

"No matter what it looks like, I couldn't bring myself to hurt you."

"You think I'm stupid, that I won't use this?" Lelia shoved the gun close to his face. "Your lying ass is in a sling and you still want to play me for a fool?"

Angry at himself, at the situation, he bit back. "It runs deeper than that."

"You lying son of a bitch."

"Damn it, if you're going to wave a gun around at least put the damn clip in."

Tears, uncertainty brightened her eyes. She drew her arm under her runny nose, eyed the gun, then him.

Trust got shot to hell the minute she saw his chain. He prayed to God he could change things. "You have no reason to trust me. Protect yourself. The clip's in my left pocket."

Suspicious, she slipped out the bayonet, held it up. "Move to me and I swear I'll slice your throat."

She let the chain fall, placed the gun on the ground behind her. The palm-leaf covering shifted. She dug the clip from his pocket, then drew back quickly. Knife sheathed, fingers trembling, she tried to put in the clip.

"Flip it the other way."

If looks could kill, she'd have buried him. She loaded the gun and aimed it back at his head.

"You're a fast study."

"The hard knock school taught me to be ready for anything. Snakes can slither from the most innocent-looking places."

He attempted to keep her in focus. "I haven't thanked you for saving my life."

"Don't. It's not saved yet."

"You won't shoot me. It's not in you."

"Try me." Her finger tightened on the trigger.

"No." His gaze fused with hers. "You're not like me."

"Didn't I say shut your mouth? You adding deaf to your dumb act?"

Elijah hoped she would hear him out. "Unlike you, I never wanted to save the world. I wanted the bumpkin-seed life. The sappy stuff. Apple pie on the windowsill. A house in the country, hammock out back and all the corny trimmings."

More lies. They rolled off his tongue like melting snake oil. Lelia inched out of arm's reach, blanked her expression.

He was an expert at detecting weaknesses. She couldn't show it, but he'd hit a nerve. Somehow he'd uncovered her yearnings, verbalized her secret fantasies. He'd strummed her forgotten dreams.

Monsters played many tricks.

Elijah's voice took on a distant tone. Unable to resist its pull, she was lulled into his tale.

"I thought I was bound for my little slice of paradise. Had the girl, a future mapped out. I couldn't want for more. I'd banked on going to college, but money was tight. I couldn't ask Ma and Daddy to help, so I signed up for the Marines. I married Dawnett before I left, promised her the world."

A quick pull tightened Lelia's chest. The diversion came right on time. Was she crazy? Believing his lies got her into this mess, cost her dearly. She'd let him rattle on, hang himself.

"The first year, Dawnett stayed with my parents, finally we got family housing, then the baby was born." His soft chuckle turned to catching hacks. The pull clenched her chest again, then his breathing quieted. A smile stroked his words.

"My girls. I was the only man in the house and didn't stand a chance. Dawnett owned half my heart, my daughter had the other.

"My commander kept on me about the special forces, said the action was what dreams were made of. I turned him down. I held my dreams every night. With the GI Bill, college was in the works. We were going to settle in that country house and stop base-hopping. I was the richest man in the world."

A somber note staved his voice. "I was called to the Philippines. My family moved back home with Ma. Dad had passed away by then. The day I left, I placed half my heart around my wife's neck and half around my daughter's, told them how much I loved them.

"Six months into my tour, my riches turned to dust.

Mama got a call through. Dawnett had died. Cervical cancer. She never told me. Told Ma she could beat it, that she didn't want to worry me."

Torment, confusion plagued his features. "When she died, I think I died along with her. When my tour was over, I didn't re-up, told myself I needed to be strong for my child. I made her my life." These weren't lies. His pain was real, etched in every groove on his face.

"At first, I wouldn't let her out of my sight. I was terrified of losing her. As time passed, the hurt from losing Dawnett, the terror of losing my baby, didn't ease.

"The more she grew, the more she looked like her mother, the more the walls crashed around me. One day all I could see was my wife in my child's face. It was painful waking up every day, knowing I couldn't stop mourning Dawnett. She was stamped on my baby's face. I felt like I was losing my mind. I tried to cope, blocked everything out, became the walking dead. My baby needed a father. Not a zombie."

The memory quaked his body. The palm leaves shuddered over him. "The thought of mentally scarring my baby because I couldn't bear to look at her ate at me like acid. I couldn't hold it together. Ma knew. Told me to go away, get myself together and come back to them healed.

"I took the special forces training, told myself it was only until I could pull it together, be the father I needed to be. I volunteered for every crazy assignment in every Godforsaken hole they sent me. Ma took care of my daughter and financially I made sure they wanted for nothing. But that wasn't good enough. They needed me to protect them and I wasn't there."

The palm leaves rose and fell deeply on his chest. He closed his eyes. "Ma always had a soft heart. She let a third cousin, Darryl, stay at the house. He said he was down on his luck." His nostrils flared, his mouth hardened. "Ma still won't tell me what the bastard did to them. But I know. Joella wrote letters to me. She'd never mail them. Darryl wouldn't let them near the mailbox. I found them after..."

He took a shaky breath, told her what was in the letters.

"I was in Ghana when I got the second worst call of my life."

Elijah's gaze fell on her. The misery in his eyes sliced her heart.

"My baby, Joella, was missing. When I got stateside, I called in every favor, contacted every missing child organization I could, I banged on every door where I thought she might run. Nothing came up. Seven months later they found my baby dead. On the way to L.A. I kept praying it was a mistake, right up until they pulled the sheet from her face.

"I stood over her, begged God to take me instead. It didn't seem real until I touched her cheek. I remember her being cold. So cold. I took off my jacket and wrapped it around her, just held her and cried like a baby."

Lelia watched him close his eyes against the memory, turn his face away. "A cop was waiting outside the morgue. He was trying to tie Joella's shooting to a drug kingpin they'd been after. He asked me if I knew any of Joella's friends. Told me about a girl they'd found at the scene. A Jane Doe.

"He took me to a hospital room. I stood over you, watched you breathing as he told me you took my baby to the trash heap she'd died in. He said you were probably a runner or hooked for the scum that ran the crack house."

He looked at her, his eyes earnest, pleading for her to understand. "One day I held all the cards. In an instant the deck blew apart. My dreams were being lowered into the ground, first my wife, then my baby. I swore to my girls I'd make it right. Swore whoever killed my baby would never be rid of me.

"I tracked the others down, waited for the right time. They got their due by their own hands, though. That left you. I followed you, thought your hero life was a lie. I wanted to snuff you out, but it wasn't right. You weren't right.

"That night you handed me the hot dog and soda outside the hotel in D.C., my heart yelled that I was wrong. My head, my hate tuned it out.

"When you got mixed up with Deng, I thought I'd hit the mother lode, called in some markers, followed you to Sudania."

He shifted, his voice sounded tired. "I had the opportunity to finish what I'd started, but my heart wouldn't let me hurt you. You breathed life into me. I began to care for you and hate myself, hate what I'd become."

Lelia looked away from his gaze. The pain in his eyes was too real.

"I don't expect you to ever forgive me." His drowsy voice captured her attention, she pulled her gaze to him. His eyes closed, he'd be asleep soon.

"I love you, Lelia."

Gun lowered, she watched him sleep. She scooted to the pile of palm leaves drying by the fire, spread them out and laid down, her face toward him.

The image of him looking over his wife and daughter's graves kept sentry in her brain. Her heart bled for him. A product of misery, the tragedy shaped the man, had destroyed him.

She'd seen it before. Lives molded by pain. Each kid she'd helped had his own terror-patterned existence.

Forgiving their anger, their trespasses, loving them back to life came easy. She'd given her heart, risked being hurt. Sometimes paid the price.

Elijah wasn't a child. She hadn't given him her heart. He'd taken it. Abused it. Forgiving him was a risk she couldn't take.

The price was too high.

For two days, the poison's fire toyed with Elijah's body, battered it. Lelia kept an unrelenting vigil. Forced him to eat the Eboga root, sponged the sweat from his brow, prayed while he choked down scants of water and Red Cole broth.

The third day his fever broke. The writhing ceased. He slept like the dead. Day four, his color was back to its cocoa hue. He'd slept on and off. Mercy, she wished it was more on than off.

Four nights of little sleep left her feet clumsy and her hands trembling. His nearness only worsened the affliction. Under half-closed lids, his eyes spoke of love, of desires that made her nerves stretch, her insides implode.

When he closed his eyes, his chest rose and fell in a deep, rhythmic stroke, she escaped to the stream.

At the water's edge, her rubbery legs gave way. She sat, looked at her reflection in the shallow, serene ripples. A weak-hearted fool stared back. Could her heart bear the torment? Exhaustion slumped her shoulders.

"Why can't I escape you, Elijah Dune?"

Four days of grit and sweat pricked, itched her skin, snapped her from the daze. She plucked the gun from her waistband, set it down, then peeled off her shirt. She splashed her neck and face, then closed her eyes. Foreboding straightened her spine, made her reach for the bayonet. She spun.

A glinting gun barrel dominated her view. A dirt-stained finger drew back against the trigger.

Tremors skirted through her, quaked her frame. Heart slamming, chest heaving, her gaze trailed up her seizer's arm. Unmasked rage set Elijah's eyes. The trained predator imprisoned his quarry with his gaze.

His gaze flicked to the knife. A sharp, quick nod, he snapped his head toward the ground.

She lowered the knife. Strange, she couldn't bring herself to anger. She battled down the fear and watched him through calm eyes.

She'd allowed him in. Trusted too much. Now, she'd bear the sentence.

She dragged in a heavy breath. He drew closer.

"Never underestimate your target. Always be ready. I could have capped you before the water touched your skin."

He released the butt, the trigger loop circled his finger. He palmed the barrel, then handed over the gun.

Sweat beaded his mustache and forehead. His color was slightly ashen. He took a shaky step toward the water and dropped to the ground.

Instinct had her reaching for him, propping up his bulk. He leaned over the stream. Hand trembling, he cupped the water. By the time it reached his chapped lips, half the liquid had sloshed from his palm.

He straightened. "Thank you."

"How'd you get here?"

The corner of his mouth lifted to a tired grin. "Started off walking, ended up crawling. Thought I was a goner waiting for you to notice me." His eyes barely skimmed her body, then closed. "The beautiful scenery inspired great strength."

Her heart leaped from the smoldering contact. "Come on. Let's get you back."

Arm around his waist, she staggered back to his pallet and eased his quaking body down. He closed his eyes as soon as he touched the ground. Inherently, she reached to place a hand over his forehead, then stopped.

Inherently, he turned toward her touch, smiled. Before she withdrew her hand. He covered hers with his own and bought it to his damp brow.

Inherently.

No matter how she denied it, they were part of each other. Sensing each other's thoughts, feeling each other's pain, knowing each other's frailties.

She felt he still carried the burden of guilt over Joella. Blame laced his voice whenever he spoke her name. They were two with the same souls. She tried to ease his.

"Don't blame yourself for Joella's running away. I never faulted my mother because I ran. Joella didn't blame you. She treasured the pendant you gave her. She loved you very much." She slipped her hand away.

"Thank you," he said softly as he drifted off.

While he slept, she inched closer, placed her hand on his brow, and prayed for the strength to leave him when the time came.

The days drew on. Elijah grew stronger, more restless. Lelia found him sitting up most of the time, propped against a tree trunk.

The stronger he became, the more unsafe she felt. The

veiled glances, his lingering fingers on hers, every cordial nicety sharpened her guard.

I love you, thank you, were his constant ballads. A melody she couldn't shake from her spirit. With each passing hour, his loving homage ensued, weakened her resolve. Her heart breathed again, pulsed again. His love song mastered each beat.

She gave herself a mental shake when she entered the clearing. Where was he? "The lethal Peabo Bryson."

"He's one of my favorites."

His deep voice bounced from nowhere. Lelia jumped, the water from the gourds she carried spilled down her shirt. She twirled around. He lounged against a trunk inside the clearing.

"I'm sorry. I can crawl to the stream and get some more."

His eyes twinkled. He looked like he was enjoying the view of her clinging shirt. Not sorry at all.

"Forget it." She spun to head back for more water, for escape.

"Lelia, before you go, I need help...please."

She turned slowly. He held out his hand, his bold eyes swept her. That look. It was a trap.

"I promise to be on my best behavior." His gaze dropped to the gun at her waist. "Trust has to be earned. That's why I wanted you to keep the gun. In case you felt you needed protection from me."

A trap, sure as she was breathing. Yet he never asked

for help. If anything, she was always on him for over-extending himself. She leveled her shoulders and walked to him. She stooped. Eye level, she let him hold her gaze.

"What do you want?"

"You..." Slow, sure, he raised his hand and cupped her chin. "...were too far away."

Gentle fingers smoothed down her throat. Deft fingers, so hypnotic, so soft, she allowed herself to be drawn by the caress. The fire in his eyes imprisoned her. She leaned into the warmth her body desired.

With lightning speed, the gentle storm changed. Sharpness snapped his eyes. He seized the gun from her waist, grabbed her arm, wrenched her to his side. He held her immobile. The strong hold against her skin surprised her.

His betrayal didn't.

She struggled against him. "You..."

"Be quiet."

She glared at him, noticed his eyes weren't focused on her. Gun aimed at the trees across the small clearing, a deadly sentinel, he didn't move, didn't seem to breathe.

His body, quieted, hers turned rigid as stone, each muscle on edge. Fear fluttered her heart, she trailed his line of vision.

Each minute stoked her horror. Finally, with a grumbled sigh, he relaxed. His head lulled against the trunk. Eyes closed, he didn't release her, just loosened his hold.

Dutifully, he held out the gun. She snatched it up and

pointed the barrel to the trees. She scanned the brush.

Nothing. Duped again. She'd never learn.

Rage stomped out her fear. "Try that crap again and so help me—"

Movement in the thicket choked her words. She steadied the gun at the motion. Marcellus stepped into view.

Humiliation burned a hole in her stomach. She felt the fool. Elijah was still protecting her. She glanced at him. He could have reclaimed the gun at anytime, but he put his life in her hands. A sacrifice of guilt, or love?

Marcellus walked up to them, rolled the grass stem he chewed to the opposite corner of his mouth. If he thought the situation strange, he didn't let on.

"Hey cuz, playing house, I see. Can I join the tea party?"

Marcellus dropped his duffel bag and crouched beside Elijah. Nonchalant, talking nonstop, he took Elijah's pulse, ran his hands over his skull, down his limbs.

Elijah brushed his hands away. "I'm fine." His weary voice held a tone of softness. "Had the best doctoring in the world."

Almost as if he hadn't seen her before, Marcellus swung his gaze to her. Lelia saw the worry in his eyes, but he smiled.

"And what a doctor indeed. Sweet cheeks, no running leap into my arms, no 'I missed you desperately?'" Dimples intact, he eyed the gun and winked. "That's the ticket to survival. Everybody needs one of those when he's ailing."

She waved the back of her hand, dismissed his comment. "What happened after you left? How'd you find us?"

"I love it when you're forceful." Marcellus turned back to his patient, thumbed down one of Elijah's bottom eyelids then the other. "Hitched a ride on the logging road. Got the parts I needed to patch the bird, then came back for you."

He palpated Elijah's stomach, eased back when he winced. "When I got back to the village, Mubadu and his boys were hog-tied in the middle of camp. Apparently one of Mubadu's boys started singing like Aretha. Turned coat on the lot of them. Aunt Lou told me what happened."

He took the stem from his mouth and pointed it at her. "She sent a scout out to make sure y'all were all right. Mubadu and his crew are getting their tails exiled as we speak. Jackasses."

He threw the stem down, then looked at Elijah. "I think we need to see how good you can move, old man." He stood and hoisted his cousin to his feet. "The bird's about three quarters of a mile hike. Can you make it?"

They hobbled around the clearing several times. The ashen color re-infused Elijah's face, sweat beaded his brow, he looked whipped. Marcellus shook his head and maneuvered him back to the trunk.

"Man, that was pitiful. Hey, no sweat. I owe you one." He winked and moved off to the trees.

Within thirty minutes, Marcellus had Elijah rigged up to a homemade gurney.

It was ending.

Anguish, disbelief settled over her. Part of her believed if she walked away, she'd never lay eyes on Elijah again, never have her dreams fulfilled.

Part of her feared if she released her heart, she'd end up an empty shell, relive the hell that overtook her life.

Whatever the verdict, she was powerless to stop the damning tide.

Mind made up, tired, hurting, she turned to distance herself from the pain. "Marcellus, are there markers to the helicopter?"

He looked puzzled. "Yeah, sweet cheeks, over there." He pointed to the tree carvings, then stepped toward the brush. "I'll be back. I'm going to fill the canteens."

Left alone, she felt Elijah's gaze beckon her. She turned to him, poised to let go. Afraid to say good-bye.

Elijah watched her come. He reached out, grasped her hand, brought it to his lips. Tears brightened her dark eyes, the good-bye churning there tore at him. She tried to move her hand away. His fingers tightened, afraid she'd say the word.

"Honey, don't. I can't stop your tears. I can't stop my own." He placed her hand over his heart. "Give us a chance. I'll never put tears in those beautiful eyes again."

"No, Elijah."

She tugged at his grip. He applied more pressure.

"Loving again scares the hell out of me, too. But letting my heart die again isn't an option. Staying dead is not the answer for you or me."

"How can two broken halves make a whole?"

The words made Lelia's heart cry. She loved him, but she couldn't trust in love.

Not again.

"What I love won't slip through my fingers. I won't let it happen."

Her mistrust made his heart bleed. He wouldn't lose love. Not again. He held on to her, caressed her palm. Prayed she'd give them a chance.

They gazed at each other for an eternity. Her lips never said the words he longed for. He squeezed her hand, then allowed it to slip from his grasp.

"It's not over, Lelia." He kept his face blank. He was dying inside. "I always get what I want."

She fingered the pendant on his chest, placed the gun and knife in his hand, remiss of her touch.

"Not from me, Dune."

Her trembled whisper tore at his heart. She turned and strode to the markers. Without a backward look, she walked out of his life.

Elijah palmed the pendant, watched her go. Soon, he'd take back his dreams. He'd have her. All of her.

Only the jungle heard his whispered promise.

"Yes, Lelia...from you."

CHAPTER TWENTY-SEVEN

It's not over.

Lelia almost wished the words were true. They lingered in her dreams, beset every waking thought. Two months earlier Elijah had spoken them softly, with determination.

Elijah.

She never did escape him. Now she knew she never wanted to.

He kept his promise, brought her back to the States, protected her to the end. All business, he and Marcellus made things happen. Things she didn't want to know. Midnight trips to private airstrips, whispered talks and handshakes with shadowed faces. Modern-day Moseses, they parted the Red Sea and strode through.

At a small airfield in upstate New York, Elijah was carted away by a cagey doctor. She still pictured his anger-filled face, his eyes denying their good-bye.

Marcellus escorted her back to L.A. He saw her to Big T and Nana's door, squeezed the life from her bones with his bear hug, then slipped into the shadows.

She'd walked into an empty house, breathed in the aroma of home-cooked meals, cinnamon potpourri, of home.

The front door creaked opened hours later. Nana, Big T and Bernard walked in, fussing about their ignored petitions to the State Department.

A starving soul, she'd looked them over, drunk in each expression, every movement. They were all fine. Tears fell as she stepped out from hiding.

"So, what's for dinner?"

Nana jumped. "Holy Jesus!"

Everyone stood motionless, stared at her as if she were an apparition.

With jerky steps, Nana moved forward. Shaky fingers touched Lelia's face. That familiar warmth opened the floodgates. Sobbing, they fell into each other's arms.

Bernard rushed over and embraced them both. "Baby girl, when I saw you, I thought I'd lost the last worn-out string of my mind."

Big T didn't say a word. His thick, wide arms hugged them all, smashed the breath from their lungs.

After a few smothering seconds, Nana batted his arm. "We can't breathe. We just got our child back. Don't go sending her to the hospital now."

He eased the pressure, looked down into Lelia's eyes. Nana and Bernard fired off questions. Big T stopped their tirades with a wave of his hand. Tears glistened his dark eyes. "Little sister, hell's fire or high tide, we were coming for you."

They fell silent, content to be together again. Her family had surrounded her, supported her.

Not that she needed much nurturing. She was stronger now, things had changed. Elijah had been the catalyst to that change.

Nana had urged her to get help to battle her demons. Lelia's last mission was to revisit the stripped lot that once was The Freeze. Fingers looped through the chain-link construction fence, she rested her forehead on her wrist and let the last bit of guilt and fear ebb.

Now she was at home, back at ChildSafe with her kids, wiping her hand over her brow from her Friday night dance challenges. Everything seemed normal, yet she wasn't completely at peace.

"Little sister, they're calling you." Concern edged Big T's voice. Teen ruckus mixed with the thumping bass beat of a hip-hop tune vibrating off the walls.

Big T's tall bulk blocked her from curious eyes. She looked into his face. A master at keeping his features neutral, tell-tale worry lines peeked around his eyes.

"You okay?"

"Yeah, I'm fine." She placed a hand on his arm, saw the lines fade slightly. "Have I told you how much I love you?"

The lines vanished completely, his dark eyes twinkled. "Nana always said you were a con artist. I'm going out back to show the boys how to really shoot hoops. Your fans are waiting." He nodded past his shoulder. "Looks like Team Diva won."

Lelia stepped around her human barrier. The kids in Team Diva strutted about, gave one another high-fives, spun off their final dance moves. Team Looks So Good wasn't living up to its name. One of them stomped over to the boom box and snapped off the music. Cackles and moans filled the room.

With a wink to Big T, Lelia moved into the hoopla, raised her balled fists toward the ceiling.

"Victory! You all were taught with a quickness. Don't player hate!"

She walked over to Team Looks So Good, hugged each member. Sore feelings and frowns slipped away, reluctant smiles returned. Someone cranked up the boom box. Soon the kids were plotting their secret moves for the following week's challenge.

Everything she'd endured over the past months was worth it. She had a different kind of love for her kids. Now she loved them just to love them.

She drew a finger in front of her throat. "Cut the music! Dinnertime. Losers, clean up; Team Diva, go eat."

Two kids still carried chips on their shoulders over losing. She cornered them, tough-loved out the fire before a fight broke out. Behind her, a pubescent voice piqued.

"Hey, man, what's up? Can I help you?"

"I came for the dance."

The deep, familiar tone stroked Lelia's body. She spun; molten eyes held her captive. Love, desire brimmed their depths, quickened her pulse.

Elijah never took his gaze away from hers. "I have a partner, if she'll have me."

Oooos, uumm-humms, and *you go, girls* erupted. Lelia barely heard them. Her eyes, beggars at a feast, devoured him. Jeans riding low on his hips, white tee stretched over broad shoulders. There ought to be a law against a man looking so good.

"Yo, Lelia. Say something."

"Yeah, cut the brother some slack."

She wiped her moist palms over her jeans, glanced around the room then jerked her thumb toward the back door. "Everybody out!"

"Aw come on!"

"Out. Now."

Two thumbs ups, loud smacking kisses, and raunchy winks were sent her way as the kids took their time to mill past. Once the room cleared, dread inched in. Her heart was unguarded, being alone with Elijah was dangerous.

"Hi." His deep voice bounced around the room.

There ought to be a law. A tremble ran through her. Could he see the way her pounding heart rocked her body? Hands shaking, she jammed her fingers in her back pockets. "Hi, yourself." That sounded weak.

He moved toward her. She turned away, tripped over her feet to the disheveled pile of mats in the corner.

Feet acting crazy, dang hands wouldn't stay dry. She ran her hands along the sides of her T-shirt, stooped to gather the tattered cushions.

"Running won't save you, Lelia."

She stood, let the mats fall.

His breath feathered the back of her neck. "Do you love me?"

A candid question. The answer was equally simple. Yes.

Uncertainty strangled the admission in her throat. How many times had her mind dismissed what her heart knew to be true?

Light and easy, his hands drifted over her shoulders. She closed her eyes, repose in the feel of his touch, then stepped away. "I can't."

"Neither can I. I can't stop wanting you, needing you, loving you, Lelia."

His heat infused her clothes, grazed her back. Mutinous, her body swayed toward the warmth, obeyed its command. She glimpsed his arms bracketing her shoulders. A strained thickness rode his words.

"There was an empty vessel, no love no peace inside. Hurt was its cork-tight closure, fear guarded every side. My heart was this lone vessel, pain destined to subdue, until the day, God showered down the blessing that is you."

Tears pooled, overflowed. He lowered a sparkling gold pendant in front of her. Two half-hearts welded to form a whole. The delicate metal skimmed her collarbone, his knuckles brushed her nape as he secured the clasp.

He covered the charm with his palm, pressed it to her chest. "Please, make us whole. Make us one."

Under the gentle pressure of his hand, she eased back into his embrace. In her mind, he'd held her like this a thousand times.

"I love you, Lelia Freeman."

His fingers fanned her stomach, fitted her snugly to him. She wrapped her hands over his arms, felt his pulse beat in unison with hers.

Uncertainty dissolved, she basked in his embrace, content to be held, content to be loved. Heart victorious, she couldn't fight the need anymore.

"I love you, too, Elijah. I love you, too."

His chest heaved against her back. He shifted, his hands smoothed down her arms. He brought her left hand back, brushed it with his lips, then slipped a heart-shaped diamond on her finger.

"We're getting married."

Déjà vu. She stiffened at the roughneck proposal. Still, there was nothing she wanted more. She'd settled the score, then she'd be his forever.

"Married!" She spun out of his arms.

"I want you, Lelia. Not part. All."

Confusion and hurt clouded his features, proved her undoing.

She grinned. "We've been down that road before and all hell broke loose."

Relief relaxed his muscles, fiery eyes sparkled. He lunged toward her. Too slow, she sidestepped, shrieked when he caught her, molded her to his frame. He captured her hands and drew them around his neck, then cupped her face.

His thumb slowly traced her bottom lip, his veiled gaze held a potent promise. "Whether hell's breaking loose or not, you'll always be mine, baby."

"Yes."

He lifted her off the floor. Feather soft, his mouth touched hers, tasted like paradise. His deep rumble of satisfaction vibrated against her lips. Blood boiled, slow, thick.

The loud crack of a slamming door blew the mist from her brain. Lelia loosened her arms, looked past Elijah's shoulder. At a more leisurely pace, Elijah eased her down his body, then turned.

Big T filled the doorway. Brows bunched, murder glazed his eyes.

Elijah dropped one arm. "Is there something you need to tell me, baby?"

Her palms were getting sweaty again. "There might be a slight problem."

Elijah's eyebrow raised. She peeped over his shoulder again. Big T moved in, fingers clenching, unclenching.

If that mug was any indication of the grilling he was about to whip up, she wondered what Bernard would dish out.

A woman saluting her man before he went off to war, she pressed a quick kiss to Elijah's lips. "Uh, make that two slight problems."

CHAPTER TWENTY-EIGHT

Sweet, clean air rolled through the passenger's window. The rambling country road seemed familiar. Lelia had a strong sense of coming home.

Elijah maneuvered the rental car down the tree-lined drive to Bernard's house. They drove up to the cedar-and-brick ranch. Elijah cut the engine. Big T and Nana pulled in behind them. As Big T unfolded his legs out of his King Cab, Lelia intertwined her fingers with Elijah's.

"Bernard's been the father I never had. Big T, too. They might be a little overprotective."

Elijah eyed the rearview mirror, then slanted her a suspicious look. "Honey, I think I've driven halfway across the country to get ambushed."

She slapped his shoulder, then opened the door. "Get out."

"Not down the aisle yet and she's already abusing me."

The whack of the wooden screen door diverted everyone's eyes to the house. Bernard appeared on the porch. He moved toward the car.

"Uh-huh, ambush," Elijah said softly.

She ignored him, smiled back at Bernard as he enfold-ed her in a tight hug.

"Hey, baby girl. It seems like years, not weeks, since I've seen you."

Lelia pulled back. "It's only been three months and you know it. Now before you go on, let's get something straight. Big T already interrogated Elijah enough…"

"Baby girl, there's something I need to tell you." The smile vanished from his face, his features determined. "You need to know…"

"Bernard, who is it, suga?"

The smoky voice behind them sounded different, but unmistakable. Low and smooth as sweet tea, Lelia would recognize it anywhere. How many years had she prayed to hear that voice?

She searched Bernard's face for answers, only pain and the question, *can you forgive me?* rested there.

The second crack from the screen door vibrated through her like a bullet. The air seemed to thin. Lelia struggled to draw it into her lungs.

Bernard's worried features blocked her view of the per-son on the porch. Lelia pushed out of his arms, stepped away.

"Mama?"

Lelia looked into the face she'd only seen in her dreams over the past ten years. Shocked eyes stared back. Her mama's jaw fell open. She looked at Bernard, betrayal, then fear slashed her features. She raised her hands as if pushing back her past, took a step backward, then rushed through the door.

"No!"

The harsh command barreled from Lelia's throat. She raced after her, through the house, back door, then into the yard.

"Mama!"

Rubinell stopped in front of the fence. There was nowhere else to run.

A few feet from her mother, Lelia stopped, too. She stepped closer. Mama's shoulders rose and fell, her body tensed, seemed poised to run again.

Lelia reached out, touched her shoulder. "Mama, please. No more running. No more hiding for either of us." She stepped around her mama's stiff body, faced her. Tears streamed down her mother's face. The mama she remembered never cried.

"I've missed you so much. Why didn't you answer my letters, Mama? Why didn't you let me know where you were?"

Her mama's gaze never met her eyes. "This was Bernard's doing, not mine. I didn't want it to be this way. I wanted to wait for...for..."

Lelia's heart banged against her ribs, dread rode up her back. She touched her mama's chin, turned her face so she looked into her eyes.

"For what, Mama?"

"For my prayer that you'd never lay eyes on me again

to be answered. I wanted to give you what you needed. For you to forget about me."

Lelia's hand fell. Anger replaced fear and doubt. "How do you know what I need! You never knew what I needed, Mama. All I ever wanted was for you to love me. Can't you understand that?"

Mama's gaze turned away.

Lelia swiped the tears blurring her vision, waited for her mama to speak.

Nothing.

What did she expect? Why did she hope on the impossible?

She left her mama standing in the yard, walked away from a love that never existed, same as she'd done years before.

Numb, she re-entered the house, looked at the faces gathered in the living room. No one noticed her.

Brows bunched, Nana jammed a finger at Bernard. "How long has Lelia's mother been here?"

"We've been together for quite some time."

"Why didn't you tell Lelia?"

Bernard ran a hand over his face. "Do you know how many times I wanted to tell her?"

Nana folded her arms. "Want isn't good enough. The child had the right to know."

"Look, Naomi, I love those two more than life. If I sacrificed one, I may have lost them both."

Anger and frustration laced his words. "I didn't know

Lelia had run away all those years ago or I would have used every penny I had to find her. When I stopped getting her letters, I thought Rubinell had put a stop to that, too. I knew they needed help, I could feel it, but there was nothing I could do."

He lifted his hands, dropped them again. "When I got the call from the hospital in L.A. about Lelia, I was on the next plane.

"One day Rubinell showed up on my doorstep. Said she'd gotten letters from Lelia in L.A., said she needed help to get her life together so Lelia would love her again." He rubbed the back of his neck. "I thought my prayers were answered. I put Rubinell in rehab; she slipped once but she's been sober ever since."

His eyes yearned for understanding. "I thought once she beat her addiction, she'd make contact with Lelia. She never did. Every time I'd push her to come with me to see Lelia, she'd get this frightened look on her face, like death was at her door. She said she'd make sure Lelia would never see her again.

"I couldn't stand to see the pain in Lelia's eyes each time I mentioned Rubinell's name, but I knew both of them had to face this. This was the only thing I knew to do." He nodded, resolved. "If I lose them because of what I've done, they weren't mine to begin with."

"Don't blame him, Nana."

All eyes turned to Lelia. Some held compassion. Some held pity. The one thing she never wanted.

"Bernard can't force my mother to love me. No one can. I tried. It doesn't work."

Fresh tears stung her eyes, her chin trembled. She sought out Elijah. His eyes flashed with anger. He held out his arms. Silently, she walked into his embrace.

"Baby girl?" A gentle hand cradled the back of her head. "Can you ever forgive me?"

She turned her face into Elijah's shoulder and nodded. There was nothing to forgive. The only thing she wanted to do was forget.

For two hours, she sat on Bernard's sofa, wrapped in Elijah's arms. The front of his shirt was damp. He'd let her cry until the tears ran dry.

His voice rumbled through her. "Honey, if I could change what happened to you, I'd battle hell to do it." He lifted her chin, gazed into her eyes. "You're hurting, but you can't leave here without straightening things out with your mother. Holding on to the pain, denying it exists will only kill you slowly inside. We both know that."

He kissed the tip of her nose. "One very stubborn, very beautiful woman once told me that we were over. I never gave up on the love I wanted. I needed." He brushed his lips across her mouth. "You shouldn't give up on a love that you've wanted all your life."

"Lelia?"

The soft, smoky voice sounded behind them. Lelia sat up, ran a hand down her clothes, felt the need to be presentable. She stood. Elijah unfolded his legs, mimicked her action. He kissed her forehead, then retreated to another part of the house.

Her mama held her gaze for a moment, then moved around the room, straightened things here, repositioned things there.

Lelia closed the distance between them, pulled a figurine from her hand. "Mama, stand still. We need to talk."

"Lelia, I...I don't know where to start. How can I explain something I don't understand myself?"

Rubinell fingered a button on her dress. "I always wanted you to make something of your life. To be strong and fearless. When the world pissed on you, I wanted you to piss right back."

A sad smile lifted the corners of her mouth. She reached for a new figurine, put it in another spot. "The kicker was that you already had all those qualities. My little girl was perfect, and it wasn't from a thing I'd done. I looked at you and saw everything I wasn't. Deep down I needed you to be proud of me, but I'd look in the mirror and know there was nothing you could be proud of.

"Sometimes I got angry. All those wonderful things you'd accomplished on your own. I was afraid that one day you'd see just how special you were and you'd up and leave me. So I tried to keep you tied to me instead of opening my hands and letting you soar. I didn't realize what I'd done until long after you were gone."

Tears trembled her voice. "When you left, I thought you were just mad and would be back once you cooled down. After a couple of weeks, I realized you weren't coming back. I got scared. I didn't know what to do, so I did the only thing I knew how. I drank. The pain went away long as I was drunk. Everything went to hell the first two years, until I got a letter from you. I thought I was given another chance."

She turned her back, moved toward the window. "I stayed sober long enough to find Bernard. He helped me dry out. He stuck with me until I was totally clean."

She spun around, her eyes pleaded. "Please don't blame him for any of this. He talked, threatened, did everything short of dragging me to L.A. to see you." She worried the button again. "I kept promising Bernard I'd come and see you in my time. He accepted that for a while, then he'd start pushing again. He put his foot down, I freaked, got scared and left, threatened that neither of you would see me again. I didn't want to mess things up for you, I didn't want to poison your life again. You had good people who'd raised you. I saw how your life was going. I was so scared you'd look in my face and hate me forever." Lelia moved to her mama. She couldn't open her heart fully, traces of the hurt child still remained.

Mama's mouth trembled, lifted into a smile. "Your father would have been proud of you."

The sentiment warmed her. It wasn't enough.

"Mama, are you proud of me?"

"Come here, Lelia. I need to show you something."

She allowed her mother to grasp her hand. It was a new

feeling. Her mother never touched her, never hugged her.

She followed her to a room at the end of a long hallway.

A montage of pictures and newspaper clippings surrounded her. Pictures of her graduation from the GED program, of her bachelor's and master's ceremonies. Her adult life covered the walls.

"This was my connection to you. Bernard always took pictures and brought them back. I never lost track."

Her mama's fingers trembled, felt warm on her face. "I was always proud of you, Lelia. Always. Please forgive me, suga. Please."

Lelia opened her heart all the way. "Oh, Mama." She stepped into the embrace, she'd waited all of her life to receive. "I'm finally home. What is there to forgive?"

CHAPTER TWENTY-NINE

E lijah twisted the doorknob and slipped into the room unnoticed. He eased the door closed, and his gaze found the room's lone occupant.

God, she was beautiful.

Lelia stood with her back to him, seemingly lost in thought. Her slim hand held back a white billowy curtain as she looked at the Pacific through the large bay window.

Sunlight played along her glossy jet curls. Yards of pearl satin kissed the glow of her maple skin. His heart swelled at the sight.

He'd be tarred and feathered if anyone caught him there before their wedding. He had to touch her, had to know she was all right.

His gaze trailed to the ocean. He blanked his face, but couldn't block the tight bands that clamped his chest, churned his gut.

Lelia's slight movement drew his gaze. She tilted her face to the sun, then closed her eyes. A look of total peace graced her features.

"I love you, Mrs. Elijah Dune."

The low, emotion-filled declaration rumbled through her. Lelia turned, caught her breath.

He was beautiful.

A dark gray tuxedo stretched over his broad shoulders. He'd cropped his dreads. A close-cut crew framed his face.

Shy under his intense gaze, she busied her hands, smoothed invisible wrinkles from the full skirt of her dress. "You're a little premature, dear sir."

He stepped toward her. The hunger in his eyes turned her palms moist.

"Now or an hour from now, you'll always be mine."

Strong palms smoothed around her waist. He lifted her off the floor, cradled her to his hard chest.

She slipped her arms around his neck. "Your cousin went to borrow some mascara. She'll be back any minute."

Soft as a gentle caress, his eyes swept her face.

"I know. I thought she'd never leave. You have more lipstick?"

"Yes."

His breath fanned her lips. "Good."

He took her mouth, strong and passionate. His fiery liquid gaze held hers, made the urge to close her eyes impossible.

Too soon the touch was over. She eased away. "Thank you."

"What are you thanking me for?"

"For finding this beautiful place. For arranging to have the kids brought here. The caterer, the servers, everything." For each deed, she placed a kiss on a different part of his mouth.

"You forgot the limo."

She brought her lips back to his.

"And the decorations."

She licked his top lip.

"What's a wedding without the wine and nut cheese balls I slaved to get."

Teeth bared, she nipped his bottom lip. "No need to get bigheaded."

"Ungrateful wench." He grinned as he lowered her to her feet. "It was nothing. A friend offered this place for the wedding. No big deal."

"Well, I still think my husband-to-be is wonderful."

She slipped her arms around his waist. When her hand brushed the hard object beneath his jacket she stopped, pulled away.

"Why are you carrying a gun?"

She searched his eyes. An unreadable expression flashed across his features, then was gone. He cupped her face, leaned down to take her mouth in a tender kiss, then rested his forehead against hers.

"Elijah?" She clasped his hands. "Your hands are shaking. No secrets, remember? What's going on?"

A callused thumb rubbed her lip. He closed his eyes. "I..."

"Elijah Theodus Dune!"

He stiffened against her. She looked toward the door. Four angry women stood, glared at him from the archway.

Sierra, Elijah's cousin, headed the group. Arms folded at her chest, lips pursed, neck crooked to the side, fixed in a defiant pose.

Nana's hands were balled, glued to her hips, her heel tapped a rapid staccato on the floor.

Mama closed her eyes, clamped her hand over her forehead and raised her face toward the ceiling.

Another silver-haired beauty's eyes shot fire. She looked as if she were contemplating which of her shoes to throw.

A fifth woman rounded out the entourage. She sat propped in a wheelchair, one weathered hand covered the other which lay gnarled on her lap. One corner of her mouth drooped, but the other was turned up in an unmistakable smile. Her eyes twinkled with warmth and mirth and love. Lelia knew her identity immediately.

Elijah was truly his mother's son.

Lelia turned back to her husband-to-be, tickled to see his sheepish expression.

Her tension banked at the comical sight. Elijah looked at her, his eyes pleaded for backup. She pulled a straight face and slowly drew out each syllable. "The-o-dus?"

Elijah's eyes turned murderous.

"Don't you look at her like that, buster. You have some explaining to do." Nana's irritated voice cracked like a whip.

"That's right. What were you thinking, Boopy? It's bad luck to see your bride before the wedding. You know that." The silver-haired beauty's Creole twang lashed stern, unyielding.

Elijah's neck disappeared into his shoulders. He looked like a little boy caught tracking mud onto new carpet. What happened to the tight-lipped roughneck that gave her the devil in Africa?

A proper fiancée would save her man, but watching her strong solider squirm was too fun to be legal. She placed a hand on his shoulder and patted it comfortingly. When he turned a look of gratitude her way, she couldn't resist. "Boopy?"

He pointed a finger at her nose. "You keep quiet, turn-coat."

"No, you keep quiet." Wielding the mascara, Sierra's petite frame rushed across the room, cornered him. "I spent thirty minutes putting the finishing touches to Lelia's makeup. Now look at her lips! You ate off her lipstick."

Her eyes pinned him, she spoke over her shoulder to the silver-haired woman. "Ma, Boopy chewed off Lelia's lips. I have to start all over."

Lelia cleared her throat quietly. When the mayhem ceased, she looked to Elijah, lifted an eyebrow. "Boopy?"

Nana sliced the air with her hand. "There he goes looking at her like that again. If I had my spoon I'd crack his head one!" Cheeks puffed out, she pointed toward the door. "Get out!"

Elijah opened his mouth, then clamped down on his words when all the women pointed toward the door.

"Get out!"

Elijah cast a gaze to the woman in the wheelchair. "Ma, help a brother out here."

Mirth still warmed her eyes. Slowly, she raised a finger toward the door.

"Traitor," he grumbled, but graced her with a loving wink.

He took a dejected step to leave, then spun and grabbed Lelia close for a lip-feasting kiss. "One for the road. I'll be back once the A-Team clears out."

Lelia heard someone gasp. Laughing, she spied him plant a quick peck to his mother's cheek, then dodge the slaps to his broad shoulders as he sprinted out.

When the door closed, Lelia's stomach drew tight with worry. She rubbed her palm, tried to find solace in Nana and Mama's knowing gazes.

Besides Sierra, she'd never met the women of Elijah's family, the women of Joella's family. She skimmed their faces. Did they know her connection to Joella? Did they understand how much she loved the child? Would they judge her?

The silver-haired woman stepped from the group. A smile lit her elegant face.

"Lord, what we gonna do with that man? Hello, dawlin'. I'm Marjorie, Marcellus and Sierra's mama." She wrapped Lelia with a motherly hug. "Welcome to the family."

"Thank you." Lelia's voice sounded weak. She tried again. "Pleased to meet you, Mrs. Dupree."

"Naw, che', none of that. You're family now. Family calls me by my middle name, Lissette."

"Okay, Miss Lissette."

"No, baby. Aunt Lissette will be fine."

Lelia smiled. "Yes, ma'am."

"A quick learner with beauty to boot. Boopy did just fine. Come, child. There's someone special I want you to meet."

Aunt Lissette clasped Lelia's hand and drew her across the room. They stopped in front of the woman in the wheelchair.

"Lelia, this is Elijah's mama, Della."

Lelia bent in front of the wheelchair and folded the woman's frail hand in her own. "Mrs. Dune, I want you to know how much I love your son, how proud I'll be to call him my husband. I'd be proud to call you Mother, if I may."

Della disengaged her hand to lay cool fingers against Lelia's cheek. Her drowsy voice inched stiffly over each slurred word, but her sentiment rang clear.

"When Dawnett died, my boy's soul died. When Joella died, his heart died, too." She paused, heaved in a breath. "Now his soul and heart are back." She lifted a finger, tapped above the scooped neckline of Lelia's gown. "They were born again, right here. My boy is back. I thank you."

Humbled, Lelia tenderly embraced the woman's narrow shoulders, then straightened. Mrs. Dune's tear-brightened gaze met hers, freed her earlier fears.

Sierra's words cut through the melancholy. Wiping moisture from her eyes, she bent to kiss the woman's cheek. "Okay, Auntie Dell, cut it out. We'll all need more makeup. Come on, Lelia. We have to fix the damage."

Lelia moved to follow, but Mrs. Dune grasped her wrist.

Lelia looked into the woman's unwavering cinnamon eyes. "My grandbaby, Joella, died with you?"

A taut silence enveloped the room. Lelia's heart jumped to her throat. She straightened her back. "Yes."

Della nodded, closed her eyes. Relief washed her face. "My baby wasn't alone. God answered my prayer. He sent an angel to watch her till He came for her."

Tears flowed anew. Lelia bent to kiss Della's wrinkled cheek. Della gave hers an awkward pat.

"You get ready for my boy, now. He'll be waiting for you." Aunt Lissette wheeled her out. The other women slowly filed in behind her.

Sierra lingered. She touched up Lelia's makeup, then stepped back to view her handiwork.

"Perfect, if I do say so myself." She put down her brushes and took Lelia's hand. "I'm so happy for you two. I haven't seen a smile in Elijah's eyes in years."

She squeezed Lelia's hand. "Girl, don't start. We can't mess up these makeup jobs again. I'll run out of face paint before you get to the altar. I'm going to check and see if the pastor found his way before the waterworks start flowing again."

Lelia smiled, watched her move away.

Sierra placed her palm over her forehead. "I forgot to give you this. I'm sorry." She dug into her suit jacket and pulled out a small package. "I was so angry with Boopy, it slipped my mind. A woman gave it to me, made me promise to give it to you before the ceremony."

Lelia turned the intricately carved wooden box in her hand. The craftsmanship was astounding.

Sierra nudged her shoulder. "Well, open it."

Lelia untied the fine gauze ribbon and unscrewed the circular top from its base. A small sprig of paper sprung from the casing. Lelia caught the paper, read the neat script.

True friendship transcends time. Lasts forever.

Her gaze fell to the small box. Snuggled on a bed of satin lay the delicate chain and half-heart she'd worn for years.

She put down the note and the box and lifted the chain. Makeup forgotten, tears streamed down her face. She held up the pendant. It twirled, caught beams of sunlight, gleamed in the rays.

"Asha." Lelia clasped the chain and ran to the door. She pulled it open.

"She's gone, Lelia. She told me she couldn't stay for the wedding." Sierra's soft voice floated from behind her. "I have no idea who she was."

She checked the corridor again, then closed the door, placed her hand against the wood. Asha had saved her life and now had given her a gift more precious than gold.

Lelia turned, looked at Sierra. The sight before her made her grin, then chuckle, then laugh. Black mascara stained dark circles under both eyes, made her look like a beat raccoon.

"What's so funny?" She caught her reflection in the wide mirror. "Lord, give me strength. I've got to start all over again." She grabbed up the case filled with her touchup arsenal and rushed toward the door. "Let me straighten this disaster out before Marcellus pops up and starts snapping pictures. I'll be back, sweetie. And if Boopy comes back, tell him he's dead meat when I finally catch him."

Lelia chuckled, saluted. "Yes, general."

Glad to be alone, she walked to the vanity and sat down. Necklace in hand, she unhooked the clasp and placed the pendant around her neck. The look, the feel of it was like welcoming a friend home.

She thought of the life she was about to start with Elijah, the love they'd found, the pain they'd shared. She lifted the pendant, placed it against the scar it created.

Two hearts formed one. The heart fell to her chest, she placed a hand over the pendant, closed her eyes.

So many blessings had been granted to her. Now she was truly whole.

Lelia heard the door open, then close, heard the soft footfalls.

She leaned her head back, smiled. His devilment was going to be the death of him. The family women would make sure of it.

"You are cruising for a bruising, mister."

She opened her love-struck eyes.

In the mirror she gazed into the eyes of madness.

CHAPTER THIRTY

"Hello, Miss Freeman." Deng's cold stare held her gaze in the mirror.

Lelia flexed to stand. The barrel of a gun bunched the skin at her temple. Long, cool fingers clenched her throat, forced her down.

"I give the commands. You obey them. Yes?"

His grip tightened on her windpipe, welled tears in her eyes. She nodded.

"Excellent. Your eyes tell me you understand how critical this situation is. Are you listening?"

She squeezed her lids closed, pressed her chin against his fingers.

"Very good. When we leave this room, we will say good-bye to Mr. Dune and your guests. Your loved ones will be ushered into the lovely reception room." He eased the pressure on her throat. "The doors will be barricaded behind them, of course. A gas leak will ensue. You and I will be transported to safety. They will succumb to the fumes."

402 <small>ALICIA SINGLETON</small>

His touch turned to a sickening caress. "Once we are at a protected distance, we will push the spark detonator, together. Today your guests will meet their creator. We will enjoy the spectacular inferno from the helicopter."

He tapped his forefinger against her jugular. "I have planned for your name to be immortalized. *Street Angel Dies at Nuptials.* That will be the caption to your obituary. The press-release has been typed. It will be sent to the media this evening."

Lelia couldn't stop the shudder racking her body, the tears rolling down her cheek.

"Not to worry, Miss Freeman. Fortunately for your loved ones, I am a reasonable man. Their deaths will be quick and painless."

He managed to add a saddened look to his crazed features. "Do not look forlorn. You have yourself to blame. If you would have kept to your business and not meddled in my country's private affairs, your precious family would wake tomorrow instead of being scattered ashes across the ocean. I informed you earlier, I do not leave loose ends.

"When we were first introduced I informed you, never allow your enemy to see your fears. They will use them against you."

He bent close; his breath moistened her ear. "Thank you for supplying your terrors. They were most useful. I warned you what your disloyalty would cost." He rolled his fingers down her throat, clasped her half-heart pendant in his palm. "Apparently disloyalty is rampant in my ranks. I assure you, they will be eliminated. You, however, will live long enough to receive the proper punishment for your betrayal."

His lips curled into an unnatural smile. He ran the nose of the gun across her breasts.

"You go to hell."

"I will. I plan to send you there long before I grace the flames."

He wedged her arm behind her, jammed the gun back to her temple. "Shall we go?"

He forced her out of the door, along the corridor. The faces she loved exploded in her mind. Their features twisted in pain, marred by fear, death.

All her fault.

They reached the garden. Deng camouflaged her behind the entry door.

A contrast to her misery, soft, soul-filled notes stroked the air. The voice from her past sang a hymn she'd always loved. Amazing Grace.

A woman stood on a raised tier, her onyx hair shone, cascaded down her back. She glowed. Angel's voice strummed sweet as Lelia remembered.

Angel ended with amen. Elijah walked over, lifted her hand, indicated she take a bow.

Another gift from him.

Lelia pressed her eyes closed, caused salty drops to run down her face.

"How touching you cry for a funeral dirge. Most fitting."

Deng jerked her arm higher. Fire ripped through her shoulder blade. "Let us start the festivities, shall we? I plan to make your nuptials, how do you say it? A stone gas?"

A single gun blast commenced the bedlam. Death thickened the air. Shrieks mixed with thunderous staccato bullet spray.

Then quiet.

He thrust her into the sunlight, shielded his body with hers.

Six of his men materialized, pointed automatic weapons at her loved ones cowering on the ground.

Elijah stood tall, his gun, his unfaltering stare trained on Deng. Marcellus pointed his gun at one of the henchmen.

Deng dragged Lelia to the altar, near the pinnacle of the bluff.

A heavy accented voice boomed over the breaking waves. "Everyone, inside!"

No one moved.

Shots cracked the air again, bought everyone to their feet. Their confused, fear-laced eyes darted around for an escape route. The gunmen rough-herded them into the house like cattle.

Deng yanked Lelia closer. "Mr. Dune, you are a thorn in my side. I was disheartened when Mr. Frankel informed me that you have arranged a meeting with certain government officials about possible human rights injustices occurring in my country. By my hand. I cannot allow that to happen. Can I, Mr. Dune?"

He motioned his head toward Marcellus. "Instruct Mr. Dupree to drop his weapon and follow the others inside or I will kill your precious fiancée."

Elijah didn't respond. His gaze never wavered.

Deng crammed the gun harder into her temple, forced her head to tilt.

"Tell him now, Mr. Dune."

Elijah took a step toward them.

"Mr. Dupree, your cousin is being foolish. Stand down or I will find someone inside you do care about."

His voice held a sardonic tilt. "My men love to sample feminine favors. Some tend to be rougher than others. All the women can be sampled. You will hear their screams before you die."

Marcellus didn't drop his gun.

Deng shouted something in quick dialect. One of his men's lips curled into a perverse grin as he headed toward the door.

"All right." Marcellus lifted his hands, released the clip from his gun. The heavy thump of the weapon hitting the earth echoed, haunted.

Deng shouted, the thug turned from the door, strode over to Marcellus. He kicked the gun from Marcellus' feet, raised the butt of his rifle, brought it hard against Marcellus' skull.

"That leaves you, Mr. Dune. Put down your weapon. Or she dies."

"Then she dies with me."

"Mr. Dune, I will grant you one last wish. I will take good care of your almost wife."

The steady beat of helicopter blades piqued the air. Grew louder.

Deng maneuvered her to the side of the cliff. Elijah followed each step.

The henchmen ran from the house, lined up on either side of them.

From the corner of her eye, Lelia could see the helicopter. A ladder lowered from the opened cockpit. Dirt, flowers, decorations cycloned from the ground in the chopper's gale.

It started a low, evil rumble, escalated to a maddening frenzy. Steel clawing glass, Deng's crazed bark of laughter ran cold down her spine, sealed their fate.

"Say farewell, Mr. Dune. She is mine now. She was never yours to begin with."

A blast of fire discharged from the cove below, shot through the sky. The flame smashed into the helicopter. The bursting inferno fell from the clouds.

Loud pops vibrated around her. Toppling chess pieces, Deng's men sprawled to the ground in gruesome succession. One man fell over the cliff, the rest at Lelia's feet. Blood pooled, stained her slipper crimson, soaked the earth.

Deng's muscles tensed. His jerked reaction moved her body a fraction. A fraction too much.

The high-pitched whine whizzed by her head, breathed on her cheek. Something warm, wet splashed her face. The heavy weight of Deng's body yanked her to the edge of the cliff. He toppled over the guardrail.

A scream filled, squeezed her lungs. Pain ripped up her arm. Her wrist, then her shoulder popped from the pressure. She stared down her arm at Deng dangling over the cliff. Wide, gleeful eyes stared back. Eyes ringed with ice, edged with insanity.

The wind stirred the heat from the crash fire below, flamed her body, all but her wrist, which stayed cold underneath Deng's hand.

Strong hands gripped her waist. Elijah's fingers jammed between her skin and Deng's hold, he pried the cold fingers free.

The icy manacle released. Deng plunged into the flames.

Elijah hauled her into his arms and buried her face against his quaking shoulder. Somewhere behind them, Marcellus said he'd check on the others.

Everyone was safe. Still, something barred her peace.

She needed to know all her nightmares were finally over. She pressed against Elijah's hold, then looked over the bluff.

The fire licked at the helicopter fuselage. Among the wreckage, waves lapped at Deng's crumpled body. Far out in the cove, a midsize boat rode the billows. Several men stood on its deck, raised their hands in salute.

A small figure stepped from the cabin. The men turned, bowed to the new arrival. The person walk to the helm, looked up to the cliff. She nodded her covered head, then waved a farewell.

Asha.

Lelia touched the half, then full heart at her throat, watched the boat power up, disappear around the bluffs.

Elijah's arms encircled her. This time she didn't resist.

Nightmares defeated, she planned to stay there forever.

EPILOGUE

A mellow breeze stirred the supple fragrance of summer blooms. The day lazed warm, inviting. The familiarity of it enticed her smile. Green, shiny leaves clapped gently overhead, a grand applause to the sweet overture. Finally, she was home.

They swung in a wide hammock roped between two magnolias. Father, mother and infant rested in its netted girth.

Lelia nestled farther into the crook of her husband's arm then gazed over to the miniature cherub sleeping rump up on Elijah's chest.

Their daughter.

The baby seemed content, cradled in her father's large hand, lulled by the low grumblings of his soft snores.

Droopy-eyed, she rose and fell in time with each swell of his chest. Her tiny mouth slipped opened, formed a small circle when she succumbed and drifted to sleep.

Lelia reached over to smooth the shiny black curls of Danielle Joella Dune, their pip-squeak.

The day she was born, Elijah held their precious gift to his heart, and tears of joy brightened his eyes. Lelia wept, too.

Time balmed their pain. God had given them a second chance.

Lelia shifted, felt Elijah's arm tighten around her, indicating she stay close.

No, she wasn't going anywhere.

She drew in a deep breath, clasped the delicate heart pendant at her throat.

She would live here. She would love her man, raise her children here. She would die here.

Nothing and no one would change that.

ABOUT THE AUTHOR

Born and raised in Philadelphia, the Howard University graduate embraced the written word at an early age. She credits this to her loving, older sister whom, while they were youngsters, made the author eat lotion on a regular basis. Realizing the need to sound-out the ingredients on the lotion label, Alicia stopped the lotion-eating practice, but continued to read the labels of the concoctions her sister brought for her to try. This early necessity to read flowered into a passion; hence, a writer was born.

Alicia resides in Maryland with her wonderful husband and son. Still an avid reader, label or otherwise, Alicia is currently at work on a new novel.

Visit the author at www.aliciasingleton.com, www.facebook.com/aliciamsingleton or http://twitter.com/aliciasingleton.

IF YOU ENJOYED "THE DARK SIDE OF VALOR,"
PLEASE BE SURE TO TRY

In Times of Trouble

BY YOLONDA TONETTE SANDERS
AVAILABLE FROM STREBOR BOOKS

CHAPTER 1
A Minor Issue

It took Lisa a few minutes to fully regain conscious-
ness when she woke up and found herself in the
living room. She hadn't meant to fall asleep. Tucked
away in an eastern suburb of Columbus, the Hampton
household had been relatively quiet last night. With her
mother and daughter out, Lisa took advantage of the
solitary Saturday evening and just relaxed. Considering
the many late nights she'd worked the previous week,
she needed the break. Lisa spent the evening in her blue

satin pajamas curled up on her cream plush sofa where she had apparently fallen asleep.

The sound of snow humming on her flat television screen was irritating and she quickly used the remote to turn it off. Noticing the time was 12:49 a.m., Lisa leapt up and ran through the kitchen to see if her car was in the garage. Nope, just her mother's car, which meant that Chanelle, her seventeen-year-old daughter, had missed her midnight curfew!

"Don't jump to conclusions," Lisa said to herself as she reached for the phone, flipping through the caller ID. She hoped Chanelle had tried to call when she was asleep, but was disheartened to find no evidence supporting her theory. She quickly dialed Chanelle's cell phone, hearing the hip-hop music selection that preceded her daughter's voice mail. She didn't bother leaving a message.

Dashing up the stairs, Lisa knocked on her mother's bedroom door as a courtesy, but didn't wait for a response. "Mama?" She peeked inside.

Hattie lay like Sleeping Beauty underneath a tan comforter that blended in perfectly with her light skin tone. She looked so peaceful that Lisa really didn't want to disturb her. She stood for a split second, admiring her mother's beauty. Though she was in her mid-sixties, Lisa's mother looked great—still-mostly-black hair, a shapely size ten figure and no wrinkles. Lisa hoped she'd inherited her mother's genes and would also age gracefully. So far so good, but if Chanelle kept working her nerves, she'd surely look old and gray within a few years.

"Mama!" Lisa spoke with more force.

"Huh?"

"Sorry to wake you…I want to know if you've heard from Chanelle."

"No, why? She's not home yet?"

"No, but don't worry. I'll find her."

Her mother quickly sat up. "Did you call Jareeka? Maybe Chanelle accidentally dozed off over there."

The girl's name was actually Gericka, like *Erika*, but Lisa didn't bother correcting her mother, who was notorious for renaming people. "Calling there is my next step. I wanted to check with you first."

Lisa ran back down to the kitchen where Chanelle's best friend's telephone number was posted on the small magnetic bulletin board attached to the refrigerator. By now it was a few minutes shy of one.

The phone rang several times before Marlon Young, Gericka's father, answered.

"Hi! I'm sorry to call your house so late. This is Lisa."

"Yes, what can I do for you?"

"Is Chanelle there?"

"No, why do you ask?"

Lisa's throat tightened. "She's not here yet. Do you know what time she brought Gericka home from the movies?"

"I don't know what Chanelle told you, but she didn't

go to the movies with Gericka," Marlon firmly stated. "Gericka and Karen went to Louisville on Friday to spend the weekend with my mother-in-law."

"I'm sorry...I thought. Never mind. I'm sorry I woke you."

"It's okay. I'm sure you're concerned about your daughter. I pray she gets home safely," he said, before hanging up.

With no other options, Lisa reluctantly dialed RJ's number, which she had unfortunately memorized by now. She *hated* calling her ex-husband, but figured the situation warranted such an action. It was a waste of time because he hadn't seen or heard from Chanelle either. As if his presence would calm Lisa's nerves, RJ had offered to come over and wait with her until Chanelle arrived.

"No, thanks!" Lisa quickly declined. He always seemed to be looking for an excuse to be near her, but the only man occupying her time was Minister Freeman, whom she had been out to dinner with on several occasions.

"Please let me know the minute you hear from her," RJ requested.

"I will," she assured.

He had some nerve, acting like a concerned father when he was the reason why she and Chanelle had left Baltimore and come to Ohio in the first place. Had she known several summers ago when she moved here that he would follow, she would have accepted another job elsewhere.

Feeling her blood pressure rise with each passing second, she went back into the living room and sat on the couch. She began fiddling with the charm on the necklace she never took off, which had become a habit whenever she became nervous or angry. The time was exactly 1:07 a.m. and that meant her daughter was now sixty-seven minutes past curfew. Lisa was fuming!

Though the "God, please don't let anything bad happen to her" prayer cycled through Lisa's head a few times, she honestly didn't feel a need to panic. For some reason, Lisa knew Chanelle was okay—wherever she was. Chanelle was okay now, but Lisa couldn't promise that she'd be later when she finally brought her behind home and parental justice kicked in.

She did not understand why Chanelle would intentionally lie and violate her curfew. She was fresh off of punishment for talking back earlier that week. Lisa had asked Chanelle to get off the computer so she could type some information for work, but Chanelle had defiantly replied, "No!"—as if Lisa had really given her an option. Already stressed because of her work challenges, Lisa controlled the urge to snatch Chanelle out of the chair by her ponytail and threatened that if she didn't move of her own accord, she would be moved. Chanelle got up without further objection but her attitude had struck Lisa's nerve, so Chanelle had been placed on punishment.

Hearing the sound of her mother's footsteps descending the hardwood stairs, Lisa leaned back on the sofa so as not to appear overly anxious.

"Chanelle still hasn't made it home?" Her mother's wire-framed glasses rested at the tip of her nose while a large green robe concealed her body.

"Nope…"

"Did you call Jareeka's?"

"Yes, her father said that she and her mother are away for the weekend." She felt herself tensing with every word.

"What about RJ? Have you called him?"

"He hasn't seen her either."

"Well, don't come down too hard on her. Maybe she didn't know Jareeka was out of town and when she found out, she decided to hang with one of her other friends instead. Now she should've at least called and told you, but she was probably so happy to get out the house that she forgot. Poor thing; it seems like she's always on punishment. Sometimes I think you're too hard on that girl. I don't want to meddle—"

"Then please don't," the thirty-eight-year-old interjected in the most respectful tone that she could conjure up with a clenched jaw.

"All right. I'll keep my opinion to myself, but I was merely going to say that you may want to consider extending Chanelle's curfew. She's practically an adult and it's time you start treating her like one. Maybe then you'd be less likely to run into this problem."

An electrifying jolt shot through Lisa's body. The way she disciplined Chanelle had become a constant point of contention between her and her mother. Thank goodness Hattie would soon be moving into her own apartment! Lisa could not wait!

"That makes absolutely no sense!" she fired back. "What she is, is irresponsible. Why should I reward her for not being able to honor her curfew? And anyhow, she wouldn't have been on punishment recently had she not been so smart at the mouth."

"I wonder where she got it from…" her mother replied cynically, quickly disappearing into the kitchen and returning moments later. "Good night."

"The same to you," Lisa replied, continuing to stew as the clock read 1:21 a.m. The only other noise she heard was the emptying of the automatic ice machine until ten minutes or so later when a car pulled into the driveway. Lisa's heart began racing when she saw flashing blue and red lights from the window. It wasn't her car as she had thought, but a police cruiser. A gut-wrenching fear fell over her. Had something horrible happened to Chanelle? She felt guilty about being so angry and the missed curfew was now a minor issue compared to the concern that her baby might be lying in the hospital somewhere. Lisa was horrified by the unlimited possibilities of things that could've happened to her daughter. The pit of her stomach knotted as she sprang from the couch and raced to the front door.